PRAISE

"Dahlma Llanos-Figueroa's *Daughters of the Stone* sings as few novels can. It also tells us of a culture and nation that is underrepresented in our literature: Puerto Rico. And it does so with brilliant flourishes, in a narrative both gripping and intimate. Conveying a wide sweep of history, as witnessed by several generations of women, the book has the warmth of autobiography while sustaining a firm and stately control of technique and language."

— PEN/ROBERT W. BINGHAM PRIZE 2010 FINALIST

"This first novel traces the lives of succeeding generations of Puerto Rican women from the 19th century onward. Though its ambitious historical narrative is reminiscent of the Latin American boom writers, it has a distinct personality of its own. In particular, I enjoyed its feminist perspective as well as the author's tender loving care about language, a quality I find badly wanting in many a book published today."

— OSCAR HIJUELOS
Pulitzer Prize winning author of *The Mambo Kings Play Songs of Love*

"Rejoice! Here is a novel you have never read before: the story of a long line of extraordinary Afro-Puerto Rican women silenced by history. In *Daughters of the Stone*, Dahlma Llanos-Figueroa rescues them from oblivion and richly, compellingly, magically introduces them to literature—and to the world. *¡Bienvenidas!*"

— CRISTINA GARCIA
Author of *Dreaming in Cuban: A Novel* and *Here in Berlin*

A lyrical powerful novel about a family of Afro-Puerto Rican women spanning five generations, detailing their physical and spiritual journey from the Old World to the New.

It is the mid-1800s. Fela, taken from Africa, is working at her second sugar plantation in colonial Puerto Rico, where her mistress is only too happy to benefit from her impressive embroidery skills. But Fela has a secret. Before she and her husband were separated and sold into slavery, they performed a tribal ceremony in which they poured the essence of their unborn child into a very special stone. Fela keeps the stone with her, waiting for the chance to finish what she started. When the plantation owner approaches her, Fela sees a better opportunity for her child, and allows the man to act out his desire. Such is the beginning of a line of daughters connected by their intense love for one another, and the stories of a lost land.

Mati, a powerful healer and noted craftswoman, is grounded in a life that is disappearing in a quickly changing world.

Concha, unsure of her place, doesn't realize the price she will pay for rejecting her past.

Elena, modern and educated, tries to navigate between two cultures, moving to New York, where she struggles to keep her family together.

Carisa turns to the past for wisdom and strength when her life in New York falls apart.

The stone becomes meaningful to each of the women, pulling them through times of crisis. Dahlma Llanos-Figueroa shows great skill and warmth in the telling of this heartbreaking, inspirational story about mothers and daughters, and the ways in which they hurt and save one another.

DAUGHTERS OF THE STONE

Dahlma Llanos-Figueroa

A hardcover edition of this book was published in September 2009
by THOMAS DUNNE BOOKS, an imprint of St. Martin's Press.

Dahlma Llanos-Figueroa, llanosfigueroapublicity@gmail.com
www.DahlmaLlanosFigueroa.com

DAUGHTERS OF THE STONE, Trade Paper Edition published 2019.
ISBN 978-1-7326424-0-9
e-book ISBN 978-1-7326424-1-6

Book Cover and Interior Designed by Cristina Castro Pelka

Cover Artwork by Dudley Vaccianna

Production by Artea Creative, Inc.

Published by Dahlma Llanos-Figueroa

THE LIBRARY OF CONGRESS HAS CATALOGUED THE HARDCOVER EDITION AS FOLLOWS:

Daughters of the Stone / Dahlma Llanos-Figueroa.—1st ed.
p. cm.
ISBN 978-0-312-53926-9

1. Plantation life—Fiction.   2. Women—Family relationships—Fiction.
3. Matriarchy—Fiction.   4. Puerto Rico—History—Fiction.   5. New York (N.Y.)—
Fiction   I. Title.

PS3612.L36 D38 2009
813'.6—dc22   2009013474

DEDICATION

To the storytellers of my life
who still whisper their tales into my ears:
my Mom, Carmen María, my abuela, Sofía,
my titis Betty, Cani, and Melin.
And to the ladies on the hill. Mil gracias.

ACKNOWLEDGMENTS

My sincere appreciation to my Ladies Group for walking my life path with me. Thank you to Linda Molier and Ruth Lessuck, my untiring and ever-encouraging readers. A very special thank you to Nydia Lassalle Davis and Cesar M. Negron. My deepest appreciation to my friend and colleague, Vivian Monserrate Cotte. Above all, thank you to my husband, Jonathan Lessuck, for living with this book almost as long as I have, and for being my greatest supporter and a most unexpected gift.

My special thanks to Carol Dixon and the John Oliver Killens Workshop in Brooklyn, the Bronx Council of the Arts, the International Women's Writing Guild, and Dr. Marti Zlatchin.

To my readers,

Thank you for keeping this book close to your hearts and for sharing it with your friends, families, and colleagues for the past 10 years. I am so appreciative that so many local and national book clubs embraced the book from the very beginning. Inviting me into your homes and private spaces was amazing to me, a first-time author who was used to working alone in my tiny office with no guarantee of anyone ever reading my work. I could feel the love.

I cannot adequately express how gratified I am that PEN America shortlisted my novel for the 2010 PEN/Robert W. Bingham Prize. It came as quite a surprise and meant so much to have the critical acclaim of my fellow writers. I am still beaming.

I am grateful for the colleges and universities that continue to use *Daughters of the Stone* in their coursework. *Mil gracias* to all the professors who saw the value of studying the world I have created within the novel. Without your support, this newly edited trade paperback edition would not have come to fruition today.

I am so happy that my words have touched so many people from so many cultures in so many places. It is a testament to the universality of the human condition and a rejection of the divide-and-conquer mentality that has recently permeated our world. We all suffer and are elevated by our common human experience.

A note about language: Every novelist's aim is to immerse you in a world of his or her creation. I wanted to present you with characters that seemed real and compelling. I was particularly focused on bringing the reader into 19th century rural Puerto Rico with all its complexities and contradictions. My intentional use of Spanish in many instances was, and continues to be, a vehicle to draw the reader into the society I am trying to recreate. I strove to make sure the content of the narrative would be clear to all readers and bring them to a more intimate understanding of that world. My intent was not to make you just an observer but an emotional participant in that society.

I hope you continue to treasure Fela, Mati, Concha, Elena, and Carisa as I have for well over 10 years.

Muy agradecida,

Dahlma Llanos-Figueroa

Dahlma Llanos-Figueroa
New York City
February, 2019

PROLOGUE

These are the stories. My stories, their stories—just as they were told to my mother and her mother and hers. They were given to me for safekeeping, and now I give them to you.

They may be visions that shimmered on the horizon at sunset, on the banks of the River Niger. They may have ridden in the evening song of the *coquí* in a long-ago Puerto Rico when rich men feasted on the sweetness of sugarcane, the bitterness of coffee, and the hearts of other men.

These are the stories of a time lost to flesh and bones, a time that lives only in dreams and memory.

No matter.

Like a primeval wave, these stories have carried me, and deposited me on the morning of today. They are the stories of how I came to be who I am, where I am.

BOOK ONE

FELA

1 ARRIVAL

A gray braid falling over each shoulder, Tía Josefa stuck her head out of the window of Las Agujas, the embroiderers' cabin located just behind the main plantation house. The wagon returning from town swung around the main house and came to a final halt in the *batey* of Hacienda Las Mercedes, a sugar plantation near the northern coast of Puerto Rico.

She recognized Romero, the mulatto *mayoral*, sitting high next to the driver. His shadow crawled over the supplies that filled the wagon behind him. The man wore all black, even under the scorching sun. The brim of his black hat, tilted forward, hid his eyes, leaving only his pointy chin and beak of a nose visible. The bony shoulders under his black cape looked nailed to the blue sky beyond. He gripped his whip, handy, ready.

In her day, Tía had seen many black people come and go, but there had been no new ones in a long time. She knew Don Tomás had recently acquired a new *parcela* and needed more hands to work it into cane fields. One thing Tía knew for sure, where there was more work to be done, it would be black hands that would do it. So she stretched her skinny neck to take a good look at the men hoisting the monthly supplies—sacks of flour and rice, bolts of cloth, sides of smoked beef—out of the wagons.

Then came the rest of the cargo—frightened young boys, stone-faced men, and hesitant women. Almost as an afterthought, they poured out into the courtyard, brown and slow, like molasses, the human purchases of the day. Tía searched for Fela, the tall woman she'd heard about and couldn't put out of her mind. She was the last to descend, a young woman in her early twenties. There was something familiar about the girl. But Tía couldn't place it and was too drawn to the scene to think about it for very long.

There was much activity in the yard—men unhitching horses, curious children scurrying about, Romero assigning quarters to the new slaves. The young woman eyed her surroundings from her height of over six feet. The others were herded into the cabins that stretched out beyond the wagons. Fela began to follow when Romero, the overseer, blocked her way and pointed his whip to Las Agujas, where she would be living. The woman just stared at him.

"*Vamos, muévete,*" Tía Josefa heard Romero command "*¿Qué? ¿No me oyes?* Are you deaf as well as dumb, or just another stupid *negra sucia?*"

Fela examined him as though he were an unreliable animal. She didn't move. Romero stood directly in front of her and shouted his command into her face. But the woman Fela held her ground.

Never known for patience, Romero snatched his whip and swung it overhead. But his hand froze in midair, the whip swinging impotently in the morning breeze.

"*¡Maldita sea!*" he growled.

Fela still hadn't moved. She showed no sign of fear or even apprehension. Romero's arm remained frozen in position. He looked from his arm to the whip and back to his arm. Confusion and then rage twisted his face.

Finally, Fela turned and walked in the direction he had indicated. As soon as she moved away, his arm dropped. By the time the *mayoral* recovered from his moment of confusion, Fela was making her way up the slope that led to the main house.

Romero gathered himself to his full height. Adjusting his hold on the whip, he was about to advance on her retreating figure when a commotion suddenly filled the *batey*.

The horses had spooked and reared, toppling supplies that were still being unloaded. Bags of beans exploded under the trampling hooves. Sacks of flour burst into clouds of white, covering the yard in a layer of ghostly powder. Children ran. Men cursed. Drivers struggled to get the teams of horses under control. Frantic voices filled the air.

"*¡Corre!*"

Men ran to help.

"*¡Mira, nena…!*"

"*¡Ven aquí!*"

Women pulled children out of the way.

"*¡Cuidado!*"

Warnings rang out as huge containers toppled over and spilled corn meal, olives, and oil on those standing nearby.

"*¡Ay, Dios mío…!*"

A man was pinned under the weight of several huge sacks of rice.

Romero glared at the pandemonium and then back at the woman who was now beyond the whip's reach. "*¡Carajo!*" he yelled.

He wound his whip and hooked it onto his belt. Before turning to the commotion, he propelled a long stream of spittle in the direction of Fela's retreating figure.

As Tía watched this scene, her breath caught at the audacity of the young girl. She could almost feel Fela's and Romero's wills clashing in the air overhead and had braced herself for the outcome.

Fela approached Tía's window and stopped just on the far side. For a moment, the old woman got a glimpse of the sadness that collected in the outer corners of Fela's eyes and weighed them down. But immediately the girl's face shut tight against the old woman. Her eyes, shiny as steel doors, were dressed in armor. Such stubbornness was familiar to Tía, like a long-forgotten melody of her youth. A finger of cold fear crept into Tía's heart. She knew that a slave, any slave, would have to yield or be broken.

Tía wondered how long this young woman had been a slave and how much longer she would be able to stand so tall and distant. For black people, pride was a sin punishable by death.

The two women stood at opposite sides of the window as each examined the other. Tía went around to the door and motioned Fela inside, holding out her hand in welcome as the girl entered the room.

"*Entra, entra m'hija.*"

Fela walked in, squeezing by the older woman and avoiding her welcoming arms.

* * *

Don Tomás, son of Don Aurelio and master of Hacienda Las Mercedes, stood at his second-floor rear window and watched the action below. The tip of his *cigarro* burned orange as he watched. He inhaled the acrid smoke, having noted the palpable tension between his overseer and the new woman. He'd heard the neighing horses and screaming women and Romero's curses. He took note of all the activity, but the tall black woman who walked away from it all with not as much as a halting step or a backward glance captured his attention. She never broke her stride, ignoring the danger coiled and growing inside Romero, moving on as if she lived on another plane altogether.

He had bought this woman because of her hands. The auctioneer said she had magic fingers, and his wife, Filomena, insisted she needed another woman in her *taller*. He had granted his wife's wish, barely glancing at the woman before paying the man and moving on with the rest of his more important purchases. But now, now he watched her as she towered over everyone, her back stiff and shoulders pushed back, breasts held aloft. She looked straight ahead as she made her way up the incline toward him, to Las Agujas, her torn rags barely covering her body. Despite her position, she carried herself with no less dignity than his wife in her silk and lace gowns.

Don Tomás drew on his cigar and let out a satisfying stream of smoke. He shifted his weight from one foot to the other, slipped his hand down the front of his breeches, and let it linger there. He heard footsteps in the hallway and quickly adjusted himself before turning to face his approaching wife.

2 LAS MERCEDES

The storyteller's stool lies abandoned on a road. A dead woman wears a familiar face and torn flesh. A lone child wanders lost in the bush, its screams mingle with the caw-cawing of the huge birds swooping down from above. Imo sits with the ancestors, his back to her. She struggles to join them but her feet are bound to the earth. The image before her begins to fade. "No! Imo! Don't leave me!" Then the words explode in her head...my fault...my fault...my fault...

Fela bolted up on the cot, drenched in sweat, mouth gaping. She took in huge gulps of air, trying to control the heaving that had wrenched her awake. On that infernal boat she had woken up in terror night after night, her screams exploding into the fetid darkness. Now it was much worse. Now her empty mouth left her with nowhere to put her pain. Since she had no way to shape it into words, she swallowed it, choking on its bile.

She sat in the dark and the memories came rushing back to her. She thought of that other dream she had had long ago as she waited for Imo by the river. Mother Oshun, goddess of the river, patron of women, of motherhood, of fertility, had come to her in that dream, leaving strange images, sharp, piercing Fela's brain—the river flowing backward, the skies opening and crying down on the flaming forest, sparks alighting the village, aimless spears broken and hanging in midair, and over everything a heavy, deadly silence. The images had stayed with Fela as she came out of her dream. She was puzzling over them as Imo came up to her in the moonlight.

This was to be their night, the full moon, the childstone—all was ready. Four planting seasons had come and gone and still her flat belly proclaimed her failure. She was tired of the sidelong glances of the younger women with fertile wombs, the whispered words that followed her when she attended every child naming. No more! It had to be done that night. So she had folded Mother Oshun's strange images and put them aside. Just for a little while. Mother Oshun would understand her woman's heart. After their ritual, she would go to the elders and tell them of her dream.

Now, in the dark in this new place, Fela squeezed her eyes, trying to erase the other memories that came rushing back. She had put herself before all else. And it had cost her everything and everyone in her life. The village was burned, the people were taken away in chains, and Imo was gone forever. She remembered being dragged away, clutching her pouch as she tried to fight off the attackers.

Fela rocked back and forth, the thud, thud of the pouch around her neck, the stone lying inside, the only thing left of her old life. She had paid dearly for that stone. So she rocked into the night and wondered when she would be released. Finally, she fell back in exhaustion and thankfully found an empty sleep.

* * *

"*Levántate, m'hija.* Time to get up and get to work." Tía Josefa handed her a gourd of sweet black coffee and a thickly buttered hunk of bread.

It was the first morning of her new life.

Tía Josefa introduced her to the women already eating their breakfast under the mango tree that stood between their workshop and the main house. The needlewomen worked at this table every day from sunup to sundown.

"Fela doesn't talk, but it's hands we need here." Under her breath Tía muttered, "Sometimes I think we have too much talk."

Then Tía got Fela settled at the long worktable just outside Las Agujas. She set down a basket full of needles and threads, then set a stack of unworked clothes on the table in front of the girl and handed her a finished napkin. She watched as Fela examined the piece. The girl then threaded her needle and began embroidering the cloth she had been given. Tía was impressed with the tiny stitches and the steady hand.

She looked down on Fela's head. As a *ladina*, Tía had been born on the hacienda but she knew of others, *bozales* like Fela, who had had lives of freedom before coming to this place. The thought took her to a past she had tried so hard to put to rest. And she lost herself in that memory until she felt the tugging at her skirt.

Fela held up the piece she had been working on. There was a perfect rosebud embroidered on the white cloth. But it was different somehow. Around the edges of the flower, Fela had embroidered a single, almost imperceptible strand of gold thread. The effect was one of sharpening the image, making it three-dimensional. With this subtle addition, the flower came to life.

"*Muy bien*. But next time, don't make changes in the work. All pieces must be exactly alike, a set, you understand?" Tía held out the finished napkins. But Fela stared out at some undefined point. Tía tapped her shoulder and softened her voice, "I see you are a true artist. Later, I'll want to see more."

Satisfied that Fela was as good as she had heard, Tía prepared to go on with her chores. But before moving on, she offered advice.

"*Suave, m'hija*. The first day is always the hardest. I know you don't believe me, but it will get better."

Fela still sat immobile. As Tía passed on her way to the big house, she bent down to whisper, "We all carry heavy loads. But even the strongest of us cannot guard against our dreams."

* * *

The hacienda on the hill was called Las Mercedes. A double row of royal palms extended from the front of the house to the river road. A wide avenue of white tiles sank into the dark earth between the trees, and on either side of the walkway, startling white gardenias led to the front steps.

The large windows were left open in the morning, shutters falling back against the outer wall. Lace curtains billowed out, huge butterfly wings quivering at every window. The mosaic floor was washed early each morning, a cool expanse for the rocking chairs that sat gently swaying on the *balcón*, which wrapped gracefully around the front and sides of the mansion.

The heavier mahogany and cane furniture of the interior of the house was polished to a high sheen with layer after layer of lemon oil, so that the intricate pattern of the inlaid floor was reflected on the paneled china closets. By midmorning, the sun had burned the crispness out of the air and warm breezes carried the scent of gardenias throughout the house.

The scent collected in the entrance hall, gathered in the corners, and rubbed up against the tall murals. It spread like heavy perfume around polished guitars, plump cushions, tasseled bellpulls, and fringed French lamps, before going on to the high sparkling chandelier in the dining room. It pushed down the corridors and through the private rooms, where it curled up on canopied beds and inside newly washed chamber pots and then moved on, to the guest rooms with their ruffled curtains and expectant vanities.

It took many hands to create the illusion of lightness and freedom of movement projected by the big house. These hands washed and

ironed. They boiled and fried and cut and served. They applied Doña
Filomena's makeup, sorted her personal linens, twisted her hair into
elaborate ringlets and braided fantasies. These were the hands that
carried pails, polished silver, scrubbed soiled sheets, and plied needles
endlessly through expensive cloth. They worked for weeks creating the
dozens of lace shawls and festooned ball gowns that dwelled in the
world of Doña Filomena's hands, which lifted nothing heavier than
Spanish playing cards, china teacups, or French hankies.

Then there were the hands that butchered hogs. These hands
heaved and hammered, scraped and painted, hauled and hewed.
They gripped the machetes that struck at the sugarcane. Calloused
and bleeding, they pushed the wheel that chewed the cane into the
golden liquid that eventually quenched the thirst of their masters,
fashionable young men in silk shirts, who offered compliments to
the fashionable young ladies who strolled around the plaza on balmy
evenings. These hands were the black hands that stoked the fires that
fueled the machinery that was the essence of Hacienda Las Mercedes.

These were the hands of bodies that never wore satin ribbons or
danced on mosaic tile. They never dined at the table or smoked fancy
cigars or rode fine stallions on Saturday afternoons. These hands were
the ones that created the beauty and hospitality for which Hacienda
Las Mercedes was renowned. Their owners lived behind the back of
the main house, where they never got to enjoy the scent of gardenias.

* * *

The back of the main house looked down on a double row of *chozas*,
cabins that housed the plantation slaves. In this world, the houses had
no names. This was *el batey*, a low flat stretching from the house of
the *patrón* on the north hill to the house of the *mayoral* on the south.
From the elevated windows of these two-story structures, everything
and everybody on the plantation was kept under constant scrutiny.

The *chozas* were raised one-room shacks made of woven palm fronds for roofs and wooden slats for walls, all tied together with knotted rope. The two rows of *chozas* faced each other, eight on each side; one for each slave family on the plantation.

Across from each other and perpendicular to the back of the big house sat the only two slave dwellings that shared the north hill with the mansion. One was the kitchen and the other was Las Agujas, which housed the women valued for their embroidery skills. These women were particularly important to Doña Filomena. Their skills provided the clothes and decorative cloth for the plantation. But, more importantly, their needles created the intricately worked finery that was highly prized by wealthy women of the county and even the capital. Their labor provided *la patrona* a great deal of pride, as well as a good deal of personal wealth.

*　*　*

From sunrise to sunset, the needlewomen worked at the table under the mango tree. When there was a backlog of work or when ball gowns needed to be done for a specific day, the women worked well into the night. Long hours of detailed work made for soreness that could lead to costly mistakes on precious fabrics. So, every morning, *la señora* had a basin of water and a blue bottle of coconut oil set out in the sun at either end of the worktable. During the day, the women took turns at the basins relieving the stiffness in their fingers.

Three days after her arrival, Fela still sat at one end of the table by herself. She watched the other women from under lowered eyelids and listened. Their constant chatter filled the air as their fingers moved incessantly over the cloth.

One of the women, Belén, looked around to make sure they were alone before she whispered, *"La curandera* warned him. But that bastard Romero couldn't wait for the birth healing before he dragged Paquita back into the cane field."

"They say he pulled her off her cot and pushed her out the door."

"*¡Ay, Dios mío!*" Margó made the sign of the cross as she continued, "I heard she barely had the strength to pick up her machete."

"*Muchacha*, two of the men had to carry her home at midday, weak and bleeding."

"*Hijo de la gran puta*," Pola knew no caution in her speech. "That Romero will get his one day! I just hope I'm there to help send him to the hell he came from."

"What *cañita* have you been drinking? More like he'll put us all in our graves before he goes to meet his master—*el Diablo*!"

"I tell you," Pola said, "I've dreamed of it many times. In my dream, I enjoy feeling my scissors sink into his chest. I give them a good twist and make sure they hit the mark. I watch the blood pulse out of his body and wonder why I didn't do it sooner."

Fela listened as they complained, reported, teased, and gossiped about their world. She wondered how these women could live like this. How could they forget who they were and where they came from? She would never be like them. Never!

Margó and Belén got up from the table, shaking out their fingers and making their way to one of the basins. Margó soaked her hands in the warm water, letting the heat dissolve away the tension in the tired muscles. Then Belén began the ritual, massaging away the stiffness with coconut oil.

Fela watched and kept herself apart. When her fingers cramped and she could no longer make her tiny stitches, she hid her hands in her skirt and rubbed discretely, knowing she would never ask anything of any of these women. She would only be here a short while. She needed no one.

When the sun was directly overhead and the heat of the day was at its worst, the other women set their work aside and shared the food from the big *ditas* that had been set out for them. The smaller of the two gourds held a dozen boiled eggs. The other contained *batatas, yautías,* and *yucas*. The starchy tubers had only that morning been pulled out of the ground behind the *chozas*. A stack of even smaller gourds made for individual bowls.

Fela still sat alone at the far end of the table. Margó called out to her but Fela shook her head no. Ignoring the rebuke, the woman walked over carrying a bowl of boiled yams and two eggs, but Fela wouldn't even look up to acknowledge Margó's kindness. Stroking Fela's shoulder, Margó set the bowl down before the new woman.

"*Mira*, Fela, you'd better eat something," she urged. "Pride may feed the soul but never the belly. Besides, you need to keep those hands steady for the work."

Fela continued embroidering, ignoring both the words and the offered meal. Margó shrugged her shoulders as she walked away, leaving the food on the table. "You'll learn."

Fela waited until the women turned their attention elsewhere before she pulled the bowl closer and twisted away. She hunched over and ate her portion, her fingers scooping up the food quickly. When she was finished and thought the other women were still engrossed in conversation, she got up and returned the empty *dita*. Then she went back to her seat, carefully wiped her hands on her skirt, and picked up her work once again.

Tía monitored the activity under the mango tree for several days. Each day, Fela kept to herself, refusing to join the other women. At first they attempted to engage her, but by week's end the women were visibly annoyed by what they took as Fela's aloofness. Margó alone still tried to include her in their activities.

"Come on, Fela, the shade is good over here and there is a nice breeze. You can't work without eating, and the sun will fry your head if you don't wear that hat."

Seeing that Margó's concern was once again met by indifference, Pola, who was always hungry and never tactful, admonished her friend, "*Olvídate, mujer*, you bend over too far, you show your ass."

The women snickered. Rudely directing her comment to Fela, Pola didn't bother to hide her annoyance.

"*Mire*, Doña," Pola charged the title with heavy sarcasm. "If you want the food, fine; if you don't, that's fine, too. More for the rest of us. But let's stop playing games."

"*Ay*, Pola, you have such a sharp tongue."

"*Esa pobre muchacha…*" Margó tried to defend Fela.

"*¡Pobre, mierda!* She's no better than the rest of us. Look, *señorita* Fela, *princesa negra*. You're too good to eat with us? *¡Pues jódete!*"

Pola had risen, her anger flashing in her voice and her face. As she started toward Fela, Belén stepped in Pola's path and handed her a bowl of food.

"*Cálmate*, Pola. No point in getting all excited. *Ya, déjala.*" Belén's big body and soft words deflated Pola's anger. "She'll come around soon enough. Come on. Food's getting cold."

Pola turned away. The tension was broken as the other women got their portions and moved into the shade, leaving Fela to bake in the sun and eat or not, as she chose.

* * *

At dusk, the women put away their things. The married women made their way down the hill, toward their *chozas* and their families. The single women, who lived in Las Agujas, set about preparing their own dinner. While some prepared their meal, the others put away their baskets and laid out their work for the following day.

As the women left the table, Tía Josefa lowered her heavy body onto the bench across from Fela. She pulled over the nearest water basin and reached for Fela's hands. The younger woman resisted but Tía held on firmly. Fela finally relaxed, surrendering her hands to Tía, who took them and placed them gently into the still-warm water.

Pouring from the blue bottle, Tía worked the oil into Fela's hands, softening the knots, easing the pain.

"You think you can live alone? *Aquí nadie vive sola.*"

Fela looked at this old woman. Why did she always begin a conversation as though it was a continuation of an earlier talk? Tía spoke as though she was just thinking out loud. It unnerved Fela because it cut through the distance she worked so hard to build.

"Here there is no living alone. All we have is each other. You think I don't know? The new ones, all day long they think about home—the old place across the big water."

Fela's body tensed.

"That's it, isn't it? You still carry the old place with you. Now, I'm not saying forget. You never will. But hear me. You live here now and you're never going back. Never."

Fela tried to snatch her hands away but Tía was too fast for her.

"Set your mind to this. You won't make it if your body's here and your mind's back there all the time. Just because you learn how to live here and now doesn't mean that you betray what came before. It just means you have to live."

Tía dried Fela's left hand with a soft towel and started working on the right palm. She began at the wrist and worked her way down, still kneading, still talking.

"You remember from home how the village worked together? Put your mind to this: This is your new village and we are your people. Here, too, we work together. We all have stories. Sometimes the pain lies so heavily inside us that it can only be whispered. Sometimes it can't be spoken out loud at all. So you think you're different? There are many silences. You've got one kind, but each of us has her own. Listen and you will hear them all around you."

There was an edge under the soft words.

"You're not alone in your pain, never have been. We're all part of each other's pain and can be a part of each other's healing, too. But when you clutch on to the first, you'll miss out on the second. Can't you see that?"

Tía wiped her hands and patted Fela's hands lightly.

"*Ya.* I'm done here." With that she got up and took the basin away.

3 Remembrances

Among all these new people, Fela had one constant that gave her solace. Whenever she could get away from the others, she slipped into memories of happier days of the distant past. The moon was her best friend. She'd look into its roundness to find memories that sustained her.

She always went back to that night. She had welcomed Imo to the clearing by the river and pulled him down to her. Pushing him onto the grass and using her hands, her tongue, she worked her way down, stopping to stroke a nipple and caress the belly and apply pressure around his moist roundness. She continued fondling, licking, until she felt a shift in him, then a familiar tension growing. But he wanted to delay the moment.

It was his turn. She let him slip his hands down her face, closing her eyes gently. He kissed each lid, kissed the bridge of her nose, her cheekbones. He pulled at her earlobe with moist lips, found the pulsing vein in her neck, gifted her with a necklace of kisses. Her body shifted, softened. She surrendered herself to the feelings until she thought she could stand no more.

They came together, bodies rolling, wreathing, arms and legs snaking, mouths engulfing. She opened herself to him. At that moment, everything else stopped. Life existed only between and within their bodies, pulsing, heaving, finally exploding into an incoherent syllable.

When it was over, he reached for the nearby stone, the childstone they had selected so carefully. For a moment they held it together and thought about the illusive baby they had wanted, the one that they hoped would hear their call through this ceremony. Imo used the stone to stroke her face, her breasts, her belly, her thighs. He worked slowly, drawing symbols, secret messages for their child on her skin. His tongue followed the path of the stone. He parted her legs and used his tongue to gently push the stone into place. Their childstone, guardian of their unborn baby's soul, was to sleep there, protected, bathing in the best of each of them until it would be placed on the altar of the ancestors, where it would be welcomed by them. That would seal the ceremony.

When it was all over, Fela snuggled into Imo's arms and let herself drift away. The last thing she remembered before falling asleep was Mother Oshun's voice rushing in the river. The water was choppy and the moonlight fractured. But Fela was too happy to let anything spoil her evening. The images she had stored away were a distant memory. *The goddess will understand*, she thought, *Oshun will, she will, she must!* Fela believed that. She had to believe that. It only took a moment to convince herself of it. Again, she closed her mind to anything other than her moment. So she put all images from the goddess aside and let her contented weariness pull her into a peaceful sleep.

The message was never delivered. All was lost and now Oshun exacted punishment. Fela would have to do her penance.

* * *

For several nights, Tía Josefa sat up in the dark and watched Fela in her sleep. What was there about this woman that touched her so deeply? What was it about her that Tía *remembered*?

The thought had nagged at her night after night as she sat and watched. But on the fifth night Tía, exhausted, stretched out on her own cot and fell into a half sleep that brought her an image she had tried to push into the shadows of her mind for many years. During the day she succeeded, but in her dreams it slipped back like an old lover or an armed enemy who knew its path well in the dark.

Back then things were different. Don Aurelio, Don Tomás' father and a man of hot temper, was the *patrón*. Young Romero, already the *mayoral*, delighted in inflicting pain even then. Each man, master and overseer, took his role in the "disciplining" of the slaves seriously—the *patrón* because he knew he was superior to the black horde and Romero because he feared he wasn't. For this reason, Romero was even more dangerous than his master.

Don Aurelio owned more land than any other *hacendado* in the district. For a time, it seemed that every month there was another wagonload of slaves to work the increasing number of fields. Among them was Clemensio, a *bozal* brought directly from Africa. He came to the plantation a grown man when Josefa was just beginning to sprout breasts.

Clemensio was a big man. He seemed to burst out of the rags that covered his body. He was a head taller than any other man, black or white, on the hacienda, and his massive shoulders rolled under a layer of blue-black skin. When he looked around, he appeared to be surveying his own land rather than bowing to the ownership of another. It seemed as though someone had forgotten to tell him that he was a slave here. Not knowing the new language, he said nothing and kept to himself.

Josefa never tired of looking at this giant. He had to bend down and slide sideways into the men's *choza*, the doorway not nearly big enough for his frame. And when he entered a room, he took up all the space and most of the air. She had trouble breathing whenever he was around. His eyes drew her in like warm honey. One of his hands could easily wrap around her arm and yet once she saw him pick a flower with such gentleness that it brought tears to her eyes.

She thought, *God must look like this*, strong and broad as the trees. So much better than the God of the *patrones* with his sickly pale body, skinny and helpless on his cross. But if Clemensio was a god, he was one of flesh and blood. She was always aware of his presence. Whenever she could get away from her mother's eyes and Romero's increasingly frequent call, she stole away to watch Clemensio work, eat, or sleep. She loved to watch him bathe in the moonlight. The water bounced off his shoulders and ran in rivulets down his back. She wondered what his skin tasted like.

Once, she hid behind the men's *choza*, watching him as he drank a huge gourd of water at the end of the day. The water ran down his neck and onto his chest. He caught her peeking and motioned her over. She went to him without shame or question. She just had to touch, to feel the silky blackness of him.

It was the first time she had ever heard him laugh. He said something in his language and laughed again, his arms wrapping around her. She knew that she wanted this man with all her young girl's heart.

She remembered the fear that had seized her the day he was whipped. Everyone knew from the moment the two men met that Romero would try to squash the open disdain that lived on Clemensio's face. The only surprise was that the beating had not come sooner.

Along with all the other field workers, Josefa was herded into the clearing around the whipping post and forced to watch the lashing. She remembered the swish of the lash as it whistled through the air, the multiple rubber tails biting into his flesh. She remembered the welts that rose like magic roads across his back, and then filled with red. She remembered the twisted muscles at his throat as he clenched his teeth to keep from screaming.

He withstood the first few strokes but the fifth had brought him down on his knees. Even dripping blood and already weak, he struggled to get back on his feet. Why didn't he stay down? Maybe he didn't realize that the more he got up, the angrier the *mayoral* became; or perhaps he knew it all too well, for he made sure to look straight into Romero's face each time he got up. After the first fall, each stroke knocked him to his knees and after each one, he struggled up again and stood, bent but still towering over his tormentor, dripping an acrid mixture of sweat and blood. The whip came down on his back so many times that the other cane workers, forced to be present, turned their eyes away and prayed he would pass out before Romero killed him. Drops of his blood sprayed on them each time the whip came up again and again.

When Clemensio could no longer get to his feet, he dragged himself up to his knees and looked up at the mulatto standing over him. Spattered with Clemensio's blood, Romero stood heaving with the effort it took to torture the black man before him.

But the contempt that still lived in Clemensio fueled the *mayoral* to go further. With one final blow across Clemensio's face, Romero knocked him flat. Then he ground his boot into the back of Clemensio's head, hoping to grind the scorn on the black face into the mud once and for all. Shards of pain shot up Romero's arms and across his shoulders. Suddenly his legs were heavy and his head clouded, but he was relentless. So much sweat and blood covered him that a casual observer might confuse the torturer for the tortured.

Romero glared at the crowd, making sure that his victory had registered with them, before removing his muddy boot from Clemensio's head. Then he staggered away as quickly as he could, not trusting that he could stand on his own two feet much longer, so exhausted was he from the beating.

"*¡Recójanlo!*" He shouted the order over his shoulder as he headed for his house, leaving it to others to clean up after him.

The cane workers rushed to Clemensio, who now lay unconscious. Josefa had watched from the fringes of the crowd, but now she broke into the circle and was the first to reach him, cradling his head as the men picked him up and carried him to the *choza* of the *curandera*.

Josefa sat outside the cabin door until nightfall. When the healer came out to wash the bloody rags, she took pity on the girl who leaned, half asleep, against the cabin wall.

"Go home to your mother, child. This will take time. But this I tell you. He is a bull of a man and he will not die. There is nothing to be done now. He needs rest so his body can begin the healing work."

Don Aurelio had heard about the beating as soon as he rode his new stallion in from town. He'd gone down to the cabin of the *curandera* and seen the work of the *mayoral* for himself. After a few moments, he stormed out and yelled for Romero to be brought to him immediately. As he waited in his library, he paced up and down the stately room, his riding boots making staccato noises on the polished tiles. His leather gloves strained as he opened and gripped the riding crop he still held. The *mayoral* stood nervously silent by the door.

Romero was still covered in blood, sweat, and mud. Exhausted, he had fallen asleep as soon as he sat on his bed, awakened only when he was summoned to the big house. The urgency of Don Aurelio's order to appear before him left Romero no time to clean up.

Seeing the condition of the overseer, Don Aurelio needed little explanation. But he barely controlled his fury long enough to give the man the opportunity to explain.

"I...I...taught him a lesson he'll never forget. Had to do it before he can be of any use to us...you, *patrón*." Romero started to boast about the good job he had done, but reading the face of his *patrón*, he thought better of it and adopted a more conciliatory tone.

"*Patrón*, discipline is part of my job and you know I take it seriously. These *bozales* need a strong hand. They need to be broken in, like any wild horse. They need to know who's *jefe* around here."

"And just who do *you* think is *jefe* around here, Romero?" Something about the control in the old man's voice alerted Romero to his mistake.

"B-b-bueno, *patrón*, of course you are the b-b-boss...that goes without saying...I just..."

Don Aurelio lost all control.

"*¡Maldito sea!* You're goddamn right, *I* am the *jefe*. *I* say what is your job. How many times have I told you, a dead slave is a waste of my money? You know how much I paid for that black savage? You almost killed him, you *hijo de puta negra*. There are other ways! He'll be useless for weeks. *¡Coño! ¡Carajo! ¡Puñeta! ¿Esto me la vas a pagar, me oyes?*"

Don Aurelio was beside himself. Red-faced and hoarse from the barrage of curses he'd let fly in Romero's face, he could barely control his hands as they itched to strike this man before him.

"*Pero, patrón*—" Romero's voice shook.

"That slave cost more than what you make in a year. NO! This time you will pay. You will forfeit your salary every month until the *bozal* gets back to the fields. And don't even consider leaving before you finish paying your debt, or I'll see to it that you will never work as an overseer again."

"*Pero, patrón*—" Romero raised his voice and tried to impose his right to be heard, but it was too late. His voice seemed barely a whisper compared with the booming tone of Don Aurelio's rage.

"*¡SILENCIO!* I'll see you groveling in the streets before you work again. *¡Vete, estúpido!* No, wait! One more thing. I want no more whipping of this slave. Do you hear me? ANSWER ME!"

"*Sí, patrón.*" Romero could only get out a shaky whisper.

"You have a problem with him, you find another way to solve it. I spent a small fortune on him and I want to get my money's worth. *¡Carajo!* He's got to be able to stand and work in those goddamned fields…unless you want to do it for him?"

"*No, patrón, pero, por favor*—" Romero spoke through trembling lips.

"And if you ever whip another one of my slaves into uselessness again, it will be *I* who will wield the whip and *I* who will know no mercy. *¿Me entiendes?*"

"But, *patrón, déjeme explicarle*—"

Don Aurelio's arm shot up menacingly, the riding crop still in it. Romero's last attempt at an explanation was thwarted before he could get the words out.

"*¿Me entiendes, sí o no?*"

"*Sí, c-c-claro que sí, p-p-patrón, pero…*" Romero finally gave up and accepted the old man's fury. He lowered his head and thought about how he would get even with that black bastard who caused him all this trouble.

"*Pero, nada, VETE.*" Don Aurelio dismissed him as he would an animal in the field.

With that the old man turned his back on his overseer, flinging his riding crop on the mahogany desk as a reminder of his fury. It had taken all his control not to send it slashing across Romero's face.

Romero stalked out of the house and into the *batey*, releasing his rage in a sudden kick at the whipping post he had used just hours before. His shriek rang out in the night as he fell over clutching his foot. The same *curandera* who tended to Clemensio's back was called on to tend to Romero's broken foot.

The next morning, the slaves could barely control their glee. They watched Romero hobble from one spot to the next as he went about his work, the excruciating pain produced by every step carved into his face. The *curandera* stood in the doorway of her cabin watching him. She hid her smile and went back to the business of serious healing. The man would never again walk without a shard of pain shooting up his leg. She'd seen to that.

* * *

Clemensio did not die. *La curandera* made sure the herbs she applied to his wounds worked slowly, giving the man's spirit, as well as his body, a chance to recuperate. And Josefa was part of the healing. Every day she stole away to the healer's cabin. On more than one occasion she nearly got beaten herself for disappearing from her duties. But the cook wasn't so old that she couldn't remember the madness of young love. So she found reasons to send the girl to the cabin of the *curandera*—strong black coffee, a bowl of broth, a pilfered piece of meat. Soon Josefa was at the healer's elbow every evening. She was the one who held Clemensio down as he bit his lips to keep from crying out in agony. Later, when he was stronger, Josefa alone washed him and applied the healer's balm before dressing his wounds.

By the time Clemensio was healed enough to go back to the fields, Josefa had long been sharing his bed. The couple yearned to live together as man and wife in one of the empty cabins. But Doña Rogelia wouldn't hear of it unless they had the blessings of the church. So each of them got a new set of clothes from *la patrona*, and the old padre came in his black skirts to say his words.

The couple moved into their *choza*. They worked hard all day and loved hard into the night. Clemensio being her first lover, Josefa marveled at the new sensations he brought out in her. She loved him all the more for helping her find unimagined facets of herself. No matter how tired she was from the day's toil, she always welcomed him into her arms, ready to explore his body and have him explore hers. Many times he was too exhausted, and then she watched him as he fell into a dead sleep. Just touching him, whether he was conscious of her or not, was enough to keep her mesmerized for hours.

Romero, chastised, never beat Clemensio again. But there was a silent, menacing energy between the two men, like lions waiting to lunge at any moment. Clemensio would not surrender to Romero's will. He did his work, but didn't bother to disguise the contempt he felt for the overseer. Josefa knew that Don Aurelio's interests superseded Romero's hatred. Clemensio would be safe as long as he was healthy and strong, a sound investment. Don Aurelio looked at Clemensio as he would a feisty prized stallion that had to be watched and carefully reined in. Josefa observed the men who ruled her life and said nothing, but fear became her constant companion.

* * *

The price of sugar bottomed out. Competition from other islands was taking its toll on the smaller plantations in Puerto Rico. Expenses began to outweigh profits. Don Aurelio had overextended himself. His investments in *mano de obra* had been unwise. He would have to liquidate property. Selling land was out of the question.

And there were other problems. There were whispers of troubles in nearby islands. Although the haciendas were isolated, the blacks had their own ways of finding out news. There had already been rebellious outbursts on some outlying plantations, and Don Aurelio was taking no chances. He was not a fool and wasn't willing to risk unrest because of one rebellious slave. Clemensio's body had been punished but his spirit had not been broken. And as he learned the new language, he would spread his brand of defiance to others. In short, Clemensio had become too dangerous. Best to get rid of him before he caused any more trouble.

One day, while Josefa was in Las Agujas, she saw Clemensio being led into the *batey* by two white men. She looked up at the sky. Odd for them to be back from the north field so early. The sun was only half way up the sky and the morning chill had not burned off completely. It was nowhere near noon. She heard the big wagon pulling into the *batey* and noticed that the two white men looked familiar. Then she remembered who they were.

She dropped her work and ran out just in time to see Clemensio forced onto the wagon. His eyes, still flashing defiantly, momentarily softened to a silent goodbye when he saw her. She ran after them until she saw him shake his head no. The wagon pulled away, leaving her in a cloud of dust. *NO!* Her scream was drowned out by the sound of the wagon wheels. She turned this way and that, seeking what? And then she saw him, grinning as he stood just under the fruit trees—Romero, chewing on his cigar, celebrating the departure.

Josefa looked at the man who had been her husband's worst enemy. She wanted to plunge her scissors into his face over and over again until she destroyed the smugness of it. She wanted to rip him apart. But none of that would bring back her Clemensio. There was only dust now where the wagon had taken away her husband and her life. She felt herself falling and tried to get up, but then the world went away and there was only darkness.

Her mind was gone for days. She didn't remember much about the morning that her husband was taken away. But what she did remember—what she would remember for years to come—was the look in his face and the rattle of the side panels of the wagon as it pulled away. She would hear that rattle every day of her life—every time they went for provisions, every time a casket was taken to the cemetery, every time a doctor was called for, every time a delivery was made. For years, every day of her life she lost him again and again.

The sound of the wagons rattling out of the *batey* had taken Clemensio out of her life, with his defiance still shining in his face. It was that same sound that brought Fela, with that same defiance living in her face for all the world to see. Josefa awoke with a start and suddenly understood the fear that had crept into her heart when she first laid eyes on Fela. She looked over at the young woman asleep in the nearby cot and knew that this would be the first of many sleepless nights.

* * *

"*Aaaah!*" Again Fela jerked awake, bathed in a blanket of sweat. This time she awoke to find Tía Josefa sitting by her bedside. The old woman sat weaving on a lap loom by the light of a small lantern. She stopped long enough to hold out a small gourd half filled with a brown liquid. Fela pushed it away.

"Do you or don't you want to calm the pounding heart?" Tía's brows shot up, questioning. "Want a quiet sleep?"

Fela turned away and burrowed into her pillow. Tía shook her head and returned to her loom. "Suit yourself."

By the end of the week and after two more heart-pounding nightmares, Fela reluctantly drank down the bitter liquid. It burned as if she had swallowed the lantern itself, searing its way down her body. Tía smiled and went back to her weaving without comment. Soon the tension started melting away and Fela fell into an uneventful sleep. When she awoke the next morning, Tía was gone, the loom was gone, and the cup was gone. It was as though the events of the previous night had never happened.

When Fela approached Tía for her basket of threads, the old woman went about the preparations as usual, making no mention of the incident. Fela struggled with her need for distance and her appreciation for the woman's kindness. Tía walked away and left Fela standing there with nowhere to put her gratitude.

* * *

Tía Josefa was in the habit of walking through the slave quarters late at night. The older she got, the harder it was for her to find sleep. Walking in the darkness often gave her a better view of the world than open observation in the daytime. She knew the secrets of the night. Heard the muffled sighs of release, the cries of agony, and the moans of delight. She had listened for the tail ends of Fela's nightmares. She had taken to leaving the tea by Fela's cot now that the woman accepted her help willingly. This freed her to continue her nocturnal walks.

As she came up the incline she found Fela, eyes closed, bare feet in the grass, arms outstretched, her white dress washed blue in the moonlight and fluttering in the night breeze. Her hair, which Tía had never seen loose, stood out over each ear as though her braids had exploded into freedom and taken a life of their own. Her entire body swayed back and forth, rocking to an inner rhythm. Her face, smooth and tranquil, lifted to the moon. A gentle smile rested on her lips. It was the only time Tía had ever seen Fela look completely happy.

Tía approached carefully, but the slight sound of her step was enough to break Fela's mood.

"I'm sorry. I didn't mean to…you seemed so happy, so much at peace. What were you thinking of? Home? Family?"

Fela immediately snatched her hand away, closing her fist on the stone. Her annoyance was drawn in the lines of her face. But seeing the genuine kindness in Tía's face softened the edge of Fela's irritation at the interruption. She remembered Tía's quiet persistence of the past few weeks. Slowly, Fela opened her hand and offered up its contents.

"*¿Qué tienes ahí?*"

Tía plucked up the stone and cupped it in her hand, stroking as if it were a small bird.

"Oh! It's beautiful. I've never seen a stone like this."

Something shifted and Fela found herself yearning to tell this woman just how precious a stone it really was to her. As though she heard her thoughts, Tía pressed it back into Fela's hand.

"You've kept it safe all this time?"

Fela nodded once and returned it to its pouch.

The old woman placed her hands on either side of Fela's face, "That must have been very hard to do." Another nod.

Fela allowed the old woman to stroke her cheek. "It's getting late and we have to be up early." Tía slipped her hand around Fela's arm and together they turned and headed back to Las Agujas.

4 PENANCE

Although the *patrones* were never very far away, the women who worked the cloth were left to themselves most of the time. Tía Josefa held the keys. She distributed the costly supplies—needles, scissors, and embroidery hoops. She received and distributed the expensive cloth, made assignments, and was responsible for meeting deadlines.

It was her business to record changes that would have an impact on their work. She knew the names, tastes, and measurements of all the ladies of the district and kept track of the dates and locations of all the major social events in the county. She knew which *señoritas* lost weight after failed love affairs and who gained after months of secret rendezvous with unacceptable *caballeros*. She knew when to take in waistlines and when to let them out, how to augment the scarce and when to reduce the abundant. Stays needed here, well-placed pleating there. She saw and heard everything and said nothing. Doña Filomena knew that she could trust Tía without reservation. The umbrella of that trust shielded all the women of Las Agujas. Their days were fairly predictable and uneventful.

After weeks of wariness, Fela began to breathe more easily, move a little more freely, trust a little more. But although she relaxed somewhat in her outer world, her true self lived in a seductive and inviolate inner world. Her dreams brought her less and less the atrocities of her past and more and more the hope for redemption in the world to come. There was nothing in this world of slaves and masters for her. But Oshun was an unforgiving Mother. Fela risked everything and everyone to bring a baby into her old world and now she would only be granted release when she brought one into this new world.

* * *

One evening after dinner, Fela stole away from the others and sat alone on the far side of Las Agujas, overlooking the *batey*. She fingered the pouch around her neck as she surveyed the scene before her.

Each *choza*, on either side of the path leading away from the main house, was supported by four poles, which raised the cabin a foot off the ground. The doors and windows were simple wooden planks, which were barred at night for privacy and during the day to keep out the heat. The harvest was almost done and as *tiempo muerto* approached, field workers returned to their cabins in the evening.

The older women who were no longer able to work the fields did the cooking for the rest. Three women sat peeling the last of the *viandas* while two others bent over bubbling *calderos*. These were set over trios of large stones that supported the large kettles.

The *chozas* were set in the hollow between the two larger houses on the plantation, so very little air circulated in the slave quarters. The smell of cooking food blended with the stench of animal and human waste during the rainy season, when the land around the *chozas* turned to mud, adding to the fetid air.

The rankness clung to Fela's hair, soaked into her clothing, and hung in the air like a heavy blanket. Armies of mosquitoes bred and hovered over *el batey*. Children scratched at infected and festering scabs, with no relief from the insects. Not even the *curandera* could concoct balms strong enough to soothe their discomfort.

During *tiempo muerto,* when the cane was gone and the ground not ready for the new planting, the men worked at the *trapiche*, extracting the last drop of cane juice in preparation for fermentation. This sticky sweet smell of *melao* was superimposed on all the others and turned Fela's stomach.

From her vantage point on the rise, she slapped at the hovering mosquitoes as she looked out into the distance at the large corrals that stood behind the overseer's house. Beyond these, an uninterrupted expanse of harvested sugarcane fields on the right, and smaller fields of fruits and vegetables on the left.

In the far distance she saw a large cloud of steady smoke that sat over the area. It came from the large vats of molasses that were part of the sugar processing that went on twenty-four hours a day, every day, until the end of the harvest. There would be two work crews that alternated day and night. She knew that during high *zafra*, the workers, women and children as well as men, labored continuously. This was a particularly dangerous time because exhaustion made their work more hazardous than ever. Sometimes workers died in the fields or sugar mill, trying to meet a shipping date imposed by the merchants who had never held a machete in their lives. Many emerged burned or maimed or worse. Sometimes a careless worker was crushed or burned to death.

The sounds of the returning workers brought her back to the scene before her. She watched the stream of people who fed the sugar monster. They moved slowly, heavily, their long machetes resting on their shoulders, their shadows creating a moving, throbbing field of pointy stalks on the ground beyond them. Their legs were wrapped tightly in old rags and secured by ropes, protection against the sharp leaves, rodents, and snakes. Their heads were wrapped in old rags as well, soiled gray and soggy from the perspiration of the day. Many wore frayed straw hats to beat off the scorching sun. As the ball of the sun set behind them, a trick of light made the lower border of the yellow ball appear to sit directly on their backs. They carried the heavy weariness of those whose work was never-ending. Their eyes never left the ground.

Fela thought about her task. It was clear that she must find a man to help her finish the work of the stone. She owed this to Imo, to Oshun, to her people. And once done, the payment of this penance, she would be released to go to her husband.

Unconsciously, Fela's hand wandered back to the pouch while her eyes searched for the men whose bodies had not yet succumbed to the ravages of the fields. One man towered over the rest, defying the sun and denying his weariness. But his height didn't hide the start of a stoop in his shoulders. He was stronger or newer to this place than the rest, but even he would eventually bow to the brutal labor. She looked, searched, evaluated. She'd have to find a powerful body and a strong will because her child would need his strength.

Riding high on his horse, Romero cast a shadow on the group before him. His black cape fell on either side of him like huge wings. He sat motionless on his steed, his only movement his eyes darting continuously in his brown face.

Romero was not the first mulatto Fela had seen. But in him, the black and white features clashed in a constant war that left him looking more animal than human. The indelible imprint of black that could not be beaten out of his yellowish skin or wiped from his warring features was the seed of his hate-filled existence. The white of him presented itself in his golden lion's eyes that looked through everyone rather than at them.

Fela studied him openly for the first time. Her eyes traveled down to his whip, its bulk always discernable just beneath the cape. His eyes were never far from the men beneath him. And, she had heard, his hands were never far from the women. They said he was as cruel and unforgiving with his body as he was with his whip. The man thrived on taking and breaking everything around him. She shivered.

What protection could any one of these men offer her child? Which one of them could see to it that her child's life would be better than his own? How could she protect the baby girl, for a girl it would be, from the white men and this not-so-white man who sat before her? Oshun had chosen her penance well.

* * *

Fela balanced the huge basket on her head. Her bare feet carried her from the beaten earth of the cabins past the gardens and the swept avenue of her master's home. She took the river road into town to deliver Doña Gertrudis' new gown. Although the walk was long and her load heavy, Fela welcomed being away from the hacienda and she loved traveling alone. She had made this trip many times. Tía usually brought her along to carry the heavy dresses, make adjustments, or deliver finished pieces. But just this morning, Tía had hurt her leg, and Doña Gertrudis needed her gown for that evening's Society Ball. This was the first time Fela had been allowed to make the trip on her own.

She worked her way into the town, passing through the squalid, unpaved streets of the poor to the more fashionable, cobblestoned streets of pastel houses and fringed and canopied *carruajes* with their shiny stallions and uniformed coachmen.

As she neared the square, her feet took her past the black craftsmen selling their woven hats from wire stands. Old women cupped their deft hands around *alcapurrias,* the dumplings sizzling as they sank into the boiling fat. One woman bowed her head to Fela in greeting. On the next corner, the *piragüero* worked at shaving the block of ice and pouring the *tamarindo* before handing a frosty treat to a waiting child.

Finally, Fela came to the square proper. On the far corner, the cantina was already opening its doors. She walked by quickly. Stopping to look would only encourage rude comments. The *bombonero* was setting out his flaky delicacies on white doilies in the window. The *militares* had just finished their exercises, their shouted commands carrying through the armory arches.

As Fela approached the next corner, a group of *señoritas* came out of the *teatro*. One of them thoughtlessly snapped open her blue parasol without looking to see if there was anyone walking by. Fela stepped back, barely avoiding a blow to the face. In doing so, she lost her balance. The young woman in the blue outfit looked down at the large bundle that now lay in the street. Her annoyance distorted her pretty face.

"*¿Qué? ¿No puedes tener más cuidado?*" she sneered as she brushed past Fela and joined her friends who had already moved on.

Luckily, the dresses had been well wrapped in muslin. Fela gathered up her bundle and deposited it back into the basket. An old man walking by helped her adjust the weighty basket on her head. As she continued on her way, Fela was too preoccupied with her own seething anger to notice the men sitting in the square.

The white men who habitually sat there drinking aged rum or discussing the buying and selling of crops stopped their conversations and turned to watch Fela move up the opposite side of the street. They watched all women, but the daring of their commentary depended on the complexion of the woman's skin.

At the first comment, Fela braced herself. She pulled the basket down from her head and rested it on her hip. Raised arms caused her breasts to push up and out. She chose to ignore the lust that dripped from the corners of the men's mouths. She could feel their eyes on her skin, and the hair at the nape of her neck stiffened under their scrutiny. Their eyes searched out her waist, her thighs, the dark secrets they imagined lay within the folds of her skirt. These men smelled like overheated irons left unattended. And the smell reached out for her, clung to her hair.

She caught a glimpse of Don Tomás as he approached the group. Looking away, she pulled herself up straight, more contained within herself, beyond them. She locked her jaw, willing herself not to bare her teeth, not to spit.

As Don Tomás approached the men seated on the benches beneath the *flamboyán* trees, he watched Fela. The men, whose attention was on the tall black woman across the square, didn't notice his approach.

"*Coño*, that Fela makes my blood boil every time she waltzes by. I sometimes catch myself wishing…," said Don Porfírio Díaz.

"I can just imagine what I could do with…," his neighbor chimed in.

"Don't even dream of it. *¡Carajo!* I've tried to buy that slave bitch from Filomena many times, but you know how she feels about her precious needlewomen. Their needles protect them like no guard ever could. This one in particular is beginning to forget that she is a slave. If she were mine, I'd teach her a lesson or two." Don Porfírio rocked his pelvis as he drained his glass.

"Be careful. You don't want to antagonize Filomena. Your wife loves those damned dresses as much as mine does." There was general laughter. But Porfírio was not amused.

"One day Tomás will regret the power he has given his wife. These matters should be left to the men, as they always have been. Tomás is a fool." Porfírio's eyes flashed.

"Yes, but a very wealthy fool…," his neighbor pointed out cautiously. Throats cleared all round.

"Oh! Tomás. *¡Hombre!* We didn't see you coming."

"Evidently not."

"We were just admiring your woman Fela."

Biting down on his premium cigar, Don Tomás said nothing, but his eyes, like those of the other men, followed Fela's tall figure. She wore an ordinary humble dress, no different from that of any slave, except that she had covered the bodice and hem with yellow embroidery. The bleached cloth gleamed in the midmorning sun, contrasting with the dinginess of the streets around her. She had tied a long yellow ribbon around her waist that trailed her as she made her way up the opposite sidewalk. Her workbasket, now nestled in the curve of her waist, accentuated the movements below and the swaying hem of her skirt, teasing the air around her ankles. The men watched her until she reached the top of the street and disappeared around a corner. The yellow ribbon was the last glimpse they had of her.

* * *

As Fela turned the corner and climbed up the tree-lined street, she continued to hold herself in. No trace of cigar smoke came her way, no too-close, too-fast footsteps fell behind her. No creeping shadow joined her own on the cobblestones ahead of her. Only when she was sure no one had followed did she allow herself to release her breath.

Recovered, she continued up the street, pulling the basket back up to her head and permitting her hips their natural sway. She didn't have to send her senses to scout around her now and after a few moments her breathing regained its natural rhythm. She knew she was safe as long as the women wanted her dresses more than their husbands wanted her.

* * *

As one of Filomena's slaves, Fela lived only a few yards from Don Tomás' back door. But *because* she was one of his wife's needlewomen, Fela was unapproachable. This irony worked on Don Tomás so that he found himself looking out of his rear window dozens of times during the day. He lingered out back more than ever before. Taking on some of the foreman's tasks, which he had always hated, he hoped he could possibly have a glimpse or a smile from the woman. Fela, who recognized the look on his face, deliberately made herself scarce whenever Don Tomás was around. Often, he would catch sight of her just as she left a room or closed a door.

One night soon after the incident in town, Don Tomás, restless in his own bed, told himself he was going out back to get some air. He came upon Fela in the moonlight behind Las Agujas. She sat on a bench, her feet soaking in a basin of soapy water. He could see the white lather clinging to her calves and imagined his tongue lapping up the salty taste of those muscular calves. She had hitched up her dress and caught it between her thighs, and she now leaned back against the side of the building, lost in thought. Her head was held at an angle as though she was listening to some far-off music, her face turned to the full moon above. When she arched her body forward a little, head tilted, the look on her face was joyous, expectant, eager. He had never seen that particular look on her or any other slave before. Her self-absorption gave him the opportunity to watch her unguarded and vulnerable, at his leisure.

Makes my blood boil, he remembered the words of the men in *la plaza*. He had always hated that mentality, held by most men in his own class. Their violence and cruelty had always been distasteful to him. After all, there were more than enough willing women, why bother with the unwilling? But he could not deny the pull he felt for this particular girl. In the last few weeks, he had visited his usual haunts more than he had in many months. But those women, well paid and well trained, had not erased this slave from his thoughts or the ache in his loins.

So he set about to win her over. He made it his business to frequent the *batey*, always managing a "*Buenas tardes*, Fela," or directing a warm smile her way. She barely nodded and went on with her activity, escaping his presence as soon as possible. He wondered if she wasn't getting his meaning. So one day he slipped into Las Agujas and left a pair of satin slippers on her cot and waited to see if she would warm to him. But the next morning, he walked out to see one of the other women wearing his gift as she stood, scrubbing at the dirty clothes at the huge tub. The muddy puddles collected below had already saturated the thin slippers he had taken so much care to select.

He decided he would be more direct. Sunday mornings were dedicated to God on Hacienda Las Mercedes. Doña Filomena insisted that the workers be herded into wagons on Sunday mornings and taken to church. Only the most pressing need would excuse a slave from attending mass.

One Sunday, Fela was left behind to finish embroidering a shawl that was needed for that evening. Don Tomás stood at his bedroom window, watching Fela from above as she sat at the worktable. He loved observing her when she was relaxed and unguarded. But as he watched, Tomás noticed a man slipping out from behind the cabins. He recognized Romero's bulk in his stealthy approach. He moved slowly, catching Fela unawares and springing on her from behind. Tomás shot into action. By the time he reached the *batey* Romero was twisting her arm as Fela fought to defend herself.

"I'll make you pay, *¡hija de puta!*" The words were grunted as he struggled to subdue the woman. "I haven't forgotten. And I'll break that look on your face if it's the last thing I do."

Tomás' voice boomed out, *"Pero, Romero, ¿qué carajo pasa aquí?"*

The stunned overseer quickly stepped back, releasing Fela, and trying to control himself before turning to the *patrón.*

"¿Patrón? I didn't know you…" Romero licked his lips repeatedly. "I was just…well, you know, she asked me to…"

Without a moment's hesitation, Tomás felled him with a backhanded slap. "How dare you?" His voice thundered. He could barely control himself. *"Descarao,* get up and don't you ever even think about coming anywhere near her again. Do you understand me, *carajo?* Get out of my sight."

He waited until Romero was gone before turning to Fela. He couldn't take his eyes away from her exposed breast, now showing through her torn bodice. She pulled the shawl over her shoulders, trying to cover her nakedness. Suddenly he realized he was shirtless and barefoot. She flinched as he reached out to reassure her. She pulled away to a safe distance behind her worktable and waited.

Remembering his original intent, he reached in his pocket and pulled out a small velvet box wrapped in a satin bow and placed it on the table between them. Fela let herself down onto her bench and sat staring at his face, not even glancing at the offering he had put before her.

"I thought you might like this."

Before she could move or say a word, the wagons pulled in from town, bringing Doña Filomena and the others into the clearing. *La patrona* held up her parasol and shielded her eyes. She took in Fela's defensive posture, her torn clothes, her husband's state of undress, and the fancy box on the table between them. She said nothing, but stared at her husband until he walked away from the table and joined her. They walked into the house in silence. Fela never doubted that he would return. She recognized the inevitability of her position. *Not again*, a silent prayer, *please, not again.*

* * *

The more distance Fela tried to put between herself and Don Tomás, the more he tried to convince himself that, as the master of the hacienda, he had certain rights. And while philosophically he didn't agree with the men in the square, he recognized that on a baser level, he was one of them in regard to Fela. Their words came back to him, exploding in his head and fueling his imagination. *If she were mine...*

Sometimes Tomás convinced himself that perhaps he should be more forceful, but the moment his eyes fell on Fela his forcefulness disappeared in the face of truth—he did not want to take this woman. He prided himself in that he had never forced himself on any woman. He wanted Fela in particular to come to him of her free will.

He'd seen the sadness in her eyes, had watched her for months, sitting apart, working by herself, alone even when surrounded by others. She was as out of place in her world of slave women as he was in his world of violent men.

The gifts continued to appear—a bit of lace here, picked flowers there, a tiny bottle of perfume or a hand-painted fan in her basket. She knew exactly where these gifts came from. Who else could afford these gifts? What man had access to these places at odd hours of the day? Who else had time for such things?

Although she rejected his gifts, Don Tomás was on Fela's mind. She didn't understand this *patrón* who courted her as he would a white woman. Other *patrones* would have helped themselves to whomever and whatever they wanted. She was astounded to realize that Don Tomás was *wooing* her. Could it be possible that he actually cared how she felt about him?

* * *

One hot Sunday morning, Tía begged a crippling headache and Fela was allowed to stay behind to tend to her while everyone else on the plantation left for church. As they heard the last of the wagons pull out onto the road, the two women gathered some clothes, picked a bar of the scented soap that had materialized that week, and headed for the river.

The current wasn't very strong that morning so they took a long leisurely swim. Fela had looked forward to scrubbing herself clean of the week's grime. When she was finished washing, she joined Tía, spreading out on the flat rock that sat in the middle of the stream. They lay side-by-side, letting the breeze dry their bodies and the heat of the sun-warmed rock ease the tension in their backs. They rarely got this kind of privacy or solitude.

Tía's soft snoring and the warmth of the sun had lulled Fela into a half sleep when she heard a rustle of leaves on the nearby bank. She opened her eyes just enough to catch the flare of a match. The sharp smell of tobacco floated over to her in the stillness of the morning. Slowly she sat up and looked directly into Don Tomás' eyes. He made no attempt to hide his open appreciation of her nakedness.

She pulled her legs up and wrapped her arms around her knees to cover herself. They stared at each other for some moments. She expected to see lust but instead she saw a moment of *genuine* admiration before he tipped his hat, inclined his head, and went on his way.

Fela was shaken. This *patrón* was so different from the other white men she had encountered, offering rather than taking. Slowly, very slowly, a thought started growing in her like a tiny bud.

Not far away, another man stood in the shadows watching the exchange. He spit before turning away, the tail of his whip dragging behind him.

* * *

Don Tomás tossed in his bed until the sheets were a tangle around his legs. He was too hot and restless to sleep. He padded to his dresser and poured himself one, then another, and then a third generous drink and looked out the window. The sounds of the plantation had long ago ceased. There was no movement in the night. The cabins were still. Even Romero's lanterns were out. He looked in on Filomena to see her sleeping soundly in her room. After gently closing the door connecting their rooms, he slipped downstairs.

He rushed out into the night hoping to find a cool breeze, but the air hung still and humid. The drinks made him lightheaded and he struck out for the river. Its cold waters would soothe him and then maybe he could sleep. As he was walking across the *batey*, he was startled to see a figure standing at the doorway of the embroiderers' cabin. She stood frozen and ghostly in her loose garment. Her height and her posture gave her away.

"*¿Quién está ahí?*" It was an unnecessary question.

Fela stepped out into the moonlight. She took in his appearance, a strong man, fit, not like the other *patrones*, grown fat and sloppy with excesses. She wasn't afraid, but stood openly assessing him. She held her head high and returned his stare. She could see his state of excitement and knew that the seed of an idea that had been growing in her mind would come to be on this night. She hadn't consciously planned for this. Maybe the goddess was guiding her down this path. It didn't matter. At least this time she would have as much to do with what was about to happen as he did. She would not be taken. This time it would be her choice.

She remembered that other *patrón* on that other plantation. The scene flashed through her mind with such vividness that it stopped her for a moment. She remembered the pounding, the violence in that barn. She remembered tensing her body against him. She hadn't seen the gash in his neck until later, but the leaden taste of his blood dripping down her chin was still living in her mouth. The blow to her jaw—the loose teeth that she spit out just before the final blow that left her sprawled on the barn floor—still haunted her. The searing hot pain that had torn apart her groin cut through her still. She remembered his rancid breath on her face.

Afterward he left her there, as he would an animal that had performed her task. Fela pulled herself up and stumbled out to get help. On her way, she heard voices on the porch. In her naiveté, and thinking another woman would surely understand, she presented her bruised body to her mistress.

"*Señora, el patrón*, he do this. You know?" Fela flung the words at the *patrona*. "Your *marido*…do this to me…"

The wife was amazed at the audacity of this slave woman to even address her, much less in front of her visitors. She glared at Fela, but the undeniable violence that clung to Fela's clothes told the whole story. She knew her husband well and had no doubt about what had happened. But this scene was intolerable.

Fela's rage blinded her to her position. She refused to be put off.

"*El patrón*…he…he…look, *señora*…"

The *patrona* would no longer endure this black woman who obviously hadn't been taught her place yet. She shook in her fury.

"Where is that damned overseer? Finally! It's about time. Take care of this."

Strong hands dragged Fela away, still screaming her accusations. The male hands muffled her screams. The embarrassed women on the porch hesitantly returned to their card game. They secretly cringed at the thought of their own husbands' frequent absences from their marital beds. Nothing else was said, but that evening the *patrona* lost every hand.

The card party ended early that night. The *patrona* was the ever-gracious hostess. But as the last coach pulled away she could barely contain herself. Her husband didn't bother denying the whole incident and left her to deal with Fela's accusations in her own way. She was not to mention it to him again. In the end, it was not the *patrón* but his victim who paid the price. To keep this impertinent slave from spreading tales about her husband, the mistress gave the order to have the woman's lying tongue cut out.

Since Fela was a valuable piece of property, she could not be allowed to bleed to death. So the veterinarian was summoned to minister to her wounds. And as soon as she had healed, Fela found herself on the auction block once again. It was expected that, given her mutilation, her owners would lose money in the transaction. But oddly enough, her inability to speak seemed to make her more desirable to bidders than her skill with the needle.

Don Tomás bought her on Doña Filomena's request. And while the new *patrona* had the young slave housed in the embroiderers' quarters, where she was given privileges she had never known before, proximity to the family could have its own dangers, as Fela well knew. Regardless of the niceties of this new *patrón*, he could do whatever he wanted. Sooner or later, his patience would wear thin and he would take what he hadn't been given.

So when she saw Don Tomás in the *batey* that night, she wasn't terribly surprised. But this time it would be different.

As they stood face-to-face, he reached for her hand and led her away. Fela yielded. *For you, Oshun, for you.* It would be over soon. This man who had bought her body would unknowingly release her soul.

Fela pulled her hand free and stretched to her full height, walking side-by-side with the *patrón*. She never looked back. Tía Josefa, sleepless as ever, watched the whole scene from the window of Las Agujas. She had seen the looks and the gifts and had known that this evening would come. She sat next to Fela's cot and waited.

* * *

The two made their way through the fields, away from the main house. Fela's resolve never wavered as she felt herself being led toward the river. Her step was sure-footed and determined. Then she felt the moist earth beneath, heard the river as it flowed in the background. She let him do as he chose, focusing on the white shoulder above her. And, unexpectedly, the details of that other night came back to her like a sudden blow.

She could feel the slap across her face, hear the crack inside her skull, smell his strong tobacco clawing at her like sticky fog. He had become a great rutting bull ramming into her, again and again. She remembered struggling on the floor of the barn, tasting the bits of earth and hay that had somehow gotten into her mouth—fertilizer, manure mixed with soil; the bitterness that had started in her mouth had permeated her body and stayed with her for months.

Don Tomás' voice brought her back.

"I don't want to hurt you." She turned her head away, neither resisting nor aiding in what was happening to her.

Fela felt nothing of what was occurring with her body. It didn't matter anymore. She sent her senses beyond this place, over his shoulder to the moon, and got comfortable there. It wouldn't be long now. She would join Imo and the others. Oshun would be appeased

and the ancestors would welcome her. She would be released and all
this would be over.

She thought of that other river, the promises, the images, the will
of Oshun, and her own clawing need back then. She and Imo had
begun something that night that she would have to finish by herself. *For
you, Oshun, for you. Only for you. My debt will soon be paid in full.*

When it was over, Don Tomás tried to get her to rearrange her
clothes, tried to speak to her of his feelings. But she was in her own
world. He simply didn't exist for her. Now that the effects of the rum
had subsided, he could see that he had been dismissed. He suspected
she had never let him come anywhere near her secret self. Don Tomás
realized that there were many ways of not having another person.

He covered her the best he could and carried her inert body into Las
Agujas. As he placed her gently on her cot, the other women pretended
to be asleep. But Tía sat in her chair and watched his every move.

"I don't know what's wrong with her. She just...she..."

Tía said nothing but stared hard, tears caught in her lashes.

"She must have the best care. You understand, the best."

He found it difficult to look the old woman in the eyes, so he
stormed out without another word.

No sooner was Don Tomás gone than Fela got up and went to the
window. She fastened her eyes on the moon and refused to lie down.
Tía washed her and combed the leaves out of her hair as Fela stood
there, gazing at the night sky.

5 AFTERMATH

Don Tomás had avoided the slave quarters, but Fela was constantly on his mind. The memory of that night waited for him every time he looked out his window. While Fela hadn't encouraged his attentions, he believed she had waited for him, followed him of her own free will. Obviously, she wanted it as much as he did. But he couldn't forget that although she hadn't fought him off, she hadn't encouraged him, either. She hadn't responded to anything he did. He had done what he wanted but he had never felt so superfluous in his life. He tried to shore himself up with the idea that she was, after all, only property, his to do with as he wished. But this argument rang hollow and he knew it.

He tried to see Fela only once after the evening in the field. Tía Josefa met him at the door of Las Agujas, a silent and impassable presence. The other needlewomen took their places behind the old woman, effectively blocking his path into the room. Beyond them he could see Fela staring back at him. She slowly turned her eyes and then her body away. The last glimpse he had of her was her rigid back as she settled into her cot. He could have easily pushed his way in. But he hadn't. He had done enough.

* * *

On the first moonless night, Fela searched the sky and, finding no moon, lay down and slept straight through until morning. At dawn,

Tía Josefa woke to find her searching for her workbasket. Fela prepared to join the women at the worktable, as though nothing had happened. If she noticed that weeks had gone by, that her unfinished work was completed, that the other women stared at her, surprised at seeing her up and about, she never showed it. She remained a lone figure at the end of the worktable.

She seemed to live more and more in an internal world that ran parallel to the one in which everyone else existed. No one remarked as the changes in her body became obvious. Tía kept her heart open and her mouth closed, waiting to see what Fela needed from her. Fela slipped more and more frequently into the world of her ancestors and stayed there for longer periods of time.

* * *

Ten-year-old Cheito Muñoz sat working on one of his pieces when the mute woman with the sad eyes and the big belly walked into their *choza*. Fela had come to see his father, Melchor, because she wanted him to make her a box. She drew lines on the floor to show the dimensions she wanted. When his father brought out the pieces of leftover wood from the various projects he had completed on the plantation, she closed her eyes and ran her fingers over each piece. She stroked the grain and tested the weight. Finally, she brought the wood up to her face and sniffed at it until she found the one. Then she placed it in Melchor's hands and nodded.

Cheito had carved many pieces but he had never seen anyone handle wood the way this woman was doing. When she left, he asked his father, "What was she doing?"

"Sometimes I think I haven't taught you enough, my son. You still know nothing of the old ways. *Oye bien*. This piece of wood is more than just wood. Once it lived in the forest and, like every living thing, had a spirit. Here men cut down trees without a thought. But, in the old place, we knew that the spirit of the tree must be addressed before the cutting. Fela wanted to make sure that the wood spirit would accept the purpose for which she is using it."

"You mean she asked its *permission* to be used."

"Yes, I suppose that's one way to look at it. *Hijo*, if you're truly meant to be a master carver, you have to learn that nothing is what it seems on the surface. What we see is only the face. Everything that lives or ever has lived has a spirit, an inner life. We may disturb that spirit for our own needs, but first, we must acknowledge its existence, its importance, and pay due respect. A master carver has to have more than just skillful hands; he must also have a grateful and humble heart, as is needed for all who do the work of the soul."

Cheito picked up the wood and felt for its spirit the way Fela had, but all he felt was wood.

When Melchor had finished the box, Fela picked it up and felt its smoothness, its firmness, and then she carried it to Cheito's table and held it before him. She motioned toward his tools. At first he had no idea what she was asking for, but then he understood.

It wasn't easy working for a woman who couldn't tell him what she wanted. But after a while they developed their own language and worked well together. It took weeks of stolen time to carve every inch of the box and then find the dyes to paint it in the colors she indicated. Cheito carried the finished box to Las Agujas and placed it before Fela. She picked it up, brushing her fingers over the surface. She smiled and bowed her head to the young carver. Cheito ran all the way home to tell his father.

* * *

Nine months after that night in the fields, during the women's evening meal, Fela left the table and went into the cabin. She was tired and wanted to lie down. Her lower back had been bothering her all day. During the night, she felt the warm liquid spilling out of her and knew the time had come. She made sure the others were asleep. Even Tía was snoring softly.

She pulled the box out from under her cot and examined the contents one last time. She removed the pouch from around her neck and poured out the stone. There, in the middle of her palm, lay the one legacy she and Imo could leave for this child, for it was, finally, their child. And this, too, she placed into the box just before she doubled over with the first flash of pain.

> Not yet…oh, please…Oshun…I know I have no right…but please not yet…Great Mother, everything is almost ready…but I must get to the place…your place, Mother…give me strength…guide my feet on this long journey back to you, back to Imo, back to the ancestors…

Fela picked up the box and walked into the night. With every step she felt the heaviness pressing down between her legs. She closed her eyes briefly to ground her resolve before making her way beyond the house. As she neared the river, she saw two full moons. One hung in the sky while the other rocked in the water. Both waited patiently for her as she worked her way to her chosen spot.

Here the earth was rich and brown and soft. Every evening for the past week, she had slipped down here and turned the earth, removing stones and making a soft cushion for what was sure to come soon. Now she set the box down on the turned soil. She removed the cover and took out the things she knew she would need—the scissors, the cloth, the threads, the oil—and laid them out where she could find them easily. Then she sat down on the ground, keeping her eye on the silvery reflection floating nearby. She listened to the sounds of the river as she waited for the next flash of pain to cut across her belly.

Hours passed and Fela became well acquainted with the many faces of pain. She lay on the ground by the river, knees up, her back pushed into the earth to relieve the spasms that seemed to settle there.

Soreness had grown to cramps. Cramps had grown to shooting shards, which gave way to the grinding, constant pain and later to the rending fire-red spasms that made her body twist and contract into positions she had never been in before. She tensed as the waves of pain came faster and faster. She began to regret her decision to do this alone. Tía would know what to do, how to ease the coming. She could judge if this was taking too long. She would know how to ease the vise that gripped Fela's groin and would not let go.

Another contraction pulled her body to an almost seated position. Everything rigid, neck, back, legs. She was losing herself to the pain that cut across her belly and settled itself between her legs. The pressure grew. She could barely breathe. Every muscle had been contracted and stretched to its limit. Then it all came together in one enormous contraction. Excruciating pain filled her world. She lost time, place. Nothing else existed.

* * *

The moon was Fela's only companion as a pale baby girl finally slid out of her and onto the bed of earth. She hoisted herself up and picked up the baby, rocking the tiny body from side to side

I've done it. Imo, our daughter—ours, yours and mine.

She was joyous, filled with light and love. But there was still work to do. She tied the cord with silk thread and used the scissors. Then she picked up her wet and slippery baby and sank back as the last of her energy gave out. As she rested there, she felt the final contractions. The afterbirth slipped out of her and lay between her legs, now cold and useless, while her daughter, warm and beautiful, lay against her breasts.

She rolled over to cushion her child in the crook of her arm. She reached down to feel the movement in the little chest and stroked the child's body, waiting to hear the sound of her daughter's voice. *She is perfect and she is mine…the only thing in this world that is mine…*

She pulled the cloth out of the box and wrapped her baby. Then she pulled closer to the river, took out another soft cloth, and, dipping it in the dark waters, slowly wiped the baby clean. She dug in the box for a small bottle and carefully anointed her daughter with fragrant oil. To her surprise, the childhood songs she had heard so many years ago came back to her, turning around and around in her head. It saddened her that she couldn't sing them to her daughter as they had been sung to her. But she followed the songs in her head and believed the child could hear them all the same.

She swaddled the baby in her white and yellow dress, her best one, which she had set aside just this night. The baby made little sounds as she lay quietly sucking her small fist. There was one last thing to do.

Taking out the pouch, Fela pulled out the black stone. She dipped it in the water and rubbed it over the baby's body making the markings, leaving a secret message on the child's skin as Imo had done to her a lifetime ago. She thought she had forgotten the symbols the *babalaos* had given them. But they came back to her and she gave them to her daughter, the only protection she could offer. She closed her eyes as she finished the ritual and prayed that it would be enough.

When she opened her eyes the baby was watching her with the eyes of an old soul. They stared at each other for a flash of a second before the child went back to being a newborn baby. She waved her arms and legs in jerking motions.

The baby's face broke up and she began whimpering. Fela lifted her to her breast, where she began sucking immediately. Fela cradled her daughter and sat back to enjoy the moment.

When the child fell asleep, Fela listened for her breathing and took in the earthen smell of her hair. She reached out to her daughter with all her senses.

It is time.

Instantly she sat ramrod straight. She knew there was no one around. Pulling her child closer, she watched the reflection of the moon as it danced on the surface of the river, and listened to the river sounds.

She thought about that other night, near that other river, about the village and Oshun and Imo and their childstone and her need and about her new baby. Fela knew the time had come. She had planned for it, prayed for it, desperately sought release. But she hadn't counted on this. Yes, she wanted to go…and yet…

She looked down on her baby and felt a pull. Too soon, it was too soon. She'd only just been born. How could Fela let go now? She clung to the child, felt the tiny hairs of her head as she tried to breathe in the child's scent.

The lapping water became more agitated. She could see it racing, fairly spraying the banks. The reflection of the moon broke into shards of light, taking on changing shapes and colors. She heard the message in the rushing water. Mother Oshun couldn't be that callous.

It is time.

Not yet. Please, not yet…I need more…I'm sorry…It was my fault they were all taken…I know it…atonement…but not yet…not this…

The river current became violent. The water ran over the banks, rushing toward her and her child. Fela tried to rise but was rooted to her spot. She clutched the baby. *No!* Her whole being screamed it. It wasn't a thought as much as a total body reaction. This was her child, hers. She wouldn't let her go. She belonged to her.

Fela's temples exploded. The voice thundered in the water, *DO NOT TRY ME!* Light flashed off the river surface, blinding her. The sound of the rushing water drowned out all other sounds. Trying to ease the pain in her head, she covered her ears and closed her burning eyes. The eruptions in her head blocked out all thought. She reeled. Through the pounding in her ears came another voice, a familiar, soft caress.

You have done well, Wife. It is over now.
Your task is done. Time for you to come home.

Imo. She had yearned for him for so long, needed him so much. But how? How to choose between husband and child? How could she leave her? This was asking too much.

As she sat weighing her dilemma, Fela noticed a shift in the child's weight. The baby's arms and legs went limp. Her tiny head fell to one side. Her chest stopped moving. Frightened, Fela shook her daughter. No reaction. She brought the child up to her face. No breathing. Panic seized her.

NOOOO! Please, I'll do anything, anything you want. Go whenever you say, just please, please, I beg you. Bring back my baby. She's yours, all yours. Just…please!!!

Fela was pulled out of her hysteria by the child's cries. Screaming, gulping in air, pumping her arms and legs erratically, the baby had tears streaming down her cheeks, and her crying filled the night.

Fela breathed a sigh of relief. She comforted the wailing baby, rocking her against her breast, letting her feel her mother's warmth. She blew streams of air against the child's face to calm her.

Once the child settled down, Fela tried to collect her thoughts. She had thought that her life of slavery was her greatest test, but she was wrong. She could never have guessed what a difficult sacrifice this would be. She sat, shoulders slumped in resignation, all the fight beaten out of her.

Finally, she placed her hand on the child's chest for a moment, offering her blessings before lowering the small body in the box. Using the floss and a few pieces of silk she had collected there, she created a cushion for the newborn.

She looked down on her night's work and smiled. She picked up the stone and slipped it into the baby's hand. The child clutched it tightly in her fist and promptly fell into a quiet sleep. Fela watched the tiny chest rise and fall rhythmically.

Afraid to touch her daughter, Fela looked longingly at her. At last, she placed fine netting over the box to keep insects away. When she was convinced she had done all that was necessary, she lay down on the soil and curled her body as close as she could around the box. She looked up at the night sky, knowing she was done here. Then she closed her eyes.

They found her there the next morning. She left behind a box of trinkets, some threads, a few old pieces of silk, a yellow and white embroidered dress, and my great-grandmother Mati clutching a little black stone in her newborn hand.

BOOK TWO

⋙⋘

MATI

6 THE GIFT

Mati spent every day outdoors. Her carved box sat on the spot that her mother had occupied at the table. She lay under the trees, where she was cool and safe, while the women worked. Their voices lulled her into a quiet sleep. When she awoke hungry and cranky and the milk was gone, the women would pull *guanábanas* from the trees and squeeze the mushy pulp between their fingers, letting the juice drip into her little mouth.

But as much as Mati was a well-loved child in the *batey*, she was also an unsettling presence. Usually quiet, she would fret when placed on her stomach, where she couldn't see the faces and colors of the world around her. Once seated upright, she examined that world with enormous eyes. Even Tía was startled when she turned around to find Mati unexpectedly staring at her with uncanny awareness. She never discussed her uneasiness, but others were well aware of the strangeness of the child.

One day all the women were busy with preparations for the Fiesta de Cruz the coming weekend. This was one of the most important dances of the year. They worked furiously but they were far behind and focused on getting their work done. They carried in coals for the heavy irons, set out muslin to protect the fine fabrics from the heat, and scrounged for paper to hold the long folds of the freshly pressed hoop skirts. It was late morning and they worked quickly to meet the daily deadline. Fifteen ball gowns had to be pressed, wrapped, and delivered to the homes of prominent women in the area before the Saturday afternoon siesta.

In all the commotion, Mati was forgotten. Earlier she had been fed, changed, and left sleeping soundly in her box. But the women lost track of time and Mati woke up hungry and wet, her whimpers soon turning to cries and cries to screams when no one responded. The child's face burned red as she wailed, waving her arms and legs uselessly in her perch. When Tía realized that the time for the next feeding had come and gone, she ran out to tend to the baby. She heard the wailing long before she reached the yard.

"*Ya, ya voy.* I'm sorry, *nena*! I'm coming!"

But as she ran toward the worktable she was amazed at the sight of heavy fruit, mottled mangos and rock-hard *jobos* dropping from the trees. Coconuts dropped like cannonballs from their majestic palms and unripe banana bunches crashed to the ground. The fruit fell with heavy thuds all around the basket. One after another, the ripe *guanábanas* burst *splat!* as they hit the ground. The hard *jobos* pummeled the earth as they dropped and rolled everywhere in the *batey*. The cracking sounds of crashing coconuts filled the yard. Miraculously, the baby's box still sat untouched on the table, but the child's screams rang out and even at a distance, Tía could see Mati's tiny limbs shaking with rage.

As Tía rushed to protect the baby, she shielded her own head to avoid the falling fruit. She ran weaving around the yard, avoiding the coconut and banana trees with their lethal burdens. When all the trees were barren and she could finally get to the child, Mati was furious. No amount of cooing or holding calmed the baby's uncontrollable cries. She waved her arms, pushing Tía away with the purposeful actions of a much older child. Tía stood there holding the screaming child as she looked, openmouthed, at the field of broken fruit. She looked from Mati to the trees and back to Mati again. She stood speechless, trying to quiet the screaming baby as others commented on the devastation and looked warily at the angry child. Tía carried Mati away quickly before the questions started.

Unnoticed by the adults, Cheito Muñoz stood at the edge of the *batey*, stopped dead in his tracks, the *guava* he had been eating frozen halfway to his mouth.

* * *

As the years passed, the people of the *batey* got used to Mati's odd ways. Young as she was, eleven-year-old Mati took her place among the women at the worktable, and she turned out to be even more skilled than her mother at working the cloth. One day, as the women of Las Agujas were having their midday meal, Mati wandered toward the back of the *chozas*. As she passed the pigsty, her eyes were drawn to the sounds of a pig surrounded by her litter. The sow lay in the far corner, her young greedily fighting for her teats. In another corner, a tiny piglet lay ignored and immobile. Mati climbed over the lowest slat and crawled over to the lone animal. She gathered the small body into her lap, examined it, and found a bloody gap in the animal's belly. She rubbed her hands together until they were warm and then carefully covered the pig's wound with them. She closed her eyes and concentrated on the inert animal on her lap.

A short time later, Margó, who had been searching for the strayed child, found her. The strong scent of freesias spread over the *batey*. Mati was seated in the pigpen, her hand still cupped over the tiny pig. Though there was much commotion around her, Mati seemed unaware of it. After some minutes, she lost the focused look in her eye and released the animal, which moved slowly at first, and then began to climb up her chest, burrowing under her arm. She laughed and the moment was broken. She was just a little girl playing in mud.

But Margó, who watched Mati's face and took in the scent of flowers strong enough to overpower the stink of the sty, would not soon forget the look of absolute concentration on the child's face. There was no doubt. This girl had the gift.

The story of the piglet reached Tía Josefa in Las Agujas, who did not interrupt her work to go see for herself. She didn't doubt that the story she heard was true but she held her tongue. That evening, as she helped the child prepare for bed, Tía parted the girl's thick hair and began the plaiting. As her fingers worked, she turned to the thought that had been worrying her all day.

"So the piglet is better now."

"Oh, yes, Tía, after I touched it, it ran and played and fought for its mother's teat just like the others."

"So you are pleased?"

Mati did not like the color of Tía's words. There was something withheld. Her face was tight and her words were heavy.

Tía put down the comb and turned Mati's shoulders so that the girl faced her. She sat the child down next to her and placed a protective arm around her shoulders, pulling Mati close.

"Have I done something wrong, Tía?" Mati asked.

"No, *m'hija*. You've done nothing wrong. Be still a moment. Now, you know you are a special girl. You can do things other little girls can't. But there are things you should not do…"

"You are angry about the piglet?"

"Mati, listen! Don't interrupt! You can do much good with your gift, but sometimes animals, and people, too, are meant to die. Their time here is finished and they must leave us. Sometimes, even if we love them very, very much, we must let them go. Maybe the pig would have survived, maybe not. The same power that gives you the gift gives all of us life. When that power takes life back, you cannot interfere. Even with your gift. That would be wrong and it would bring much suffering. So you must learn to listen; not just to me. Listen to the voice inside. The same power that gave you that gift will let you know how to use it. You must learn to trust it. Let it guide you. I wish I could tell you how to do it, but I don't know how. It's something you must find for yourself. It will come to you and you will know."

Two days later, Mati came to understand Tía's words. The child had healed the tiny animal, but the litter was too big and the sow could not feed them all. The same piglet died of starvation. No one had the time to sit and nurse one small animal. So the pig died a worse death than if she had not interfered at all. Mati began to listen for the power that directed her gift. She learned to look beyond the immediacy of what she *could* do, to measure what she *should* do. It was the first of many hard lessons.

There were times when she felt cursed and cried in her pillow and let only Tía Josefa see the pain. Tía held the child, listened, and watched.

* * *

From the time she was a little girl, Mati had always had dreams that she kept to herself. She dreamed about the Lady Oshun who told her stories. The Lady spoke in a language Mati had never heard before and yet Mati understood everything she said. The Lady Oshun spoke about a long-ago village, about Mati's mother, Fela, and father, Imo, and her grandfather, the keeper of tales. She spoke about the drummers and dancers and the gods and goddesses that ruled life. She told Mati about the ancestors who would always be waiting. And she told her about the stone that her mother had brought with her from her village. She spoke of its journey and of its power. One only needed to believe, she said.

> There is a movement in the trees and then there she is. She sits hovering a few feet above the ground, suspended in a globe of blue water, her dark skin shiny, her hair floating about her head. She wears shells around her neck and a skirt of luminescent scales. She is adorned with golden earrings that brush her shoulders and braided bracelets that jingle when she moves. Her jewelry flashes in the yellow light. She beckons me with her left hand as she lowers her right to release a black stone. It rolls out

of her hand and toward me. I bend down to pick it up and when I come
up again, she is gone, leaving a whisper behind: It is time.

Mati hadn't dreamed about the Lady Oshun in a long time. And
now this. The dream brought back memories of the stone that Tía had
spoken about long ago. But she hadn't mentioned it in many years.
Mati remembered Tía putting it away under her bed but she never
asked about it. Still, she wondered if the stone really could be magic.
She didn't mention the dream to Tía, but the thought of a magic stone
intrigued her. She thought about it at the worktable, during dinner, as
she bathed in the river. It even followed her into her dreams.

One day, when she had completed her morning's chores and the
others sat down to their midday meal, Mati slipped back to Las Agujas
and pulled her box out from under the cot. She'd dreamed about the
stone just the night before and was determined to explore its mystery.

Mati dug through her box, pushing aside the old threads and bits
of fabric left by her mother, until she found the pouch. She carried it
out behind the cabin where she wouldn't be seen, and sat in the sun,
her back against the warm wall and her legs stretched out before her.
She held the pouch in her lap, hesitating before she poured the stone
out into her hand. It felt cool. She held it in both hands and closed her
eyes, searching, concentrating, reaching out to find its special meaning.

Soon the noises of the women at lunch became faint and she could
feel the sun burning into her skin until it itched. This sensation, too,
became faint and soon the wall was gone and she was no longer where
she had been.

Instead, she stood on the crest of a hill, a grown woman. Above
her, clouds moved slowly, masses of white, one growing out of the
other, as though each one was unable to contain the next. Her skirt
blew around her legs and caught on the bushes that grew lush on the
hillside behind her. She was surrounded by *yerba buena, anamú, menta,
rompe saragüey*, and other plants of healing. She could smell them all,

but the odor of freesias was strongest and it enveloped her like a heavy veil.

Her hands grew warmer and warmer until they throbbed. Holding her arms out before her like antennae, she moved forward. The plants she left behind swayed in her direction, their leaves rising from their stems and floating up horizontally, as though she was a magnet pulling them in her wake. The ground was hot and moist. She raised her face to the sky and closed her eyes, her body taking in the energy of every living thing around her. She could hear the plants rustling, smell the rain that was about to fall, feel the movement of the clouds on her skin. She became a part of them, feeling how the clouds dissipated as the rain fell, the tug of the earth on the roots of the trees, the movement of the insects in the soil. The rays of the sun filtered into her body through the pores of her moist skin. She gave herself up to it, becoming one with the energy. She lost herself in it until she felt a huge shift.

When she opened her eyes, the stars shone overhead and there was a chill in the air. The earth no longer pulled. Shadows filled in the spaces between the trees. In the distance, a light called to her, growing as she approached the side of the hill. The mouth of a cave welcomed her.

As she walked past the entrance and toward the inner glow, the walls, moist and mossy, quickly changed from the green of the forest to deep sea blue, to the orange of the sun's outer rim, to fresh blood red. Still she walked. At the very back of the cave she found the glowing soft yellow of afternoon light emanating from a pond of iridescent water. Fascinated by the dance of the colors in the water, she approached the pool. Looking into swirling water, she saw images, a series of moving pictures evolving one into the next. She knew nothing of the world flashing before her and yet she knew everything about it. Here were her ancestors, the long-ago Africans, the world the Lady had spoken about in her dreams. But here also were people she hadn't met yet. She saw old men and women sitting with their grandchildren and great-grandchildren. Here was Tía Josefa, old and tired and ready to go to her rest. The face of a beautiful young man looked up at her with sad eyes and turned away. With a certainty she couldn't explain, she saw her children and grandchildren being born, maturing, and passing on from the world. There were even white men in the depths of the well, shadows with pleading eyes and outstretched arms. Then there were dozens, then hundreds of faces floating in a sea of red— sinking, struggling, and screaming.

Mati scrambled all the way to the back of the cave, next to the yellow wall, shaking as she inched herself up. Her heart pounded. There were too many pictures, too much to see. Good and warm pictures, yes, but also the frightening and the disturbing. No, she didn't want to see. She didn't want to know.

She ran as fast as she could, out of the cave and into the night air. And still she ran, through the valley and into the forest of protective trees. She ran until her lungs could take in no more air. Her legs gave way and she slid to the ground, dropping her head to her knees and trying to control her breathing.

"Mati...Mati..." She heard her name called in the wind. There was another shift and she was once again aware of the stone in her hand. Her skin was hot and sweaty and the wall behind her had dug painful grooves into her back. She didn't know how long she had been there. She heard the others, familiar voices coming closer. She opened her eyes and she was back.

She sat, mesmerized, unable to pull herself away. She remembered her dream. Was this the legacy left by her mother? She secured the stone within the pouch, pulled the drawstrings, and then hung the pouch around her neck. She was still shaking as she walked to the worktable.

When Mati went out to join the rest of the women, Tía noticed the pouch immediately. Because Mati had stopped asking questions about the stone long ago, Tía thought she had forgotten all about it. Looking at the girl's pale face and her trembling hands, Tía could see Mati was seeking her own answers.

As Mati approached, Tía noticed that the weight of the pouch accentuated the two growing mounds on the girl's chest. Her hips had taken on a firm roundness lately. She walked straight, sure, her muscles moving easily under the dress that had grown too snug. The girl was growing up. It seemed as though the changes in the girl's body had led her to introspection. She was developing the private life of a young girl beginning to explore her womanhood. It was only natural.

Tía felt the conflicting feelings of a parent. Mati was healthy and beautiful and soon would be bursting with a fertile glow. She would be starting her own family. Tía fought the feeling that she was losing something valuable. She pushed away the thought and tried to go back to the work at hand.

* * *

Cheito Muñoz had been Mati's best friend for as long as she could remember. But once he had joined the world of the *macheteros*, he seemed to forget about her, preferring to spend his time with the older men who had other things in mind.

One evening, Cheito was returning from the field with the other cutters. Mati stood at her window and watched. The men had finished cutting the last of the year's crop and the *patrón* had given them a day of rest. They had finished days before the *macheteros* in surrounding plantations. The men slapped each other on the back, congratulating themselves as they made their plans. One caught sight of Mati as they went by.

"Cheito, there's your little *amiguita*. Maybe you should stay here tonight and help her sort her threads." The men laughed, continuing their teasing. "After all, we're going down to Lola's and have other games to play. Maybe you'd better stay here where you can't get into trouble."

"Who? Me?" Cheito sounded offended. "Look, I told you, *yo soy un macho hecho y derecho*. A grown man, *¿entiendes?* I have no time for playing games. What do I need with a girl when I can have a woman? I'll be the first one there tonight. Don't you worry about that. *¡Hasta luego!*"

Mati heard the banter and turned away with a tight heart. That evening Cheito tapped on the door of Las Agujas. It was hot and the women had gone down to the *chozas* to celebrate the end of the cutting season. Mati came to the door with a stone face.

"What are you doing here? Isn't Lola waiting?"

"Mati, please. I'm sorry I hurt your feelings. Those were just big words." Silence.

"I didn't mean to…it's just that…"

Mati stood still, her anger, impassable. Yet just beneath the layer of hurt lived an undeniable desire to have him say the magic words that would restore their friendship. Still, there was her pride. And her pride won out.

No matter what he said, he could not get through to her. He tried again and again but he, too, had conflicting emotions. His desire to join the men's celebration made him impatient with her unreasonable anger. After all, she was just a girl. Exasperated by her stubbornness, he grabbed her arm and tried to force her to follow what he was saying.

Mati saw his mouth moving but heard nothing. Soon she was only aware of the mounting heat. Her head pounded. Her skin became a coat of fire. The heat blinded her to everything else.

She never knew exactly what had happened during those few lost moments but when she focused on Cheito again, he lay on the ground, his right leg twisted under him. She rushed to help him but he cursed her and cried out at every move. When she finally got close enough, she could see the thighbone pushing out at an unnatural angle. The agony in his face and fear in his eyes told her all she needed to know. This was the first time her gift had gotten away from her, the first time she had ever hurt anyone.

"*Dios mío*, Cheito. Damn it! Why did you grab me like that? I didn't mean to hurt you. Here, let me see."

She held her hands out to him but he instinctively shrank from her touch. "Get away from me. *¡Una bruja!* Those who call you a witch from hell are right! Don't touch me."

His words stunned her and she pulled back, shaking at the vehemence of his rebuke, which added to her own guilt at having caused him so much injury. She wanted to push away that part of herself that made her different. Was it a gift or was it an uncontrollable curse? It made him fear her, creating distance where she had dreamed of closeness. For a moment, she was put off by his burst of anger and his cutting words.

Yes, there were some people who were fearful of her and she knew that some, even after years of knowing her, approached her with hesitation. But she had never expected Cheito to be one of them. *¡Bruja!* The word stung her deeper than he would ever know. She pushed her own feelings aside. He lay in pain, needing the very thing he had cursed. She brushed away his words and followed her instinct to help, to heal that which she herself had injured.

"Cheito, listen. Let me help you. I can fix your leg. You know I can."

His face contorted in pain but he still wouldn't let her touch him. She searched for the words that would make him listen. "What kind of a *machetero* will you be with a crooked leg? If I don't tend to it, it'll be the end of your *palero* days. You want to be a cripple? What will your *panitas* think of you then?" He hesitated and she went on, "You'll still be in the cane fields but you'll be with the old men, gathering up the stalks after the others do the cutting. Is that what you want?"

Cheito pictured himself with a useless leg. He heard the derision and, worse, the pity in the voices of the able-bodied men. He imagined the look of disdain on the faces of the women he wanted so badly to impress. *El cojo*, they'd call him. He shivered at the thought.

Cheito did not understand Mati's ways, but deep inside he knew she hadn't meant to hurt him, not like this. She might be angry but she wasn't vicious. He also knew that she could heal him better than anyone else. He nodded, closed his eyes, and braced himself.

Relieved that he had given in, Mati placed her right hand over his eyes and concentrated. She gathered up her will and focused on him. Soon his body relaxed and lay inert. While he was unconscious, she worked on his limb. Back rounded, head bent slightly to one side as though she were listening with some inner ear, she worked on him, her fingers carefully pulling and kneading and stretching until the bone was back in its original position. She wrapped her hands around the repositioned leg and sat back, eyes closed, energy coursing through her, into his leg, and back to her again. She envisioned sealing the bone, knitting the ligaments, soothing the muscles. When she was sure everything was in place, she removed her head wrap and secured the newly repositioned bone. Later she'd find boards and stronger cloth to bind the leg until it finished healing.

7 Changes in the Wind

Cheito's life had changed drastically after his leg injury. Yes, Mati had healed his leg. But he found that he could no longer work all day with the other cutters. He could swing his machete with the strength he had before, but his leg now buckled in the follow-through. Romero, whip in hand, was more than ready to deal with what he saw as laziness. Don Tomás intervened just in time to spare the boy the beating Romero was ready to administer. *El patrón* decided Cheito would return to the wood-carver's *choza* to work with his father. Romero seethed but held his tongue. He wouldn't make the same mistake twice. His disdain for his weak *patrón* was well guarded. He kept his opinions to himself.

When Cheito returned to his old workbench, the wood seemed unfamiliar, flat, and unyielding. Everything seemed reduced; furniture and tools were too small to accommodate his outdoor body and massive hands. His fingers were stiff and unused to working the small tools. His hands had forgotten the play of strength and delicacy needed to coax out the natural beauty of the wood.

It took time to get reacquainted with this type of work. He cursed his clumsiness and flung his tools across the shop. Melchor watched his son's struggle. One day, as the younger man entered the work shed, he found that his father had made him a new bench, better suited to his new proportions. Melchor had also spoken to Don Tomás, and soon

Cheito had larger tools that sat better in his hands. It took weeks, but as Cheito surrendered himself to the wood, his hands remembered where to apply pressure, how deep to carve, when to leave the wood alone. As he worked, he slowly began to recapture the pride he had taken in his early work.

A few months later, Doña Filomena ordered a large box for her newly acquired jewelry. Melchor turned to his son for the design. Cheito, pleased at the confidence his father showed in him, designed a chest carved in mahogany and inlaid with mother-of-pearl. The design was so clever that no joints or openings showed anywhere. The closure was hidden within one of the leaves that covered the lid. *La patrona* was delighted when the case was delivered to her, freshly varnished to a high sheen. She was so impressed with the results that she summoned Melchor to thank him for his fine work. When she was told that it was Cheito and not his father who had worked the box, she wanted to see more of his work, so she ordered another piece.

One evening she approached her husband with an elaborately carved bowl. Her hands stroked the smooth *caoba* as she entered the room. Don Tomás shook his head in frustration, preoccupied with the pile of papers at his desk.

"*¿Qué te pasa,* Tomás?"

"The price of sugar…"

"The Cuban markets again?"

"*Sí, mujer.* I don't know what to do. We can't go on like this." He got up and paced the room. "I'll have to go to the capital again. Maybe the bankers…"

"*Quizás,* but do you think maybe it is time for a change in the direction of the hacienda, Tomás?"

"Meaning what?" He was half listening to her as he made mental notes and alternative plans.

Filomena knew her husband well. They both knew that she had always been the better manager, and he had always been content to let her run the plantation. It had allowed him freedom for the indulgences of his youth. Her practical head had saved them time and again while he was busy with his own interests—horses and the occasional visits to the mountain towns. She had never wanted, nor did she need, credit for the changes she had brought about on Las Mercedes. But times were different now. As his aging body was unable to keep up the carefree lifestyle he led as a younger man, Don Tomás stayed home more and redirected his energy to administering the farm. He needed to feel that he was the guiding force behind the hacienda, so she had withdrawn from its day-to-day management. Instead, she spent more time with the needlewomen and supervising the household chores, only stopping by the library occasionally and dropping suggestions that led him down a path that he could easily follow to a given end. He made the decisions. Silently and subtly, she made sure he made the right ones.

"*Perdóname*, Tomás. You know I would never presume...of course, it is your decision..."

Whenever Filomena became so cautious around him, Tomás listened. He had learned to trust her in these matters. Although he would never admit it, he couldn't match her head for business. She had never failed him. He stopped pacing and put down the papers he had been examining.

"It's your choice, *claro*," she continued, "but there are other, shall I say more creative, ways of keeping this hacienda afloat. You could lease the western fields, reducing costs and increasing revenues. We have nothing to lose in that situation. Ignacion Concepción has been asking to buy our people for his *almacén*. I'm not suggesting a sale, but we can send them into town and hire them out to do their work there. Craftsmen are in demand and will bring in a pretty penny. We can keep enough hands here to bring in enough cane for domestic use. We'll keep some pickers for the fruit and vegetable crops and send the rest into town. Our costs on the farm will go down and our profits in town will double. Times are changing. The money now isn't in the fields but in the towns."

Tomás sat down. "I'm listening."

"We have talent here that is going to waste." She put the bowl down on the desk. "Why keep our *artesanos* here when there is such a demand for them in town? Many *hacendados* have sent their workers to the capital. With proper supervision, they have done quite well and have filled the pockets of their *patrones*. The Cubans and the Jamaicans will keep underbidding us until we break. Things will only get worse. We don't need all these workers here anymore."

"But all I know is cane. Besides, even if we send all the workers into town, surely that won't bring in enough...?"

"The number of quality families in the capital has exploded. They always need servants. They need blacksmiths and stevedores and carvers, just like they have needed my needlewomen all these years. Let the Cubans have the European markets."

He listened carefully to her suggestions and spent the whole evening pacing in the study. Urban slaves. He'd seen them in town, knew of others who had gone this route. They would be carefully supervised. Their earnings, except for a small living wage, would come directly to him. They'd save a bundle just on living expenses for the relocated slaves. They'd need only a small force to produce a smaller crop, and just the other day Don Xavier had approached him about supplying cane for his rum factory in Corozal.

He pulled out his ledgers and reviewed, calculated, planned, and projected. He made lists, contemplated outcomes, and anticipated earnings. It would be a gamble. But by the end of the night he was sure the idea that had been planted by Filomena hours before had come from his own foresight. Filomena sat in the parlor and smiled. She waited for her husband to tell her of his new idea.

* * *

"I have to go now." Cheito had put off this moment for as long as possible. He knew that Mati had heard of his departure and he wanted to avoid the hurt he now saw in her face.

Mati felt like a part of her was being torn away. "I…" She could barely get the words out.

Heartbroken at having to leave friends and family behind, he tried to sound optimistic.

"It isn't as bad as all that. I'll be back."

"But I…" She couldn't bear to look at him.

"Mati…please."

She clung to him and shook her head in denial. Finally, he had to break away.

"Mati, you know I have no choice…*patrones* who can't sell their crops, meet, talk, and then black people are gone, sold off, and are never seen again."

He saw the fear in her eyes and relented. "At least I'll be nearby. I can come back and see you. Every person I care about is here." His eyes bore into hers. "Every person I love is here. Mati, I don't know what's waiting for me in the capital. But I know this. There's no future for me here. Maybe there I'll have a chance. At least I won't have Romero's eyes on me all the time. I've heard that some black men there are allowed to keep some of the money they make for their *patrones*. Some have even saved their money and bought their freedom. Mati, can you imagine that? Can you imagine? It'll take time, I know. Maybe…you…maybe we…"

She shook her head again. There was nothing she could say. These things he said were madness, things to make her feel better. It had been decided long before now. They were lucky they had time for goodbyes.

"The leg…I know this is all my fault." She couldn't keep the guilt down anymore. She couldn't forget the look on his face after the accident, the accusation in his voice, the word *"bruja"* hanging between them.

"How many times do I have to say it? It wasn't your fault. I...I was scared and said stupid things. That was so long ago and it's all over now. Besides, the accident got me away from *ese bruto de* Romero. I was sure one of us would kill the other. So, in that way, you saved my life."

He looked down at her. "Please...I need to remember you smiling. Your smile will bring me back."

Mati managed a reluctant smile and wrapped her arms around his waist. She knew that to him she was barely more than a child, but she had already given him her heart.

He returned her long embrace before walking away. As the darkness closed around him, Mati turned her back to keep herself from running after him.

8 PASSING ON

Early on a sunny morning, seven years later, one of the maids went in to awaken Doña Filomena and found the still-warm body of *la señora* propped up in bed. The bedclothes were neatly tucked around her. Her braid, now shot with gray and laced with a lavender ribbon, lay peacefully over her right shoulder. Her rings had not yet been removed. The open account book lay facedown on the coverlet. At the side of her bed, her slippers were carefully aligned on the floor. Her robe, at the foot of the bed, had been positioned within easy reach. The only sign of anything being out of place was the child's rattle found clutched in her left hand. A frayed blue ribbon hung from the handle.

Don Tomás locked himself in with his wife's body all day. At a loss for what to do, Tía called for Romero who sent a boy into town. The priest was summoned, but he could get no more reaction from behind Filomena's locked door than the maids. At nightfall, Tomás finally opened the door and let the women in to make the necessary preparations. He sent Romero into town to notify the authorities. The oppressive heat and Tomás' daylong delay necessitated a hasty burial. Word was sent to the Superior Casket Company in the capital. The coffin arrived the next afternoon highly polished and inlaid with European tiles and ivory chips. Cheito, a master carver by then, was sent to accompany the valuable coffin.

Mati dropped the basket she had been carrying out to the worktable. She watched, rooted in place, as Cheito rode into the *batey*. All traces of youth were gone now. He was a broad man, sitting straight-backed on the high seat. She could see his thick moustache and heavy lips. It had been so long, but she would know him anywhere. She raised her hand and was about to call out to him but didn't. She could wait.

* * *

Much later that evening, Cheo, not the diminutive Cheito of the past, but Cheo, the master carver, came to her. He came walking out of the same darkness that had taken him away seven years before, the moonlight playing on his shoulders. Shadows danced on his blue-white shirt and he carried a smile on his lips. Throughout the entire burial ceremony, he had stared at her. And she had stared back, the tie between them stronger than ever. Neither heard a word of what had been said. Neither had approached the other in public. It was fitting that their meeting came under cover of night.

She didn't know what to do or say. As he approached, she watched his figure getting larger and larger until he was standing directly before her, filling her field of vision, looking down at her from the height of his full manhood.

He remembered the young girl he had left behind, now a grown woman. Her body had softened into pleasing curves. She was all inviting ripeness.

"I would know you anywhere, Mati," he said, picking her up, light and easy. She let him, relaxing into his arms, taking in his scent once more. She had been afraid that he would be different. But the sound of his voice and the familiar scent erased the years.

She pulled herself up to him and wrapped her legs around his waist. Together, they moved away from the cabins. He held Mati in his arms, her head buried in the crook of his neck, the wide skirt of her dress floating around his knees as he carried her into the night.

* * *

They had needed no words. Much later, they lay side-by-side, exhausted but unwilling to break the moment. The sun was well on its way when he started speaking and once he started, he couldn't stop. He spoke of his town life and the freedom he had found there. Of the feeling of pride at getting his first wages. Of his making his own arrangements, lodgings, board, selecting his own clothes, buying his first cigar, his first hat. Of work; men like him, black, and white, too, working together. He told her of his pride in his work, describing the unusual woods—mahogany, ebony, oak, cedar, teak—that came to them as huge logs in the big ships that choked the port. And he told of how their hands transformed the wood into carved furnishings, sturdy cabinetry, and fancy decorative pieces.

The men lived together, ate together, laughed and played together. They began making names for themselves. Cheo's style was distinctive and his work prized. People paid a lot of money for his pieces. The *patrón* got most of it, of course, but some of it came back to him. For the first time, he saw his value measured not in years of toil but in money that he could save or spend as he wished.

He spoke of the Casita Pueblo where he lived. It was an old stable owned by María Candela, a free black woman who had been the mistress of a high official. Over the years, she had been well rewarded for her attentions. Now an older and wiser Doña María had transformed the stable into a hotel for city slaves, the craftsmen and women who poured into the city as the price of sugar plummeted and the cost of maintaining a plantation soared. *Jíbaros*, most of whom had lost their farms, came down from the mountains. Starving and desperate, these men who had never seen the city found themselves sharing living space with skilled slaves and poor *libertos* in the backstreets of the capital.

Cheo spoke of other *libertos*, the free black men and women who lived in modest houses near the docks. Some even had servants. Unbelievably and shamefully, there were rich *negros* who sometimes had slaves of their own. And there were former slaves who had bought their freedom and had begun to build their own lives. It seemed Cheo would never stop talking. Finally, he slowed down.

"Mati, I've got two presents for you…I hope you like them."

Struggling to get something out of his pants pockets, he finally pulled out a crumpled piece of paper and presented it to her.

"Open it slowly now, I don't want you to lose them."

The bundle held two small shiny objects that flashed in the sun. They had tiny hooks on the top and little golden balls hanging from the bottom. Mati's mouth dropped open. Only white women wore such things.

"Well? Do you like them? Aren't they pretty? I saved and saved for them. I thought they would be beautiful for you. They're not exactly new but they're real gold. They're small, I know, but one day…"

Mati put her fingers over his mouth to quiet him and slipped into his arms again. She thought about how long he must have worked to buy such a gift. She couldn't find the words to tell him how she felt, so she showed him.

* * *

"Remember I said I have two gifts?"

"But I don't need anything…"

"No, I haven't told you the best yet." Cheo paused for a moment and took a deep breath. "Mati, I can read and I can write." He whispered it slowly, like a prayer. The pride in him curled in his smile and glowed gently in his eyes. "Not just numbers, Mati, I can read words. And I can teach you."

Listening to all his stories, Mati had been introduced to a new world. She was carried along on his excitement, on his flights of discovery. But this last sentence brought her to a complete halt.

"I don't need to learn reading and writing. Why would I? It is a thing of *los blancos*."

At her reaction, the smile left his face. "Mati, they write down everything that is important on their papers. They write down when somebody's born, when they die, when they get married. They write down what they buy and sell and whom they want to leave things to when they die. They write down their past and present. They write down their lives. They write down their messages to each other that we don't know anything about. Many of their own, their poor ones, can't read or make their mark on paper. Some of their women can't, either. Only a few, the ones with the power, can do this thing. No wonder they keep it for themselves, like their jewels and their money and their land. Just the fact that they don't want us to have it tells me that we *must* learn to do this."

"I never thought of it that way before. I never thought of it at all before. I don't know…"

But Cheo never got a chance to convince her. Two days after the funeral, he was sent back to the capital. When Cheo pulled out of the *batey*, Mati was heartbroken. Who knew when they would see each other again?

* * *

"Well, don't just stand there. *¡Ven aquí y déjame verte!*" beckoned Don Tomás.

He had taken to his room since the funeral two months before. When he refused to let the maids in, his meals were left outside his door. Sometimes the food was gone and sometimes it wasn't. He hadn't had his bath drawn. He would allow no cleaning or airing out of his bedroom. Every morning, the maid found his chamber pot outside the door, but none of the house slaves had actually seen him in all that time.

The stench in the room made Mati gag and she longed to run out into the fresh air. But her feet were glued to the spot as she watched the figure on the bed. Mati had never been in this room before. She knew this man had taken her mother out into the fields one night and she knew she had been born nine months later. But she had never thought of him as her father. She had seen him on the plantation, of course. He was the *patrón*, but she had never been summoned into the house.

Now she forced herself to step into the room. She couldn't believe that the skeletal body in the bed was the *patrón*. Gone was the well-groomed *caballero*. Even in the dim lantern light, she could see that his shiny black hair had turned white and his clean-shaven jaw was now covered in matted facial hair. The thin nightshirt emphasized his sunken chest. His nails were yellow and clawlike and his papery skin had death written on it. The cloying stench of decay hung in the air.

"Come closer," he croaked.

Mati took a few steps, standing halfway between the bed and the open door. It took all her willpower to stay there. Only her promise to Tía Josefa would make her go to this old man's room.

Standing there, Mati felt it in her stomach, the desperation Fela must have felt that night when she followed this man into the field. He was her best avenue of escape. If she could only get through that night, she could complete her task and find release.

"I suppose you know you are my daughter." Don Tomás' raspy voice grated on her.

Mati's skin crawled. The acrid taste of vomit filled her mouth. She swallowed and said nothing. She could smell death waiting for him in the darkness. She noticed the pleading in the corners of his eyes and focused on the sound of his voice instead. He squinted and beckoned her closer.

"Fela...," he started to explain.

"Don't you say her name." The words flew out before she knew she had spoken. Forgetting he was the *patrón*, she looked at him as the man who had taken her mother on the ground, like an animal; a woman whose severed tongue silenced her words of revulsion. Mati wouldn't listen to him speak of her.

He tried again. "I only..."

The crack in her armor closed, sealing her away from him behind her wall of silence again. She was her mother's child.

"You hate me, don't you? You think you know what happened? It wasn't what you imagine. No force…there was no f…"

No, I won't listen. She was about to turn and run when she noticed movement in the corner of the room. There was a stirring in the curtains. The shadows shifted and the scent of freesias filled the room. Slowly, the lines began to settle into a more distinct and familiar pattern taking on substance. A woman's figure emerged, dim, commanding Mati's attention. A dark hand motioned Mati to stay. She knew this was her mother, Fela, the woman who sometimes came with the Lady. Mati froze where she stood, afraid that she would lose the illusive figure.

She felt dizzy and closed her eyes for a moment. Trying to steady herself, she reached for the doorframe. When she looked again, the image of Fela was still there.

Mati had forgotten all about Don Tomás. But Fela's insistent gesturing became more urgent. The man's wheezing broke into a hacking cough that filled the room. It took all her effort to look away from the figure and focus on the bed. She noticed his now outstretched hand holding a sheaf of papers. Cautiously, inching closer, she reached for the papers he held out to her.

In a burst of unexpected energy, his other hand shot out and locked on her wrist. Before Mati's fingers closed around the packet of papers, she was his prisoner. She tried to snatch her hand away, but his clenched fist was a vise.

"We wanted a son, but Filomena wasn't able…even a daughter would have done. But after the epidemic, cholera…." He was breathless, getting out the words in short spurts that only frightened Mati more. In the dim lighting, she could see that his eyes went away for a moment before focusing on her again.

"After the boy died, there were no others…we tried…she really wanted…miscarriages…so many…

"But you're here...and you're all I have. So it'll be yours, you know—the house, land, animals, everything. You'll be a rich woman. You'll be free to do what you want, go where you want."

So intent on trying to get free of him, Mati hadn't really been listening. But now she stopped, his last words sinking in slowly. The man must have lost his mind. She looked at the dark corner where Fela's image nodded yes, pointing to the bed with more urgency. Mati's eyes fell on the papers again as though seeing them for the first time.

As soon as his hold loosened a fraction, she snatched the papers with one hand and twisted out of his reach with the other. Mati clutched the sheets to her chest and pulled all the way back to the safety of the doorway. Searching out the corner, she could see the figure already receding into the shadows. As the darkness and the cold of the room closed in once again, she felt a tremendous sense of loss. Fela was gone, smoke dissipating into the darkness. Mati took one last look at the man in the bed before turning her back on him.

She ran as fast as she could away from the room, away from the old man, her father. She ran through the *batey*, past the cabins and into the fields of tall cane. She fell to her knees, gulping for air. When she finally caught her breath, she realized the papers were still clutched in her fist.

* * *

As he listened to Mati run down the corridor and out of his house, *her* house soon, Tomás lay back on his damp pillows and relaxed. He heard music, the calliope echoing in rooms that had never been used. He heard Filomena's young and happy voice, singing old lullabies. Below her voice, he could hear the squeak of the rocking chair that held the new mother and her nursing baby. He could see her hands on the dressing table, small veins pulsing. He watched as she went through the drawer full of tiny clothes. He saw the hem of her ball gown and heard the swish of the silk on the tiles as she came to him. He felt himself slipping his arms around her and stepping out to the strains of the *danza*, pulled in by her heady perfume...

Those were the last images that flashed through his mind before the vein burst in his brain.

* * *

Weeks before, Tomás had called Dr. Rigoberto Calderón; his attorney, Don Anselmo Álvarez; and Padre Bartolomeo. The papers were prepared and ready for the signing. He needed men of unquestionable reputation as witnesses. His last will and testament had to be unassailable.

"What can I say to dissuade you from doing this, Tomás?" Don Anselmo didn't bother to disguise his exasperation. On several occasions he had tried to make Tomás see reason. His client was as stubborn as ever. How could he be so blind? Why did he always have to take a different path from everyone else? After dismissing every other attorney in the capital, Tomás had hired Don Anselmo and had been his client for years. Tomás was a hard man to represent. His stubbornness and radical ideas made him an outcast among his own class. Even to the end. As he was leaving this world, he cared nothing about the chaos he would leave behind. If he didn't care about himself, at least he should consider the damage he would do to the others.

"I don't want to hear another word about this from you, Anselmo. I came to you for a service for which you will be well paid. Your opinion on this matter was not part of the package. I know what you and the others think. I know what you want. It has nothing to do with me. You run your haciendas as you see fit, and I would appreciate it if you would let me run mine my own way."

Anselmo exploded, "Padre, you talk to him. Perhaps he'll listen to you. He certainly has never taken my advice."

"*Hijo...*" The priest stopped. The scorn on Tomás' face left little to be said.

The doctor interceded. "Tomás, you mustn't upset yourself. Your health will be further compromised."

"Doctor, I have no health left. I need you here for other reasons. My end is approaching and there is nothing you or anyone else can do about that. Do me the courtesy of being honest."

There had been heated discussions. Tomás had little regard for these men. Their hypocrisy dripped from them. Their public faces hid the lechery and cruelty he witnessed in them in more private arenas. They sported a veneer of civility that shielded greed and absolute self-interest. But he needed men who would not be challenged. And there was the law. He looked at the circle of faces around his bed and hoped that all would go as he planned. They didn't agree with his plan but he hoped that the payments he had made were sufficiently large to ensure that each of these men would honor his word.

But in the end, it did not matter what Don Tomás had written down. Papers could burn and so they did. Lawyer, doctor, and priest, all of whom were slave owners themselves, had too much to lose with the disruption of order that Tomás' plans would wreak upon them. As soon as they left his room with the signed papers, they agreed that Tomás' will, drafted during his prolonged illness, was the work of a man touched by madness. When he finally died, it was reported that there was no will found among his belongings.

* * *

Mati got up early the day of the sale, put on her big hat, and headed for the town square. She wanted to be there when the men began to arrive. Now she was standing in the sun, a solitary female figure, waiting. She could have stood more comfortably under the shade trees in the plaza, but she wanted a good, close look. She wanted to see their faces, wanted to see their eyes as they did this to her. And she wanted them to see her.

She thought about the papers she had pushed to the bottom of her box, under all the threads and bits of fabric left to her by her mother. She remembered Cheo's words: *They write down everything...what they buy and sell and whom they want to leave things to....* She couldn't read the papers, no, but she knew well enough what was written there. She remembered the words of the *patrón,* too. *It'll be yours...the house, land, animals.* In the end, those papers meant nothing. The *hacendados* were about to take it all away. The papers were no protection after all. She would have to find another way. And so here she was.

The men began to arrive in little groups, on horses or in carriages. These were men she had seen many times, *hacendados* of the district. Most did not even notice her standing there and others merely ignored her presence. One man nearly knocked her over. *"¡Salte del medio, negra estúpida!"* He pushed her out of his way as he walked by with a group of drunken young men.

His name was Don Próspero Herrera y Torres. Mati knew about this man, although she had never actually seen him. She knew the savagery in him had been inbred for generations. His family had owned Fela before she went to Las Mercedes. It was his father's lust and his mother's fear that silenced Fela's voice. *They silenced her songs.* Mati's eyes fell on him and took in his saunter, his white teeth biting down on the fat cigar and his lewd laughter slicing through the noise of the crowd. A sharp current of hate crept up her spine.

The men gathered in a circle under the cool of the *flamboyán* trees, taking up all the shady spots. They shook hands, offered each other cigars, exchanged friendly comments. They discussed their newest boots, the price of coffee, the latest shipment of saddles. Mati stood in the sun, just outside their circle, and watched them.

Then she noticed a face across the square. The black cape and hat were unmistakable. The sneer on his face sent a chill up Mati's spine. What was Romero doing here? He couldn't possibly expect to outbid any of these men. Still, there he was, his eyes boring into her. She could almost hear his laughter. The stench of his cheap cigar cloyed her senses even at this distance.

But the tone of the conversation in the circle had shifted to the business at hand, and she had more important concerns than Romero. The auctioneer stepped up to the center. Don Próspero took his place in the circle and soon the bidding began. The men divided up Las Mercedes as they wished, not even bothering to seriously challenge one another's bids. Everything had been prearranged. Mati's mind wove in and out of the sale. *They had taken her body.* Don Próspero bought the largest parcel of land, which included the river near where Mati had been born. *They had taken her words.* This was the river where Fela washed her baby—*they had stolen her lullabies*—the land where Fela was finally laid to rest.

The sun beat down on Mati's head and shoulders. Its heat penetrated her straw hat and bore down on her head. Her scalp baked under the hat, sending rivulets of perspiration down the sides of her face, dripping onto her bodice and sliding between her breasts. The moisture on the nape of her neck traveled down, sticking her sodden dress to her back.

The stored heat of the scorched ground permeated the soles of her shoes. She was broiling, but she withstood the sun, standing in her place near the bidding area, just outside the circle of men who talked, smoked, and socialized as they helped themselves to the land that had been left to her. She strained to see their faces, hear their voices, register the timbre of their laughter. She took the moment in, wrapped it, studied it, saved every detail. Later she would take it out again and savor it in private. It would feed her resolve. It would guide her. It would help her win.

Her head was pounding and her mouth was parched. She was having difficulty breathing. Each time Próspero bid on another parcel of land, her breathing became more labored. The air she breathed seemed seared by both the heat of the day and the greed of the bidders.

By late afternoon, all the bidding was done. The men had bought everything. The cane fields, cattle, and machinery were all gone. The sale was over. *"Salud, dinero, y amor."* The men toasted their good fortune with golden rum. They slapped each other on the back and smiled. Don Próspero pushed the papers for the lands he had just bought into a weathered saddlebag, a self-satisfied look on his face. White teeth flashed everywhere. *They had taken her tongue.* They walked away without even glancing at the woman whose land they had stolen.

Mati's knees were locked and her body felt too heavy to move. She must have stood there a very long time. The sun was low in the sky and the shadows of the trees stretched far beyond her. The plaza was empty except for someone tugging at her shoulder. She looked at him for a while before she realized it was Padre Bartolomeo. His hands were clammy. His mouth was moving as he pulled her away from the plaza.

* * *

Mati had never been in the rectory before. Now she sat in one of the padre's heavy chairs. He sat across the large table from her, a huge crucifix hanging on the wall behind him. His mouth was still moving. He was aware that Don Tomás had given her certain papers. The man started fanning himself. No, that had been a mistake. The priest was aware of the fact that there was a "special" connection between Mati and the deceased, but she had misunderstood Don Tomás' intent. He got up and opened the window and returned to his seat. There were legal issues she could not possibly understand. The padre assured her that only through his intervention would Mati be allowed to keep the house and the land and cabins immediately behind it. It was only at his insistence that all the slaves on the plantation would be given their freedom. With this act, the priest bathed himself in good conscience. He had upheld Christian teachings while securing his own and the other planters' interests. No one could ever blame him for what had happened here.

The *hacendados* had not set much opposition to the priest's plan. There were rumors of slave rebellions sweeping nearby islands. Incidents involving rebellious *cimarrónes* had risen alarmingly in recent months. Tomás never had the *cojones* of a good master. His leniency with the blacks was one reason he was never really trusted by the others. None of the *hacendados* wanted to deal with Tomás' slaves, whom they believed had been coddled and spoiled for years. Integrating the blacks from Las Mercedes into their own workforces would cause any number of problems. Tomás' blacks could give their own slaves dangerous ideas. But as freedmen, on their own, they'd be too busy trying to scratch out a living to cause much trouble. Even if they did bring in a small crop, who would buy from them? Besides, they'd be too exhausted to congregate for talk of rebellion. Let them have their scraps, so long as they kept to themselves.

So the slaves on Las Mercedes were to become *libertos*. The buildings and grounds immediately surrounding the house itself would go to Mati. It was expected that she would be grateful for that. The priest finally held out a pile of papers across the desk, more papers she couldn't read.

"You are a free woman. The others have their freedom as well. The house is yours. It says so, right here." He shook the papers at her as if she hadn't seen them. "They're yours."

Mati sat in the big chair in the rectory and looked at him. He was growing impatient.

"Take them." He threw the papers on the table as though they held some contamination. They slid across the polished surface and fell on the floor at her feet. He pointed. "This is what you all want, isn't it?"

She kept her eyes on him while she stooped to pick up the papers. She was still watching him as she made her way to the door. The ball of rage was already collecting deep inside.

* * *

She had to think about what had happened in town, of the priest's words. How could she trust in the words of these people who had always lied to her? She felt for the papers she carried in her pocket, the ones that, she was told, would give her the house, that would give all of them their freedom and a home. But were these papers as useless as the ones the *patrón* had given her? How could she trust such a thing? What to tell the others? What to believe? Where to go?

Mati arrived at the plantation wrapped in her thoughts. Her "father" had died and she felt nothing. She looked up at the big house. The padre said this was her home now. She could enter and leave it at will, change it, burn it if she wished. She walked around to Las Agujas, the only home she had ever known and the only place where she could find the peace to think.

She sat at the worktable, alone, quiet. Wearily, she leaned forward and rested her face in her folded arms and let everything out—fear, suspicion, frustration, pain. Her shoulders shook uncontrollably.

She thought about her father, her *soul* father, Imo, who never did see her, and she cried. She thought about Fela, the terrible silence of her life and the mysterious silence of her death. And she cried. Mati cried for the ones who had been beaten to death and the ones who never survived the voyage. She cried for the women who lost their men, and the men who lost their dignity, and the children who would never know their mothers' voices. She thought she would never stop crying.

* * *

The sun was burnishing the horizon and the ochre glow spread over the rooftops at Las Mercedes. It would be a night of celebration. Mati changed into a fresh dress and combed out her hair, letting it spring loose and free. She felt refreshed and rested. She looked out over the *batey* and knew there was one thing to do for Fela, for herself, for them all.

Peeking through the window, she just glimpsed the man's shadow as he passed Las Agujas and headed for the big house. He moved stealthily, stopping every few steps to make sure the trail of liquid fell continuously in his wake. She saw the tiny flame and then heard the commotion as the men followed, chasing him with bats and machetes in hand. "Romero, *¡mírenlo ahí!*" The first match blew out. Discovered, Romero could not keep his hand from shaking as he struck the second match. It, too, missed its mark as he turned and ran from the advancing crowd of angry men. He made for the far incline toward the dark bulk of his own house.

Mati followed the men across the *batey*, where the women had been preparing the evening meal. The pots bubbled over fires that burned hot and bright. Mati was the first one to pull out a burning stick. The other women joined her. The far incline was steep and rocky, but their feet were steady and their objective clear. One after the other, the women and children grabbed logs, brooms, sticks, and canes, tipped them into the fire, and joined the men who already surrounded Romero's house. As they approached, they spread out around the two-story building. Then, one after the other, they tipped their torches onto the ground floor of Romero's house. The little flames caught and began working their way up the outer walls.

Fleeing the menacing crowd, Romero ran out his back door and headed for his mount. He could have easily ridden away, but he couldn't resist a final confrontation.

"So you got the old bastard to leave everything to you, ah? *¡El gran pendejo!*

"First the old fool Aurelio. He wanted a job done but tied my hands. Gave me all the whips I wanted but then stopped me from wielding them. And then the other one. The young *patrón*"—his sneer distorted his face—"rolling and fucking in the fields like the animal he was.

"And *they* thought themselves better than *me*? I did his dirty work and he got all the benefits. What hypocrisy! You and your mamá both thought yourselves better than me. *¡Hija de la gran puta!* Your mother was a whore and you are the whore's litter. Was that the best he could do? Produce a half-yellow bitch?

"And now this. They're all cowards. They caved in. Gave it to you...ha! What are you going to do with it? A sow in a silk dress. Ha, ha, ha...still...not a bad deal. Your mamá spread her legs for him just once and you get the whole thing. That must have been quite a fuck. Maybe she really was a witch. She sure bewitched him, *¡pendejo, estúpido!*"

Mati, hand tightened on the torch, was poised for battle, the flame growing hotter and hotter.

She grasped at her pouch, visualized the stone in her hand. Her breathing came in deeper and deeper drafts. She pulled into herself, went deep within, mining her strength, finding a new well of fortitude that fed on a core of crystalline loathing.

"You're a strutting *mulato* bastard who can't stand to look at his own face. Who was *your* father? How was my mother any different than yours? And what gives you the right to even speak of her? You think yourself up to challenging me?"

Romero backed away as he continued spewing his curses, "*Me cago en tu madre. Maldita sea ella, y tú también.* I hope the black bitch is rotting in hell where she belongs."

Romero's hair flew around his head as he continued to rant. Mati stood very quiet, but the fire at the end of her log danced in agitation.

"You should be careful, Romero...very careful."

In the last light of the evening, Romero thought his eyes were playing tricks on him. Mati's face shifted and suddenly there was Fela, and then the lines shifted again and he saw a face he hadn't seen in years but recognized immediately. The guttural, multi-tonal voice coming out of her mouth was as much Mati's as it was Fela's as it was his own mother's.

"I see I have your attention now. You maimed and tortured and killed and took pleasure in it. You raped and stripped and flogged and enjoyed every minute of it. Well, it's your turn now. With the power of Oshun and all the blessed ancestors, I curse you with living for many years. *Óyeme bien, hijo del Diablo,* you listen and believe this. I want you to live a good long time, longer than anyone has ever heard of; long enough to pay, long enough to know the agony of a putrid and bleeding body. I curse you with a living death and I pray that my words will haunt you every night of your miserable life. Every time you close your eyes I will be waiting for you. And mine will be the last face you'll see before going to the gaping hole of hell where you belong."

He smelled it before he felt the heat, the little tendrils of smoke that rose from his hat, his shirt, his cape. And then he felt his clothes begin to warm. In a panic, he slapped at himself. Looking down, he saw Mati's face, still smiling, still watching. *¡Bruja!*

He turned and ran for his horse. He could see the barrel of his rifle sticking out of the saddle. But by now all he wanted was to get away, to stop the increasing heat of his clothes. As he approached his horse, the animal reared and galloped away, wild-eyed and frenzied from the growing fire that was now consuming the first floor of the house. Romero was left standing alone and unarmed against the advancing mass of black bodies.

They watched as the ashes settled on him and the first flickers of flames caught on his hair. The last they saw of the man who had tortured them for years was his smoldering silhouette as he ran for the river.

They turned to his former home, swinging their torches, increasing the speed and range of the arcs as they surrounded the house to finish the job they had started. The torches, a garland of pendulous lights, filled the clearing. The first torch flew through the second floor window. The flames caught the curtains. Other torches were flung onto the porch, on the stairs, around the baseboards. Within minutes the house was consumed in flames.

The crowd roared as they watched it go up, lighting the night. The sound of the crackling wood drowned out the cheers. The bedding floated up in fiery clumps. They heard glass bursting in the heat.

Papers, like burning bat wings, blew in the breeze. Flames danced along the rooftop. An explosion sounded, then flaming items flew everywhere—a charred crucifix, scorched ledgers, and a black cape reduced to blackened bits of fabric like feathers hanging above them. In the midst of it all, long serpents of fire danced in the air, spiraling, consumed by flames. They finally landed, motionless, blistered and smoldering on the ground before them. They weren't snakes at all, but the many whips that Romero kept on hand, ever ready to bite into black flesh. These were the whips that hung by his door, draped over his saddle, waited in his brutal hands. The people stared at the remnants of these whips in silence as they melted into the earth. Then a low rumble grew from their throats and burst into a jubilant cheer that spread over the fields.

* * *

During the fire, Josefa stood in front of Las Agujas and watched. When Mati finally came home to bed, Tía Josefa knew the young woman wasn't aware of her charred clothing, her blackened hands and streaked face. Tía Josefa prepared Mati's bath, helped her get rid of the ruined clothes, and laid out fresh garments. When Josefa was done braiding Mati's hair, she helped the young woman into bed and sat and watched over her during the night, as she had done for Fela years before. While Mati slept, Tía bent down to smell her newly washed hair. She remembered Mati as a baby. She stroked her face and sang her all the lullabies she could remember until she lost her voice and could only hum.

She remembered the set of Mati's shoulders as she confronted Romero. The man who had always seemed so big, powerful, and unbeatable lost his stature as he stood before her little girl. Tía Josefa remembered Mati as she lit into him, followed him in his retreat. She didn't need to worry anymore. Mati had grown into the strong woman Tía had always known she'd become. *I did the best I could, old friend, and I think I did well.*

* * *

When Mati woke up the sun was beating down on her face. Perspiration slid between her brows and down the ridge of her nose. Her lips were salty and her throat dry. Before she opened her eyes, she remembered the events of the previous night. *Everything will be different now*, she thought. But as she became more aware of her surroundings, she sensed something was wrong. It was too quiet in the cabin.

She sat up and looked around. Tía Josefa lay on her bed fully dressed. Instead of the usual braids, she had wrapped her hair in a spotless headdress, and she wore a clean white gown. Her nails had been scrubbed clean and her hands now rested on her chest, modestly securing her best shawl around her shoulders. She wore serenity on her face like a mantle. She had readied herself for important company and had slipped away when Mati wasn't looking. Tía had even spared her the need to cleanse her body.

Mati dropped down onto Tía's cot. She picked up one of the old woman's hands, touching her as if she were made of the most fragile crystal. Mati nuzzled into Tía's neck and tried to capture her scent. She looked down on the old face, wrinkled, burned black after so many years in the sun. The once thick lips had diminished to a thin line. She strained to think of the first words she remembered coming out of that mouth, the first admonishment, the first smile. Too much to remember it all. It all fell away and blended into a feeling that filled her with warmth. When the other women woke up they found Mati lying side-by-side with Tía's cold body.

9 Visitations

When Cheo came back to Las Agujas after Tía's funeral, he found a different Mati. There was now a heaviness to her movements, and the light had gone out of her smile. He had heard that Tía Josefa had died and knew that Mati would need him. As a *liberto*, he should have been able to leave. But the warehouse foreman would not pay him his wages until he had finished his current pieces. Once done, Cheo collected his pay, packed his clothes, and left for Las Mercedes.

Cheo had plans now that he was a free man. He intended to take Mati back to town with him. He could offer her marriage, a family, a home, and the respect that his craftsmanship could buy them. He had made a name for himself, and now he could use it. Others had done it, so would he. He had been saving money to buy their freedom. Now he could take that money and open a small shop just outside town. They would marry and live in the back of the shop until he could buy her a little house of her own. They would begin a new life together.

When Mati saw him, she took him in her arms and clung to him for a long time, not knowing what to say or where to start. So much had happened.

Later, when she was calmer, they had time to talk.

"I've been thinking about the way it's been with us." He took her hands. "Mati, I had so many plans. I was saving my money little by

little and I thought…*el patrón* would have…I could've bought…you…"
He was having so much trouble getting the words out. "But now…the
way things are…we don't have to wait anymore." He grew excited.
"Mati, people—important people, rich people—like my work. I've
been thinking that with the money I've saved we can buy a workshop,
not much at first but maybe a little place, maybe not right away…but
if you'll come with me…"

Mati smiled and shook her head. It was a smile fueled more by sadness
than joy.

"Come with you? Cheito…Cheo, it all sounds wonderful and I
love you for thinking and planning it, but I…I can never leave here. I
have plans, too…I owe…"

"Owe? You *owe* nothing." He pointed to the big house. "They owed
you. You and your mother, and me and my father, and all of us who
have been slaving for nothing. *They owed us.*" Cheo's voice grew hard.

"Exactly, and this is where they will pay. Cheo, listen…the land…
he left it to me. They cheated…"

"*¡Qué locura!* I've heard about this so-called land of yours. Did you
really think they'd let you have it? That land is gone. It was never
yours. You're lucky, Mati. *We're* luckier than most. We can go where we
want, do what we want." He was growing impatient.

"But I *will* get it back—for me, for you, for the rest of us. They took
us away from our Home Place. So we must build a new home. They
will give it back."

The words came out of her mouth, fast and sure, as though they had
lived there for a long time. There was no hesitation, no doubt in them.

Cheo's eyes opened in amazement. "Are you crazy? Don't ever say
such a thing. Someone will hear you and…"

"Look at me, Cheo," she said. "You know that I have ways of
getting things done. There are things I know I can't change. But if I
say I'll get my land back, it *will* be mine again. I'll do whatever I have
to, to make sure of it."

"Again! *Your* land! It was never yours. Do you think they will ever admit that you're his daughter? You're a slap in the face of every one of their women and proof of their own lechery. You think you can win against these 'honorable *caballeros*'? You'll find yourself in another district, enslaved again, in a place that will break your spirit as well as your back.

"Didn't you learn anything from Fela's life? These men will shut you up any way they have to. You're going to get yourself killed, Mati. The men who took your land won't hesitate to take your life and think no more of it than they would of killing an annoying mosquito. Mati, please, I beg you, come with me. I can give you a home, children. This revenge you're after…"

"Revenge has nothing to do with it. It is a matter of balance. You are right about one thing—they owe me, and they will pay."

"But Mati…"

"I've made up my mind." She turned and walked away, refusing to discuss it further.

Days later, after trying again and again to convince Mati to go back to town with him, Cheo finally gave up and left Las Mercedes alone. He couldn't stay there any longer. Too much had changed for him. He couldn't live there with its memories of the past around every corner. Just as Mati was determined to make her life there, he was determined to start living as a free man in town. He had always hoped she would be part of that. But the most he could hope for now was the hasty visit, when they could come together and forget the rest. When he set his feet on the road again he left his heart behind and, although he wouldn't believe it, Mati's heart went with him.

* * *

By age twenty-five, Mati had shown no romantic interest in any men in her community. As much as the locals were attracted to her physical attributes, Mati's gift made them extremely uncomfortable.

She read their intentions easily, sometimes understanding her suitors far better than they understood themselves. Some of them resented Mati for being so unapproachable. Those who had tried, in vain, to charm themselves into her bed angrily accused her of putting on airs just because her father had been *el patrón*. *"¡Se cree muy especial!"*

Mati had nothing against them. It wasn't that she rejected them as much as that she never considered letting them in. She was lonely, but Mati had never met a *curandera* who didn't live the solitary life. Even if years went by without a visit from Cheo, she reserved herself for him alone. She often thought of him in the darkness of her loneliness and hungered for his sporadic visits when, instead of feeling different and apart, she felt loved and treasured. When he was gone, she felt as though a piece of her was gone with him.

Mati didn't choose to become a healer. It was not something she *could* choose, but rather something that chose her. The old *curandera* had healed the black people on the plantation for more years than anyone remembered. When she died, people simply began appearing at Mati's door. They brought her their warts, broken hearts and broken bones, breathing ailments, jealousy, unrequited love, grippe, infidelity, nightmares, spasms, fears, infertility, sleeping sickness—on and on. She could see into the hearts and bodies of people and was able to heal the hidden hurts.

They approached her with a *respeto*, tinged with a healthy dose of fear of the unknown. They were driven by their needs. Many of her people carried with them an unspoken or half-forgotten memory of the old African religions. They had a sense of the powerful healing force in nature and respected its use. But the old ones, the ones who *knew*, the ones who were brought in ships, were almost all gone now. The younger ones, *ladinos*, no longer fully trusted the old ways. So they approached Mati with a silent hesitancy, a half-hatched fear.

Mati's ability to help people was whispered throughout the district. Her name was passed from one mouth to the next and often she tended to the slaves of neighboring plantations. Sometimes, the white *jornaleros* who seasonally worked the fields found their way to her door with a toothache or twisted limb.

In critical situations, when their white doctors in their white hospitals could not solve their problems, even *hacendados* who had heard of her knowledge of herbs and remedies sought out her skills.

In time, her name and her work were known to a great many people. Because she had so many ways of dealing with injuries of the body and soul, and because she knew so many of their secrets, not many would cross Mati, black or white. So when the men who had cheated her out of her land at the auction unexpectedly began taking to their sickbeds, folks nodded their heads, looked at each other knowingly, and waited.

* * *

Mati's eyes were closed and her mouth open. As she stood before the altar in her room, she chanted in a long-ago tongue that she herself did not understand. Tendrils of *sándalo* incense curled among the freesia that sat on the freshly dressed table. The candles had flickered to stubs: the smaller green ones to ensure Mati's own curative powers, the large yellow one to honor Oshun and call on her wisdom.

Mati dipped the neatly aligned stems in her right hand into a bowl of clear river water. She circled her hand three times around her head to the right, then three to the left, sending droplets of water flying around the room. Then began the rhythmic cleansing ritual of brushing herself, alternating between the right and the left side of her body, beginning with her shoulders and working her way down each side until she finished at her feet.

She began the ritual at sunrise. When she finally opened her eyes, she could tell by the way the light fell on her things that noon was fast upon her. She placed her fingertips on the table and smoothed the cloth, again closing her eyes for a moment to find her center. Then she was ready.

When the sun was directly overhead, Mati stood at the front gate of the Herrera y Torres plantation. Don Próspero's wife, Doña Sara, had sent for Mati after all the doctors of the district, and even some from the capital, had come and gone, their black bags hanging heavy and useless in their hands. Even Padre Bartolomeo, who came daily now, held out little hope for the *patrón*. Mati had been summoned under the secrecy of night. She had responded in her own time, in the light of midday. She stood before the gate, hands in her skirt pockets, the *remedio* she had been asked to bring clutched in her left hand.

Pucha, the young girl who had been sent to get the *curandera* a few nights before, was sweeping the wide steps as Mati walked up.

"*Buenos días,* Mati. Doña Sara *dice que pases por atrás.*"

"*Buenos días,* Pucha." Mati smiled and returned the greeting but remained where she stood, ignoring the instructions she had just been given. Her days of going to the back door were over. The girl had gone back to her sweeping but the broom slowed as Pucha realized that Mati wasn't moving. She looked up, confused, and was about to repeat the message when she realized Mati's intent. The lines of confusion softened and melted into a look of astonishment.

"Mati, no," she whispered. "You mustn't. The *patrona* will be furious."

Mati stood her ground. "But I have no *patrona*, not anymore. And never again." She stood motionless as Pucha watched her, openmouthed.

"But..." It was no use. Mati was impassive.

Finally, the girl leaned her broom against the wall and ran into the house. When she reappeared she walked three steps behind her mistress.

The blond woman stood on the porch, holding her hand up to shield her eyes. Pucha stood just behind, nervously twisting her apron.

"*¿Qué es lo que te pasa?*" The woman called out.

Mati heard the annoyance in the woman's voice. Nonetheless, she waited. Doña Sara sent the girl down to open the side gate. Pucha held the gate wide open and waited, her eyes pleading. Still, Mati did not move.

"Mati, *¿qué pasa?* Are you deaf or what?"

Finally, clearly exasperated, the woman marched down the path. Pucha got out of the way. Doña Sara stood just inside the wrought-iron fencing at the front entry. Elaborate metal curlicues separated the two women as Mati, a full half foot taller, looked down calmly at the white woman before her. Doña Sara looked up, hands shielding her squinting eyes, and repeated her question, her voice cutting through the afternoon quiet.

"*¿Qué es esto? ¿Qué pasa? ¿Dónde está mi remedio?*" she demanded.

Mati looked at Sara's bejeweled hand on the ironwork and waited. Finally, the woman understood that Mati was waiting for her to open the gate. The indignation in the woman fairly jumped out of her eyes. "*No!*" The word exploded between them.

Doña Sara whipped her hand out and stuck it through the fence, fully expecting Mati to hand over the vial. Mati looked down at the woman and then back at the hand. Then she tipped her hat and turned to leave. Doña Sara's belabored smile, more like a grimace, faded as she watched Mati start down the path. A black woman had never turned her back to Sara before. She couldn't, wouldn't allow such an insult, especially in front of her own slave. She, Sara, mistress of Las Colinas, was being dismissed by this *negra*. She couldn't believe the insolence. This was intolerable!

While Sara fumed, Mati took her time making her way down the path and was about to turn onto the public road. Sara thought of her husband, who lay dying upstairs. They had tried everything and nothing had helped. Finally, Próspero had asked for this woman. Sara thought he must have lost his mind. But he truly believed Mati was his last chance. Sara herself didn't put much store in the tales about this woman as a healer. But she had never questioned her husband's judgment before and she wasn't going to start now, when there was so little time left. Just when Mati was about to step out onto the road, Doña Sara called after her.

"*No.*" Doña Sara was more controlled now. "*Un momento.*" She had adjusted the volume, subdued the edge of her voice.

Mati stopped and turned to look at the woman. Only when Doña Sara unlatched the gate and held it open did Mati walk back up the manicured path to the front of the house and through the open gate. Doña Sara's head was held high and rigid by the tight cords that bulged on either side of her neck. She bit her bottom lip hard and her eyes flashed. But she held the gate open until Mati walked through.

"*Pasa.*" It was a grudging invitation.

Sara went ahead to the open front door, but as she stepped through she sensed that Mati wasn't following. She turned to face the black woman, who stood by the porch furniture, waiting. Mati eyed the rockers. Clearly, she was not ready to enter the house yet. Controlled anger was once again replaced by fury as Doña Sara understood Mati's intention. The small veins on her temples pulsed visibly. Her hands gripped the ends of the elegant silk fan, previously hanging from her wrist, now bowed, arched, and ready to snap. This time she couldn't trust her voice. Again, the image of her husband in pain mediated her rage. After a moment, her hands loosened into a quick motion of the fan, indicating a nearby seat.

Mati pulled her shawl around her shoulders and sat down carefully, not on the straight back chair offered, but in the cushioned rocker that was in the cool shade. She stretched her tired legs and rested herself after the long walk. Sara stood over her, impatiently twisting her fan, but Mati, with more grace than her hostess, motioned for Sara to have one of her own chairs.

"*¡Esto es el colmo!* Who is the slave and who is the mistress here?" Doña Sara spit out.

"You forget. *I* am not a slave, *señora*. After all, it was *you* who sent for *me*. I do have other things to do. If you don't need me...?" Mati's eyebrows rose in two arches.

"No." Doña Sara swallowed and took a deep breath in an effort to calm herself. She took her seat as Mati had indicated.

"It certainly is warm today. A good day for a glass of *limonada*, especially after that long walk over here," Mati said, never taking her eyes off the woman who sat seething across from her.

Mati's face was smooth and calm. Her black eyes looked directly into Sara's green ones and did not flinch. She seemed quite comfortable, slowly examining, evaluating, measuring the mistress of the house. Sara's attention was drawn to the pricking pain in her hands. Her nails had dug into the fleshy skin of her palms. Even through the pain, her hands itched for a riding crop, a whip, anything that would allow her to beat the equanimity out of this smooth brown face before her. This house was her domain. Here her word was law. She was the *patrona*. Yet somehow, she had lost control of her own house to this *negra*. There was a moment's hesitation before her voice rang out.

"*Pucha!*"

The girl appeared instantly.

"*Señora?*"

"Bring something to drink...and fast."

"*Sí, señora.*" The girl could barely hide her delight as she ran to the kitchen.

* * *

Mati put down the glass. Sara had watched impatiently while Mati drank her lemonade, waiting before broaching the subject on her mind.

"If you are ready now, I would like to have the *remedio*. My husband is very ill..."

"No one knows that better than me. That's the whole point, isn't it?" Mati rose to her feet and eyed the front door. "I'm ready to see him now."

"Surely, you don't expect to go…he's in his bed!"

"Then I am wasting my time here." Mati bent down to gather her shawl from the rocker.

"All right, all right! Maybe he'll see you."

"I thought he might," Mati said quietly to herself but loud enough for Doña Sara to hear.

The woman turned to go inside and Mati followed. They crossed the foyer, a circular area that opened onto a large room on either side. A long curved staircase led to the private rooms upstairs. Their skirts made a swishing sound in the silence of the house as they made their way to Don Próspero's room.

"Espera aquí," Doña Sara threw the words over her shoulder.

Mati waited as the woman went into the room. In a few seconds, she came out again and closed the door behind her.

"I don't know why, but he will see you now. Don't be long. He needs his rest." She escorted Mati into the room and hung back as the *curandera* approached the bed.

It was a large room, dark and cool even though outside the day was warm and sun-flooded. After the brightness of the noon sun, Mati strained her eyes until they adjusted to the dim light. The drapes hung heavily, obscuring shuttered windows and giving the room the tension of a prison, the silence of a tomb, musty, old, and airless. Half a dozen protective angels painted in glossy hues glowed dimly from the vaulted ceiling, barely visible in the lantern light. Above the bed, a large cross was affixed on the wall. The muscular body of the Christ on the cross had turned brown with age.

Mati didn't see the man at first, but finally her eyes found Don Próspero's bulk amid the crumpled nightclothes and newly soiled linen on the bed. His smell hung in the air. His once long and shiny black hair had fallen away, leaving patches of bald spots amid matted strands of gray. His moustache had grown into the tangled beard. His face looked pasty, like wet clay. His cheeks, which Mati remembered as being rounded with good health, had sagged. The white teeth, which had gripped the thick cigars he was known for, were now an opaque yellow. He lay very still until he opened his eyes and found her in the dim light.

"Finally! Where is my *remedio*?"

Mati said nothing. Instead, she looked around the room until her eyes stopped at Doña Sara. For a moment, he didn't understand why she hesitated, but he soon grasped the situation as he looked at the resolute black woman.

"Sara, *déjanos*," he commanded his wife.

"*¿Cómo que déjanos?* I'm not leaving you alone with this one."

Mati squared her shoulders and focused on him.

He reacted quickly and forcefully, "*¡Mujer, que nos déjes! ¡Ahora!*"

Sara flinched. His voice came out sharp, strong, commanding.

"*Está bien, hombre. No te agites,*" She immediately acquiesced, leaving them alone.

"*¿Qué quieres?*" he asked.

"What do *I* want? We'll get to that later. I believe it is you who are in need."

"All right. *Mi remedio,* how much?"

His hand snaked out of the linen folds and disappeared into a box that sat on the bedside table. She heard metallic shifting and then the click of the coins as they were thrown at her feet.

"There, that should be more than enough for your efforts."

The lantern light fell on the scattered coins on the floor. She looked down at the *reales* and wondered at what price he valued his life. He misunderstood her hesitation. His hands did more searching and three more coins fell at her feet.

"And not another *centavo*! Now give me my *remedio* and you can go." His hand gestured impatiently toward the door and he started turning his back to her.

She still didn't move. "It is not a question of money."

"Not money?" His voice was laced with genuine incredulity. "Well, what do you want, then?"

She thought he would understand by now without her having to say it. But he was dull and stupid and required the words.

"I only want what is mine."

His eyes searched her out, impatience being replaced by the beginning of anger. "*¿Pero qué diablos?*"

"I think you know. Your mind has not left you yet. You have something of mine that I want back." He still stared at her uncomprehendingly.

"I want my land back. I need my home intact. That, and only that, is my price."

"*¿Cómo?*" His eyes were gone for a moment, trying to place her face. Memory and then comprehension smoothed out the creases in his face before anger brought him a new store of energy.

"*¡Nunca!* I will never...*your land...?* That is my land. *¡Presumida!* Where do you get the nerve to...?"

"We both know whose land it was."

"I bought it legally with my money. And I am protected by the law."

"There is your law and then there is justice. Can your law protect you from illness, from death?" Her eyes bore into him knowingly.

"*¡Estarás loca!*"

"You think so? You have a very bad memory."

He remembered the rumors, the mystery that surrounded this woman who seemed so sure of herself. He said nothing, clamping his lips together as though keeping something dangerous from coming out.

"I see you do remember."

"Superstitions! That's for *ignorantes*. You can trick them. But as for me, I'll never give up what's mine. *Nunca*, you hear me, never! I'll rot in hell first."

"Really?"

Mati had hoped it would not come to this. She looked at this man she despised, and focused on her purpose. She visualized the inside of his body. She saw the organs inflamed and tender. In her mind she watched them shifting slowly, pulling, straining, twisting. Don Próspero's face contorted, his features disappearing into the deep folds of his loose flesh. His words were cut short by a gnawing anguish as he folded into himself, a quivering mass of pain.

Mati's eyes flashed. She looked down on the helpless man before her. She calmed herself, took a deep breath, and released. The man fell back against his pillows, wet hair plastered across his face. The odor of sweat and feces filled the room.

It took him a while to catch his breath after the unexpected attack. He desperately tried to reconcile all the different parts of this experience, his mind trying to understand what he already knew in his body. Reason told him this was an impossible situation and he grasped at the last vestige of logic.

"You're the daughter of ten thousand *diablos* from the bowels of hell. *Bruja mala…*"

Mati froze. She appeared to grow several inches before his eyes. Her hands balled into stone fists at her sides, all her concentration going out to the man before her. His last words were choked by screams of agony as his body arched into a human bow on the bed. His arms and legs went taut. His head jerked back. His entire body was rigid, every nerve and muscle stretched to the limit of its endurance.

Doña Sara burst in the room at the sound of her husband's screams.

"*¿Qué pasa aquí?*" The sight of her husband stopped her short. "Prós—" Then she was speechless. As she stood there, her eyes glued to her husband's spine arched into an impossible position, Mati stood motionless, untouched by the spectacle before her.

Doña Sara's terror multiplied as she looked from Mati to her husband and back again. "*¡NO! Por favor.* Anything, you can have anything you want. Please! I beg you." Doña Sara lost all control. Mati looked at this woman who wore arrogance like a suit of clothes. Then she looked back at Próspero, still arched in agony. She had as much compassion for them as they had always had for her people.

Still, she released him, giving him a chance to recover. He fell heavily onto the bed, gasping for air, as his wife rushed to cover his limp body. Mati stood at the foot of the bed, hands relaxed now, waiting. Finally, Don Próspero recovered enough to focus on her again.

"*¡No más! ¡Está bien!*" he gasped. "You'll get…your land."

Mati dug in her apron pocket and pulled out a small vial. She held it out but stopped, hand in midair, for a moment.

"Don't even consider cheating me. If you do, I won't be back when you sicken again, and you *will* sicken again. Then there will be no more discussion of this matter. You do understand me?"

Her eyes held him. He was no match for her. There was no other way. He would give her whatever she wanted, just as long as she got out of his room. He nodded his head in defeat and sank back into his pillows.

"*Sí, sí.* You will have…the land back," he said quietly.

Mati placed the bottle on the bedside table, not looking at the man who desperately grabbed for the vial as soon as she released it. She walked past Doña Sara, who jumped as Mati brushed by her. Marching out of the room onto the landing and down the stairs, she opened the front door, leaving it wide open. She crossed the *balcón* and made her way down the front steps.

Mati walked away from the house, leaving the gaping gate behind. Her feet took her down the wide avenue and around the bend in the road. There she stopped to lean against a *ceiba* tree. She took a deep breath, releasing her exhaustion, acknowledging her victory. She felt for the stone around her neck and tried to calm her beating heart. She knew she would have to pay a great price for this afternoon's work and wondered just how payment would be extracted.

* * *

One after the other, the neighboring plantation owners who had taken her land developed ailments for which the doctors could find no explanation or remedy. Each man began to waste away. The gentry offered masses for the improvement of their health. Local doctors were replaced by specialists from the capital. The druggist made a fortune filing prescriptions that never worked. Lawyers were summoned, paraded in and out with ink-stained fingers and newly witnessed documents. Distraught wives were tortured by nightmares of hearses and shrouds of black silk. When the situation seemed hopeless, words were whispered in the dark. And then there would be a nocturnal knock on Mati's door. Soon after, a visit from Mati and an understanding. By the end of the year, every man who had stolen a parcel of her land would sign it back in exchange for her elixirs. The land she was given always coincided exactly with the land left to her in Don Tomás' will. She never asked for or was given a kilometer more or less. Shortly thereafter, the ailing man's health would improve and all would, apparently, be well. It would be years before anyone noticed that none of these *patrones* fathered any children after their mysterious illness.

* * *

It took two years, but Mati finally got all her land back. The people at Las Mercedes prospered. They pooled their resources and worked the land for themselves. They sold their crops as a collective to ensure the best prices. Of course, the best markets were closed to them by the organized *hacendados* who held the lucrative contracts with overseas buyers. So the Colectiva Las Mercedes started its own local markets in nearby towns and sold to townspeople who had forgotten how to plant, sow, and reap and had traded land for city life. They worked hard and lived modestly but better than they ever had as slaves. They worked their own land, lived in their own homes, and answered to no one but each other.

10 REARRANGEMENTS

While the white people owned it, the big house was called Las Mercedes. But as soon as Mati moved in, everyone called it Caridad. Where Las Mercedes was a genteel lady, Caridad became a big, handsome woman of a house. All the many windows, no curtains now, were flung open in the morning to welcome the outdoors. The fruit trees that wrapped around the sides spread like ample hips. They provided shade for the children who played around their trunks, privacy for the young people who made love beneath their branches, and a cool refuge for the old men who chewed tobacco and dreamed of their youth on lazy afternoons.

The *batey* now bustled with the life of the black people working for themselves. It was a private world into which outsiders were seldom invited, not in an attempt to hide the ugliness of its previous life but rather to preserve the spirit of community that now lived there. People who had never had privacy or the joy of sharing openly with their neighbors now took those gifts very seriously and protected their privacy in many ways.

Amapola bushes grew right up to the house, sometimes even extending limbs onto the *balcón* and into the dining room windows. Everywhere, there were bowls of fruits and baskets of wild flowers. It was as though Mati was trying to bring the outdoors, which she had always associated with life, into this house that she had always associated with death.

Las Mercedes had been a house that had always been kept by many hands. When it became Mati's, there were only two hands to tend to it. When a house's needs outweigh the owner's ability to care for it, it begins to die. So Mati began to make changes to keep it alive by sharing its treasures with her community.

Pieces of the big house had found their way out the back door to the newly built houses of the black families. The path from the *batey* became a conduit for distribution. The French crystal glasses traveled down from the formal dining room of the big house to Mariana's home, where they lived among the rough-hewn furniture left over from the *choza* days. The simple benches of Tibursio's family now sat on a thick Persian rug, the edges curled up against the floorboards. Rosalba's humble windows were now hung with lace and silk curtains. Embroidered napkins now served as diapers for brown babies who had always gone bare-bottomed. People who hardly had enough to eat before now ate their beans and rice and pigs' feet from fine china plates and sipped their *mondongo* from silver soupspoons.

Men who had owned nothing but poorly mended shirts now wore elaborate *guayaberas*. Old women who had never worn shoes in their lives now owned Italian leather ones. Young women with courting beaux squeezed their feet into too-small satin dance slippers. Mati sent all these things out through her back door.

Mati filled her house with her own work. Although she couldn't read or write and didn't do a lot of talking, she was a great storyteller. Her stories flowed from her needles. The people who populated her dreams came to life in the pieces she hung on her walls.

The first tapestry she ever made was one of the Lady Oshun. It was the hardest to do because the Lady had come to Mati in so many guises that she didn't know how to limit herself to just one. So she filled the surface with different figures. First, there was the young woman, naked from the waist up, wading into the river. Mati worked her loose hair using three strands of thread and making tiny knots to simulate the thick texture of the locks. The figure wore a string of seashells, and for this Mati sewed actual shells onto the heavy fabric, one connected to the next with twisted metallic threads.

Then she worked an image of a mature woman standing on the seashore, every inch of her skin covered with fluid outlines of sea creatures. A diaphanous shirt flowed over her low-swung breasts. Her lips were broad and her eyes huge. She stood as in the midst of a dance, arms extended in invitation, one hip higher than the other, the skirt swirling around her bare feet. She carried a large tray filled with fruits and flowers.

In still another section, the same woman had grown older. Her body was less defined but the garments still hinted at her roundness here and there. She carried a staff, wore a head wrap, and held a pipe in her mouth. Her many bracelets and long hanging earrings glimmered. A large mirror hung from her belt, half visible among the folds of her skirt.

All of these images floated on a background of a blue-green cloth and were framed by long, winding strings of seaweed. It took Mati months to complete but when she was done with these she turned to the other pieces that now filled her home.

There was a large tapestry of Tía Josefa as a young woman. It wasn't Tía's face as Mati remembered her, but as Mati dreamed her to have been sitting in a rocker, dressed in a white gown embroidered in pale lavender. The little table next to her held the tools of her craft. Mati worked this piece with the sharpest colors, as bright and crisp as her memory of Tía Josefa.

Finally, there was the piece that hung in her bedroom. Cheo's tapestry was placed on a wall all by itself. Mati worked his figure as he came to her, night after night in her dreams. It was a huge piece, of a man over six feet tall with muscular arms and legs, big hands, and a poet's soul beaming through his eyes. She had dyed the white thread until she got the color she wanted, experimented with cinnamon, allspice and honey, mahogany and ebony powders, clay, and ink. Finally, she found just the right combination of dyes for his skin tone and spent hours, hundreds of stitches, on his hands. She copied the cuts and bruises faithfully, symbols of his craft and his livelihood. She worked and reworked stitches for the tendons on the feet and the hairs on the chest. She used thin fibers to work the creases in the face. After many months, when she was satisfied with her work, she often sat back and visited with his image late into the night.

* * *

Cheo stood at the foot of the path that led up to the garden. This would be the first time he'd walked up to the front door of this house. He stepped onto the carefully tended path and hesitated before going up the stairs and across the tiled floor to the mahogany rocker on which sat the lady of the house.

Mati's rocker was nestled at her favorite spot, the corner of the porch near the lemon trees, her old box of threads just by her feet as she examined the half-finished tapestry on her lap. She put it up to the sun to gauge the effect of her color choices in the light. She was pulling out a length of goldenrod thread and preparing to work the tiny French knots required in the next section when Cheo's shadow fell across her work.

She could hardly believe it. She hadn't set eyes on Cheo for over ten years and here he stood before her, citified and different, but her Cheo nonetheless. She stood slowly. Her breath caught in her throat as she reached for him. She lost herself in the warmth of his body, the feel of his moist skin. She found her favorite spot on his neck and sniffed. The years between them melted away.

They pulled back, each inspecting the other openly, noting all that the other had become, and ignoring the fact that youth was long gone.

Cheo wore a straw hat, nothing like the *pava* that had kept the sun from his eyes in his cane-cutting days. Now he wore a panama hat, stiff and tightly woven by expert hands, a Sunday hat. Much had changed about Cheo, but his hands had not. They were the same scarred, strong hands of a carver. The tiny cuts were those of the artisan, not the slashes of the machete. She would know his hands anywhere.

Mati knew she had changed since the last time they'd met. She retained her high bosom and ample hips. But now there was more of her, a buxom woman. She smoothed back her hair, now shot with gray, as she motioned him to sit on the rocker across from her own. Her eyes never left his face.

Cheo had been anticipating this moment for weeks. He sat back now and feasted on Mati's face and her body. His hands itched to undo her beautiful new hair and smell it. He didn't want to say anything yet, just wanted to get his fill of her. But his body betrayed him and he reached out for her again. And then they went inside and closed the door.

* * *

He was still watching her as they ate their breakfast. They had said very little all night and this was the first time he had had a chance to sit back and really look at her in her world. Sitting on this *balcón*, there was no doubt that she was the mistress of the house. Lounging on *her* porch, sitting on *her* furniture. He shook his head.

"I just can't believe my eyes. This is your place, Mati. Yours? I'm sorry, but I just can't understand how you can live here, in the house of the *patrones*, among their things."

"A house is just a house. And this one is my house now."

"Is it so easy to wash away everything that went before? Aren't *they* still here, hiding in the crevices, under the floorboards, in your memory?"

"Yes, *they* are still here. But they're only a small part and they're not alone. The others are here as well. Mamá Fela is here and Tía Josefa and your father. And all the others that lived and died working here are still here with me. Their names are back there in the graveyard. But they come and sit here, take coffee with me in the afternoons, and keep me company at night."

And because she had heard the condemnation in his voice, she added, "They were here and kept me company when others disappeared." The accusation hung humid and dense in the air between them. Her words had struck home.

"All right, Mati. You made your point."

Not now, thought Mati. She really didn't want to have that talk now, *not here in the sunshine, not the first day.*

Her next words came out softly, more like the Mati he remembered, "Come and stay with me in my house, and get to know us both. Then we'll find a space of comfort between us again."

* * *

Cheo had been back two weeks. Uncomfortable as the house made him, he had moved his slippers under Mati's bed and his tools into his father's old workshop. It would have to be expanded, but for now it would do.

He looked out on all the land Mati had retrieved and wondered how she had managed it. How had she managed to get those men to give up their properties? Just how far had she gone to get what she wanted?

One evening Mati closed their bedroom door for the night and started preparing for bed. She was brushing out her hair when she caught sight of him in the mirror and returned an unwavering gaze.

"What is it?" she asked. But she knew.

"Tell me about the land."

She had been expecting this. Her neighbors were good people, but there was little to do in the evenings but sit and talk. Gossip was the cheapest entertainment. They respected her and came to her when in need, but they never could quite understand her strange ways.

"Mati, what did you do?" The words came out slowly, carefully.

"I got the land back."

"Mati…"

"I did what I had to do."

"Mati, did you…"

"And I paid the price."

"What are you talking about, Mati?" There was already an edge, the sharp edge of a question already answered.

"There are things you wouldn't understand."

"Then why don't you explain them to me?" The chill that had moved in behind his words was not lost on her. She wanted to hold and reassure him. But she wouldn't let herself. If he was to be a part of her life, then he would have to accept that some things couldn't be explained. Words were too small.

"There are things you have never understood and will never understand."

"You'd better try, Mati. You'd better try real hard." He crossed his arms and waited. His words were taut, a string of unspoken accusations. He used them as armor and Mati had no weapons to pierce them.

"Words…you want words from me now. We have never needed words before. I don't have words…they have never come easily to me. You'll have to learn to trust me."

"I still don't understand." He had wanted this woman for as long as he could remember. But he couldn't stand the thought of what she might have done to persuade those men to give her back her land. He wanted to hear that she had been forced. He wanted her to put a face on the enemy.

"I did what I had to do. I don't have answers for you…I made choices…accepted the consequences."

He tried to remember that she had been left alone, that he had no claim, no right to question her decisions. He wondered just how much she had been forced to do to survive, how much she had been willing to do to make a place for herself, for all of them. But this was too fantastic. Was she a liar or was she truly a witch?

"I used my gift to bring pain and fear into people's lives. A gift that had always been meant for good, I used to get my revenge. I felt justified in breaking the rules. I had made my decision and I wouldn't stop. The gods were the gods but we lived here. We needed our own place and this is where they all were—our past, our memories, Mamá Fela, all of them. We could never go back home. So this would be our Home Place and it was worth whatever price I had to pay."

Cheo sat speechless. His mind tried to take it all in. Finally, he pulled the covers over his head and turned away from her.

Mati finished brushing her hair in silence. When she got into bed she reached for him, but Cheo had gone far away. So they didn't touch each other. Long into the night, they lived in their own thoughts. Finally, Mati fell asleep, but Cheo's eyes were still open when the sun came up.

He looked at her, trying to find the woman he thought he knew so well. He stroked her hair, losing himself in its texture. He had waited for this woman his whole life. She was his world. There was no other place for him. For years, he dreamed about giving her so much. And now he had come home to this. She was right. She had done what she needed to do. He would have to take all of her, even the parts he'd never understood. Or he'd have nothing. So he tried to push away his doubts. Finally, just when Mati was starting to get up, he stretched his arm around her and held her back.

* * *

Mati thought of Padre Bartolomeo and his complicity in the stealing of her land. She remembered his white face sweating as he tried to convince her that she had no right to what had been taken from her. She thought about the church in the town where her people were never welcomed. And she turned her eyes away from these when she thought of her upcoming wedding.

Likewise, Cheo could not see asking this man, who owned slaves himself, to bless their union. He remembered delivering heavy pieces of furniture to the rectory and having the priest haggle over a price that had long been agreed on. He remembered the blow he received when the warehouse manager found the discrepancy between the amount on the priest's bill and the amount of money paid. It had been easier to strike a slave than to question the padre's honesty. The difference was taken out of Cheo's wages. He ended up working for almost a year without pay. No, this Padre Bartolomeo would have no place in their marriage ceremony.

So they found the oldest couple among their people and invited everyone else to meet them at the river on the evening of the full moon. There the elders chanted ceremoniously in a tongue that no one knew anymore. Their song rose up to the sky and out over the water and across the fields. Then the eldest woman placed her hands on Mati's head and the man placed his hands on Cheo's head and they sang a whispered melody into the younger couple's ears. After this they raised their voices once again to the crowd. No one understood the words, but the melody seemed more of a benediction than anything any of them had ever heard before.

Even though a large crowd was present, the ceremony was intimate and very brief. But the celebration went on all night and into the morning. So the *batey* was full of the smell of *lechon asado*, on the spit since daybreak, and *batatas* roasting slowly on the firestones. The cook boiled huge pots of pinto beans until they were tender and juicy, big chunks of pigs' feet floating in the sauce, heavy with fatback, garlic, and cilantro. And the *morcillas* sizzled in big frying pans. The children sipped sweet lemonade and munched on crispy *chicharrones* and sugarcane sticks. The men brought out a barrel of *cañita* with the fermented fruit lying deceptively harmless at the bottom.

After the elders' blessings, the drummers brought out their instruments, the *tumbadora, congas, tumbao*, *timbales.* They played the secrets of Africa in their complex musical lines, each type of drum providing a different voice until, in unison, they became a chorus that drove the rest of the instruments. Their music was a pulsing, breathing creature that lived on air and wood and stretched hides. Next came the *maracas* and *güiros* made from their own *higüero* trees and a handful of seeds, adding the swish of the ocean as an underpinning, a female softness to the male drumbeat. Other men brought out a *tres* and a *cuatro* and a guitar, the strings of which added lyricism to the festivities. One young man brought out the *clave*, a counter beat in the music.

Brown bodies glistened in the heady scent of pleasure sweat rather than work sweat. The bodies moved, swayed. Women's hips pushed the night air, side-to-side, buttocks firm, pendulum-like and dangerous. Men's thighs twitched, enticed by the undulations under wide skirts, insinuating themselves between the modest or openly willing columns of female flesh hidden there. The older dancers—stately men holding their heads up, and their gray-haired women—danced the controlled dance of long-ago courtships, holding their shoulders straight, their knees bent, ignoring the stiffness of a life's worth of working in the fields.

The men wore their *guayaberas* open at the neck. Women twirled in wide, colorful skirts, *amapolas* tucked seductively behind their ears. Children practiced adult moves, giggling, playing the little men, little women—all added the sounds of their bare feet on the newly constructed platform to the sounds of the musicians. The music lines wove in and out. The *coquís* stopped their own music to listen to the sounds floating up from below. And they were jealous of the sound of human celebration.

Book Three

CONCHA

11 EXPOSURE

Concha learned her world through her feet. She was a baby when she first became aware of them. Even before she explored the face of her mother, Mati, or the mustache of her father, Cheo, she knew her feet. They fascinated and entertained her in her crib world. She had been watching them a long time. She wanted to *feel* these things. She pulled and twisted and wrapped her small hands around them. She got familiar with them and started sucking on the little parts. And that felt good. She hated it when Mati insisted on covering them.

As soon as she learned to remove her socks and shoes, she found every opportunity to free her feet and run around exploring an even bigger world. She found that she could do many things with her feet that other people did with their hands. After dropping something on the floor, she much preferred using her toes to pick it up. She had a game she loved to play, picking up larger and larger twigs with her toes and moving them to different places. Soon she could pick up spoons, forks, even small marbles with her toes.

But most important, she found that her feet gave her information. They were like antennae, receptors that picked up on the slightest changes. She could read people's footsteps like other people read faces. She identified people by the size, shape, and depth of their footprints. When she followed her mother around, she could tell Mati's mood by the degree of warmth left in her tracks. As she got older, she learned to read more from each imprint and found that she could also do this with other people who were close to her.

Once, when Concha was six, one of the women in Las Agujas went missing for hours. Concha slipped off her shoes and quietly found and followed her tracks to a remote clearing near the river. The woman had fallen and hit her head, apparently as she was preparing to bathe. She lay naked and unconscious by the water's edge. Concha went home and told the others of the sleeping woman who would not wake up no matter how much she shook her. The little girl led them to the still-inert body.

* * *

Seven-year-old Concha sat on the high bed, bare feet swinging, brushing the fringed bedspread while she watched Mati part her hair down the middle with a wide-toothed comb. Her mother twisted each half until it looked like thick rope and then wound it round and round until it became a tight bun.

It was herb-gathering day. People in the barrio came by every week to consult Mati about all their troubles. None of them trusted the town doctors with their white coats and cold metal instruments. They understood the warmth of the earth and the smell of the green. And they trusted Mati. They brought her their out in the open problems: headaches, heart palpitations, warts, toothaches, stomach troubles. These could be laid out in the light of day for everyone to see. They had names, histories, causes. For them, Mati found easy cures.

But then there were the troubles that couldn't be seen or heard, the ones that lived deep in people's hearts—loneliness, envy, man worries, empty wombs, sadness. Some people who brought her these could put no name to their troubles. They suffered from *"los nervios."* Others could only whisper the names in the darkness of their rooms. Still others didn't want to name them at all, fearful that doing so would court disaster. These were the hardest troubles to cure, because they could only be found by reading the tiny clues that lived behind the rigid masks and smiling faces of the sufferers. In these cases, her mother had to work extra hard to give a face to the sickness, so she could find a cure. Concha believed that her mother could see through people's skin and find the meaning behind their words even before they were spoken.

Mati pushed the last hairpin into her buns and then topped them with her old hat. She picked up her basket and turned to Concha, who she knew had been watching. She stretched out her hand in invitation, *"¿Me acompañas?"* The child nodded eagerly and jumped off the bed, excited about spending the morning with her mother. They left the backyard, hand in hand, and headed for the woods.

Mati became engrossed in picking the plants she would need. Concha quietly pushed off her sandals and began carefully sweeping her foot from side to side in a circular motion. Eyes closed, the girl stepped out tentatively, stretching her bare foot before her and repeating the arching motion. Once she detected what she sought, she walked directly to a plant and began cutting. Observing her daughter, Mati wondered if Concha had any idea what was happening. The child was getting older. Surely she must have some questions.

"Concha, *¿qué haces?*"

The child responded without hesitation, as though she had been having a conversation with her mother all along.

"I'm looking for the right plant for Doña Migue's swollen ankles, Mami."

"¿Cómo sabes cuál es?"

"It tells me."

"¿Cómo?"

"Well, I think hard about her ankles, all puffy and purple. I close my eyes and ask the forest to show me which plant will make her better. And then I feel the ground. I follow the pulse there and it always takes me to the right plant."

"*¿Cómo estás tan segura?*"

"Because you told me. You told me I was right."

"*¿Yo…?*"

"Yes, I used to find the plants like this all the time, but I wasn't sure. So I waited to see if you picked the same one. And you know what? I was right every time. So now I know the forest is never wrong. Just like you. You are never wrong, either. What I don't understand is how you can find the plants with your shoes on, Mami."

"There are many ways of knowing, Conchita. I have mine. I see you have found yours."

The gift of healing had come for Concha as it had come for Mati herself, like breathing, and the child needed no instruction from her mother. Mati was proud that there was so much of herself in the child. But as she watched, she felt a sadness. *Curanderas* paid a great price for their gift. She wondered just how much her child would have to pay for hers.

The child had asked to carry Mati's basket at the beginning of their walks, swinging it easily, but as they collected their plants, the basket grew too heavy for her. So Mati got her daughter her own little basket, which Concha carried and then dragged as she filled it with her cuttings. Mati could have helped her carry it but didn't. The child had to learn to pace herself, to gather only what she needed, when she needed it. Carrying it home was an important part of the lesson.

Once the gathering was done that morning and they made their way home again, Concha knew her mother would be lost to her for most of the day. They carried their baskets onto the back porch and Concha added her cuttings to her mother's basket. Mati took the herbs into her *consultorio*, where she prepared the *remedios* for the people who came for advice. Concha wanted to follow her mother into that room but was never allowed to. That was her mother's domain.

"Concha, people bring their deepest secrets to this room and trust me into parts of their hearts that they show no one else. What happens here is private. When I have finished making their *remedios*, you can come in, but for now, you must find something else to do. Go out to play and I'll see you later this afternoon."

Mati didn't miss the disappointment in her daughter's eyes as she turned away. But the child must learn limits, and Mati's work called to her. It was already late. Before she closed the door to her *consultorio*, she noticed Concha running, not toward the fields, but toward her father's workshop at the far end of the *batey*, where Cheo had been hard at work since early morning. Mati smiled to think how close the little girl and her father had grown in the past few years.

* * *

"Mati, I don't want to argue about it anymore. I've decided and that's that!"

"No, that is *not* that! She's my daughter as much as yours. So *we* will discuss *our* daughter as long as it takes and *that* is that!"

Cheo turned away from his wife, exasperated at her stubbornness. This time he wouldn't give in. This time it would be his decision. But not wanting to be arbitrary, he tried to reason with his wife. He wanted her to agree with his choice.

"Mati, there are a lot of things you know about. You amaze me every day. But you know nothing of the changing world out there. I lived in town. I know the changes that are coming. Concha must go to school. Don Peyo is taking children younger than her in school every day."

"I don't trust this book learning you're so bent on. The child has her own way of knowing and you must respect it. It's true and real. It comes from inside. You should celebrate it, because it isn't given to everybody.

"Those books you love so much—what lives in there and who put it there? The only knowledge we need is all around us. The trees and the plants…there lies the truth. Where is the sun and the wind in your books? Where are the plants to heal and cure? Whose way of knowing is in there? For what purpose?"

"Mati, this is ridiculous. The child must go to school."

"But, Cheo, *I* never went to that school and neither did you and we have a good life. Please, the child is happy. She has all she needs here. She's free and safe here. Let her be.

"Out there, what is there for her but misery? Those people don't understand us. They never will. What did living in town do for you? You're back here now. You're happier here than you ever were there. Why should she be any different? She has us—"

"And when you and I are gone, Mati," Cheo interrupted, "how will we protect her? What will we have given her to help her make her own way through life? She needs to learn the new ways."

"She has the stories, the stone, the gift. Those are all she needs."

Cheo threw his hands up in disgust. "And what will that 'gift' do for her? It can't buy anything, it can't help her read and write and figure numbers. It can't—"

Mati stopped dead in her tracks, "Don't you dare dismiss what you don't understand, Cheo."

He took several breaths before continuing in a more subdued tone. "School will show her her place in the world, give her strength, guide her through the pain and the suffering and the struggle. It will set her feet on the right path, pave the way, give her direction, and strengthen her."

"Show her *her* place? These books, they are the things of the *blanquitos de la capital*. Are you telling me they were thinking of us when they made these books? I've seen them. There's never a picture of anybody who looks like you or me or her. What place can they show her? In whose world? What path will they lead her to? They will teach her to be what they want her to be. They will teach her how to be a slave again, teach her to be less than what she is. They will destroy the beauty she sees in herself and her world. They'll make her laugh at us and all we stand for. The books will make her weak and twist her thinking until she doesn't know our ways or theirs. And then she'll be really lost." Mati shook her head, unconvinced. "No, Cheo, this is a bad idea."

"Mati, listen to me. It was because you couldn't read and write that your land was taken away from you so easily. Think how different your life would've been if you had been able to read and write, not just because of the will. Think how hard it was later, trying to run this place when you couldn't sign a contract, make good business decisions. Think of all our people who were cheated out of their land, their property, because of this."

This stopped her argument for a moment. She faltered because she did remember how they had manipulated her. She remembered how her face had burned with frustration at not being able to decipher the marks on those papers. Maybe Cheo had a point. But deep within her, she was still fearful for her child.

"We've done all right, better than most. Besides, you can teach her to read and write right here at home. She doesn't have to go out there for that."

"Mati, the world is changing too quickly and getting more and more complicated. Concha needs to learn more things than we can teach her."

"But I don't think…"

"Look, you can help her so she doesn't lose sight of her gift. She'll have two ways of knowing and two ways of living, all right? Mati, that's why we're here—we can help her find a way of walking both paths."

"I don't know of any way to do that," she said quietly. She knew her position of absolute certainty was shaken. Much of what Cheo said sounded right, but her heart was screaming inside. She tried, but she couldn't find the words to explain.

"We'll find a way." He seemed so sure.

She couldn't explain where her fear came from or why, but it was there, alive and waiting, every time Cheo presented another argument.

She knew what she knew, even if she couldn't convince him of it. She studied her husband for a moment.

"You have never trusted the old ways. I see it in your eyes."

"Mati, I have decided." His voice was weary, but determination made it firm, unshakable. "You can teach her your ways as much as you want and I'll teach her mine. You can teach her whatever you want at home, but tomorrow morning, I'm taking her down to see Don Peyo and she *will* start going to school."

He walked out before Mati could say any more. She felt helpless. This was one battle she had already lost. She was no fool. Mati had watched Conchita rejoice in her every discovery, run freely through her childhood, unaware of the dangers that waited just beyond the horizon. But in her heart of hearts, she had to admit that things *were* changing and the child *would* need more.

When Mati had embraced her own gift, she had committed herself to using it in the service of others. Her people, especially the old ones, trusted the past and feared the future. Mati was their lifeline. These were things she couldn't explain to a child. There were times when Mati had to shut her out. But Conchita had the selfishness of a child grown used to having her mother at hand. Lately, she had become more and more resentful of the time her mother spent with the others. The child was lonely. Mati saw the pain in her face. She knew Conchita needed more. She needed other children, other people in her life. And yet, Mati was afraid of losing her daughter.

Now there were these new ways Cheo believed in so much. He said Concha could walk both paths, but Mati didn't believe it. What if instead of both, her Conchita ended up with neither? Mati hadn't felt fear like this in a long time. Now it came back and moved into all the old familiar places.

* * *

Concha was very excited when her father told her about school and her excitement multiplied as he walked her to the school door. But by midmorning, she knew this place was not what she had hoped it would be.

The children went to recess under the eyes and within earshot of their teacher. While the boys ran around the clearing hitting, pushing each other, and playing, the other girls stood in circles, chanting rhymes and making elaborate rhythms with their clapping hands. Concha watched girls smiling, hugging, and playing with each other's ribbons. She waited for them to ask her to join in. But the invitation never came. She sat for a long time. She looked hard from one girl to the next, willing them to like her. Occasionally, they looked her way and broke into giggles and hand-shielded whispers.

Concha was confused. She had looked forward to making new friends, but here she was, surrounded by many children and feeling lonelier than she ever had at home. There had always been Mati's herbs and Cheo's wood for company. Now Concha watched the children watching her from a distance. When she couldn't stand their whispers any longer, she turned and wandered into the safety of the wooded area bordering the school property. She didn't understand these children, but she understood trees and plants.

As she walked into the nearby woods, the trees reminded her of her walks with her mother. She had always felt at home surrounded by wild greenery. She removed her shoes and sat down to think about her feelings, about the children who had pushed her away. *Why? Why?* She looked at the tall trees, the wildflowers growing nearby. And all the while the question circled around her head, *why?*

She sat in a beam of sunlight that filled a clearing, closed her eyes, and concentrated on the question that wouldn't go away. Her feet began to feel a familiar sensation. She stood up, feeling the pulse of the ground traveling up her legs, loosening the calves, unknotting the knees. The warmth of the sun spilled over her head and around her shoulders. When it settled in her chest, she released herself to it. Her body was totally at ease, freed into the golden light of the sun. There was no breathing anymore, no body, no scent, nothing to distinguish her from the life around her, nothing to delineate her borders. She floated, then soared, became one with the light. There was no time, no place, no person—just peace, an overwhelming oneness of being. Then a sense of awareness came crashing in on her, her eyes snapped open to find herself surrounded by her classmates.

"*¿Qué te dije?* I told you she was out here. She was looking up at the sun and talking to the trees; I saw her. And then she started dancing around and singing by herself..."

The whispers, "She is so strange..."

"She's not strange. She's just a *bruja.*"

"*Sí,* I heard my mother talking about her mother...that's right. And all you have to do is look at her. She looks like a witch, wild and crazy. Just look!"

The accusation. "*Bruja, una bruja loca.*" They chanted and danced around her, making faces and jabbing at her with sticks.

Concha looked down at herself, trying to see what they saw. Her clothes were covered in leaves and twigs. Her braids had come loose, wildflowers dangling from the ends. Her throat was parched, her lips dry. She couldn't remember anything after the warm sensation on her legs.

Suddenly, she just had to get away. She broke through the circle of taunting voices and kept running. She ran, fast and far. But their words followed her all the way home. "*Bruja, bruja ¡tu madre es una bruja!* You, too, you'll be a witch just like her. Maybe you are already. Run, hide, the *bruja* came to school today.*"

* * *

Nine-year-old Concha ran into the house. Pushing her sandals off and leaving them at the door, she headed for her bedroom, schoolbooks clutched against her chest. She had been sent home early because she had a pounding headache and could no longer function in class. All she could think of was finishing the history exercises she had to do for school so she could go to bed.

But on her way to the back of the house, she caught a glimpse of her mother in her *consultorio*. She stopped, standing barefoot, at the door of Mati's room. She hadn't been in the house at that time of the day since she had started school. Now, her headache forgotten, she stood at the doorway and watched, unable to pull herself away.

This was the room where her mother saw the people who came seeking help. The large table, draped to the floor in a pure white cloth, supported a crystal bowl full of clear water. At either end of the table stood a huge vase of fresh-cut flowers. The scent of freesia filled the room.

She watched as Mati, kneeling on the floor, waved her arms over a pot of river water and chanted words in a language Concha didn't understand. She hadn't seen her mother do this for a long time. But today she stood in the doorway, drawn by the flickering light and the heady scent.

Mati knelt, surrounded by her Catholic *santos*—Santa Barbara, San Lázaro, Santa Clara. But it was the wooden representations of the parallel African gods who inhabited her mother's mind and spirit that drew Mati into her trances. Concha looked at the altar and remembered the names she had learned as a small child, the names with the beautiful sounds—Chango, Yemaya, Elegua, Ogun, Oshun.

She didn't realize she was mouthing these names and that as she did so she was taken in by the chanted words and glow of the many candles that gave the room an illusion of a pulsing movement, almost as though the walls themselves were breathing in and out and in again. Mati was chanting, *Mbe, mbe, ma yeye, mbe, mbe, l'oro…mbe, mbe, ma yeye, mbe, mbe l'oro….* They were soft, mysterious sounds, a lullaby that flowed over Concha, making her drowsy.

It started with her feet again, a vague tingling sensation that intensified to soft vibrations, which lengthened into longer, smoother throbs. Concha could scarcely form the thoughts. *No, not again. This can't happen*. But it was too late. With the throbbing came increasing heat. She felt it coming to her in waves, beginning at the soles of her feet and working its way up her legs. She felt her body soften, relax. She felt something loosen inside, felt herself lose solidity. She felt a release of weight, a drifting, a swaying to a timeless rhythm in her head, yielding to the soft light. She was becoming feather light, her body becoming a whisper.

The sound of her schoolbooks scattering snatched her back. Still dazed, she slid down, welcoming the feeling of the floor tiles, cool and hard. In her confusion, she found her mother's hands, helping, bringing her back.

"*¿Estás bien?*" Concha tried to focus on Mati's worried face. "*Siéntate, nena*. Rest for a moment before you try to get up. Take one breath. Slowly. Now another. Slow. Good. Hold my hand. I'm here. Feel me. I'm just next to you. Look…look at me. Focus. There…that's better."

Concha sat on the cold floor and held on tightly to Mati's warm hands. She needed the orientation. Her mother's face slowly came into sharp focus.

"Mamá, what happened?" Concha asked haltingly, as she massaged her temples.

"You'll be fine. It's just…the old ways that came to visit when you were least expecting them. Has this never happened before?"

Still confused, Concha tried to focus on what Mati was saying. Slowly, she felt understanding, memory, edging itself in.

"Mamá, I tried to stop it but I couldn't. It just kept happening and…"

"I know, *m'hija*. I know."

"I just came in and you were talking and…Mamá, what were you saying?"

"Conchita, I don't know. I never remember what I say. It just happens. I've been told that I speak the language of the ancestors, the tongue of the old ways. I don't choose the words. They come to me from long ago. I don't think we ever forget the past. We may misplace the memories, but *they* find *us*."

Concha sat perfectly still. She remembered the warmth, the throbbing, the release, and then the awakening. She realized that she had lost time; she had lost control of her body. Could this speaking in tongues happen to her, too? She imagined unknown words lying deep within her, imagined one day opening her mouth and having them all come tumbling out in front of the children at school. She remembered the first day of school, remembered the laughing, scornful faces and the barbed words that followed her all the way home. Had it happened already? Was that why they all stayed away from her at school? All this time and they were still afraid of her?

Sitting there with her mother, Concha recognized the fear she had been holding at bay since that day. It had grown with her, taken up residence in her heart and become a part of her.

Mati tried to soothe away the fear but Concha knew her mother had no *remedio* for this problem. Concha saw clearly, perhaps more clearly than Mati, that her childhood had ended the day she started school. And she knew, too, that she would have to guard against this "gift" that came at her when she least expected or wanted it.

12 Losses

Concha woke up screaming. She could barely catch her breath. Her heart felt like it would burst right through her nightshirt. It took a long time for her brain to start working again. She was sitting up on her bed and knew that she had been dreaming but she could not control the screams that kept shooting out of her. Then she felt strong arms holding her, reassuring her that all would be well.

"Don't worry. I'm here." Mati sat on her daughter's bed and tried to soothe her. "You're all right. It was just a dream…I—"

As soon as Concha realized that Cheo stood nearby, she pulled away from Mati and threw herself into her father's arms. He held her close. She smelled the wood sap that clung to his skin. Immediately, she relaxed in his embrace.

Father and daughter didn't notice when Mati quietly left the room.

* * *

Mati knew that Cheo loved her but he didn't love her gift. He had seen the goodness of it when she had healed him, but as time passed, he had come to resent it. Sometimes, Mati would be in her *consultorio* all day, tending to an endless stream of neighbors needing her help. Some traveled all night to knock on Mati's door at dawn and wait their turn.

For Mati, those sessions were private and sacrosanct. Usually the petitioners were gone by the time Cheo came home in the evenings, but sometimes he had to wait for his dinner, or entertain Concha until Mati finished her business. So he began to resent that which had always been a part of his wife.

One morning before the sun came over the rise, Cheo was washing up in the backyard before heading for his workshop. He never had breakfast, but that day he felt like a little coffee to clear his head after a bad night's sleep. He had an important delivery in the south and needed to be wide awake to put the finishing touches on the piece. As he came through the back door, he heard the shuffling of feet and the whispered voices. He had to thread his way between the double rows of chairs lining the hallway. A dozen petitioners looked up, smiling at him and waiting their turn patiently. Mati would not be done with these people until well after noon, and there were sure to be more arriving during the morning hours.

He had always known they were there. Perhaps that was why he had gotten into the habit of skipping the morning meal. On most days, Mati packed a light lunch for him and he chose to stay in his workshop until dinnertime. But on this day he wanted Mati to be there for him, and these people were a wall that kept her from him. Resentment simmered within him. He made his way through the people and headed for the room where Mati was already at work. Barely containing his anger, he opened the door a little too forcefully.

Mati sat in front of the altar, candles ablaze behind her, a bowl of steaming, green water, with herbs still floating in the dark liquid, before her. She had just dipped her hands in the bowl and was about to anoint the head of a very old woman who faced her, eyes closed, lips murmuring a silent prayer. The interruption broke the moment. Both women jumped as the door slammed and Cheo stood before them. He tried to get hold of his temper when he saw a familiar face.

"*Permiso,* Doña Serafina." He had to control his anger before this elderly woman whose age alone forbade him his offensive behavior. He stood there shuffling from one foot to the other, obviously waiting. Out of *respeto,* he knew he couldn't ask the woman to leave, but she was no fool.

"No, no se preocupe, Don Cheo." She addressed him using formal language. "We were just about finished. *No se moleste.* It wasn't important." She picked up a battered purse.

"Buenos días, Doña," he said as she was about to leave.

Mati was horrified at his rudeness. "I'm sorry, Serafina. We'll talk soon."

Mati and Serafina kissed on both cheeks and the old woman let herself out, shutting the door quietly behind her and leaving with not so much as another glance at Cheo.

"What has gotten into you? Since when do you barge in…?" Mati whispered, very much aware of the people sitting just outside her door.

"Mati, *carajo,* I can't even walk around my own house. I come out half dressed and there they are. Doesn't a man have any rights? All I ask for is a little consideration."

"Cheo, lower your voice. *Cálmate. Yo…*" Mati's controlled tone only angered him more. She glanced at the door, knowing his voice carried.

"Cálmate, mierda! I'm sick and tired of this, Mati. You are my wife, but I have to share you with damn near the whole world at all hours of the day or night. I can't even have my breakfast in peace when I want it. And these men here. Why aren't they out working like I'm about to? What's more important than a man doing his work?"

Mati got up slowly and began wiping her hands on her apron. She kept glancing at the door, knowing that the people on the other side of it could hear every word.

"Cheo, we can discuss this later…"

"Later? Later…why do I always have to wait? Why are my needs less important than everyone else's? It's always 'later' for me. Well, not this time. This is my house." His anger had taken over and he didn't care who overheard him. The veins on the sides of his throat popped. He pounded on the altar, unsettling the bowl of water.

Mati could feel herself losing control as well. She tried to stop his fist, but before she could do so, one of the larger statues toppled over and smashed at her feet. He continued yelling, not even glancing at the damage.

"Cheo. *Cálmate. Siéntate. Óyeme bien.*" The words were clipped. She had stopped moving and her eyes bore into him. She felt her self-control slipping. He wasn't listening. Still, she tried to reason with him.

"You know, you've always known that I've got responsibilities others don't. And that will never change. People need my help."

"What about me, Mati? When do you take care of me, my needs? This has got to stop."

"Cheo, this is not the time and place for this conversation."

"Mati, who's the man of the house here? Either this stops, right now, or—"

Something in Mati broke. Her voice took on a sharp edge.

"*Or what?* Are you giving *me* orders? Since when? Did you forget that this is *my* house?" The words were out before she could stop them. She looked at her husband's face and knew she could never take them back. She knew Cheo well enough to know that the wound that she had opened in his chest would never be healed.

Cheo stumbled back and stretched his arm out to steady himself against the wall.

"*Your...*" He barely got the words out. "You are so right, Mati. Stupid me. I really thought that we were working together, that this was *our* home. For a moment I forgot this isn't and never will be *our* house. This is the house of *la nueva patrona.*"

It was worse than a physical blow. She'd never been referred to in those terms, never thought of herself in that role.

Everything stopped in the room. Something huge had shifted and couldn't be righted again and they each knew it.

In vain, she tried to find healing words, tried to think of what she could possibly say. But before she could say another word, Cheo was gone.

He needed to be out of that room, out of that house. He needed air, the sky, the sunlight, things she couldn't control, things that were too big even for her. He ran as far as he could, trying to get away from *her* house. He ran until he was off *her* property and then dropped down on the grass under a *ceiba* tree. He sat there for hours.

Mati was right, of course. It was *her* house, *her* world. There was no arguing with that. Who was he in this world of Mati's? What was he doing here? Where did he fit in? What could he give her that she couldn't get for herself? The same thoughts looped around and around in his head. These questions plagued him. And those questions brought back others that remained unanswered. How *did* Mati get her house? Why had those men returned her the lands? Who were they? How many? And how long did it go on?

He'd heard the rumors about the sick white men who had sent for her in the night. What kind of powerful magic had Mati worked on them? She got their land. *¡Bruja!* The word came back to him as he thought of her. He hadn't used that word in years because he knew Mati hadn't deserved it. But now he wasn't so sure. He felt that she had taken over everything and everybody. And if he didn't get away from here, she would take *him* over, too.

He thought about all the years when he had been owned by another man. He had worked and worked until he had found a way. He had sacrificed and saved. He would buy his own freedom and then hers. And then he'd be his own man, with a wife and a family of his own that couldn't be taken or sold away. Those were the things he wanted to give her.

And then the word came that he was free, that they were all free, because of her. Instead of him buying her freedom, it turned out to be Mati's gift to him. She had robbed him of his greatest dream. She had a house of her own and a good living. Then she got the neighboring *hacendados* to give her all that land. Somehow she had gotten everything she wanted. What could he possibly have to offer her now?

He had tried. He really had tried. But he felt that he had gone backward, back to being just Cheito—peripheral, unessential—once again. He wanted Mati to be Don Cheo's wife. Instead, Cheo was Mati's husband. Her words had proven it.

* * *

Concha had been standing outside the door when her father ran out of the room. It wasn't the first time she had overheard them fight. Cheo's loud voice and Mati's tightly controlled one didn't clash often but when they did, Concha knew there was danger beneath the surface. The words jolted her where she stood, leaving her feeling unstable. Then it started. Deep inside, she could feel her innards begin to pull together, like strong fibers twisting into a tight, quivering knot.

She watched Cheo as he streaked by her. She wanted to run from the house and follow him into the fields, where there was sunshine and light and trees. She wanted everything easy and uncomplicated. She watched him disappear into the trees. He'd come back. He had to come back. She would wait for him until he came over the rise again and welcome him home even if her mother didn't. She'd make him laugh to make up for the unhappiness Mati was causing. Her father would come back to her, for her. Yes, she would wait and everything would be all right again. The knotting began to ease.

Mati hadn't realized that Concha had overheard their conversation. She worked in the *consultorio* all morning and into the afternoon. Long after the last patient was gone, she sat in her room. All day she had pushed away the terrible scene with Cheo. Now it came back to her full force. The accusations that had flown out of their mouths carried the weight of truth. She had worked hard to build this life, her life, and she wouldn't give it up. He felt that he needed to be her center. As much as she loved him, she couldn't give him that.

Mati finally got up to cook dinner. But when she called out for Concha, there was no answer. She called out across the *batey*; no answer. She went out to Cheo's workshop but there was nobody there. Then she noticed that Cheo's tools were gone and she sat for a while, taking in the reality of his not being there. But then a terrifying thought propelled her out and around the property. Heart pounding, she searched for Conchita everywhere. She knew she'd lost Cheo, but she couldn't lose her daughter as well. Mati searched for Concha for hours and finally found her at dusk, curled up and asleep under a tree. She shook the child gently.

Concha sat up with a start and looked around. "¿Papá?"

"It's all right, *nena*, it's me. Come, let's go home." Mati tried to put her arm around her daughter, but the child pulled away.

"Don't touch me. I want Papá. You sent him away."

"Conchita, everything will be all right. He's just gone for a little while, but he'll be back soon." Again Mati reached out for her daughter.

"No. I heard you. You sent him away! I hate you. I hate you. Why couldn't he wait for me?"

At that, the child started sobbing. Mati looked at her daughter, and, more than anything, wanted to gather her up in her arms and take away the pain. But she knew the girl would reject her every effort. Finally, Concha went limp, still sobbing at her loss. Mati waited until Concha cried out her misery. Then she pulled her up and they started for home. As Mati put her child to bed, Concha pulled as far away from her mother as she could and promptly went to sleep.

Mati sat with her sleeping daughter most of the night. *She's almost grown, not my baby anymore.* She kissed her and lingered, wondering where her little girl had gone. She wondered what she could have done to avoid the distance that had grown between them.

Mati finally put out Concha's light and went to her own room. Her daughter weighed heavily on her mind, the child's pain, the anger. And then there was Cheo. His missing tools told the whole story. Mati took off all her clothes and stood in front of her mirror. She was amazed that her reflection showed no trace of the hole that now lived in the middle of her chest.

13 NEW LIVES

Toño had had a very uncomfortable morning. As he walked down the road he kept rubbing the back of his neck to offset the irritation of his overstarched *guayabera*. His mother had gotten up at first light to iron it and now it shone under the sun, its pleats wilted after hours in town. He limped a little as his country feet tried to make peace with his city shoes.

He recalled how the young men had passed by his house that morning, their machetes sitting on their shoulders and their voices ringing out in the stillness. He couldn't distinguish between them because the sun was barely up over the trees, but he didn't have to.

"*¡Adios,* Toño*!* Good luck in town."

"*Sí, hombre.* Don't let those city hips keep you too long."

"No, Pepe, his mind is only on the cane."

"It's not his mind I'm thinking about!"

"*¡Cállate, muchacho!* Watch your mouth. Don't you think Doña Pepa can hear you?"

"*¡*Toño*, mira,* Toño*!* Get some of that perfume for men they keep talking about. I could use a little help declaring my love to Olgita."

"If you get something a little more interesting than perfume, get some for me, too."

"Shh, she heard you for sure now. You're such a horse's ass!"

"Ah, ass, that's closer to what I had in mind."

"What did you say? I didn't hear you!"

"Never mind…lucky for you he didn't hear…Hey, Toño, just don't get too comfortable in town and forget about your brothers in the field."

"*Adiós,* Toño. "

"*Te veo,* Toño. "

Their teasing and mock fighting were familiar. As they made their way to the fields, Toño had stood at the window, his hands itching for his own blade. He'd rather be on the road with his friends than preparing to go into town. He only did so when absolutely necessary.

Toño hadn't been ready to take on his father's role, but he had no choice. Now he was the man of the house. He had to go into town and sign contracts for the sale of their crops. He was a simple man with simple needs, and he wanted to get this business over with as soon as possible. There was no competitiveness in him. He would go after the modest local business and he would come back to the barrio where he belonged.

Now, on his way home, Toño couldn't wait to get into his work clothes. The fancy shoes were chaffing him and his shirt was sticking to his skin under the afternoon sun. He was anxious to get back to the farmwork he loved.

As he limped along the road he looked down the ravine to the river below. He could hear the young women as they did their wash. Toño knew Concha would be there and hoped to get a glimpse of her. As children they had played in the same bend in the river where the women were now scrubbing the clothes.

He'd been there her first day of school, when the other children had ridiculed her until she ran away in tears. And he was there the next day when she came back, mouth set, ready to face them again. He quietly left his seat and took the empty seat next to her. It was his book that they bent over when she didn't have her own. They ran and laughed and walked to school together. But they weren't children anymore, and something else was in the air between them now. As he approached the women at the creek, he wondered how he could get to talk to her alone.

The women, busy at their task and their banter, didn't notice him watching. Concha sat with her pile of clothes, quiet among all the chatter. Too shy to approach Concha when she was surrounded by so many women, Toño walked away, the image of her still playing in his mind. He sat down under a *ceiba* tree, still thinking of her as he had seen her just a few days before.

He'd been sitting with some friends at the cantina when Concha walked by. It was late afternoon and she was coming home from town. He had made a study of her body as she walked away. He watched the thin fabric of her blouse stick to her back and taper down to an impossibly small waist.

The *nalgas* below rubbed against each other as she walked, each pushing up and over toward the top of the other, stopping just before the beginning of a reciprocal move from its neighbor, so that the motion became an unending pulsing of the muscles, a rolling game between the two. This walk was the earthbound, fluid walk of the women who worked with their bodies and carried their futures in their pelvises. This walk carried life—pain, lust, pride, invitation. Its rhythm was the rhythm of the tides, of wind sweeping through fields of cane, of the coming and going of the seasons, of breathing, of heartbeats. If he could set her movements to music, the sound would be the steady beating of a drum.

Her legs were heavy and, unlike the style of city women, unshaven. She wore no stockings, letting the cloth of her skirt wrap around the legs free and smooth against the bareness beneath. Those legs guaranteed that once their owner decided upon a spot in which to stand, no one could dislodge her from her position. When not walking, they stood far apart and ready for the unexpected.

Concha's feet were wide and had a high instep. When shoes were forced upon them, they fought against the leather, refused the laces, and strained at the seams. Those feet hungered for the soil, the water, the sun. He could never understand why Concha kept trying to force those healthy feet into the tied shoes that she habitually wore. But on wash day, she wore the more practical thick-strapped sandals she had today. These were the sandals that came within his field of vision as he rubbed his own tired feet.

"You're not going into the fields now, are you? The day is half gone." Her voice was husky, as substantial as the rest of her.

"I thought I would, but those shoes have ruined my feet and I can barely get my boots on."

"Maybe you shouldn't go. Maybe you should take the afternoon off and relax a little."

"And what would you suggest I do all afternoon?" He looked up at her, a mischievous smile dancing on his lips.

"I don't know. I'm finished at the river and I thought I'd just sit under a *flamboyán* and rest for a while before going back. Maybe you could use a rest yourself after that long walk to town and back?"

"Maybe. You know, my favorite spot is not far from here. You want to see it?" He stood up, shoes in hand.

"*Sí, cómo no.*"

* * *

By the time she was a teenager, what Concha wanted most of all was to be like everyone else. She covered her feet at all times and denied her special ability even to herself. When the other girls fussed and argued about the best shade of lipstick or the best perfume, Concha looked longingly at the tiny bottles of nail polish. She saved her pennies over seven months so she could buy just one bottle. On Saturday evening, after her bath, she brought out a tiny bottle of scented oil. She took her time rubbing the oil onto her moist heels and brushing the polish onto her toenails. It was a weekly ceremony that gave her a private delight. No one ever saw her feet anymore, but she pampered them in secret.

When Concha married Toño, that privacy was more difficult to achieve. There was no way to keep her feet fixation from her new husband. She was afraid he'd laugh at her, but it turned out that Toño loved her feet. He saw them as a sensual part of her and couldn't wait to explore the possibilities. They devised a ritual that they celebrated for years.

She gathered fragrant leaves in the morning, boiled them down to a strong brew, and added her treasured oils. Then she'd set the mixture out in the sun to keep it warm. When Toño came home from the fields and saw the pot, he knew how their evening would go. First they bathed together. Then he sponged her legs and feet in the fragrant water, dowsing them over and over again, and then dried them carefully, taking his time, enjoying the feel of her skin. He massaged the prepared oils into her feet, stopping at each toe, rubbing around each nail.

Then it was Concha's turn. Sitting on the headboard above him, Concha began with his chest, using her freshly oiled feet and dribbling additional drops of oil over him as the massage progressed. Her toes burrowed into his chest hair, stopped to stroke over and around each nipple, and then inched down the sides of his body, tracking every curve and hollow.

When she got to his waist, she shifted to the foot of the bed, facing him. She stroked and rubbed his body using the sides and bottom of her feet. When he was ready, she began the milking motion, using her toes around his penis, cradling the shaft between her feet. Starting at the root, she worked her way to the very tip and then back again.

Her feet knew every inch of his body better than her eyes, better than her hands. She had heard that blind people "read" people in this way, by touch. She considered herself lucky that this man understood her need to do this. Their ritual brought them closer. For their anniversary, Toño fastened a gold ankle bracelet around her ankle. She stared at it in disbelief. She'd never seen or heard of such a thing. She kept her anniversary present a secret between the two of them and it became a part of their ritual.

* * *

They enjoyed their intimate games for several years before Concha got pregnant. She feared the lack of privacy that would come with a baby. But once Elena was born, Concha could not wait for the midwife to go away and leave her to get acquainted with her daughter. After weeks of family visits and constant attention, she was left to tend to her baby in peace. Every day she waited until the breakfast dishes were done and most women were busy with their clothes or vegetable gathering. When she was less likely to be interrupted, Concha bathed Elena and took her out to the back porch. There she spread out a thick blanket and set her baby on the floor in front of an old chair. She placed a foot on either side of the baby's torso and rocked Elena from one foot to the other. She continued the motion until she felt the child relax into sleep. This was her favorite time because she felt that there was a special connection between her and her new daughter. This child was the second person in her life to whom she owed no explanation and who took her exactly as she was.

* * *

As the years passed, Mati's *consultorio* door was closed less and less. Cheo had been right. The world had changed, and Mati's way of knowing was in much less demand. While the older people still put their faith in her healing, their children preferred going into town for medical treatment. Mati's house got much quieter.

Once Cheo left, the house changed forever. A heavy silence had fallen over Caridad. The old women at Las Agujas, growing older, eyesight failing and fingers misshapen after years of work, tried to pass on their skills to their daughters, who preferred the classroom to the workroom. Many younger women left home now to work in *fábricas*, foreign-owned businesses that produced shoddy, inexpensive reproductions of the painstaking work Las Agujas had created for so many years.

Only the wealthiest old families kept coming to them for tailor-made linens and personal garments. For the rest, the stores had an endless supply of cheap, flashy goods that caught the eye of many a young woman and some not so young.

Pushed by their children, many of her neighbors in the *batey* moved away. The plantation land, which had been parceled among them years before, was now sold piecemeal. Since she couldn't maintain the land on her own, Mati herself was forced to sell part of her property to strangers who knew nothing of hard work or community. She watched as foreign businessmen who cared only for money overran the land where she had lived her whole life, the land where Fela had lived and died. She saw the fields where many of her people had lost their lives being tilled by huge machines that chewed up memories and long-forgotten ancestors. Mati looked out across the horizon and thought about her struggles with the Prósperos of the world. Yes, there had been many sacrifices. She turned her eyes away and retreated more and more into the safety of her memories and her needlework.

She lived more in the past than in the present now. Loss and regret awaited her every night when she went to her room. It had been years since Cheo had walked out on her and still Mati went to bed every night and stared at his tapestry, wondering where his path had taken him and whether he would ever come back. Concha lived in the house with her family, but she had been lost to Mati for many years. Elena was the only one who could bring Mati out of herself and into the world again.

14 MOTHERS AND DAUGHTERS

One morning, Concha folded and stacked yards and yards of carefully cut and ironed fabric on the dining room table. The heavy broadcloth lengths felt smooth and still warm as she prepared to take them to Las Agujas. There she would sew the borders and no-nonsense seams for the bed and table linens that the very rich still preferred tailor-made.

The older women, her mother's generation, had passed down their skills to their daughters, and a few of these younger women did most of the decorative work: the sequined, beaded evening dresses, the lace-trimmed lingerie, the embroidered afternoon dresses, the pleated dress shirts. Concha knew that this work was considered their specialty and brought in most of their income. But she preferred the honest seaming, the straight hems, the sturdy fabrics. She detested the slippery silks, the insubstantial tulles, and the unnecessarily ornate brocades. She worked the utilitarian pieces that the others shunned, thinking the work boring or uninspiring or artless.

As she turned off their new electric light and prepared to leave the room, she overheard voices on the porch and stopped to listen.

"I'll never get it right. Look at it. It looks all chewed up," Elena whined.

Mati continued working, ignoring the frustration in the girl's voice.

"You know, *nena*, I have always loved working with my hands, especially starting a new project."

"Abuela, look at yours. I'll never be able to make even stitches like yours. Look at this! Ugh! My stitches look all choked and pull the fabric."

"Nothing that's worthwhile doing comes easily, *nena*. You have no patience. You have to *feel* the spirit of the work. Try this. Look at the fabric really close, so close that you can see the threads in the material. Good. Now think of how you want the design to look and feel. Think of the colors and the texture. Now pick up your needle. Remember to give the thread the space it needs so it can flow onto the cloth. Trust it. Let it go. If you hold it too tight, it'll fight you. Your fingers already know what to do. Now, let them do it."

Elena picked up her hoop once again and took a few deep breaths before continuing. Deep lines of concentration crossed her forehead. Mati knew the girl was trying too hard.

"I know! What you need is another story."

Concha's shoulders stiffened as she listened in the other room.

"Abuela, I'm not a little girl anymore."

"No, don't put the hoop down. Stories have no age. They're for everyone."

"All right, but I want a good one. Where do you get them all? You have a story for everything."

"Well, this story is about Imo, and he gave me many of the stories I am passing on to you."

"That's a funny name, Imo. Who was he?"

"He was my father. I had two, you know. I had a body father. He helped my mother, your great-grandmother Fela, make my body. But before him, Fela had another husband who was my father, Imo. He helped her make my soul. And she brought this soul to Puerto Rico when she was brought here from her Home Place."

"What is the soul, Abuela? Where is it?"

"Well, you keep it in here," Mati pointed to her chest. "It is the thing you are born with that makes one person different from another. Some people have a troubled soul and they are always unhappy and make other people unhappy. Some have a strong, healthy soul. And those people bring happiness to other people's lives and at the same time have much happiness in their own. Even when they have problems, like we all do, they look for the good in themselves and others, to try to solve those problems. And the best part is that while the body wears down and the person dies, the soul lives on and on.

"You can feel a person's soul in your heart but you can't see or touch it with your body. That's why it was so important that my mother made a body, this one I have here, to go with the soul she had carried for so long."

Elena listened carefully and tried to make sense of the words. She thought hard before asking the next question. "But, Abuela, if the body is a container for the soul, and you say the soul lives on after the body is gone, where does it live? How does it live on?"

Mati looked at her granddaughter and was proud of the girl's natural inquisitiveness, her need to make sense of the world around her.

"Well, if you live your life well and you give love to those around you, a part of your soul stays behind with every person you have loved or every person who has loved you. In that way you never die. You are just shared by more and more people."

"But what happens when the people you know die and the only people left are people who never met you?"

"That's why the stories are so important, m'hija. That's one way we pass down the souls of the old ones. We keep them alive in the stories, which never die as long as someone tells them.

"The stories I give you are the souls of those people you never got to meet, like Imo and Fela and Tía and all the rest. And as long as you pass them on, too, those people will never really die."

Elena looked at her grandmother and considered this before continuing her work.

"I'm ready for that story now." And she picked up her work.

"Well…my mother Fela died before I could meet her. One night, Mother Oshun came to visit me."

"Who is that?"

"The ancestors believed that there were many gods and goddesses who watch over us. Mother Oshun is the one who watches over me. Because Mamá Fela died before I was born, the story chain was broken. So Mother Oshun came to me and told me stories that happened before I was born."

"Really?"

In the dining room Concha put down her load. How many times had she asked her mother not to fill the child's head with nonsense? But she couldn't pull herself away. She sat and listened, tapping her foot and trying to stay calm.

"Mother Oshun visited me often and told me many things over the years. She taught me much about the old ways, showed me the place she called Home Place, the place some people called Africa. She told me about a small village with chiefs and warriors and families. She spoke of those who protected wisdom, and mothers who were robbed of their babies and men who betrayed other men. She told me about the gourds and the calabashes that were used to make sacred instruments like *shekeres* and conga drums. She told me about the healers who collected plants and made potions and brews that cured people before there were hospitals and doctors."

"Is that how you learned, Abuela? Is that how you got to know so much about *remedios*?"

"Yes, but *remedios* are only some of the things I learned from her. The most important thing I learned from Mother Oshun is that stories make us stronger. She told me a whole world in stories and asked me to pass it on to the children so that they wouldn't forget."

"Like me?"

"Yes, exactly like you. You know, the most important person in their village was the *griot*. You know why? Because it was the *griot*, an old woman, who collected and held the stories of the people. The people believed that if they lost their stories they would lose their path, their way of knowing themselves. They believed that if you forgot where you came from, you wouldn't understand where you were or where you were going. The path would be blocked and you'd be lost forever. But stories may come to me in many ways—daydreams and night dreams, long-forgotten memories and family-told stories. So I pass them on to you."

"But, Abuela, Mamá never tells me stories."

"Well…your Mamá…she has so much on her mind. She must have forgotten…"

"Oh, but, Abuela, she'll lose her way."

"I hope not, *m'hija*. I hope not."

Concha had heard enough. She snatched up the broadcloth, but the force of her sudden movement knocked several other stacks of fabric off the table and sent them flying across the floor. Angrily she stepped over the mess, not bothering to pick it up. She stormed down the main corridor that led to the back of the house and then out to Las Agujas. As she passed the front door, she glanced out to see Mati and Elena, heads together, examining a piece of work held between them.

* * *

At night, the house that holds an active child settles into an unaccustomed silence. Things that are held at bay during the day crystallize, their edges becoming sharper. Concha joined Mati on the *balcón* after Elena had gone to bed. She sat opposite her mother in a straight-back, unpadded rocker.

"Mamá, I need to talk to you for a minute."

"*Claro, hija*. What's on your mind?"

"*Mira*, Mamá." Concha had trouble starting. "It's just that…I wish you wouldn't fill Elena's head with those stories. She really believes those old wives' tales and she's been having nightmares."

Mati looked up from her work, puzzled. "Nightmares? *La nena* has nightmares? Since when?" She studied Concha. The light played shadows in her face but Mati searched for truth there. "Elena's life is too full to have space for nightmares." She looked knowingly at her daughter. "Nightmares are for people who refuse to listen to their hearts. People who have lost their way, who are hollow. Fear slips into those hollow places. It is the very emptiness that draws the fear."

Concha ignored her mother's insinuations. She didn't want a scene, but…taking a deep breath, she continued. "She doesn't need to hear all that stuff about magic stones and fairy godmothers. You can keep all that nonsense to yourself."

"*¿Cómo fue eso?*" Mati's eyes flashed. "I think you're forgetting who you're talking to." Mati's voice was taut, ready to spring.

Concha bit her lip and looked away from her mother, continuing what she had to say. "Mamá, I've asked you before to stop telling her these stories."

"I only speak the truth. The truth you never wanted to know about. Elena loves the stories. Maybe you'd do better if you listened to some of them yourself. Your daughter soaks up what you have pushed away."

"What *I* pushed away?" Concha's control was slipping away from her, her voice getting louder. "Look who's talking about pushing people away." She stood up and pointed her accusing finger at Mati, who was still seated. "When did you ever make time for me? You were always so busy with your plants and your patients with their stupid little problems. No, if anyone here has done the pushing away it's been you, not me!"

Mati pulled her weight out of her chair and stretched to her full stature, standing face-to-face with her daughter.

"So it finally comes out. All these years of hard faces and stiff necks and silent accusations. You finally found the words for it. After all this time of you locking yourself away from me…"

"*Me?* I only locked myself away after you locked me out." Concha's voice was taking flight, rising above the safety zone. "You know what, Mamá, let's leave it alone. There's no point to this. Let's forget the whole thing." Concha started turning away when her mother's hand shot out. Mati's fingers closed around Concha's arm like a vise, forcing the younger woman to stay.

Mati fired back. "How many times did I try to break through your silences? How many ways did I try to get beyond your walls? Year after year…"

Concha tried to pull away from her mother's grip, but Mati was amazingly strong. The more Concha pulled, the deeper Mati's nails dug into her exposed arm.

"Oh no you don't. This is one time we're really going to talk this out. How many times did I try to come close to you only to be pushed away? You never wanted to talk out your pain. You fed on it until there was no room for anything or anyone else."

Concha tried to contain the hot anger that was boiling up in her as her mother spoke. But now the heat of that anger filled her throat. The veins in her neck and face bulged with it. And then it had no place to go but out.

"*No!* I won't listen! I know what you want. You want to confuse me. But I remember! You were never around when I needed a mother. And now that you have the time and your services aren't wanted or needed anymore, now you want to steal my daughter."

Concha lost all control, "You threw your own daughter away and now you want mine. Well, you can't have her. You can't have either of us. You drove away the father I loved and now you fill my daughter's head with *ridiculous* stories about spirits and magic and *brujerías*—"

Concha didn't see it coming until she felt the sting. The slap reverberated in her head. It was done before either woman knew what had happened. The searing fire of Concha's anger was now concentrated in her cheek. Mati's whole body shook with rage. Too late, she pulled her hand back. By then, each woman's chest heaved with anger and indignation.

"You *will not* speak of your father and me. What happened between us was between us. If you'd allowed me to come closer to you maybe we could've shared that, like other families do. But as it is, you haven't earned that right. As for your accusations of me, I'm not perfect—I've made mistakes and have much to answer for. But not to you, not like this, and certainly not in this tone.

"And the women in our family have already paid too high a price for that last word you tossed around so easily. If you *ever* set your mouth to use that word with me again, it will be the last word you'll say through those teeth. I'm still your mother—whether you choose to remember that or not. You may have no respect for my ways, but you *will* respect me. You will *not* offend me in my own house ever again. As much as I loved your father—yes, loved and still love him, whether you want to believe it or not—as much as I loved your father, I wouldn't allow him to call me that name and I certainly won't allow you to do it, either."

Mati opened the *balcón* door with such force that it slammed against the outer wall, bounced, and slammed back again. Neither she nor Concha noticed the crack, which wouldn't be repaired for many years.

* * *

For weeks there was only silence between mother and daughter. In not wanting to aggravate the situation, each grew more monstrous in her silence. While Mati worked in Las Agujas, Concha stayed in the house. When Concha cooked, Mati walked the fields. Even Elena moved carefully whenever Mati and Concha happened to be in the same room. Toño watched both women and knew there was nothing he could do. Still, he realized, things couldn't go on like that for much longer. There was almost an electric charge in the air.

15 THE STORM

Concha wrung the water out of the last piece of laundry. She hadn't done the wash in the river for years, but she had needed to get away and think. There had been no words between her and Mati all week. Things couldn't go on like this. Something had to change.

She bent over and swung the basket up to her head. The old cloth that she wound into a thick ring cushioned the huge basket that held most of the week's laundry. Her arm and neck muscles strained with effort as she centered the load on her head. She balanced it carefully as she walked across the fields, up the river road to the house. She passed the *balcón* and moved on to the *batey*, where the mound of fresh lemon leaves awaited her. She slid the basin down to her shoulder and rested it on the back porch. Rubbing her neck, she examined the sky once again. It had gotten gray since she had set out for the river this morning, and the air hung oppressively. The sun was still shining but the gray was advancing. Maybe the clothes would dry before the rain. She hated the musty smell of clothes drying indoors. So she spread out the freshly picked leaves. She shook loose each piece before swinging it out and fanning it open and letting it settle on the carpet of fragrant leaves. She looked at the sky again and judged that in two hours she could collect and fold.

She made her way up the back steps and into the house and cursed at herself as she found a pair of dirty work pants, obviously dropped earlier as she prepared to do the wash. She bent to pick them up and dropped them in the basket as she went upstairs to organize the drawers. The clothes would be dry in a few hours and she meant to put them away in neatly ordered rows. She worked until the light started to fade.

Concha peered out a window, checking the position of the sun, and was surprised to see that the gray had advanced considerably and was almost upon them. Just then, she was distracted by the sound of the children's voices. They came, not in twos and threes as they usually straggled home, but in one large group, like a brown blanket covering the entire width of the road. They carried no books or bags, and there was urgency in their walk. Over their heads she saw the advancing roils of gray. She could easily make out Elena's anxious face as she hurried home in the midst of the younger children.

Mati, too, had been alerted by the return of the children. Both women were already in the back yard as Elena came up the path.

"*¿Qué pasa?* What are you doing home so early?" Concha asked.

Mati was preoccupied, eyes glued to the sky.

"Mamá, Abuela!" Elena could barely catch her breath, "They say it's the worst one ever. *¡Huracán!* Don Peyo put on the radio and the announcer says we must all stay inside until it's over. He said the hurricane was…"

Mati stopped listening. Her mind was racing. It had been years since the last one. There was much to do in very little time. The plans that flew through her mind left no room or time for the child's words.

"*¡Apúrate, nena!*" She had not meant to yell at the girl but there was no time. "You be in charge of the house preparations. Go inside and stay there. Fill every container, pot, pan, anything that will hold fresh water. Set them by the cellar door. You'll have help soon."

Concha had been a child during the last hurricane. She remembered the panic, the rushing, endless preparations. But nothing, nothing she had ever seen or heard about hurricanes made her as fearful as Mati's face. There was no time for thinking. Mati barked orders.

"It can't be. Just like that? It must be a mistake—" Concha tried to collect her thoughts.

Mati never let her finish. There was no time for denial, even less for explanations.

"Concha, you get the shutters. Close all the windows. Secure the doors. Find all the lanterns and candles you can carry. We'll need pillows, mattresses, anything that will cushion. Take everything downstairs. That's the most important thing. I'll bring in as many fruits and vegetables as I can carry."

Concha looked at her mother, confusion still in her face. Mati had to get her moving. *"¡MUÉVETE!"*

As Elena and Concha catapulted into action, Mati's mind raced. Why hadn't she read the signs earlier? Why hadn't she been more in tune with the changes around her, the animals, the wind, the sky? But these thoughts distracted her from her tasks and she had to keep moving. Delay was dangerous. She dragged the washbasin to the vegetable garden and pulled whatever she could into it—tomatoes, lemons, avocados, grapefruit, eggplants, lettuce, cucumbers. When the tub was full she dragged it to the kitchen door. One of the men would have to carry it in.

By now Toño and the other men were guiding the cattle back over the rise. They moved a little too fast, the calves, straining to keep up with the larger animals, their mooing filling the air in the distance and adding to the commotion. One was so small, Toño had to carry it into the corral.

Mati could already hear the crowd approaching, as she knew it would. Her old plantation house had the only cellar in the area. She saw their closest neighbors pushing their children ahead of them, rushing up the road toward her house. They carried pillows, sheets, lanterns, half running up the incline to the back door.

"*Entren*, downstairs. Good. You brought your things." She pointed. "The cellar. Close all the doors!

"You boys, help me get some more food down there. No! Come here. Help me move this. Get everything down there, now! You, start taking the mattresses down. You! Go help Concha with the shutters."

The other women charged into action.

"I'll see to the little ones."

"We'll take these things down."

"Hernán, take the chickens and the ducks into the kitchen and lock up Las Agujas. Martina, get the bedpans. I'll get the kerosene stove. Put everything around the walls in the cellar. Leave the center clear. *¡Apúrate, muchacho!*"

Toño had finished herding the cows into the corral. The men that had helped him get the cattle this far ran off to their own houses, rushing to gather their families and return to the strongest house in the area. Those who had just arrived pitched in to secure the doors and windows. They gave the animals as much shelter as they could before the rain and the wind reached them.

"Concha, make sure all the windows are closed up here. I'll go down to the cellar and make sure we stock the supplies and leave room for all these people."

Concha saw Mati helping the older people down the stairs. One woman refused to go without her grandchildren. A confused abuelo kept trying to come back upstairs to get his chewing tobacco. Mati had her hands full trying to get them to follow instructions.

"Don't worry, Sebastiano. I'll get it for you. Just go downstairs. I'll take care of everything. I'll get you your chew. Yes, yes, don't worry about it. I'll make sure I go. There's nothing to worry about. Everything will be fine." Concha had to admire her steely strength. But there was no time and still much to do.

* * *

Pastora and her family came running down the road just as Concha was about to lock the door. Her old friend was buffeted by the wind and rain as she hung on to her children, who swayed like reeds in the wind. Concha ran out to help them inside. She grabbed the oldest child, a toddler, as his feet gave way under him. Pastora held the other two securely, finally making it to the doorway. By now they were all soaked.

The boards and palm fronds from the *chozas* were just beginning to be ripped away, and Concha heard the first of the shutters bang against the side of the house as they made their way inside. As she pushed the last child in, she stopped to look at the damage the house had already sustained. The gardenia bushes bent naked in the wind, their branches blown to horizontal tangles. The *balcón* furniture was whipped away, smashing into the trees and flying like disconnected sticks into the air. A loud crash brought her back to the situation at hand.

Concha hurried into the house and locked the door. She heard the crack, crack of the wind ripping at the shutters and sending one of them flying across the front yard. She ran down the corridor, making sure all doors were closed and rushing to join the friends and family downstairs. As she stood at the cellar door, she took a last look around before one of the corridor doors came crashing in followed by a gush of water.

She crossed herself instinctively. "*Dios mío*, we're all in your hands."

With that she slammed the door and worked her way down to the group of upturned faces and helping hands. For a moment she thought she would lose herself to the fear that had gnawed at her all afternoon. But Toño's strong arm helped her down the last step and held her close.

"We got them all I think. I'm proud of you, *mujer*."

She put her head down on his shoulder and let out a sigh of relief, as something heavy crashed against the cellar door.

"Mami, where is Abuela?" Elena's frightened voice rang out.

Concha's head snapped up, eyes searching the room for Mati. "Mamá?" When she realized her mother wasn't among the frightened faces in the dim circle of lantern light, she bolted. She had reached the top step before the men could stop her. Toño grabbed her around the waist and pulled her down again. "Mamá!" The word exploded out of her. She refused to be held down. Arms flailing, she tried to break free of their hold. Toño pinned her arms to her sides. They fell backward, landing on a group of women. Still, he wouldn't let go. He wrapped his legs around hers as he continued pinning her arms. "Mamá!" She kicked, heaved, twisted. He wouldn't let go. "MAMÁ!" It wasn't a word anymore. It was more like a howl. They heard the creaking boards overhead, the crashing furniture. They heard doors slam as they were pulled off their hinges, and the sound of shattering glass everywhere.

Concha struggled. "Mamá!" But Toño wouldn't let her go.

"No, Concha, *óyeme*. We can't go out there now."

"*Suéltame*, Toño." She tried to push his hands away. "Mamá!"

It took four men to hold her down. She cursed at them, strained against their arms as she tried to get loose. She tried to kick, bite, punch, to no avail.

Toño grabbed her face, trying to force her to focus on his words. "It's no use now. We can't help her. You'll only get us all killed." He struggled to find the magic words that would bring Concha to her senses.

"Mati is a strong old lady. She knows what to do better than we do. She's probably in Las Agujas right now. Probably safer than we are."

She stopped resisting, but the moment he relaxed his hold she twisted away from him and headed for the stairs again. He grabbed her and hesitated for one moment before he slapped her. Hard. He had never laid a hand on this or any other woman. He would have killed anyone who dared touch her. But she had left him no choice.

Concha collapsed with the force of his blow. He gathered up her limp body and sat back against a mattress. He smoothed her hair back and gently locked his arms around her, restraining any further movement. Elena was directly in front of him. The child sat, her little hand over her mouth, trying to hold something in. Tears hung on her lashes. She needed him. Toño didn't know what to do. He couldn't let go of Concha. One of the other women tried to console Elena, but the girl pushed her away. She crawled to her parents and burrowed her head under Toño's arm. They sat like that, huddled together, for hours. He held Concha and Elena held on to him while the winds ripped at their home. No one mentioned what was on everyone's mind—Mati. The hours passed. The old lanterns sent a feeble light around the circle of neighbors. Outside, the rain whipped through the house and sent rivulets under the cellar door. Men sat surrounded by their exhausted wives and sleeping children. Unabashedly, they let tears slide silently down their faces.

A defeated Concha still whimpered in Toño's arms. She said nothing, his handprint on her cheek. He didn't look at her again. He was afraid to let go. So he just held on and she let him.

He still held her as they all listened for the lull in the storm. When the wind finally died down, they sprang into action. The women held Concha back as the men went up the stairs.

A heavy weight had fallen across the doorway. They took turns pushing, but the space didn't allow for more than one or two men at a time. They had made little progress, an opening of no more than a few inches, when the winds whipped up again and they had no choice but to return to their places.

It seemed an eternity before the winds finally died down and the movement upstairs subsided. It took a while, but the men finally managed to hack the door open. As soon as she realized the door was gone, Concha shot out of the cellar. At the top of the stairs, she took a deep breath and started down the long hallway. She headed for the back of the house, toward Las Agujas, hope and fear pushing her along. At the back door, she looked out over a devastated landscape.

The spot where Las Agujas had stood was bare. The only remnant was the mango tree. It stood naked, its trunk wrinkled into heavy folds like the body of an old, old woman. Concha ran back into what was left of their house.

When she got to Mati's room, the others were already there. She looked in, trying to make sense of what she saw. The shutters had been ripped off the hinges, the altar was gone. She had to climb over a table that partially blocked the doorway to actually get into the room. In the corner she saw Toño huddled over. He lifted something heavy that had lain on the carved chest, Cheo's wedding present for his wife. It was the only thing in the room that appeared untouched by the hurricane. It stood intact among the rubble that was the rest of the room. Toño laid Mati's body on the floor not far from the chest.

Elena, who had been stroking her grandmother's inert body when Toño finally reached her, sat on the floor, legs sprawled out in front of her. She lifted Mati's head and laid it carefully in her lap. Her small hands stroked the mat of wet hair. She looked up at her parents, lips pouting, chin trembling.

Concha looked around the room and took it all in at once—the silent circle of friends, the compassion on Toño's face, Elena's tear-streaked cheeks and Mati's limp body. She turned to her husband for help. Then she turned back to Mati's corpse. She tried to say something but nothing came out. Her hand went out in her mother's direction, trying to erase the scene. She started backing away, slowly.

"Mamá?" was all she could finally get out before the reality of her mother's death sank, like fangs, into her brain. That one word was all, before she started a slow descent, sliding onto the floor, pulling away from the world she no longer understood. Her head tilted and her knees came up to her chest. She pulled her dress down over her legs and covered her feet. She began to sway, humming a song she had heard Mati sing in this very room. Her eyes went dead. She saw nothing, heard nothing, and, mercifully, felt nothing else.

16 LOST AND FOUND

The world is gone. I raise my voice…and nothing…

I'm dead…no, I can walk…keep walking…if I am walking, I'm alive…

When no one watches she pulls out the stone and slips her hand under her skirt…her fingers secure it in the only private place left to her…

The river is flowing upstream…fish leap into the air…eels snake up into the surface and shoot back down, aimless arrows…water spits up… making her sticky wet with green spume…she jumps back…"Mamá, where are you?"

She wraps her chain around his throat…the other women cover his mouth…she uses her nails, her teeth and finally picks up her leg and smashes the man's face over and over with the shackles he had bolted around her ankle…the other women beat him with their little weapons… it is all done quickly…

The woman wanders through the rooms listening to the echoes of the past bouncing within the walls of the house…voices come to her, sweeping sand, whispers that never take the full shape of distinct words…

The clock chimes eleven times before cracking open.

Dra. Marta Montalvo watched as the nurse brought in her patient. Concha immediately went to a corner and sat on the floor. She pulled her skirt over her knees and all the way down to cover her shoes. The *doctora* greeted her patient and waited for a response. She spoke very quietly, tried to create a place of safety where Concha could emerge from her inner world. Concha sat vacant-eyed and unresponsive until it was time for her to be taken back to her bed. It had been this way every week for a month. They had established a routine.

Week after week, Dra. Montalvo sat patiently and observed. For the most part, there appeared to be little change. She tried to find out more about her patient, but after the hurricane records were difficult to find for townspeople, let alone country people who rarely interacted with town agencies. No one had come to see Concha, and the *doctora* could get no information from the emergency workers who had brought her in. Records were easily misplaced during the chaos that followed San Cristóbal.

* * *

The blank eyes, the limp hands resting on the floor, and the lowered head all seemed signs of an absence of consciousness. Yet as soon as someone got close, the hands tensed into defensiveness. Nothing escaped Dra. Montalvo, and while Concha never focused on anything or anyone, the *doctora* thought there was much more than surrender there. The *doctora* hung on to the slightest glimmer of hope. Somewhere, Concha was still fighting. Which meant that somehow, there was a way of bringing her back.

* * *

Six weeks after her initial meeting with Concha, there had been little change. Dra. Montalvo closed the door to her office and sat down heavily. The staff meeting had not gone well. Her colleagues' smirks were barely contained as she admitted her lack of progress with Concha. They had only grudgingly accepted this modern thinker of a woman who believed in "empathy therapy," whatever that was. But now, the question of expediency came up. How long would they carry an unresponsive patient? Weren't there others who deserved their attention more? Couldn't they be equally interested in patients who could afford to pay for their care? Shouldn't they depend on the more traditional forms of therapy? Then there were these new drugs... Only the chief of staff supported Dra. Montalvo in her position. She could continue treating Concha for a time. But the *doctora* could hear the clock ticking.

* * *

Elena's eyes flashed as she addressed the *doctora*. "Who did this to my mother?" she demanded. "What kind of place is this?"

The child was furious because her mother had been strapped down. The thirteen-year-old was thin and drawn but she stood her ground. "Are you the one in charge?"

"Yes, I am your mother's doctor."

"Why did you do this to my mother?" she demanded. "Is this your idea of helping her?"

"She was violent. She needed to be restrained for her own safety."

"Mamá? *¿Violenta? ¡Imposible!*"

"Not all the time, of course. But whenever we try to bathe her she attacks the orderly and..."

"Her feet...did you touch her feet?"

"Well, of course, our health regulations..."

"You can't do that."

The *doctora* stared at the child. "Excuse me?"

"I mean, you don't understand."

She went on to explain about Concha's sensitive feet and her need to keep them covered at all times.

"Tell me more."

"Why should I tell you anything? You tie her down like an animal."

"We only restrain her to avoid injury. If she would stop fighting us, there would be no need to tie her down. But there are issues of hygiene. She must be bathed."

"Then I'll do it. I'll wash her feet when I come." The child was determined. "But I can only come once a week."

"Once a…?"

"I have to look after Papá and the house. We live far away." She almost whispered, "It isn't easy, you know."

"How can I be sure she won't hurt herself or anyone else?"

"I know her better than you. As long as you leave her feet alone she'll be fine."

Dra. Montalvo thought about Elena's proposal for a moment and then acquiesced. Better to have an ally in Concha's treatment, even if the rules would have to be bent a little.

"All right, once a week. We won't touch her feet, but you must agree to see me every time you come to visit."

"But…"

"No, that's the deal. Do you or don't you want to see her get better? Then I'll need your help."

"All right, you win, but no more ties!"

* * *

As Elena was led away to Concha's room, the *doctora* could only guess at what the girl had been through in the six months since the hurricane. That part of the country had gotten the brunt of the storm. Thousands of casualties, hundreds of homes destroyed, crops and cattle lost. The roads were still mostly impassable. It was a mess.

The girl must have been frantic about her mother's condition. The *instituto* had to be a totally alien world for her. It must have taken a great deal of courage for Elena to walk through those gates, let alone stand her ground and demand better services for her mother. The *doctora* had to admire the girl's spunk.

The *doctora* was looking forward to an ongoing conversation with Elena. For the first time in weeks, Dra. Montalvo was hopeful about

Concha's prognosis. Maybe Elena had the key that would unlock Concha's mind.

* * *

Elena rolled up her sleeves and reached for her mother's feet. Concha moaned and tried to pull her dress over her shoes. But when she heard Elena's voice, she stopped fighting. The girl kept talking as she worked, pulling gently at one leg, then the other. She held each foot for a moment before slipping off the shoe. Concha rocked from side to side, still moaning. Elena kept talking and moving slowly as she washed her mother's feet. Concha's moaning grew weaker, until she just rocked back and forth, like a child at play. When Elena slipped her mother's feet into a pair of clean white socks, Concha pulled her knees up, curled into a fetal position and went to sleep.

* * *

Dra. Montalvo observed her patient. Concha sat in her same spot and her dress was still pulled over her knees. But today the hem of her dress stopped just short of the floor, exposing the tips of her shoes. After her talk with Elena, the *doctora* caught detailed changes she might have otherwise missed. The feet sensitivity—she would start there.

* * *

The *doctora* wanted to know more about the business of the feet. Elena said that her grandmother Mati had told her once that all the women in their family were born with a special gift. The grandmother had explained that Concha's feet were her special way of knowing the world around her. But then something happened, because as Concha grew up, she made sure her feet were never uncovered.

"Your grandmother sounds like a wise woman."

"She was. You would've liked her."

"I think so. Was?"

"She died in the hurricane."

"She did? And then what happened?"

"That's when Mamá got sick."

The *doctora* stopped writing.

* * *

Concha was still not speaking and her eyes still didn't focus, but she sat with her stockinged feet clearly visible. There was a slight movement of her big toe.

"*Buenos días,* Concha," the *doctora* said. "It's a beautiful day. I am here and I am paying attention."

* * *

"Now, tell me about your father. I haven't met him, have I?"

Elena began to fidget in her chair. Toño's absence from the hospital, his apparent disinterest in his wife, and his punishing silences were hard to explain, especially to a stranger.

"No, he hasn't been here. The hurricane took everything, you see… the farm, you know…and all the work…and…but he loves Mamá. He loves me, too, really. It's just that…he's just so hurt, you see. He feels so helpless."

Elena was forced to admit to her father's shutting everyone out, even his daughter. She sat, twisting the hem of her dress and glancing frequently at the door.

"Was he always like that?"

"Oh, no. Before the hurricane, things were so different. He used to laugh a lot. And he was the only one who could make Mamá smile, even when she was moody. He would tease her until she started to laugh. Now, I don't even remember what her laugh sounded like. His, either. He used to laugh but not anymore."

"I see. Do you suppose your father would come to see me?"

"I…I don't know."

"Well, maybe one day? It would be really helpful if I could talk with him."

"Like I said, he's not much for talking."

"Okay, I think that's enough for today. I'm sure you're anxious to see your mother. I'll see you next week."

The girl got up quickly and in three steps was out of the room.

* * *

Concha sat, her breathing slow and rhythmic. Her body, relaxed, now shifted a bit. There was the tiniest upturn at the corners of her mouth, the barest hint of a smile. The *doctora* didn't know where Concha's mind was traveling, but her patient was allowing the *doctora* to watch her embark on a journey. The smile was a door left ajar.

* * *

Back in the corner, feet folded beneath her skirt, Concha moved forward and back and forward again. She cocked her ear for a moment. The movement was almost imperceptible. Then she went back to her rhythmic rocking.

* * *

Dra. Montalvo waited. Concha wasn't brought to the office at the appointed time. The nurses informed the *doctora* that Concha had fallen into a deep sleep and they were unable to get her up for her session. The *doctora* rushed to the ward. Concha slept soundly through the entire examination. Nothing was out of the ordinary, all vital signs were normal. Concha was still sleeping quietly when the *doctora* left. Dra. Montalvo left orders that her patient was not to be disturbed but she was to be notified as soon as Concha woke up on her own.

* * *

The *doctora* noticed the tremors that started in Concha's legs and spread upward. Concha jerked from side to side as though shaking off something cumbersome, all the while moaning, tears rolling down her cheeks.

* * *

Concha was agitated. She sat, eyes closed, mouth open in a silent scream, her hand covering her mouth. She shook her head until it was time to take her back.

The *doctora* wondered at the struggle going on in Concha's head. She had been making painstaking notes on her patient. The progress was slow, but definite. The fact that the inner life was slowly being manifested in her outer world was promising. The *doctora* wanted so much to say something, to help Concha out of her private world and into the more public one of the hospital and, later, the world outside these walls. But she knew she couldn't push. It must come from the patient. She must *want* to come back. All the *doctora* could do was pave the way, make it safe for Concha to return. She didn't probe. It was a script now, routine:

"*Buenos días*, Concha. I'm here and I am listening."

* * *

One lone tear inched down Concha's face and fell to her bodice. That was all. The *doctora* didn't move, not even to console. "You know I am here when you need me." Concha curled up and fell asleep. But the *doctora* wasn't worried. She hoped Concha felt safer, that this was exhaustion, not retreat. She moved closer. She understood that Concha had been through much and still had a long way to go.

* * *

Dra. Montalvo looked out the window and weighed the situation. It had been over two years since she started work with Concha. Much progress had been made. Slow and steady progress was good. Introducing such a charged item would be risky. This stone Elena spoke about could go straight to the heart of the conflict between Concha and her mother. It could be a way to jump-start her progress or it could permanently shock her into her world of escape. Elena wanted to try. The *doctora* remembered the first time the girl spoke to her, *I know her better than you.* Maybe Elena was right. Dra. Montalvo picked up the phone and asked for Concha to be brought in.

* * *

The *doctora* watched from the doorway as the girl slipped the stone into her mother's hand. For a time there was no reaction. The girl went on to wash her mother's feet as she usually did. But as Elena worked, Concha stopped rocking. Her eyes roamed around the room until they stopped at her daughter. Elena was stunned at the sudden look of recognition in her mother's face. Dra. Montalvo watched. It was only a moment and then Concha was gone again. But it was a breakthrough.

The *doctora* would monitor Concha to see whether the episode sparked any change in their regular sessions. Elena wanted to continue bringing the stone to every visit. The *doctora* agreed.

* * *

Each visit, Elena pushed the stone into her mother's hand. Each time, the moments of recognition got longer. Sometimes Concha just stared at her daughter. Other times she reached out to touch Elena's face, her hands. Sometimes she just repeated, "*¿M'hija? ¿M'hija?*" as though seeking reassurance that Elena was real and not a figment of her dreams.

* * *

Concha's sessions with the *doctora* remained unchanged. She didn't acknowledge her presence or that of any of the staff, but the *doctora* felt that if Concha could reach out to Elena, she could eventually also reach out to a wider world. Dra. Montalvo had an idea, but she gave mother and daughter time to get used to each other before introducing any new elements.

* * *

When Concha held the stone and reached for Elena's hand, there was a tiny smile on her face. But when she saw Dra. Montalvo sitting just behind her daughter, she made a sharp sound and pulled away from the girl. She turned her face to the wall.

* * *

It had taken more than two years to get the door ajar. Dra. Montalvo was furious at herself. She should have known. What if Concha never came back? She had to rein in her impatience and remind herself to follow Concha's lead.

* * *

"Mamá, I'm alone. You can come back now." Concha hadn't responded during Elena's last visit. But Elena wouldn't give up. The stone had been in Concha's hand during this whole visit and no reaction. But Elena kept talking. "I've gotten to know your *doctora* really well. We're friends, you know? I'm sorry we scared you. She just wants to help."

And slowly, Concha did start coming back. A few moments at a time. And each time, Elena spoke about the *doctora*. At first, Concha was agitated just at the mention of her name. But after a while, Dra. Montalvo became just another topic in Elena's long monologues. Concha never responded but she stopped cringing when Elena brought up inviting the *doctora* to their next visit.

* * *

Dra. Montalvo sat in the corner and watched Elena and her mother interact. Elena had introduced the *doctora* when Concha came out of her stupor. But Concha didn't acknowledge her presence, and neither mother nor daughter referred to the *doctora* during that session.

After several visits, Concha finally turned from Elena at the end of the session and looked directly at the *doctora*. She rested her eyes on Dra. Montalvo for only a moment before curling up and going to sleep.

* * *

The *doctora* was surprised when the tall man standing at her door introduced himself as Concha's husband, Antonio. He held his hat in his hand and waited to be asked in.

"I understand you are my wife's *doctora*."

"Yes, I am."

"And you know my daughter as well."

"Yes."

"Elena tells me Concha is doing better now."

"Yes, yes she is."

"May I see her now, please. I brought something for her."

He pulled out a small bottle. "It's only a little oil."

The *doctora* said, "Of course," and showed him to Concha's room.

* * *

It had been several weeks since Elena had first allowed Dra. Montalvo to use the stone in her private sessions with Concha, who now routinely opened her eyes and focused on the *doctora* for a short while before retreating.

Toño had been visiting his wife regularly for two months. He and Elena took turns visiting so that the husband and wife visits were always private. Toño was not a man of many words. He wouldn't meet with the *doctora*. He felt her meetings with Elena were enough family contact.

* * *

Concha opened her eyes and looked at the *doctora*. There was no hesitation or tentativeness. There was no uncertainty or fear. Concha simply observed the woman who had been observing her for so long.

"I'm Dra. Marta Montalvo. Do you remember me?"

Concha nodded.

"I'm glad you've found your way back to us."

Concha said, "*Sí*. You are Marta." Then she slipped off her shoes.

17 RECOVERY

Five years after entering the hospital, Concha stepped out of the car and into a new world. The neighboring farms and fields, the physical markers of her daily life, were all gone now. Behind her and beyond the car, the river flowed, naked of trees she had known, still winding down a remembered path. But the house that stood before her had the face of a stranger. It was because of the hurricane, of course, the eraser of all that had been. She took one step back and bumped into Toño's solidity: Toño, her anchor.

She squared her shoulders and climbed the steps of a new *balcón* to a modest one-story house. At the door she leaned in and looked down the long, darkened corridor that ended at a rectangle of light, the *patio*. She stepped in and walked straight to the back of the house, where she found what she needed. She let out a sigh of relief at seeing the old mango tree and Mati's grave below it, just as Toño had described it, the low branches hanging just above the headstone. Making her way down the back steps, Concha slipped off her new shoes and closed her eyes. The packed earth under her feet felt good. The cool grass as she approached the well-tended grave felt even better. She walked all around the marker and came back to face the headstone. She dug her toes into the grass and stood, head bent to the side, listening. Finally, she sank to the ground and leaned against the headstone.

Mamá. There is so much I need to tell you. And there are so many questions. So many unanswered whys. Why did you have to go and leave me? You could've…I didn't even get a chance to…I wanted…I felt you always shut me out…always left me behind…and then you did it again… slammed another door in my face…the final door that time. Oh! I was so angry…but we talked about it in that hospital. Oh my God, how many times did we talk about you and me and us? The *doctora* wouldn't give up. And now…now it's time finally…for you and me…it's time. The *doctora* said, "Time, give it time." So here I am, in this home I don't know, talking to a mother I don't know. But I'll come every day and I'll take my shoes off. And we'll get to know each other. We'll crack the door open, just a little. And then maybe…maybe we can find "I'm sorry."

* * *

Toño came into their room to find Concha sitting with what was left of Mati's tapestries. She stroked the stitching admiringly before digging into the thread box in the chest.

"These need mending. They are so old and fragile. Did you know Papá carved this for her wedding present? When I was a child, she kept all her treasures in it. She was so happy then; so was I."

She began humming an old tune, Mati's tune. Toño shifted his weight. He watched her carefully, as he did when she went out to the mango tree every day. He watched and waited for some sign. But so far, she was holding on. The first day she came home she had walked out to the back and sat for a long time. Then, shoes in hand, she walked around the house. When she finally came in, still barefoot, she went into each room and walked every inch of them, as though she was memorizing space. He knew she needed to do this, make the acquaintance of her new home. But he worried that it would all be too much and she would retreat again.

Concha looked up casually as she threaded the needle and began the repairs.

"Don't look so worried, Toño. I'm just remembering Mamá and thinking about how much we never got to share. *Ay*, Toño, all those years in the hospital. All that lost time. When I was lost in the stories, in the memories, that was the easy part. When I finally came out of it, Dra. Montalvo wanted to talk about everything, all the pain and love and resentment and anger and joys and disappointment. All the talking, all the examining—that's the part I thought would kill me. It didn't, though. It made me stronger. But now, it's like starting all over again."

"Concha, are you sure this is the right…" His voice was deep with concern. He had just gotten his wife back after so many years. His greatest fear was to lose her again.

"Don't worry, I won't go back. I can't go back. But you don't know how hard it really is. I can't stand still, and going forward means feeling all the pain again. Dra. Montalvo says I'll only truly be well again when I confront the past. She says it was the running away from it that made me sick. Do you believe that? Sometimes I think she sounds just like Mamá."

* * *

Concha and Elena hadn't said a word to each other all through dinner. Then Elena went out to the porch to sit with Pedro Ortíz and stayed there for hours. Concha sat for an hour under the mango tree visiting with Mati. Toño waited until evening when the house was quiet and the privacy of the darkness brought them closer. He and Concha lay in bed looking at the stars through their bedroom window.

"*Sabes*, Concha, I've watched Mati and you and Elena for years. And you're all so much alike. Now, wait a minute. Don't interrupt. There are things to be said. Since you and Elena seem to have so little to talk about, I think it's my turn.

"Remember the silences between you and Mati? They were like giant shadows living between you. Everyone knew you loved each other beyond words. That's where you kept your love, beyond words, in your silences. And here it is again. I see those same shadows growing between you and Elena."

Concha was about to say something when he put his finger up to her lips.

"That child never missed a visit with you whether you responded to her or not. When I was too angry to face that place, to look at what was happening to you face-to-face, Elena took her books and her diary and later her stone, and she went there. Every Saturday, rain or shine. She fought everybody—me, the doctors, the nurses—because somehow she thought she knew better what you needed. For five years she put everything in her life second and you first. Just as you did with Mati. Isn't that what your illness was all about, putting Mati before all the rest of us? Elena learned from you. Her silence and her anger are no different than yours. All you women feel too much. Everything is too big with you. You love too big and fear too big and have too much anger and too few words."

Concha swallowed. She wanted to say something. But there was nothing to say.

"Be careful. Your love burns the rest of us. Some of us can deal with the fire. And then some of us just can't."

* * *

One morning, two weeks after Concha had returned home, she was making the bed when Elena walked into the room.

"Mamá, do you have a minute?"

Concha was surprised to see her daughter and even more surprised at her request. She had been thinking about Toño's words just that morning. Maybe he was right. She looked at her grown daughter. Not a child anymore.

"Of course." She finished smoothing out the sheet and sat down on the newly made bed.

"I've been thinking about this for a while now. Mamá, I want to go to nursing school."

"Nursing school?"

"Yes. I have excellent grades. In fact, I'll be the valedictorian. Don Fernando, my science teacher, thinks I can get a scholarship and…"

"But I just got home. I thought we could spend some time together, get to know each other again."

"Yes, I know, but I can't pass up this opportunity."

"But that school is so far away…"

"That's why there is a residency requirement."

"A what?"

"I would have to live there, Mamá."

Concha was speechless. Elena wanted to move away, live somewhere else?

"Have you lost your mind?" The words just came out. "An unmarried young woman, living with strangers?"

Elena had anticipated this reaction. She knew her father would support her in this. But Concha would be the big problem.

"They are very strict about rules there. The housemother…" Elena tried to explain.

"I don't care. *I'm* your housemother. It's out of the question."

Before Elena could answer, Toño came in wondering about the loud voices. "*¿Qué pasa aquí?*"

"Your daughter wants to live on her own. She wants to move to—"

"Papá, I want to go to nursing school."

"But what about your m…"

"I want to be a nurse. It's only a two-year program and they've offered me a scholarsh—"

"When did all this happen? Does that Pedrito Ortíz boy have something to do with this?"

"Papá, Pedro has already been accepted at the university. Yes, he will be in the capital, too. But this has nothing to do with him. It's me. It's what I want."

"*¡Imposible!*" Concha was furious.

"But Mamá…" Elena's patience was beginning to wear thin. Toño decided to put some space between them.

"Why don't we discuss this later? Elena, this is a new idea to us. Give us a little time to consider…"

"But Papá…" she wasn't willing to let it go.

"*Hija*, you've obviously been thinking about this for some time, I'm sure. Don't we get a little time to think about it, too?"

"*Pero*, Papá…"

"Elena?" There was a warning in Toño's tone and she knew it was useless to continue.

"*Sí*, Papá."

* * *

"She's too young. An unmarried girl, going off by herself like that! Tongues will wag and we'll never live it down." Concha shook her head as though shaking off Toño's words.

"*Pero, mujer*, she won't be 'going off,' as you put it. She'll be going to school. And she'll be well supervised. I've looked into it. Talked to the woman in charge myself."

"I don't care. It's not right."

"Concha, you're not listening. Sit down a minute." He had forgotten how stubborn Concha could be. He knew his daughter had inherited her temper from her mother, and he didn't want them having this confrontation just when Concha was doing so well. But Concha wasn't listening. She paced the room, talking to no one in particular, venting her disapproval.

"Nursing school! Oh, I know all about that place. I've heard stories, I can tell you! Supervision? Do you know what they do in there? Young girls, *señoritas* supposedly? They're expected to tend to men, young and old, naked men. The girls bathe them, dress wounds in their privates and who knows what else. And they're in there day and night. What happens when the 'supervisor' falls asleep? Men are men and girls are weak."

"Concha! I'm ashamed of you, *mujer*. Now, I know you've been listening to *malas lenguas*, people who have nothing better to do than throw dirt on others. You should talk, of all people, who have had to depend on those very nurses to keep you alive when you gave up on yourself. Is your memory so short? Elena was at that hospital to see you every week. Don't you think she might have seen something 'inappropriate' while she was there?"

"No. She's too young. I won't allow it."

"Another thing—you forget that Elena is almost a grown woman. For months, Zenobia's boy, Pedro, has been spending more time on our *balcón* than his own. He's been coming by three or four nights a week after supper. They often go out for a walk. What do you think they do out there under the moonlight? Elena isn't a child anymore. She hasn't been for a long time now."

Concha opened her mouth to argue and then sank into a nearby seat. The fight had exhausted her, and the words came out weak.

"But I've only been home a few months and she wants to leave already."

He didn't want to hurt her. "Concha, time stopped for you but not for the rest of us. You were in that hospital a long time, and the rest of us had to go on."

Concha listened. Toño had never spoken of this before.

"San Cristóbal changed everything. Elena had to grow up fast. She gave up her childhood to become the woman of the house. There was so much to rebuild, so much to get used to. You were sick and I couldn't help you. I knew you needed more. I signed those papers, but the day they took you away, they took the best parts of me with you. There was nothing left for Elena. I'm ashamed to say, I wasn't there for her when she needed me most.

"Now we have you back and it's time for her to start thinking about her own life. It's time for her to put herself first. If she wants to go on studying, we should let her go. We should celebrate her wanting it. It doesn't mean she loves you less, just differently."

"Love? We don't even know each other. I've tried, oh, Toño, I've tried so hard, but I've lost her. I came back to a new house and a new young woman who looks and sounds like my daughter but is so… distant, so cold. She's a stranger living in my Elena's skin."

"Give her time. I'm sure…"

"You know how much I've always loved her. But first there was Mamá. Together they built a wall against me. I thought now that Mamá was gone, maybe we could…there's so much I want to say to her, to explain."

"And there's no reason why you can't. But you can't turn back the clock. Don't treat her like a child. You'll surely lose her if you do. Give her time. Give her space. Maybe this school is just what she needs. Sometimes we can see better from a distance. Let's help her prepare for the next part of her life. That's the best thing we can do for her."

Toño opened his arms to her and Concha slid in. But in her heart of hearts she knew she was losing her daughter. Maybe she had already lost her. And she had no idea how to get her back.

* * *

"Oh, here you are." Concha came into the kitchen as Elena was washing the last of the dinner dishes. "Need some help?" She picked up a plate.

"No, I'm doing all right." Elena pulled the plate out of her mother's hand and pushed it into the soapy water.

"So, when are you leaving us?" Concha stood back, arms crossed before her. She chose her words and her tone carefully.

"Not until September." Elena knew she had Toño to thank for her mother's changed attitude. Her hands never stopped moving. She was grateful for the dirty dishes.

"Good." Concha took a deep breath. She looked at Elena, who was so different from the girl she remembered. She searched her memory. No, she really hadn't understood the child back then and she certainly didn't know how to be a mother to this young woman now.

"Maybe we can get to know each other again before you leave." Concha examined the crevices in the floor, rubbing a spot with the toe of her shoe. "You have become quite a young lady overnight."

"Not quite overnight, Mamá."

Their truce was so tenuous, a crystal bowl, easily cracked.

Concha tried to introduce a lighter tone. She remembered something. "Elena, you used to love Mamá's stories, remember? Come, let me tell you one of them. The dishes can wait."

"Abuela's stories? Since when do you know Abuela's stories?" Elena's hands stopped for a fraction of a moment before lathering another dish.

"Actually, while I was sick, I remembered many of them. They kept me company. I think they were the only thing that kept me sane. They were...important."

Elena turned, soapy water dripping onto the floor, and examined her mother openly. Who was this woman? No, she wouldn't let her mother into the world she and Abuela Mati had created. Besides, it was much too late now.

"That's not what you told Abuela. You said they were superstitions. You called her a crazy, superstitious old woman. Or don't you remember that?"

Elena knew how fragile her mother was, how delicate her condition. She didn't want to hurt her. But she couldn't stop herself. Where were these words coming from?

"I remember, but I've changed." Concha almost whispered.

"A little late for Abuela, don't you think?"

Concha stared at her daughter openmouthed. Then, slowly, she started crumbling. Concha seemed much smaller than the woman who had walked into the kitchen just a few minutes before. The pain on her face was frightening. Her features folded into themselves, eyes, nose, and mouth merging into a mass of agonized lines.

Elena watched her mother cover her face with shaky hands, her whole body starting to tremble. The tremors started with her shoulders and soon her whole body shook. Her mother was collapsing right before her eyes.

"*Ay, Dios mío.*" Elena dropped the dish she was holding and sprang into action, catching her mother by the shoulders. She held on, trying to calm her mother's shaking, silently pleading, *Oh my God, please don't make her sick again. Please, I didn't mean it. It's my fault. Please, don't punish her again. Punish me. It's my fault, my fault.*

Slowly, Elena began rocking her mother in her arms. At first the tension in the older woman was raw, unassailable. But Elena kept trying, pushing gently, seeking a response, and slowly, unconsciously, Concha surrendered to the swaying. "Shh, shh, everything will be all right." She stroked her mother's hair, stroked her back in long, soothing motions. They kept rocking, the two of them inhabiting a hypnotic space of consolation and love, living for one magic moment, in a protective bubble where there was no regret, no anger, no accusations, no resentment. Each of them needed it, hungered for a respite.

"Mamá, I don't hate you. I don't. I love you. I'm so sorry, Mamá. Please forgive me."

Mother and daughter knelt, swaying back and forth and crying, trying to think of how to mend their world. Each knew deep down inside that forgiveness would take time, perhaps more time than they had left. For now, this moment was the closest they would come.

Book Four

ELENA

18 THE DEPARTURE

Elena was comforted by her father's presence as he drove the pink and gray 1950 Studebaker down the country road. The *flamboyán* branches, heavy with their red blossoms, struck the car as it made its way. It had been drizzling all morning, and the windshield wipers kept a steady beat, *"Don't go…don't go…don't go."*

She looked back at her daughter, Carisa, on the rear seat. The three-year-old sat, as instructed, knees together, in the midst of layers of pink ruffles that Elena herself had worked on for weeks. There was a huge satin bow in Carisa's hair and a tiny white patent-leather purse on her lap. The child sat very still, having none of the usual excitement that takes hold of many children when they know they are starting on a trip. Carisa sensed something new in the air. But she sat quietly clutching her bag and waiting to see what cues her mother would give her for this strange occasion.

Danilo, the baby, sat in Elena's lap, roly-poly and happy after having had his breakfast. As soon as he had settled on her lap he had fallen asleep. His weight was comforting against her breast. His cheek rested on the roll of money Elena had pinned to her padded brassiere just that morning.

Carisa and Danilo: even their names had caused problems. As usual, her mother-in-law had had her own opinion, not that she had spoken to Elena about the matter. But while putting the baby to sleep, Elena had overheard Zenobia's comments to her son.

"Why couldn't she name them normal names like María or Juan? Or pick a family name? Always wanting to be different! Never satisfied with whatever's good enough for everyone else! *Hijo*, I told you marrying her would be a mistake."

It seemed every conversation that woman had with Pedro ended with the same sentence. Elena couldn't stand it anymore. *He will have to decide which he needs more: wife and family or mother. Funny how I assumed a good son was the measure of a good husband. Live and learn.*

Zenobia Ortíz had given them the tiny *casita*, a dilapidated four-room cottage at the far end of her property, as a wedding present.

"It's all I have and all I can give you," she'd said back then. But a year after Elena finished rebuilding and refurbishing the house, Zenobia announced that she was in need of money and needed to sell the cottage. Elena's shock was quickly replaced by indignation. She turned to her husband. Pedro, too, was horrified. But always the obedient son, in the long run he acquiesced to his mother's wishes without much protest. Elena was furious and since then their marriage had been marked by fight after fight—all fueled by Zenobia's meddling.

"My mother is my mother. What do you want me to do?"

"What about your family is your family? Your wife is your wife? Your home is your home? Pedro, you're a married man now. What do you think you're supposed to do?"

"I was a son long before I was a husband."

"Thank you for clarifying your priorities."

There it was, out in the open. She finally got an answer. Not the one she would have wanted, but an answer nonetheless. So she stopped arguing.

When her mother-in-law sold their *casita* out from under them, the young family had been forced to move into the old woman's house. This communal living had been the catalyst for Elena's decision to leave. Pedro began moving their things into his mother's newly expanded space behind the old *kiosko*. Elena didn't lift a finger to help and retreated into a raging silence.

It had taken her months to come to the decision and weeks to make the proper arrangements, but she was on her way now. It had not been easy, preparing for her departure and packing in secret. It had almost broken her heart to see Carisa trying to help, handing over her toys and favorite books as the folded clothes went into the suitcase. These preparations could only be made while Pedro was out with his friends. The one thing Elena had not wanted was any more scenes before she was ready to go.

This morning, Elena had confronted Pedro as he and Zenobia were having their breakfast. As the young woman approached the dining room, she could see Zenobia seated at the head of the table. Pedro sat opposite his mother, his back to the doorway. Elena's high heels made solid staccato sounds as she crossed the tiled floor. As she entered the room, Pedro turned, a look of surprise on his face. She was usually on her way to the hospital by now. His mother, remaining in her captain's chair, looked at her daughter-in-law over her son's shoulder, a mocking grin on her face as her eyes took in not the usual white uniform, but Elena's good linen suit.

Elena focused on her mother-in-law's grin. The gaps between the teeth were visible from across the long room and she could almost hear the words slip out from the dark spaces between the gatelike teeth, "*Go...go...go...*"

"Pedro, I've decided to take the children and leave." He began to rise, about to say something. Elena put up her hand, palm facing him, and shook her head calmly.

"We're leaving for New York City in an hour or so. We'll be living with Marcelina for a while. Do you want to come out and say goodbye to the children?"

"Elena, *¿pero te has vuelto loca?*" Pedro's shock registered in the high pitch of his voice. His usual baritone had changed to an outraged tenor. "What do you mean *you* decided?"

"We've gone over this a million times! You never listen. There was no other way." The weariness in her voice was not new. "I'm tired of the endless fights and of the thick silences of our lives. You built this house for your mother. You stay with her. I just can't do this, don't want to do this, anymore. The children are waiting in the car. There isn't much time. Are you coming out to say goodbye?"

"*¡Esto es imposible!*" was all he could get out before she cleared the door.

But by the time he got up from his chair, Elena was halfway across the porch. Toño waited to drive her to the airport. He had been loading the suitcases during this scene and now awaited her by the car, keeping a careful eye on the door in case his daughter might need him.

Pedro stalked after her but modified his gait and modulated his voice once he saw his father-in-law. Still, he caught her by her arm as she stood on the porch. "*¿Cómo que te vas para Nueva York?* You must have lost your mind. You're not going anywhere! I won't allow it."

Her weariness was quickly replaced by anger.

"You won't…what? Allow? *Allow*?" She tried to control herself. "What makes you think I'm asking permission?

He took in her stiff back and her squared shoulders. He'd seen her like this before and knew he had made a serious mistake. He needed time to think, but he could see there was no more time. He never thought it would come to this. His mother had assured him that it was just a phase, that Elena would get over it and accept her husband's decisions.

He began again in a more conciliatory tone. "Come back inside, Elena. Let's talk about this. Whatever the problem is, we can work it out. Just between you and me."

"Don't you mean, you and me and Zenobia? No, Pedro, the time for talking is over. You haven't been listening for a long time. The only voice you hear is your mother's. Now, I'm too tired to talk and too angry to listen. I just want to go. Don't make it harder than it already is."

Pedro could see that his delaying tactic was not working.

"But those are my kids. That's my son. No, you're not taking my kids away from me! If you want to go, you go by yourself. My kids stay with me! Elena, don't you dare walk away from me. Elena—ELENA!"

She was already halfway down the porch steps. Pedro, in a panic, grabbed at her arm again. Elena jerked away with such force she almost toppled over.

"*¡Suéltame!*" The screamed word exploded in his face. He froze. The thoughts rushed through his head. Who was this woman who was walking away and taking everything with her? Where was his wife? She didn't look or sound like the woman he had been married to for six years. No, this couldn't be happening.

Zenobia came up behind him and put a protective arm over his shoulders, "*Déjala*. We don't need her. We never have. Let her go. Come, let's finish our breakfast."

"*Pero*, Mamá, what are you talking about, breakfast? That's my wife! Those are my kids! How can I just sit down to eat as though nothing is happening?"

"*Hijo*, you're a man and men don't beg. Besides, do you really think this little drama is real? She's trying to manipulate you by making these scenes. If you give in now, you'll never wear the pants in your own house again. Besides, she'd never leave the rest of her precious family to go off by herself."

"*No sé*, Mamá. I've never seen her so determined." He watched Elena settle into the front seat of the waiting car.

Zenobia, losing all patience, flung her anger at her son.

"I thought I brought up a man, not a sniveling boy. *¡No seas pendejo!* Confront this situation. *¡Ponte fuerte, hombre!* I taught you how to wear the pants in the house. Now wear them!"

Zenobia, seeing the expression on Pedro's face, worried that she had gone too far. Putting her arm around his waist, she counseled him in softer tones.

"*Siéntate, hijo*, let her go. I doubt she'll actually go through with this. But even if she does leave, she's never lived anywhere but here. This is her place. Let her try. She'll fall flat on her face and come crawling back like a beaten dog, her damn pride finally broken. Then she'll be ready to be a dutiful and obedient wife to you. It's time she learns that lesson. And then everyone will know who's the head of this family. Maybe this is the best thing that can happen to all of us."

* * *

"*Don't go…don't go…don't go.*" The wipers kept up the litany as they drove by the Municipal Hospital where Elena had worked for seven years. It sat in the morning light, its tall palm trees sweeping the upper windows. Elena squeezed her leather bag between her ankles. She had packed it last, taking her time to make sure she missed nothing, reading and re-reading each page—birth certificates, baptismal papers, diplomas, and marriage license. At the bottom of the bag she felt a lump, a small pouch she had slipped in at the last minute. She remembered her frantic visit to her father.

* * *

Concha had been doing the weekly ironing in the dining room. She glanced up at her daughter and pressed the heavy iron against the fabric. The sun came in through the window and fell across her busy hands.

"*Siéntate*, keep me company a while."

Concha pointed to the chair across from the ironing board. The sun fell over Elena's shoulder and kept her face in shadow. Their relationship had improved over the past few years, but Elena still kept her at arm's length.

"Is something wrong, *m'hija*?"

"Oh, nothing. I'm fine."

They had developed a truce in which neither trod on private ground. But something in Elena's demeanor led Concha to break their unspoken rule.

"*M'hija*, do you think I'm as blind as all that? Can't we talk about it? Toño won't be back until late. But…maybe *I* can help this time."

Elena had come ready to unload her worries on her father. He had always listened and given gentle advice. The idea that had been growing in her head for several weeks still didn't have clear shape. She needed help in sorting out the many conflicting emotions that left her exhausted at the end of the day.

She had been barely holding on as she made her way to her parents' house. It was too late to turn back now. Her feelings were too close to the surface, too exposed to be reined in again. So the warmth of her mother's words opened the floodgates. The words burst out, the raw and uncontrolled feelings wrapped in rage, hurt, and impotency. They had been fueled by years of suppression and now they exploded into the air.

"*¡Esa jodía vieja!* She's killing me, Mamá, sucking the life out of us. She couldn't stop us from getting married but she never gives us a moment of peace. I may have married Pedro but Zenobia has made sure he's son first, then father, then husband a distant third. She wears her mask of need and weakness to build a house of guilt and manipulate him away from us. I married a man but I live with a boy. Her meddling even creeps into our bedroom and poisons our most intimate moments. She's a spiteful, evil old woman who wants control of everything and everyone. And she hates me because I won't let her."

Once Elena got started, she couldn't stop herself. Her pain spewed out in a torrent of words. "I've tried everything with Pedro—patience, silence, reason, outrage, even sex. And nothing, nothing works. She bleeds him with her guilt and drives a wedge between us. Oh God! I give up. I can't fight her and him, too. I just want to disappear. I want to pack up my kids and go somewhere where I can build a life and no one can take my home away from me again."

Concha wanted to comfort her broken daughter. She wanted to wipe away the tears as she had done when Elena was a child, warm and open to her mother's love. But too much, or maybe not enough, had passed between them in recent years and she didn't want to do anything to break this rare moment of truth.

Concha put the iron aside and watched her daughter across the ironing board that stood between them. She listened to the anger that sparked in her daughter's words, feeling her pain.

When Elena was finished, Concha walked over and sat very close to her. Not wanting Elena to misunderstand, her mother measured her words carefully.

"*M'hija*, maybe you should do just that."

"What?"

"Maybe you should take your children and go." Concha's attention was riveted on her daughter, measuring, hoping not to be shut out again. *Dios mío, let her hear me out this time. Let her take what I can give. Let me be a mother again.*

Elena looked at her mother incredulously. Was Concha encouraging her to walk away from her marriage? Concha, who had fought so hard to keep her from going away to a school in the next district, was now encouraging her to go even further away?

"Mamá? I can't believe you're telling me to…"

"*Hija*, more than anything else in the world, I want you to be happy."

"But you never…"

"I've made mistakes. You think I don't know? I haven't always been there for you. But I'm here now. I'm listening, not just with my ears but with my heart. And I want to help. Please let me.

"I've had a lot of time to think, to put myself in your shoes. First the hurricane, then my illness, and now Zenobia. We've all taken too much from you."

Elena sat dumbfounded.

"Don't look at me like that. I'm not blind and certainly not stupid. I've learned a thing or two in the past few years and I'm not the same woman today that I was back then. I swore to myself that the next time you needed me, I'd be here, right here for you, that I'd never fail you again.

"So if you feel you have to leave here to find your happiness, then go. You go and you do what you think is best for yourself and your children. It'll hurt me to see you leave. I don't think I can be there waving goodbye. But I'll send you away with my blessing."

For years, Concha hadn't known how to reach her daughter. Now that she'd found the words, they just kept coming. And Elena, astounded, put her hurt aside to listen to this new mother that sat before her.

"Wait a minute. I'll be right back."

Elena was too stunned to move. When Concha came back, she carried a brightly embroidered pouch that she placed in her daughter's hands.

"You gave this to me once when I needed it. I think I'm done with it and you might need it back. Hang on to it. After all, Mamá left it for you."

* * *

Elena's decision weighed heavily on her for weeks. Night after night, she fell asleep holding that stone. And then one night she had a strange dream.

> An old woman is making her way into the woods. The bright sun overhead sends shafts of light through the trees. She pushes past green branches, following a narrow path. As she travels, the foliage changes from dark greens to shades of yellow, bright orange and red and, underfoot, a brown carpet of fallen leaves crunches as the woman moves on, always

traveling north. A sudden wind whips the leaves into a whirling dance. Then it was over, as quickly and unexpectedly as it had come. The sun, barely luminous, hides behind a blanket of gray clouds. The leaves are all gone and the old woman wears furs and heavy shoes, shivering as she continues on her journey. She heads for a tower rising in the distance, leaving the familiar path, to work her way into unknown territory.

Early next morning, fresh from the dream, Elena got up and began her chores with a new sense of urgency. It was her day off and she had much to do. She washed and ironed clothes all day, every stitch of clothing they owned. She didn't know exactly where she was going yet. But she knew her journey would start soon.

* * *

Carisa's shifting body brought her mother back. Elena turned to check on her daughter. She was taking her children away from everyone they knew and loved. But what did they know? What had their lives become? Raised voices and accusations and the constant struggle between their mother and grandmother? Elena had had to fight just to keep her children her own. Zenobia wasn't satisfied with being "Abuela." She had demanded that the children call her "Mamá Grande." No, these were Elena's children and they would be raised her way, in their own home, and she would do whatever she had to, to guarantee it—even if that meant taking them away from their father. She was right. She knew she was right. She had to be right.

* * *

Toño waited until she had picked up the tickets at the airline counter and gotten all the baggage checked in. He had never been a man of many words and he had even fewer to offer now.

"*M'hija*, your mother has one half of my heart and you the other. It is breaking."

"No, Papá, I think it is just beginning to heal."

Elena clung to him until the baby started to cry. Pulling away from him was painful. She stroked Toño's face and brushed her hand over his white hair. When had all the black grown out of it?

"*Última llamada para el vuelo doscientos setenta y cuatro Trans Caribbean con destino al Nueva York.*" Final call; they had no more time.

"*Bendición,* Papá."

"May God go with you, *m'hija.*"

She adjusted Danilo on her arm, grabbed Carisa's hand, and walked away quickly.

* * *

Elena settled Carisa into the window seat and focused on making Danilo comfortable. She tried not to look back at the gate, where she knew Toño would be waving a white handkerchief. She squeezed her eyes shut.

"Look, Mami...big fans."

The huge propeller blades were beginning to spin. Beyond the wing was the terminal building, and she could see a tiny white speck at the gate. It was cut off from her intermittently as the propeller blade cut across her field of vision. Her father looked so small, his freshly starched shirt gleaming in the sun. Elena wished Concha had come with them to the airport. At least then he wouldn't look so alone.

She felt the plane pulling forward and then she was looking down on the terminal, a diminishing shoebox of a building interrupting a wide band of palm trees anchored to the white ribbon of a beach on either side. She let the whoop, whoop, whoop of the blades take her off to the place in her head where the palm trees, trembling with her pain, loosened their roots and took flight after her, tiny green umbrellas pulled in the wake of the metal bird.

* * *

By the time the plane landed six hours later at Idlewild International Airport in New York City, the children had fallen asleep out of pure exhaustion and Elena was totally drained. As hard as she had tried to arrive at their new home in their best clothes and brightest smiles, a six-hour flight with a fretting baby and an airsick toddler had left her feeling rumpled and tired. Thank God Marcelina and her husband, Fonso, would take them to a warm and comfortable home. She knew she could drop all her baggage at Marci's door until she could get on her feet.

But she wasn't ready for the scene that met her in the terminal. It was a huge space filled with masses of people. They rushed in all directions, intent on their destinations. Elena stood dumbfounded. They spoke a rapid-fire English that bore no resemblance to what she had learned in school. Carisa pulled at her skirt. The child needed a bathroom. Elena reached out to a uniformed woman who had trouble understanding her. Finally, the woman led her to the bathroom door.

After she had cleaned up as much as possible, Elena found her way back to the gate, praying she hadn't missed Marcelina. She looked around. This place seemed so alien. There were no colors here— no dancing reds or bouncing yellows or singing greens. People wore moribund black, sleepy browns, tired grays, as if a malevolent spirit had drained all the color out of their clothes. How could this place ever feel like home?

Elena searched the room. Her eyes darted up and down the gate area. *Marcelina, where are you?* Where could she possibly be? *Cálmate. She'll be here in a minute, ¡paciencia!* She looked down at her children and thanked God for them, the only familiar sight in this place. She tried to calm her fears by caressing their small bodies. The one thing she wanted most was to look up and find herself surrounded by the known, Marcelina's brown face and warm smile welcoming them. But the time passed, and still no Marci.

The passengers from her flight were long gone. Relatives claimed the arriving passengers and went on their way. The arrivals area slowly emptied out. Even the staff at the gate had packed up their papers and gone on their way. An hour later, Elena was still sitting by the gate. Marcelina couldn't possibly have forgotten. Elena started toward the telephone only to remember that she had packed her address book in her luggage. The luggage!

The only thing more frightening than the mass of rushing people was the silence of the empty baggage area. She looked at the many signs and finally found the one she thought she understood. Relieved, she spotted her luggage neatly piled in the center of a small room. Four suitcases and three cardboard boxes with their ropes and wrappers more or less intact. She let herself down heavily on the largest of the suitcases and put her baby down on her lap. Danilo's round legs dangled. Carisa climbed onto another suitcase, leaned her head on her mother's thighs and closed her eyes, her thick braids now crooked in their wilted bows.

Elena caught a glimpse of herself in a nearby mirror: a too-thin young woman, her white linen suit now stained and wrinkled, her hat askew on her head, her lipstick smudged, traces of makeup here and there. Thick ladders ran up her stockings where they had snagged hours before. Zenobia's voice came back to her. *She's too proud. Always wants to be better than everyone else. She'll learn her lesson. I only hope I'm alive to see it.* The woman in the mirror now sat with her suitcases and her sleeping children, and two long trails of tears sliding down her smudged makeup.

";Mírala, allí! Elena, Elena, aquí, aquí vengo." Marcelina's voice cut through her misery. When Elena looked up and saw her friend's round face under her flower-trimmed red hat, she felt the sun come back into her world.

19 OUR NEW HOME

Elena watched her children in the blue moonlight shining through their bedroom window. Marcelina had given them a room for themselves. Their little bodies huddled together under the quilt. She slid in and they immediately molded themselves around her body. She needed their warmth as much as they needed her protection. When their breathing had returned to the rhythm of sleep and the apartment was quiet, she opened the door to guilt and let out the voices she had been holding at bay for days.

Are you crazy? You can't do that! Did you think about this carefully? What do you know about New York? How good is your English? I'm warning you...you've got a good job...how are you going to make do with two kids and no husband? What will people say? You know how she'll end up! There are no morals up there...go with God...I envy you, *mujer*. She'll find herself another man in no time. That's what this is all about. Just wait and see! They all do...so stubborn...so vain...so proud...always thought she was too good for us...just has to go up north! My advice is...a good wife endures...think it over again...are you ready for the cold? Where will you work? Reconsider...you'll be back! You don't fool me! You'll fail...you'll fail...you'll fail...

A wail grew in the distance. It kept growing and growing until it filled her head and snatched her away from the voices.

"Nooo!" She sat up in the strange dark room, her children still tucked into the blankets beside her. She was thankful her cry hadn't awoken them.

At first light, Elena slipped out from under the quilt and went to the window. White crystals had formed on the edges of the panes. Icicles, like transparent knives, hung from the iron railings that ran down the side of the building. Fire escapes, they called them. She dug in her bag and pulled out the diary she hadn't touched in years. She needed an old friend and she found it in the pages of her journal.

¿Qué hago yo aquí? No husband, no home, shivering in someone else's box of a home, high in the sky over a refrigerator of a city. Sleep finally shut off the look of confusion playing just beneath the trust in their eyes. Mami, the woman who's supposed to protect them, is now the woman who has taken them away from their Papi. They trust me but "the cold itches me, Mami. Make it stop." They love me but, "Mami, when are we going home?" and "Mami, where's Papi?" and "Why are we here?" Good questions. A better one would be, will we ever have a home again? And where?

I had to leave. Is it all selfishness? Is it only about me, my own needs, my own unhappiness? Unhappy wife, unhappy mother…or is the only consideration happy children? Which heart do I follow? Come here and rob them of their father? Stay there and let their mother die a slow death? That's what it would be. It would be killing the person I am and ultimately losing my children to her as well. No! Zenobia wants Pedro? She can have him. But she can't have me and she can't have my children! I won't let her…I'll freeze here first.

* * *

Everything seemed backward here. The bathtub sat in the kitchen, a big white boat of a thing on claw feet. It was the first thing you saw as you came in the door. There was a long metal sheet that fit over it when it wasn't in use. Marci covered it with a nice throw and used it as a table, but there was really no way to camouflage it.

The toilet was down the hallway that ran along the outside of the apartment. It was shared by all four families on the floor. You had to listen for the flushes and then rush in carrying everything you needed with you, because when you actually got in there, there was never any toilet paper and usually no lightbulb, either. Somebody on the floor kept stealing it and the super was refusing to replace it. So they carried their own bulb or did their business in the dark. Elena made sure Carisa didn't drink anything after dinner because those late-night trips down the hall were scary even for a grown woman. One night there was a strange man waiting as Elena came out of the bathroom. He refused to move aside. In fact, he made sure he was close enough to smell her as she pushed past him. She was terrified, and when she found that no one of that description lived on the floor, she vowed never to go out there after dark again. She improvised an emergency bedpan for herself and the children. Who would've believed she had left her comfortable home for this?

When Elena watched the children, arms around each other, gently snoring, she envied them their closeness. In spite of all the scenes, of the many arguments that had forced her to flee that house, she still loved Pedro and longed for his warmth.

Elena remembered that last, long walk to the car—with every step she prayed he would come after her and promise that they would have their own lives. She wanted him to turn to Zenobia and tell her that he chose his wife and children; that she, Zenobia, would have to find a life of her own because she couldn't have theirs. Every step she took toward the car was a plea, a hope, a prayer for that. But then there was the car door and the loaded suitcases. That had been the longest walk, and the loneliest. The truth was, he had been willing to let her go.

* * *

Fonso stayed with the children while Marci and Elena went out to get some things. *La Marqueta* was the major shopping area in the neighborhood. Rather than one store, it was really a series of long barnlike structures housing one after another stall of tropical fruits and vegetables, lingerie, school supplies, over-the-counter drugs, costume jewelry, dozens of varieties of rice and beans in huge barrels, ladies' clothes, men's work clothes, fresh meats, and cosmetics. The air was filled with the pungent odors of *bacalao*, smoked meats, and an array of fresh and dried *manzanilla, ruda, tilo, rompe saragüey, anamú*, and *verbena*. Elena recognized the medicinal herbs Abuela Mati had grown in their garden so many years ago, here transformed into crates of dry leaves and brittle stalks.

One stall in particular stopped Elena in her tracks. A dozen bodies, mostly women, vied for their place on the line that was constantly moving in front of the crowded display. Behind the counter stood row after row of giant religious statues, figures smiling down in beneficence at shipwrecked sailors, or upward at a presumed heaven. There were framed pictures of an open palm with a huge eye in the center and tiny images floating over each finger. There were crudely carved statues of African drummers and scores of dolls, rotund figures dressed in bright colors—yellow, red, blue, green. Overhead hung hundreds of beaded necklaces, rosaries, and amulets. And the stall was almost blocked from view by the crowd, waving bills and shoving for the next place in front of the vendor. Her faded memories of Mati's room with its candles and its incense crystallized into sharp focus. It felt as though she had walked backward in time into an achingly physical reality. Elena was rooted to the spot.

Marci had to pull her away to the next barn with its stalls of outerwear. Elena reluctantly followed, taking the image of this stall with her. Even the blast of frigid air that hit them as they went from one structure to the next didn't erase the familiar images. Suddenly, she longed for her Abuela Mati more than she had in years.

* * *

With the warm clothes the children stopped shivering and returned to their usual playfulness. Although Cari still asked about her Papi, there were so many new and strange things to distract her that Elena had little trouble turning this episode in their lives into an adventure.

At the first fresh snow, they were so excited that Cari couldn't wait to eat breakfast and get dressed in her new clothes so she could go outside. For a while she just watched the other children, but soon she was playing in the snow along with her new friends. But Dani, who started crying as soon as he felt the cold on his face, clutched his mother until she took him back inside. Elena sat at the window, a shaken baby in her lap, watching Marci join a snowball fight. She remembered Marci as a young girl, running and laughing in the sun, and was thankful for her old friend.

* * *

Although the warm clothes helped, they all came down with severe colds. Danilo especially was miserable with his congestion and constant cough. Elena went up and down the drugstore aisle and finally bought a huge bottle of aspirin. Then she headed for *La Marqueta*, where she stood on line with the other women and waited to pay for the herbs she knew would work.

Her diary became her constant confidant.

> Thank God, Danilo is much better. He's been sleeping quietly the last few nights. Today the fever broke. He murmured "Papi" in his sleep. Carisa sucked on her thumb. She hasn't done that in a long time.
>
> I climbed in between them. It was the least I could do. Keep them safe and warm and comfortable now that I have brought them here. But I couldn't find my own sleep.
>
> I lay awake for hours, staring at the semidarkness of the room, listening to the passing traffic and the distant wail of a police siren—or was it an ambulance? I still can't tell the difference. I just know that it's not

good. The night sounds died away into an eerie silence and still I sought answers among the cracks and shadows that lived in the ceiling. When I finally fell asleep, I had the oddest dream.

A woman was walking down a steep and narrow path on the side of a mountain. She walked barefooted and unprotected in the whipping wind. The slippery rocks along the way were beautiful but dangerous in their thin coating of ice. She stopped, unsure of whether to continue or to turn back to a presumably safe zone. The fact that she couldn't see her destination down the twisted path immobilized her more than the cold itself.

I woke up with a start, shivering even under the blankets. I was confused for a moment until I remembered. I pulled the children closer and rearranged the covers. Then I watched the sun rise through the bars on the window.

* * *

After the children dropped off to sleep, Marci and Fonso went to the movies. No sooner had she closed the door behind them than Elena's thoughts rushed in on her. She wondered where Pedro was at that moment and what he was doing. *Does he miss us? Is he eating well? How does he feel going home to an empty bed?* She managed to put aside these thoughts during the day, but at night she was defenseless.

Still no word from Pedro. Zenobia plays her role so well: the helpless widow, the lonely mother who gave up everything for her son, the defenseless woman in a cruel and hostile world! I'm sick of the whole thing! The woman is a snake!

I got a letter from Papá. They were happy to hear from me. I tried to make our lives here sound exciting and new and left out all my fears and frustrations. But I think he read between the lines and is worried about us. He says that everything there is fine. Mamá sends her love. She's not much of a writer, he says. I'm not surprised. We had so little to say when we lived together, what could we write now that we are apart? The business of mending is hard enough in person. It's almost impossible on paper. Still, it was great to get the letter, my first one. I can almost hear Papá's voice when I read the words.

Elena had had to put aside the problems she left behind for the needs of her current situation. Life in New York City was not cheap, and Elena's savings were running dangerously low. Marci and Fonso were great. They never asked for money, but Elena was becoming desperate for a job. Marci had put out the word all over the neighborhood. She took Elena down to see Doña Felicia, the wife of the *bodeguero*, who worked in the kitchen at a place called Flower and Fifth Hospital. The woman said she'd talk to the nursing supervisor. But weeks passed and Elena was never called.

Then there was Herminia Torres from apartment 2A, who had a cousin whose sister worked at a place called Pleasant Valley Home, in the Bronx. They didn't need a nurse but they could use an aide immediately. Elena swallowed her pride. A job was a job. She'd have to work the night shift, which turned out to be perfect because she could be with the children all day and Marci could babysit while Elena was at work. Things seemed to be looking up.

I've been working for several weeks now, and I confess, it hasn't been easy. Some nurses laugh at my accent and the doctors pretend they don't understand me. There are many nurses from other countries here who know just what I'm going through. Some forgot how they were treated when they came and are the worst tormentors. People don't seem to have any problem understanding Italian and Polish accents and they even understand the Spanish accents of the Puerto Rican porters. But when it comes to me, suddenly they don't understand what I'm saying.

I'm as good a nurse as any of them but they give me the worst jobs, the jobs for orderlies. Sometimes I have to bite my lips to keep from screaming. But I hold my tongue. Pride won't buy milk. I seal my pride with silence. I picture Cari and Dani when I have to empty bedpans and change sheets and take away trays of human waste. Every day, I show up for work in my starched uniform, my shoes spotless. I've made a few friends who are supportive and encourage me. One day things will be better, they say. I have to believe them.

On the day she received her first New York City paycheck, Elena rushed home. It wasn't much but she was thankful. She could support her children now. She wouldn't have to run back home defeated. How many times had she been tempted? She might have given in on any one of those days when she had dragged herself home spent and exhausted after a double shift of emptying bed pans and putting up with ill-tempered patients. She went into her room, closed the door, and danced around the bed, all the while holding her paycheck. She felt like laughing for the first time in a long time.

A few days later she got a telegram. She set the black and yellow envelope on the table and eyed it. Telegrams were always bad news. Marci put down the cooking spoon and joined her at the table. Elena hesitated. She took several deep breaths and finally reached for the envelope. When she finished reading the paper, she dropped it and ran into her room. Marci was frightened, *"¿Pero qué pasa, mujer? ¿Qué pasó?"* She picked up the telegram and sighed, relieved that it was good news. Pedro would arrive in two days.

20 TURBULENCE

Marci got up at dawn to press Elena's hair. It was shiny with bergamot as she smoothed it into shape, making sure the curls bounced around Elena's face. The blue or the red dress? Or maybe the new brown tweed. He'd never seen her in anything like that. So she picked that and looked at herself in the mirror. She'd lost a few pounds. She'd always prided herself on her curves. Now they were mostly gone. What would he see? New clothes, a new woman. No, same woman. She hoped he'd see that she had managed, that she was a survivor. But also that she was the old Elena, the young woman who had fallen in love with him all those years ago, who still loved him and needed him. She didn't know why he had taken so long, but was so glad he'd finally chosen her.

She went to the bathroom four times as they waited for the flight. When she returned the last time, the plane had already landed. Pedro stood surrounded by the children and Fonso and Marci. She watched him from a distance before running up to put her arms around him. She clung to him, right there at the arrivals gate. They blocked traffic. People were staring but she didn't care. She hadn't realized that much of the cold she'd been feeling had nothing to do with the climate. When Pedro put his arms around her, she felt like she was home again. He even smelled like home. She didn't know what would happen but whatever it was, it would happen to them together. Just the two of them and the children.

* * *

When the children were finally asleep, Elena and Pedro lay in bed holding each other. Elena closed her eyes and felt Pedro's arms warm and strong around her shoulders. She settled into him, but there was an awkwardness now that hadn't been there before. In the silence of the night, the questions that had been lying in wait suddenly took shape, like a photograph coming into focus. The unasked and unanswered questions that had lived within her for weeks now lay in the bed between them. She didn't want to spoil the moment but she heard her voice before she could catch the words.

Her voice said, "I waited for your letters."

No answer.

"I thought you had forgotten about us."

Silence.

Then something broke, "Did you care? Was it so hard to write?"

The questions spilled out, and she waited, praying for an answer that would wash away the resentment and allow the darkness to enfold them in intimacy rather than alienation. When there was no answer, she pulled out of his arms and searched his face.

Finally, he said. "It was you…you who walked out. So calmly…like our marriage meant nothing anymore. Then, for weeks, every night when I went to our empty bed, all I heard was the sound of your heels receding into the distance."

She opened her mouth to respond but nothing came out. How many times had she told him of her unhappiness? How many times had he not listened? How could he not remember all the fights, all the tears, all the slammed doors?

He was still talking. "Suddenly you were walking away, just like that. I didn't even have a chance to…you took my son, my children. I thought about it a long time. I discussed it with Mamá."

There she was again. Zenobia standing between them.

"And what was your mother's advice?"

"Mamá is Mamá." He went on, "But I made my choice. I chose my family. I chose you. Let's leave it at that." He pulled her close again.

Elena felt like he was trying to squeeze away her questions. He had silenced her mouth but her mind was awhirl. She tried to look beyond the words, listen for the fine shadings of meaning. What was it she heard—hesitancy, reluctance, resignation, duty? Why didn't she hear joy? It started in her chest, the tightening and pulling. She shifted her weight. Her husband was here now. He wanted her. He wanted their children. She was a lucky woman. Why wasn't she satisfied? What more did she want?

Elena, too, made a choice. She would push away the nagging worry. She would start their new lives together with a clean slate. The past would be the past. They would build for the future. She turned to her newly arrived husband and welcomed him into their new life.

* * *

Fonso had worked for years in the loading docks in the garment district. His bosses liked him because he was a strong quiet man who got to work on time and caused no trouble. He knew Pedro would need a job soon and was more than willing to help.

"*Compá*, I know it's not fancy but it pays the rent." The offer was heartfelt.

"*Gracias, compay*, I'll let you know."

Fonso was a simple man but he knew when an offer had been thrown back in his face.

"Whenever you're ready."

* * *

Elena watched as, day after day, Pedro got up, shined his two-toned cordovans, and brushed off his beige linen pinstriped suit that was too warm back home. The light fabric played well against his deep skin. But his stylish clothes clashed with his heavyweight winter coat and fedora that made him look off-kilter, like a slice of pineapple on a plate of steak and potatoes.

"How do I look?"

It was late February. She looked at her husband, who was looking for work in lightweight summer attire. Elena knew enough to bite her tongue.

But as the weeks went by, it became obvious that Pedro wasn't seriously considered for the type of downtown job he had been seeking. His countless telephone inquiries had ended in hang-ups. Doors had been slammed in his face. Prospective meetings ended in cancelled appointments. Even when he got interviews, they ended prematurely because of his language limitations.

Week after week, Elena watched her proud husband become more silent and morose. She tried to be supportive and encouraging, but it was obvious that he wasn't going to get the kind of job he wanted. She was careful not to say anything that might sound critical. But she could see this was taking its toll on him. Not even the children cheered him up anymore.

One day she walked in on Pedro and Fonso talking in whispers. She couldn't imagine what they were being so secretive about. But she was glad to see Pedro taking some interest in what was happening around him. He took the children out for a long walk and came back at dinnertime.

When she went into their bedroom, Pedro was sitting on the bed, rocking, one fist beating into the palm of his other hand each time he rocked forward. She leaned on the dresser opposite him and waited.

"Tomorrow, I'm going in with Fonso. All those years of school for this? Sweeping floors and unpacking boxes?"

She looked down at her chapped hands and could almost smell the disinfectant on her fingers.

"*Sabes*, Pedro, all day long I clean up other people's vomit and empty out their bedpans. They call me a nurse's aide, emphasis on 'aide,' not 'nurse.' I'm just a pair of hands to them—no mind, no brain. I do as I am told.

"I choose not to hear the snickering every time I mispronounce words. I put up with the whispered remarks. They think if we don't speak perfect English we must be stupid.

"I do it because I have two children who need to eat. I do this because it is the life I chose for them. I am responsible. So I bite my tongue and put up with the indignities I have to swallow every day."

She could see the pulsing in his neck. He still sat rocking, hands opening, closing, opening. Then he swung around and pounded the pillows, over and over again. "*¡Qué mierda, carajo!*"

She thought about the many times she had wanted to hit somebody or something, anything. How many times did she hide in the utility closet so they wouldn't see her tears of frustration?

She saw the veins standing out in his temples and walked over and massaged the throbbing there. Then she straddled his lap facing him and sat there rocking back and forth, holding him, trying to soothe away his and her own bitter disappointment.

* * *

Pedro worked for three months before hearing the worse words in the English language—"laid off." He had never been crazy about his job but he made do. Then one day he came home in the middle of the day. At first he refused to talk, but later he told Elena what had happened. The manager's cousin had come from Italy two weeks before and he needed a job. The manager put him to work side-by-side with Pedro. Everything was fine until the owner showed up and said he didn't need two men to do the same job. The manager, who had praised Pedro for his work just a few weeks ago, now said that Pedro was lazy and that he had been forced to hire his cousin to help Pedro get the work done. So Pedro was out.

Things were bad, and finding a new job was almost impossible. Pedro asked everybody they knew about any kind of job. He started helping out in the *bodega*, but that brought in just a few dollars here and there. The *bodega* became the community social center, with its constant dominoes game and the steady parade of unemployed men. After a few weeks there was no more pretense of job hunting. Pedro had settled into a comfortable life of beer drinking and dominoes playing with his *panitas* during the day and into the night. Elena was still working the night shift. Often, she went to sleep to an empty bed while he spent time with his jobless friends. Things weren't going well. First there was the fighting, and later the silence that grew between them became unbearable.

* * *

One Saturday night Elena woke to an unexpectedly cold room. She automatically felt for the radiator, which was ice-cold. She looked out the window to find late-night snow had blanketed the cars up and down the street. The children surrounded by their parents' bodies hadn't stirred, but when she touched Dani's forehead he was burning up.

"Pedro, wake up, it's freezing in here."

"Aha." Pedro agreed in his sleep, turned over, and continued snoring.

Elena, fueled by the memory of Dani's awful colds of the previous winter, quickly pulled more blankets from the closet and piled as many as she could on her sleeping family. Then she went into the bathroom and filled the hot-water bottle, wrapped it in towels, and slid it between the two children, making sure to warm Dani's chest. She didn't like the sound of his breathing but tried not to panic.

The next morning Elena took the baby to the doctor. He had been coughing all night. The doctor listened to Dani's lungs and assured her that it was a simple cold. Baby aspirin and warm clothes should make him right as rain. But Elena was only partially reassured. She kept a close eye on Danilo in the house and called often while at work. Pedro never left his son's side.

They had three days of winter frost. During that time, the super refused to turn up the furnace. It was March, and he wasn't about to make the landlord angry by wasting expensive coal at this time of the year. Besides, this snow was a fluke. The temperature was sure to rise in a few hours. But it never did.

Meanwhile, the family huddled around the gas stove and turned on all the heaters they had. They lived in the kitchen, the warmest room in the apartment. Still, they couldn't keep warm. By the third day, Dani's fever was dangerously high and he was having difficulty breathing. He barely moved. Elena and Pedro finally rushed to the hospital, their baby boy dressed in all his winter clothes and wrapped in multiple blankets.

They waited for three hours in the emergency room while the staff took care of the bleeding and dying. By the time they got to Dani, the doctors rushed to admit him. Elena sat by his hospital bed, holding his hand and watching helplessly as he lay under the oxygen tent. She wanted to hold him, give him her warmth, and blow her life's breath into his limp body. But he needed the oxygen more than he needed her touch. So she settled for holding his hand and watching for the slightest change in his breathing. That night, Dani's breathing became so labored that the staff pushed Pedro and Elena outside while they worked on the baby.

She and Pedro sat in the waiting room without touching or speaking as they counted the minutes. The doctor finally came down the hall.

"Nothing more we can do for him right now. We'll have to wait and see."

Nothing more we can do. Yes, thought Elena. *I've done enough already.* She thought about how cold Dani had been lately. She thought about how warm it was at home at that very moment.

Pedro said nothing, but she knew what he was thinking. *This is your fault. You brought our son here to die. Are you satisfied now?*

"Why don't you go home and get some rest?" The nurse had a kind face. Elena had said the same thing to so many families so many times. But she couldn't go back to the apartment. The bench in the waiting room became her home. She spent the night there, sitting next to Pedro, neither of them saying a word. But she could feel his resentment like a breathing being growing within him.

Elena had asked Marci to bring her her diary along with a change of clothes. The next morning, Pedro went home to change and Marci brought Elena the things she had asked for. Since Elena felt she couldn't talk to her husband, she had to find someplace to store her words. And once again, her journal was her refuge.

> Danilo is burning up, weak, not even coughing much anymore. I felt him slipping away from me. He looked so tiny in that hospital bed. And I feel so helpless.
>
> What can I do? I pray until my bloody knees grind into the bathroom tiles and still I kneel. My voice is hoarse and I pray in my head. I've cried until my eyes dry. Is it me? Is it my fault? Is this my punishment? Losing my boy? What have I done to deserve losing my baby?
>
> Dear God, I've said two hundred Our Fathers. I'm up to my ninetieth Hail Mary. I've forgotten the other prayers, but you know they're in my heart. I've run out of words. What can I offer you? Candles? I'll light a thousand of them in your cathedral. I'll do anything, anything, but please save my son.
>
> He's just a baby. Has just come into this world. Has done nothing. Nothing. It was *me*, my choice that has brought him to this.

But as much as Elena prayed, the child never recovered. She was so distraught; she didn't know what to do with the grief and the guilt, the twins that were born in her heart when Dani died. Pedro seemed so distant. There was no reaching him. So she took her pain inside and nurtured it in silence. She turned more and more inward as Pedro turned further and further away. His days began and ended away from the apartment. After a while, that seemed to make it more bearable for them both. Elena turned to her only outlet.

They put my baby in the ground. It was so cold they couldn't break into the soil. How can he sleep down there, in that frozen hole?

Where is my boy? I hear his raspy breathing. His tiny voice, "Mami, I hurt."

I looked in the mirror today. There is a woman there who looks like me but she has gray hair. Mamá?

Today I woke up to find Carisa looking at me. She said, "Mami, when are you coming back?" My eyes were so tired. I closed them and searched for Dani. Cari's voice followed me, "Mami? Mami, come back." Then there was darkness, merciful darkness.

It is too quiet now. I can't find Dani's voice anymore. Where has he gone? What will he do without me? What will I do without him?

It is nighttime. Pedro is sleeping. Is that a smile on his face? How could he? He wakes up dry-eyed and says little. But he points accusing eyes at me. I see that Marci and Fonso find it difficult to be in the same room with us.

Pedro turns to the wall for solace. Lucky him, to find such relief. Last night, I got an idea as I turned and faced the window. I wanted to fly out and find my baby. Maybe that's my solace. Maybe I don't belong here anymore. I wonder how far I would have to fall...then Carisa stirred, and mumbled something. Still asleep, she reached for me. I pulled her closer.

The warmth of my body seemed to soothe her. When she settled back into a peaceful sleep, I got up and closed the window.

The silence that moved in between Pedro and Elena grew to monstrous proportions, feeding on the grief they each felt. When it couldn't be contained anymore, the silence exploded into words, accusations bursting in the spaces between them.

It started so innocently.

Elena said, "Pedro, we can't go on like this. Let's talk."

"I have nothing to say."

"Pedro, *por favor*, we haven't talked in weeks."

"And I suppose it's all my fault?"

"I don't know...you...I—"

"Look, Elena, please, leave me alone." He didn't trust words. "Don't push it."

"Why not push it? Who are you? What are you? I live with a ghost. Where is the man I married? What have you done with him?"

"What?"

He had tried to avoid this. But now it was too late. Something broke inside. "Why don't you ask yourself where is the woman *I* thought I married? Better yet, you tell me who you are and what you did to my son. Where's my son now, the one you took away from our home and brought to this hellish place to die? Is that what you wanted all along, to take the most valuable thing in my life? No, I won't forgive you. You killed my son just as surely as if you had set him out there to freeze. I want my son back. Can you give him back? No? Then what is there to talk about?"

They were out. The stunning blast of words hung between them, a moment of quiet before the final eruption. Everything stopped. Then she crumbled onto the bed. Someone was shrieking. She looked up. Who was that woman in the mirror, the one ripping her clothes, the one who knelt on the bed, breasts exposed, arms flailing, tear-stained face contorted into a mask, ineffectual fingers curling into claws? The howling continued, drawn-out animal noises that filled the room and then the apartment.

Pedro, who had moved into his own grief, had lashed out without restraint. He had emptied himself of all the pain and misery of the past. But now, seeing the result of his outburst, he feared for his wife's sanity.

There was beating at the door.

"Elena, *¿qué pasa?*" Marci's voice was heavy with fear.

"*¿Qué pasó? Compay*, let's talk. You and me." Fonso was trying to be calm.

"Pedro, Elena, *¡por Dios!*"

"Open the door, *compay*." Fonso's voice had an edge.

"Pedro, think of Cari. Lower your voices…the neighbors, the police." Marci tried everything she could think of to defuse the situation. "Please, open the door."

Elena was now wailing. The man tried to restrain the woman in the mirror, his face contorted as well.

Finally, Pedro maneuvered his arms around her as she tore at her hair and screamed into his face. "Elena, stop! Control yourself… *Cálmate. Stop it!*"

He wouldn't let go, pinning her arms so she couldn't hurt herself anymore. He pushed her down into the mattress and used his body to hold her. Still she fought him.

"I'm not letting go until you calm down."

"Mami"—Carisa's voice squeezed through the door—"Mami, who's hurting you? Why are you crying? Mami, open the door. I'll take care of you, Mami…please." The child's pleading, her tiny voice, got through to her mother. Elena could hear Cari's pain even through her own.

Little by little Elena's cries slowed. Her rigid body began to loosen and finally went limp from exertion. She was too exhausted to fight him anymore. Pedro relaxed his arms and finally slipped them away. Then each of them lay crying. They cried for their dead son, for their dying marriage, for destroyed dreams. They lay across the same bed, but their thoughts lived in different worlds. They did have one thing in common. Each knew that something had been broken that night and neither knew how to fix it.

Pedro sleeps on his side of the bed and I sleep on mine and there is a big space in between where Danilo sleeps.

Danilo visits me in many disguises in my dreams. He lies on the bedspread after his bath. He plays with his fingers, trying to catch the sunlight as it streams down on him. I oil him all over, sprinkle powder on his bottom, and dress him in his pajamas. He is covered in tiny teddy bears playing baseball. He smiles as I pick him up, and reaches for my earrings. A shadow falls across the window, leaving us in darkness. When it passes I am holding an empty garment. It holds the shape. I feel Danilo's weight in my arms, the warmth in the cloth. I smell his clean hair. But my baby is gone. I don't know what snatched me out of my dream. I wipe my face and lie back down. Pedro is still snoring.

He's a young man now. He's tall and husky and strong. His jaw is covered in soft stubble. He's in a dark and empty room. There are no windows or doors. Just the sound of him pacing. He covers the length of the room and then back again. His speed increases. Frustration bunches up in his shoulders, in his face, his fists. He suddenly stops and pounds his fists into the wall until his knuckles are raw, until he leaves bloody prints on the surface. He screams until he runs out of energy and slumps onto the floor, motionless but for the heavy breathing. Time passes. He gets up and starts again, walking, pacing, going nowhere. Shouting at the walls, the floor, the ceiling. His voice becomes raspy, pained. Again he punches the walls, pounds out his anguish before the pacing continues...

He's a toddler lost in a snowstorm. His skin is gray white. He's not scared, only lonely and always cold and determined. He stumbles along on unsure legs. There are many feet around him. He searches for familiar white shoes. Red patent-leather sandals, red painted toenails peeking out. He moves on. Burnt brown wing-tipped cordovans. No. Not them. The child moves on, shivering under the falling flakes. Laced boots, scarred and spotted with paint. Unfamiliar. He falls over and catches himself: his hand is almost crushed under the scuffed work boots. He continues looking. But the tied white shoes he has been searching for are hard to find against the white of the snow, as is his pasty skin. As the snow continues to fall, they continue to miss each other.

What day is it today? What was it I was going to write? I forget.

Carisa climbed into my lap the other day while I sat at the table. Was it yesterday or maybe this morning? She took the spoon from my plate and fed me a cold dinner. I looked at her. Then I chewed.

* * *

Marci was worried. For the third night she watched as Elena sat, looking at her plate. Carisa was about to reach for her mother's spoon once again when Marci stopped her.

"Mami will eat on her own today. You go watch your *Looney Tunes*."

The child hesitated, not convinced.

"It's okay, Cari, I'll stay with Mami until she's finished."

Reluctantly, the little girl climbed down and went into the other room. Marci waited until she heard the television go on.

"Elena, *mírame*." She grabbed her friend's jaw, and forced Elena to look into her eyes. "I've known you my whole life, so I have the right to say what's on my mind. You may not like it but you're going to listen. Who told you you could climb down into that grave with one child and leave the other to fend for herself—worse, to take care of what's left of you?"

No reaction.

"She's only a little girl. You're supposed to take care of her, not the other way around. Or have you given up being a mother to the one child you have left?"

Elena smiled and lifted her hand to stroke Marci's face.

Marci slapped it away, "I don't need that! Look after Cari. *She's* the one that needs you. Or have you forgotten her altogether? I never thought you'd become a *malamadre.*"

The word put a crack in Elena's wall. *"Mala—"*

"For the first time in all these years, I'm ashamed of you. When that child needs you the most, you abandon her."

The words were ruthless, machine-gunning into Elena's brain, *abandonar* and *malamadre.* Marci went on ruthlessly.

"Zenobia raising your child? Is that what you want?"

"No!" Fear flashed across Elena's face.

"Well, that's exactly what'll happen if you don't wake up. Pedro will take her home to his mother. Zenobia will win and you'll lose your daughter forever."

Finally, the words broke through. Elena tried to put her world into some recognizable order. Marci watched for a moment before turning to the sink. "I have work to do." But every part of her listened to make sure she hadn't gone too far. She prayed she had done the right thing. And then she felt Elena's hands as they pulled the dish out of her hand and began drying it off.

* * *

Elena started having her meals with Carisa. Then, she started cooking for the family. She helped with the cleaning and, after a while, she did neighborhood errands, going to the Laundromat, the post office, and the supermarket.

Pedro finally found a job, pressing hats in a factory in Hartford, Connecticut. He left on Sunday nights with a carload of other men who couldn't find work in New York City. They shared a room in Hartford during the week and came home on the weekends. For the first several weekends, Pedro chose to stay in Hartford, "time-and-a-half pay," he said. But Elena knew better. Each Friday night there was a knock on Marci's apartment door and one of the Hartford men handed Elena an envelope with money for the week's expenses. There was usually a short note, "for the groceries," "for ConEd," "for the telephone." But the silences were just as thick on paper as they had been in their room.

21 REBUILDING

It was Carisa's birthday and the child was impossibly excited. Cari had planned everything: what she would wear, what her mother would wear, the type and flavor of her cake, and how many and what color balloons. Elena tried to give the child her every wish. She put on the child's favorite dress and makeup and stopped before the mirror. She had lost weight and the dress hung loose. But the makeup covered the dark circles under her eyes and the red lipstick gave her face a lift. She found her smile for the party, painted and shaky but a beginning. Maybe this was her way back: Create the illusion and reality would follow.

Weeks later she got an unexpected call from the Flower and Fifth Hospital. A new supervisor had reviewed her credentials and was offering her a position on the nursing staff. Finally, Elena would get the recognition and respect she had craved. She gratefully accepted the position. They needed the money. She felt much stronger, and work would force her to focus outside herself. Unfortunately, the only opening was in the obstetrics and gynecology division. She convinced herself that sooner or later she would have to take this step. But inwardly she dreaded delivering other women's babies into their arms when hers were still so empty.

* * *

One night Elena heard Cari talking to herself only to find that the child was fast asleep. The murmuring continued into the night and was the last thing Elena remembered as she fell asleep. The next morning, as she put a bowl of cereal in front of Cari, she asked the child if she had had a bad dream.

"No, Mami, I was just talking to my Lady."

More than once Elena had wondered if Cari created this imaginary friend out of loneliness, to counteract her mother's distraction of the past weeks. A sliver of guilt started growing in her.

"And what were you talking about with 'your' Lady?"

"I've told her how unhappy you are and she told me to tell you to look to the stone." Carisa took a spoonful of cereal.

Elena stopped midthought. "What did you say?" Cari repeated herself. The girl said "stone," not pebble or rock, but "stone." Why was this triggering something in Elena?

"What stone, Cari?"

Cari took a swallow of her milk before answering. "I don't know, Mami. She said you'd know." She dived back into the bowl.

Elena stared at her daughter and tried to place the uncomfortable feeling in her chest. The thought played in her head all day until she got into bed that night. *Mamá's stone!* Elena remembered the stone in the pouch that Concha had pressed on her just before her departure. She remembered the stone's effect on Concha in the hospital. And then she remembered Mati's stories. Elena had almost forgotten. Magic, she had once believed. Elena lay back in bed and thought about all the years and all the stories. She got out of bed and searched the dusty suitcases until she found it. Elena sniffed at the old pouch and could almost imagine herself back in her mother's house—the smell of freesia. Slipping under the covers, she fell asleep holding the stone. For the first time in weeks, Elena slept the night through without dreams or interruptions.

Yesterday, I delivered the first baby since I lost Dani. The team in the delivery room watched me almost as much as the mother. But I was all right. I wrapped the newborn in his blanket and laid him down carefully. That's when I first heard it, Dani's laugh. I smiled and said nothing but I lingered over the baby, taking my time checking his ears, his nostrils, his mouth. Everything fine. I sponged him clean before wheeling him into the nursery. Hung the tag—BABY BOY TURNER. I pushed my finger into his closed hand. His tiny warmth went through my whole body. Strong little boy, he hung on. Dani laughing again. By the time I joined the rest of the team, my face was smooth again and my hands were steady. I was fine. I'm going to be fine. Yes, I am.

Elena started carrying the black stone with her everywhere. She no longer worried about Cari's imaginary friend. She remembered Mati telling her that there were things that she would never understand. It was enough to take note and listen to the inner voice. So she listened whenever Cari spoke of her Lady and encouraged the child to share her dreams. And then Elena herself started dreaming again.

One night she dreamed of a little girl lost in the forest. Everywhere she turned she found endless tangles of fallen vines and dense foliage. The sun crossed the sky and started to set behind the western trees. Shafts of light pierced the foliage; green beams fell all around the girl. As the western light diminished, darkness crept into the trees. The girl began to get nervous as she realized that soon she'd be lost in the dark. Then there was a movement among the brush. She didn't know whether to run toward or away from it. Whatever was coming was really big. Panic climbed up her spine and was about to shoot out of her mouth when the leaves parted and a woman stepped out. She was huge and very dark skinned. She wore a complicated turban and her body was wrapped in a colorful cloth. She wore no shoes. She carried a three-legged stool under her arm and a smile on her face. The girl relaxed as she watched the woman sit down, shifting her weight around until she was comfortable. The woman held her arms out to the girl and the girl felt safe enough to go to her. Maybe this woman could lead her home. She settled into the woman's lap. A strong scent of flowers clung to the woman's hair and skin. The woman's voice filled the forest. It said, "It is the time for stories." And out they came— stories of magic and rage and love and fear and anger and loss and healing. Her voice wrapped around the trees, each sentence coming from a different direction until the forest rang with her sounds. The girl pressed her ear to the woman's chest to find the source of her words. The woman pulled her away. "No, look to yourself. Everything you need is within you. Look to your own stories."

The next morning at breakfast, Elena pulled Carisa into her lap and began. "Your great-grandmother Mati was a woman of many stories."

"Like my Lady?"

"Yes, just like your Lady. But your Abuela Mati didn't live just in dreams. She was a real person."

"My Lady is real."

"Yes, well, let me tell you some of Abuela Mati's stories. I think you'll really like them."

* * *

Elena's mind was often heavy with thoughts of Pedro. Things couldn't go on like this forever. Now she could almost understand his lashing out at her. How could he not blame her when she had blamed herself more? Maybe she still did, a little. But she had been forced to find a way of forgiving herself. Otherwise, she would have lost her mind and her daughter, too. But she didn't know if he would ever find forgiveness for her.

So the next Friday, she took his envelope and gave the messenger another in return. She asked Pedro to come home. It was time to talk. It was time to mend.

Elena had no idea how each of them would react to his return. She hoped that they could begin building a bridge back to each other.

Marci and Fonso took Carisa to the movies, a double feature, just before Pedro was due to arrive.

Then he was finally there. They sat across from each other like awkward teenagers, the table a protective barrier. Each sat in silence. Finally, tentatively, Elena reached out for Pedro's hands. He winced and she jumped back.

"No," he said, "don't misunderstand."

He reached out to show her. His hands were all blisters and pus-filled sacs. She went for the medicine cabinet and came back. He winced every time she touched him. She worked quickly and carefully as his story came out.

Recently he had been transferred to a better-paying job in which he had to use much heavier irons, which were much bigger and hotter. He hadn't yet developed the protective calluses that the other men had. She was quiet as she applied antiseptic ointment and then bandages. Once she was done, they sat down to eat dinner.

"I've missed your food, Elena."

"A good home-cooked meal always makes you feel better."

"I've missed many things."

Neither of them spoke about their last meeting. They were afraid of breaking the gossamer coating that had begun to knit their lives together again. *One day at a time*, she thought. More can be said in a careful embrace than in a hundred words. The words would come later.

Sunday night, he got in the car with the men and left for another week of work. Elena knew she couldn't live like this anymore. There must be another way.

The following weekend, Pedro came home again. His hands were better. They went to the movies. Carisa was inching her way back to her father, little tentative forays. She remembered the screaming and the silences. It was obvious he needed more time at home. With Elena's new job, his wages weren't as critical. But she said nothing. She needed to hear what was living in his head. They danced around each other, carefully, until it was Sunday night again. Another piece of the bridge. Little by little they would get there. Elena was beginning to believe it could happen.

She surprised Pedro one weekend with some papers for him to fill out. The civil service exam was being given and she thought he might be interested. He was good at exams, and his accent wouldn't be an issue. It could lead to a job that would bring him home again.

Pedro was really excited about the possibility of working closer to home. Things had gotten better between them. They were still very careful, extending themselves a bit and then retreating in search of safety whenever things got too intense. But each time he came home, they got a little closer. Elena hoped that one day they might find true intimacy again.

One day, Elena put out a picture of Dani, which she hadn't been unable to look at for many months. When Pedro came home, he didn't miss that detail. He picked up the frame, stroked the glass, and then placed it carefully back on the table, smoothing the doily beneath before walking out of the room. Elena watched and held her tongue. She picked up the photo as well, tracing her fingertips over the spot Pedro had just touched.

They still didn't discuss the baby. But at least now his image was once again part of their lives.

* * *

That fall, Elena and Pedro sat across from each other, staring at the envelope. His fingers were sweaty and shaky as he ripped it open. He read it twice before sharing the news with his wife. His grades on the civil service examination had guaranteed him a position as a statistical analyst in the post office. He could report for work in another month.

They whooped and laughed and Pedro picked her up and gave her a sloppy kiss. Elena enjoyed the uncontained happiness. When he finally put her down, she pulled out a folder from the top drawer. She had saved $453 and had clipped seventeen ads for apartments in the Bronx, a quiet neighborhood across the street from a huge park. Pedro began making plans for his last week of work in Hartford. They would have their own place and start again.

Carisa watched her parents and giggled.

October 1956

It's been almost a year since I've written in you but it seems like a lifetime. We have moved to a wonderful apartment in a totally different neighborhood. It's quiet and clean. Many people had window boxes full of colorful flowers all summer. There aren't many Puerto Ricans here, but our mostly Jewish neighbors are nice. We do a lot of smiling. I was unpacking the last carton in the back of the closet and there you were. You have held so much of my pain for so long that I thought it was time to give you some of my joy as well. So I brought you out to our hill to write in while I watch Carisa run after a ball. So much has happened that it will be hard to catch up.

First. We live in the Bronx now, across the street from a beautiful park called Crotona. This neighborhood is so much nicer than the one we left behind. The super really keeps the place clean and we always have plenty of hot water and heat. It took a while to get used to sleeping in the bedrooms at the back of the apartment. Those windows face the Third Avenue El, which makes a terrible racket. I guess we have gotten used to the noise because we don't even notice the passing trains anymore. But the front room faces the park. We have taken over this little hill and spend every Saturday afternoon here while it's warm out. The flowers are gone but the turning leaves float down every time a little breeze goes by. It's not the tropics but it's another kind of lovely. And it's wonderful to see Cari running and playing in the fallen leaves while I unwrap our picnic things.

Second. I finally got a promotion. At first I worked the night shift. Then I was really lucky that two nurses quit and another retired. So I moved up in seniority much faster than anyone expected. I work days now and almost never on weekends. It's wonderful spending more time with Cari. She'll start school next September. I can't believe how fast she is growing.

Third. Marcelina and Fonso liked our new neighborhood so much that they talked to the super and he promised them they'll get their own apartment nearby as soon as one becomes available. Oh, yes! Marci and Fonso have started their own family. So Marci watches little Benjamin as well as Cari while I'm at work. When Cari starts school, Marci will go back to work. We'll have to find someone to watch the baby and get Cari to and from school, but that's in the future. In the meantime, we are all happy with this arrangement.

Fourth. *Most important*. Pedro and I are working out our problems. Having our own place helps. What does or doesn't happen between us stays between us. Having a job that pays well, where Pedro can wear a suit and is respected, has been a big help. He loves working in the payroll section of the post office, where he can use his head and "not get his hands dirty," as he says, which is really important to him. His mother's letters still come on occasion and then he is restless for a few days, but I let it go. There are some things I can't change. We try to do many things together. We go to the movies, have picnics, and visit friends. We have a simple life. So I guess things are going well.

We don't talk about what we don't have and we try to focus on what we have created together rather than what we have lost. We rarely talk about Dani and *never* talk about Zenobia. For now, we take things one day at a time. There are rough patches, but we try to work them out. Sometimes it's really hard, but I have Carisa to think about.

Cari—we have come through so much together, especially those lonely months while Pedro was away. During the long nights when Pedro was gone, Cari and I would cuddle in bed and turn down the lights and then the stories would come back to me. I told her about the black stone. About the baby born by the river. I told her about Tía Josefa, and about Abuela Mati's gift, and the white men's mysterious disease, and the return of the land. I told her the story about Abuela Concha's illness. I told her about how a sick woman was healed with oil, a stone, and loving. I told her all the stories I could remember and then started again. She always listened. I think that even when she fell asleep my words followed her into her dreams. Once in a while, I would begin a story and Cari would finish it for me, sometimes murmuring the last words just before she dropped off to sleep.

The telling made me stronger. Sometimes I think it was more for me than for her. The telling was a healing. It helped me find my way, just as it had helped those before me find theirs. I mined those stories in the dark days. When I was weak, I dug in them for strength. When I was tired, I found tales of success. The old ones, the ancestors, wrestled with the same demons and left me a map. It wasn't easy, but my load got easier to carry. It's always easier when you know it's been done before.

And then there are my own stories, the sad ones I haven't shared with her, my Pedro stories, my Zenobia stories. Maybe, when she is older…

BOOK FIVE

⋙⋘

CARISA

22 SHOW-AND-TELL

I stood in the front of the room feeling quite proud of myself. I would have the best show-and-tell item of any of my classmates. I waited until the class was absolutely quiet and then held out my hand. I opened one finger at a time to add to the mystery. The students snaked their necks to see what I was holding. Then there it was, the black stone in my hand.

"Oh, come on!"

"Big deal, it's just a rock."

"No, it isn't," I protested, "it's a magical stone."

The room was quiet for a moment and then exploded into laughter and loud voices.

"Get outta here."

"There ain't no such thing as magic."

"Whadaya, nuts!"

"Yeah! Yeah, right!"

"Who you kiddin'?"

"She done flipped now."

Miss Santini clapped her hands and the class settled down. "I'm disappointed in you. What did we say about respect for each other's words and actions? We owe Carisa our silence, our attention, and our respect. Just like you want those things when you come up to the front to speak. Is that understood?"

I always did love Miss Santini. She cleared her throat and turned to me.

"Go on, Carisa. We're all listening."

I looked at the class and then at Miss Santini and then at the class again. I tried speaking, but my mouth was dry and my words got glued together so nothing came out. I tried to swallow but I couldn't do that, either. My heart started beating really fast, not like a clock like it's supposed to but like a drum. Suddenly I had to go to the bathroom. My hand closed around my stone. I squeezed and squeezed, hoping that the pressure in my belly would go away.

"Go ahead, honey. We're all ready now." Miss. Santini encouraged.

I shook my head and pulled back, all the way back to the blackboard. I couldn't, just couldn't do this. Miss Santini was kind, really nice. I wanted to please her. But more than anything, I didn't want to be laughed at again.

"Look at me, honey, you finish your story."

I looked into her eyes. Puppy eyes, always soft when she looked at me. Then she looked at the class and her eyes changed. Menacing, cold.

"You go on, honey." She kept her eyes on the class, which was now absolutely silent. I could still hear my heartbeat.

"There'll be no more interruptions."

"Well, uh, I mean…that's okay. I'm done."

"Take your time, honey. Take your time and tell us."

"Well…"

I looked at their faces and could hear the laughter hiding just beyond their pursed lips. I closed my eyes. How could I do this?

"Well…"

I was afraid of using the word "magic" again so I left a lot of things, important things, out.

"This…this…rock is really old. Really, really old. My great, great—well…you know, my long-ago grandmother…she brought it with her from…from far away. And it was a gift from her husband. And it was passed down from one grandmother to the next until I got it. It's sort of mag…special, because it makes me think of them, the grans, even the ones I never got to meet. The end."

The class was absolutely quiet when I stopped talking. They looked at me incredulously. One or two sat, eyeing Miss Santini, hands pressed against their lips to keep in their laughter. It was supposed to be a two-minute speech. I must have said just a few sentences. And then I was done. Silence hung in the air, forever it seemed.

"Well, that was a lovely story—a little short, but very interesting. Does anyone have any questions for Carisa? Not one question? Well, thank you for sharing it with us. Children"—she eyed them as she continued—"let's thank Carisa for that lovely story." They all clapped halfheartedly but I didn't care. At least they weren't laughing.

I walked to my seat in the back of the room and shut them all out. I looked at my desk the rest of the day. I didn't say anything to anyone. The next thing I knew, the dismissal bell was ringing. I gathered my books and got ready to go home. Home! Safety. Quiet. No laughter.

I felt a hand on my shoulder and looked up to find Miss Santini standing there.

"Carisa, I'm feeling a little tired today and I could use your help. Can you stay for a few minutes and help me close down the room? Mr. Hughes will dismiss the class."

Usually, I loved helping at the end of the day. It made me feel so special, and one of the reasons why I loved my teacher was because she knew it and occasionally singled me out for this task. But, today, more than anything else, I wanted to run home. I hesitated. She said, "Please." I nodded yes because I still couldn't speak. I was about to get up to begin washing the board when she stopped me.

"Let's forget about the blackboard for now. I'd like to talk to you for a minute. Is that okay?" I said nothing. "I'm sorry your feelings were hurt this afternoon. The class was very rude and has a lot to learn about respect for others." I still said nothing. My eyes were burning again. I looked at the hem of my dress because I didn't want to cry. I knew if I looked at her face, I wouldn't be able to hold back the tears.

"I have a feeling there is more to the story you told us this afternoon. I'd like to hear it." I looked up for the first time. Again, those soft eyes. She folded her hands in her lap and waited for me to start.

"Really?" I started feeling the excitement that had brought me floating into the room this morning.

"Yes, I would. I'd like to hear the whole thing."

I took a deep breath and told her everything I had left out in class.

"You know, my stone *is* magic. It really, really is. It's magic because my long-ago grandfather Imo was a wise man and a healer. He told my long-ago grandmother that he would put their baby's soul into the stone so that even if they were separated, the baby would be all theirs and be a very strong and special child.

"And his wife, my great-great-grandmother, Fela, hid the stone to protect it from the bad men who attacked their village. And she brought it in a secret place from Africa. And her baby girl was born with the knowing—the healing and the dreaming and the knowledge of plants and trees. And after that the stone was given to every first girl in the family, like me. That's how I just know things, not just school stuff but *real* things. Like how people feel and what they have in their hearts and why they're unhappy. I don't know *how* I know these things, but I do. And I have lots of dreams and there's a Lady in my dreams who tells me things. And sometimes she tries to fool me with disguises, you know like at Halloween, but I know her anyway and she comes and puts the colored words in my head, and she teaches me how to weave the words into stories. She says someday I will be a storyteller and many people will come to hear my stories."

When I finished, I felt good. I finally got to tell my story my way and there was no laughter. In fact, Miss Santini hadn't taken her eyes off me the whole time I had been speaking.

"That is a really charming story. It really is. But do you remember a few months ago when we talked about the difference between make believe and real?" Something in her voice started to make me feel uncomfortable.

"We all agreed that some things are make believe or fantasy. Remember that word, 'fantasy'? When we are little, we all get those two mixed up. But now you're older, the age where you have to separate the real from the make believe. Do you understand me?"

I nodded. But then I whispered without looking up, "But it really *did* happen. My mom told me all about it."

"I'm sure she really believes it, too. Sometimes, stories get passed down from generation to generation and people forget what was real and what was made up."

"But…" I was about to explain, but what she said next made me stop and think.

"My grandmother did it, too. She came from a tiny town in Italy and she believed in 'the evil eye.' She thought that envious people would take good luck away by just *thinking* bad thoughts. Now, that's just plain superstition.

"Some people still believe in stories that they brought over from their old country—like Italy or Greece or Spain…or Africa. But we're Americans now, modern and educated. Here we believe in science. No need for superstitions anymore. That's what we call progress."

"Oh." The word kind of dropped out of me.

"So when you told us about the rock, was that just a story or do you think the rock is really magical?"

"I…I…I guess maybe, it's just a story, then," I said, crestfallen.

"Yes, that's right. Now maybe you can bring something else in next time that shows something truly real, that represents our world today."

She gave me a warm smile and a big hug. I should have felt wonderful. But I felt as if I had lost something.

* * *

That night my Lady came to me in my dreams. She walked in the forest, the moon and stars shining so that I could see her clearly even in the night. She came out of the trees wearing an old tattered coat and carrying a huge dirty bag full of rags and half-eaten fruits. She walked slowly because the bag weighed her down. Finally, she reached me. I tried to help her with her bundle but she pushed me aside. She made a nest of fallen leaves and sat me down on the cushioned ground. The leaves overhead shifted and in their movement I heard her words floating in the air. *Look and learn and remember. And take what you will.*

My Lady spread open the front of her coat and immediately the clearing was aglow with light. Colors flashed all around her, illuminating her figure in the night. The jewels and mirrors and sparkling stones that lined her coat suspended her in changing hues. There were tiny bells making tinny sounds, and colored beads and dancing patterns on the cloth. And her bag was now full of painted eggs.

Most people see the tears and the dirt and the dull colors of my coat and they smell only the stench of the old and dying. But a few, a select few, will see the colors and hear the songs. They have the patience to wait and the imagination to see. You must learn to recognize these few. Start with the eyes and work your way inside. Stop here—she pointed to her chest—*and look into their hearts. And when you are ready, only when you are sure, open your coat and let them see your jewels, let them hear your song, let them see you shine.*

The next time we had show-and-tell homework, I asked my mom for something special to take to school. The following day, I took in her stethoscope. It felt hard and cold all the way to school and I forgot how to pronounce the name. But everybody loved this new toy. I got a gold star for my presentation. Miss Santini smiled broadly and said,

Excellent. My classmates and even Miss Santini took turns listening to each other's hearts, passing the instrument around.

I sat in my seat and watched them. The teacher beamed. The class was very impressed. And I had learned my lesson.

23 OLD FRIENDS

Mrs. Goldberg lived upstairs on the fourth floor. She was the only Jewish person left in our building. She had long gray hair and you could see her scalp because her hair was so thin. She wore thick stockings, rolled and held just below her knees by elastic bands. Her shoes, black in the winter and brown in the summer, were always the same style— thick heeled and tied all the way up, like her feet were choking or something. In the house she wore slippers, with which she shuffled all over the place. Her house had a sharp smell. She had little white balls everywhere. I said, "We don't have no white balls and we do okay." But she said, "I couldn't be without my mothballs." So I didn't go to her apartment if I could help it. I didn't want to hurt her feelings, but those balls sure did stink up the place!

Anyway, I didn't have to go to her apartment much because I never saw her in the winter. I don't know what happened to her in the cold months, but I only saw her in the spring, summer, and fall. She and Mrs. Jackson, who lived on the second floor, were good friends.

Mrs. Jackson had lived in the building longer than anyone could remember. She had come from Georgia with her husband and her children, and now only she was left. All her friends had moved on, one way or the other. So she was just as alone as Mrs. Goldberg.

Mrs. Jackson was a wiry old lady. She had skinny arms and legs, but they took her all over the neighborhood. She walked all the way to the other side of Crotona Park every day except Sunday, for her "morning constitutional." And on Sundays she put on a black straw hat and her flowered shirtdress and picked up her black patent leather bag. She'd sit out on the stoop early, "so's I can show off my doodads," until the church van came by and picked her up. She was going to "pay the Lord his due," as she put it. "Chile, I hope I'll be meetin' him soon and not the other one, so's I better make sure I pay the Lord his due."

Most kids didn't have time for old folks. Kids are always in a rush. Old people took their time. Since I didn't have many friends my age, I had lots of time to give the ladies. Mrs. Goldberg and Mrs. Jackson were my oldest friends, if you know what I mean. I didn't know either of them very well, until one spring day while I was doing my homework by the open window in our back room. I heard them in the backyard.

Our backyard was almost all cemented over, like all the buildings in our neighborhood. It was rectangular, with buildings along the two long sides. One short side led to the doorway where Harry, the super, kept the garbage cans. Once a week, he'd haul them out to the curb for the sanitation trucks. But the other short end at the very back of the yard had a half wall, and beyond that half wall was a patch of wild grass. It was full of trash, beer bottles, and newspapers. That day, Harry was just sober enough to sweep the alley. So when Mrs. Goldberg and Mrs. Jackson descended on him, he didn't know what hit him.

Mrs. Goldberg said, pleading palms to the sky, "So, mister, what would it hurt to let us plant a little seed, maybe?"

"Look, I don't know, lady. The landlord is kind of a pain in the a— I mean, kinda fussy about stuff like that."

"But, mister, it's no skin off your nose…"

"It's not me, lady, it's the landlord—"

Mrs. Jackson got into it. "Look, Harry, we knows you have a good heart and the Lord knows you have to put up with that nasty man who owns these here broke-down buildin's. But maybe we can hep you out. We can maybe get you a little taste now and again..."

Mrs. Goldberg stared openmouthed at her friend.

Harry stopped sweeping for a minute and grinned. He looked Mrs. Jackson in the face. "You got some..."

"Well, Harry, I guess we can get you a little somethin', somethin' once a week. This lady here and me, well, we old and live mostly on our memories. Just t'other day, we got to reminiscin' and it seems like we used to have us each a little garden, just a little patch of nothin', really. Our gardens, they never bothered nobody and this one won't, either. And if you can see your way to lettin' us use this little bit a land back here, well, we can probably see our way to findin' you a little nip here and there when our checks comes in."

"Well, I don't know..." He stood, holding the broom, not back to sweeping yet.

"Harry, I'm glad you see things our way. You'll get your first bottle next week. In the meantime, these two old ladies want to thank you for bein' such a upstandin' young man."

Mrs. Jackson grabbed Mrs. Goldberg's elbow and hustled her down the alley. The two of them waddled into the building, making plans already.

"Come on, Miz Goldberg, we in business. We need some straw hats and some old servin' spoons and a hoe, where can we get a old...?"

"But, Mrs. Jackson, he didn't say he'd let us."

"Miz Goldberg, you just don't pay him no never mind. He's the kind a man who's just waiting to do some good but he don't even know it. I just gave him a chance to redeem his soul...even if we do have to pay for it with a little hooch."

"Well, if we are going to garden together, you should call me Rose."

"And I'm Addie."

Later on that afternoon, Mrs. Jackson stopped and called out to two kids who were emptying their trash, "You boys"—she gestured at them to come closer—"can you bring one of those cans over here so's we can get rid of some of this stuff?"

"Whatcha doin', Miz Jackson?"

"We's makin' us a garden. This here's Miz Goldberg."

"Hi, lady…Miz Goldberg."

The boys brought the can over and set up some cinder blocks so the old ladies would have steps leading up to their garden. They helped each other up the incline and began picking up the papers and other debris that had been accumulating there all winter. Those two old ladies were back there every day, and soon I was out there, too.

* * *

This is the way it happened. I had been spending a lot of time in the back room. The TV was broken again and Pop had taken it in to be "fixed." I knew that meant that it would live with the man in the pawnshop on Boston Road until payday. Our tape recorder, the record player, the toaster, Mom's Bulova and Pop's typewriter had all lived with Mr. Weinstein over the years. I had never met him, but Mr. Weinstein seemed to have been part of the family ever since I could remember. Anyway, the television was gone and my homework was done and I didn't want to hear the hokey music my parents were listening to on the radio.

I heard the ladies in the backyard from our back window. They were complaining about how hot it was and that they were too tired to go in and get a drink. If they went in, they'd stay in. I looked down and saw one perfectly shaped gladiolus at the very back of the yard. Its pale peach blossom set it apart from all the gray that surrounded it on that wall. I jumped down and ran into the kitchen. I poured out two glasses of lemonade and carefully carried them down to the basement, through the alley, and to the backyard wall.

I said, "I heard you talking and I thought I'd trade you a glass of cool drink for a closer look at your flower."

"Why, precious, don't you live on the fifth floor?"

"Yes, ma'am."

"Well, then. This is your flower as well as ours. You don't need to trade nothing! Just come on up here."

I held out the glasses.

"Well, thank you, young lady. And what would your name be?"

"Carisa."

"I never met a Carisa before."

"Neither has anyone else."

"Well, we're pleased to meet'cha."

No adult had ever shaken my hand before. I felt special. Mrs. Jackson had the handshake of an athlete. I looked at her face to make sure she was as old as I thought. She was. Mrs. Goldberg's handshake was not as strong but she held my hand a long time while she talked to me and studied my face.

* * *

"So today, I will tell you a story. But the story is not free. Today I give you mine and tomorrow you will give me yours."

"It's a deal," Mrs. Jackson jumped in immediately.

Mrs. Goldberg turned to me, "Well?"

"But I don't have any stories," I said.

"Of course you do. Everyone has stories."

"I think I am too young to have my own stories."

"But you have family stories and they were yours before you were even born."

Mrs. Jackson said, "Let me tell you a secret. Those old family stories are the best ones. They get mellow with time, like fine gold, and like my grandfather's old pocket watch; they help us get through the bad times. That's when you take 'em out and dust 'em off and let 'em heal your soul. Now think. Didn't your mother ever tell…?"

I remembered that when I was little I fell asleep to Mami telling me old stories. I used to love listening to her voice as I drifted off. But then I stopped listening to that old-fashioned stuff a long time ago. I thought they were just bedtime stories.

"Yes…I think I have stories like that but I don't remember."

"Then you'd better go home and ask your Mamá. We won't give away our stories. We only trade them. I will tell no story if you don't guarantee you will tell one, too." Mrs. Goldberg pursed her lips and stuck them up in the air.

"Okay, okay."

"That's better. We'll start tomorrow," said Mrs. Jackson. "Now, you got 'til next week. Then we'll wanna hear one of yours. No excuses now."

"Yes, ma'am."

Mrs. Jackson's Story

Elijah Claudius Jackson was sittin' at his station, lookin' very handsome in his smart Pullman jacket, when I slid open the wrong door. This was the white folks' compartment. He directed me to the right car. As I turned around to find my seat, I made sure I gave a little wiggle just to see if he was watchin'. He was. I do believe by the time the Atlanta/New York Limited pulled into the station in Manhattan, I had his attention. One thing led to another and we was married. A good long time, too, 'til that po-liceman's bullet stopped my 'Lijah's heart. He was in the wrong place at the wrong time, the po-liceman said. He said Mr. Jackson looked like a man who held up a liquor store down the block. He said, anyway, a old man on a cane had no business out in the streets at that time a the night. The po-liceman threw all these no-sense-making words at me 'fore I hit the floor in a faint. When Billy came home from work, I was still lyin' unconscious on the floor.

Mrs. Goldberg's Story

I was still Rosie Cohen when my sister Hannah and me stowed away on that freight train in Ukraine. Things were bad at the *shtetl*, and our father had wanted to get us away before they got worse. We had never been outside our village and had been robbed of Papá's money before we reached Poland. That's how we ended up sneaking onto the train that now made its way west through Western Europe. All we had left was each other and the name and address (the paper safely folded in my right boot) of a relative in Marseille. We would be safe there for a time. But the train ride was long and there were many such as ourselves. Many people were traveling this way. Hannah met a boy, Avram, who had eyes only for her. She fell in love and they were inseparable. They kept warm in the freezing nights by huddling next to each other as the train rushed through the darkness.

Then one morning they were found. The track workers swung open the door and cursed at them for costing the company thousands. They were merciless with their long sticks. I was small and managed to hide among the crates. I watched as Avram and Hannah were dragged out with the others. They were taken away by the police who wore the rail company insignia on their uniforms.

I decided to wait until nightfall, when I could steal into town and figure out where they were being kept. Meanwhile, I squeezed into a dark corner of the car and waited. But I fell asleep. When I woke up, the train was moving. I panicked, thought of jumping off and running back. But there were no lights anywhere in sight. The train had picked up speed, and jumping off would probably mean breaking my neck. Every minute took me farther and farther from Hannah and Avram and closer to a frightening unknown.

All I knew was the name and address on the paper in my shoe. And so I burrowed into my tiny space and cried all the way to France.

MRS. JACKSON'S STORY

My legs were already botherin' me in fifty-four when I climbed up those six flights of stairs in an abandoned buildin' on One Twenty-Seventh Street. Been lookin' for a week. Billy would be the death a me yet. Since he came back from Ko-rea, the boy jus' wan't right. Mr. Jackson was gone already, thank God! Seein' his baby boy like that woulda just killed him for sure. They called it junk, but they shoulda called it somethin' else, somethin' more deadly. "Junk" was too tame. This stuff was a killer, a killer of women and men and babies, a killer of neighborhoods. And tho' I never laid eyes on it, it was killin' me, too. It wan't junk—junk left you alone. That there was somethin' entirely different.

Well, I did find my Billy—on the roof. They jus' left him there. Didn't even bother to call me or nuthin'. Makes no sense, 'cause it was such a beautiful spring day. Sunny, as I recollect.

Anyway, my beautiful baby boy, arm and legs all sprawled out and a-rottin' away in the sun. Needle still stuck in…what was left of his arm. I tried to hold him, best I could. And I guess I must have screamed, 'cause folks came a-runnin'. Last thing I remember was some doctor tryin' to put a needle in my arm. I was still screamin', I guess—I don't want no junk. Done had too much of that already. But all that came out were just howls. Leastways, that's what they tell me.

MRS. GOLDBERG'S STORY

It wasn't until I got to America that I finally began to feel safe. I had another piece of paper. This time my brother Pinkus knew I was coming and would be waiting for me. I had never met him. He was much older than me and a rich man. He had a factory and one hundred fifty workers—a respected businessman.

It wasn't the money I was thinking about. More than anything, I wanted to go to school. I could speak Yiddish and Russian and Polish and even a little Rumanian. But I couldn't read or write any of them. So my dream was to go to school. I had even bought myself a little notebook before we sailed so I would be ready when I got to America and they would see that I wanted to be an educated woman.

But Pinkus, he had other plans. Oy, such plans he had for me! I went to the factory university, the school of work. My first lesson was work. My second lesson was don't stop. My third lesson was shut up.

But eyes can see and ears can hear. While I worked I noticed a handsome young man. Ruven Goldberg was his name. I give him the eye and he gives me the eye. In between, after and during work, we gave each other the eyes. So one thing and another and we liked each other.

One of the things I loved about Ruven was that every time I saw him away from work he was reading or writing. In fact, my Ruven was a union organizer. I didn't know what that was, but he said that I should join the union and go to class. School. He said the magic word. Finally. And so I went to class—English class and literacy class and workers' meetings. And I saw that I had been blind and now my eyes were opened. And my Ruven, he had helped me to see with open eyes.

And that's how I ended up on the picket line outside Pinkus Panties Factory. Oy! You should have seen Pink's face when he heard my voice yelling at him along with the rest. And his paid goons came out and he came out and I made sure when I hit, it landed on Pinkus. They took many of us to jail and I remember kicking and screaming and waving my arms. And Ruven was right there next to me. Both of us bleeding but feeling good for the first time in a long time.

We were in jail for a while but even Pinkus couldn't keep us in there forever. I lost my job, of course, and I had to move in with Ruven's sister. But I tell you, I was never happier than when I saw Pinkus walking down the street, hat sitting high above the bandages that covered the side of his head. I really gave him a good one!

* * *

Mrs. Jackson slapped her knee. "That was a good one, Rosie." She wiped her eyes and they both laughed. They had gotten carried away with their own stories. But now they turned to me.

"Aw right now, precious. Don't think coz I'm a old lady, I done forgot. It's your turn now."

"Yes, *meine sheyna*. Your turn."

They looked at me, pursed their lips, folded their arms, and waited. I couldn't think of anything to say. Then I opened my mouth and the words were there.

MY FIRST STORY

Once upon a time, a couple that loved each other very much realized that they couldn't have a baby. They tried and tried and nothing. So they went to Mother Oshun and asked her to help them start their family. She promised that she would help them. First, they would need to find a special stone and then…

24 HIGHER EDUCATION

I sat across from Professor Stevens' desk and watched his bald spot. He had been on the phone for the last four minutes. I sat with my journal flat on my lap, knees pressed together, palms sweating, counting my breaths. I wanted more than anything to take this man's creative writing class. I had applied to this university because of him, only to find out at registration that he screened his students and would accept only twelve per class.

Registration was in the gym on the other end of campus, so when I first got to his office half an hour ago, sweat beads popping on my face from the run, I knew I hadn't made a very good impression. When he finally saw me, it wasn't good. He had examined me carefully: my newly trimmed Afro, huge hoop earrings, and embroidered Mexican blouse. My love beads tinkled on my bodice as I sat down in front of him. His eyes drank me in openly before he spoke.

"Excuse me, are you in the right place? The Comp 101 table is in the gym with the grad assists."

"No, that class has been waived for me."

He gave me a second look. "Oh. Really? Well then, what can I do for you?"

"I want to take your creative writing class."

One eyebrow arched minutely before he turned back to the papers on his desk and put his hand out. When I just sat there, he looked up once again, his patience breaking.

"Well?" His eyebrows shot up.

"Well, what?" I stared at him uncomprehendingly.

He didn't bother to hide his exasperation. "Your manuscript, your work?"

I stared at him. Of course! Why hadn't I thought of that? "Well...I, I didn't know..."

"Look, I rarely accept freshmen into my classes anyway. Maybe this is just a waste of your time and mine."

"But you haven't even given me a chance. I brought my journal."

I could see the course cards in his shirt pocket; blue-edged, key-punched cards that peeked at me over the pocket of his plaid flannel shirt. They seemed to stand at attention, like soldiers guarding the palace gates.

He took one look at my journal and sneered, "Is that it? How quaint." The sarcasm dripped off his tongue and stung me in places I had kept hidden for years. "Let's have it." I handed it over and looked down at my hands. *Be cool, girl.* I thought. *If I look at him, I'll cry. I'll curse him out. I'll slap him. How dare he?* But I held my tongue. Maybe I had misread him. Maybe I was overreacting. *Just wait. He might love my work. Don't shoot yourself in the foot before you even start. Focus on something else.*

Professor Stevens held my journal in his hands, odd rough hands for a writer, with jagged, dirty fingernails, cracked skin, calloused edges. They looked like the hands of someone who breaks things for a living. I stared at the three hairs growing on his pate and knew I didn't like this man. But I had read his work and marveled at how he could paint such pictures with words. I knew nothing of the world he wrote about, yet I knew everything because his words guided me into understanding. I wanted to write like that about my world. I wanted to guide people past the hard surfaces, to the soft and loving core. I knew

I needed to learn from him. His position and reputation had tricked me into trusting him.

I sat in the chair and watched his body stiffen as he read. I waited, even though everything in me told me to run. It took all my willpower not to snatch my journal away. Each time he turned a page, I felt he was examining another part of my life, and disapproving. Is that what being a writer was all about, stripping yourself bare for hostile eyes? I had thought they were just stories. But sitting in that hardback chair I came to see that my stories were the different facets of myself. Maybe I wasn't ready to share all of that with strangers. Maybe I needed to think about this more, examine them for myself before opening them up to others. Watching him, I could see how such a man could easily kill my stories, kill me. But it was too late. After only a few more pages, Professor Stevens closed the journal and pushed it back at me across his desk.

"Well, you know, Miss…" He cleared his throat and searched for my name.

"Ortíz," I helped him.

"Oh, yes. Miss *Ortiz*." He pronounced it with the accent on the first syllable. I guess he couldn't hear well, either.

"As I said, I rarely take freshmen into my workshops."

My heart dropped. Then I heard myself say, "Yes, but you do make exceptions, don't you? Rarely is not never."

"Yes, but…may I be honest?"

I nodded, my wooden face closed to him already. He continued with his sharp-edged sword of honesty.

"You need to start by reading before you attempt to write. Read voraciously. Read the masters. Read everything in every genre. Study the canon. Steep yourself in the great themes of Western thought. Study *The Age of Reason*, the classics. When you have a good grasp of what came before you, consider whether you have anything of worth to add to that exalted company. Then and only then consider putting pen to paper. If you get to that point, do try to be eloquent. And above all, rely on logic, no smoke and mirrors to tell your story.

"As to this"—he pointed to my journal—"this is a mass of superstitious nonsense, clichéd ghosts and goblins. You must understand that I'm interested in high-quality literary work. This…is just not it. This type of marginal material has no place in belle letres. There are arenas for this type of thing…"

I didn't hear the rest of his words because I was trying to gather the pieces of myself that had been blown apart. I saw them floating before me and wondered how I would ever get them back. I let him go on because I didn't trust myself to speak. His mouth was still moving.

"You might have a flare. There are some nicely turned phrases. Maybe one of the children's fantasy magazines. Their editors are always looking for stories for their Halloween issues, I'm told. But you'll have to play down some of those sex scenes. Maybe Harlequin…"

I heard nothing more. I left his office, his words trailing behind me. I slipped my journal into my coat and hugged it all the way back to the dorm. I thought it would keep me warm in the autumn winds. Or maybe I could keep it warm and protected. I felt it needed my protection and yet I felt so wounded and in need of protection myself. I ran up the eight flights, not waiting for the elevator. I thought about Professor Stevens and his rough hands. I fell asleep swearing I would never let anyone touch my journal again.

* * *

Six months later, I stood at Professor Jamison's front door. I knew I was the only freshman invited to the party, so I was surprised and honored.

Professor Jamison was my American Studies teacher and the total opposite of Professor Stevens. He encouraged me to explore the literature outside the classics. His reading list included *Native Son* and *Manchild in the Promised Land* and *Down These Mean Streets*. I visited his office several times a week, and we had had really good talks about contemporary works that reflected a wider modern reality than the canon. He liked my ideas and called on me frequently in class. On a whim, I had left one of my stories on his desk just before I left campus. After the Stevens fiasco, I'd kept all my writing to myself. It felt good finding someone who could appreciate what I was trying to do.

"Hey, welcome to my madness." He stood there in his jeans and sneakers and pulled me into the foyer. He handed me a glass of wine and said, "Mingle. It's every woman for herself."

Professor Jamison lived in a Victorian house with dozens of rooms at odd angles, and there were people in all of them. Most were drinking wine and nibbling on cheese and crackers and had been doing so for a while, from the look of them. I didn't know anyone by name so I wandered in and out of rooms. Some contained groups of people involved in low humming conversations, others in energetic disagreements. Some welcomed me a little too boisterously and others ignored me altogether. The acrid smell of marijuana floated faintly in the air. I was about to head for the foyer to hunt for my coat when, as I passed the open door to the kitchen, I heard my name.

"Miss *Ortiz?*" Accent on the first syllable. "Oh, yes, she wanted to take my creative writing class. Can you imagine?"

"I know she's been writing but I hadn't really read any of her stuff until this afternoon." Professor Jamison's soft voice was heavy with alcohol and he slurred his words a little.

"Well, what did you think?"

"She has an interesting point of view."

"Like I said, what do you think?"

"There's some potential there. It has to be honed…"

"Come on, she should be taken out of her misery. She writes about semiliterate, poverty-stricken people who have no past and even less of a future."

"Oh, come on! She does have a certain amount of authenticity…" The defense was halfhearted.

But Professor Stevens was on a roll. "And what is that mishmash that passes for style? Is that pig Spanish she throws in there for good measure? 'Cause it's certainly not Castilian, for Christ's sake. I'm sorry, but mastering some rudimentary grammatical rules does not a writer make."

"That's a bit harsh, don't you think?"

"Can you imagine anyone outside the South Bronx being interested in any of that tripe?"

"Well…"

"Give me a break, can those people even *read*? Have they any idea of the intricacies and finesse of the English language? Can they utter a single sentence without torturing the pronunciation?"

"Simon, I think you go too far. How much have you had to drink?"

"Be honest! Would you even consider publishing her work in the campus literary magazine?"

"Well, no, no I wouldn't…but…"

"Look, Bob, forget about this letting them down easy. The kindest thing you can do is let her have it, now. There's no point encouraging her. She's impossible…"

I was out in the cold and running before he finished his sentence. I was shivering when I finally got back to my room. I kicked off my boots and dived into bed. But before I could settle into the warmth, I threw off the covers and ran to my desk. I dug into the drawer until I found it. Still shaking, I got back into bed, pulling my quilt over my head. In the morning, I woke up still clutching at my journal protectively.

I stayed in bed for weeks, hugging my journal the whole time. The phone rang and rang and I never answered it. Someone kept knocking on my door. I turned to the wall and went back to sleep.

I ate whatever was in my tiny fridge and climbed back into bed. When I ran out of food, I drank water, and finally felt no need to eat at all. Time fractured. I might sleep all day and then lie awake for hours, watching the night sky.

One morning I woke up from a deep sleep. The sun had finally broken through the clouds and came blazing in the windows and onto my bed. I had been dreaming that my skin was tingling from the hot sun. The sound of the palm fronds lulled me into a half slumber. The warm water at my feet seduced me into its depths. The water lapped my calves, my arms, fanned out my hair. I let myself go and floated, supported by the salty sea. It rocked me a long while before depositing me back on the shore. When I woke up, I knew what I needed to do. I packed my bag, made two calls, and hung a sign outside my door: GONE HOME.

25 Porch Stories

When I arrived in Puerto Rico, I surrendered my weak body and bruised spirit to Abuela Concha. I walked off the plane and steeped myself in her world. The first day, she threw away the pills and prescriptions in my bag. She called her friend Teo and together they decided on my new *remedios*. Every day Abuela went into her garden and collected herbs. Then began the endless remedies: *lengua de perro* to calm the nerves, *genjibre* to ease the vomiting, and *flor de virgen* to lift the sadness. And always the candles glowed in the background for the African deities: white for Obatala, calmness, clearness of thought, wisdom; green for Osayin, general healing, regeneration of the life force, and protection from nightmares and unseen enemies; red for Chango, to break evil spells and fortify the spirit; yellow for Oshun, to attract love and well-being.

But the most important part of recovery came from community. A cot was set out for me on the porch and every day, as my grandmother went about her chores, her white-haired friends hobbled across the road and up the hill to spend time with me.

Doña Gume was a tiny woman with delicate bones and ill-fitting teeth. Doña Pastora was big and boisterous. Her voice rang out and grabbed your attention. In contrast to her huge body, she always carried a tiny bone china teacup and sipped from it throughout her stay. Then there was Doña Teo, who always waited until everyone else had spoken before adding her quiet voice to the conversation. Sometimes she sat all morning and said nothing at all, happy to just listen to friends talk.

Every morning, these ladies from all over San Antonio washed their breakfast dishes, wound their grey hair into tight buns, put on their gold earrings, and came to sit with me. Lying on the porch cot, I watched their brightly colored umbrellas bobbing in the sunshine as they approached. They bought their oils and ointments and as I lay there too tired and pained to care, I surrendered myself to their hands, wrinkled hands that missed holding babies and soothing toddlers. They brought me their love in the folds of those wrinkles, kneaded it into my body as I lay unsuspecting, and from under their nails, between their fingers, within the softness of their flesh, they brought me the gift of their stories.

* * *

The first time I met Doña Gume, I couldn't stop looking at her. There was something odd about the way her face moved when she spoke. She kept tripping over her own words. Abuela, who walked by occasionally on her way to her errands, finally slowed as she walked by and said, "*Mira*, Gume, *muchacha*, take those things out so the girl can understand you. This ain't company. The girl's family!" Then she kept right on walking.

Doña Gume looked around sheepishly, took a hanky out of her apron pocket, opened her mouth, and pulled out her teeth. Immediately, the smooth skin about her lips puckered up into a million wrinkles. She made big chewing motions, exercising the muscles that had strained to accommodate the ill-fitting dentures.

Doña Pastora, who had all her teeth, roared and slapped her knee until she nearly spilled her tea. Doña Teo smiled behind her hands, trying not to make Gume feel any more uncomfortable than she already did. But Doña Gume recuperated quickly. Her right hand shot out faster than I would have thought possible and a good right jab landed on Pastora's left arm.

"*Coño, mujer, ¡eso duele!*" The larger woman rubbed the injured arm.

Abuela yelled out, "Gume, tell her the story, *mujer*. Tell her!"

I looked back at Doña Gume, stroked her hand, and smiled.

"Don't worry. You don't have to."

"No, no, *m'hija*. I can tell you. Everybody knows anyway. Besides, Concha is right. You're family."

Doña Gume had always hated wasting money. She wanted to leave this world with more than she had when she entered it, so she saved everything. When her husband, Paco, died she saved all his things. Still had them. Good thing, too, because when she lost all her teeth, she had her husband's dentures right there. Why should she go and spend more money on teeth when there was a perfectly good pair in her top drawer? Then there were the glasses. Paco left her a good pair of spectacles, too. So maybe things didn't fit perfectly. Maybe she missed the mailman coming down the road and maybe she couldn't talk so good sometimes. She was going to save her *centavos* for a rainy day.

Doña Pastora interrupted, "It's pouring now, Gume. Go into town and let your children get you what you need. This is ridiculous."

Even Doña Teo piped in, "Gumecita, you'll really be better off. You'll be able to read Pepe's letters from Nueva York and the newspaper and…"

"All bad news. When there's good news, somebody will make sure I get it. No, no trips to town. I see and talk well enough. And that's that. Now where's that needle I just had?"

* * *

One morning, while I was writing my daily entry in my journal, Doña Gume came up much earlier than usual. "*¡Buenos dias!*" she called out from the gate. Surprised, I put down my pen, helped her up the porch steps, and settled her into her usual rocker.

"You are so early today," I said, closing my journal. "Abuela is out back collecting her herbs. You know how she is. She'll be back in a few…"

"No, *nena*. I came to see you. Are we alone?" She looked around before going on. "You see, I didn't tell you the whole truth the other day."

I was confused. "The other day?"

She continued, "About the teeth, you know."

It had been weeks since that talk, "Doña, don't worry about…"

"No, listen, *m'hija*. It isn't about the money, you know. I am careful but I'm not cheap. It's about town, you see."

Doña Gume's Story

Town is where they took my Paco's body. I lived with that man for sixty-three years. I wanted to wash him down, make sure he met his creator as clean as he was when he was with us. I wanted to be the last one to touch his body, smooth his clothes before…but they don't let us do it at home anymore. Regulations, they said. So they took him away to a *funeraria*, they call it. Who knows what they did to him there, whose hands touched him last? *Horrible.* And you couldn't see the body for all the flowers and ribbons and things. Why can't they just let us go with some dignity? A body should be at home, with the people who loved him, like the old days. You see?

Well, now they got their *new* ways! The health department says this. The authorities say that. So they took him to the funeral home and then they buried him out there, in the *new* cemetery. He didn't know any of those folks out there. He should've been buried right here in the barrio. Well, that's not a place for him. What they forgot is that we are not *new*. We're old and like the old ways. So I watched all of it and I closed up my heart. *You're so brave*, they said. I wasn't brave. I just wasn't there.

I came home, our home, his home, and I sat in the dark and I called to my Paco. At first, he couldn't find me. Maybe I didn't know how to call. But I stayed in my room for three days. Then finally he found his way home and he was there with me, in our room, like he always was. I fell asleep with his face in my mind. That's when I knew I would never go to that town again. I had everything I needed here. Paco was here so I didn't need to go there, especially not that place where they tried to take him away from me. So I wear his teeth and I wear his glasses. They make me feel closer to him. They're not so comfortable and they don't work so good for me as new ones. But they make me feel he's with me. When I come to tell you my stories, I bring him with me because he helps me remember better.

* * *

Doña Teo and Doña Gume were looking down at their hands. There was no rocking today, no fanning, and no jokes. Even Abuela stopped her work in the kitchen because there was not one sound coming from there, either. They waited, stock-still, hoping their friend could get at it. They had waited for many years to hear her say it. Now it took my asking. Me, a young girl from the seas of not-knowing asked with such innocence, "And what happened to your husband, Doña Pastora?" That's when they all fell silent.

It wasn't easy for her to tell it. It seemed she had to search deep in her memory. And when she found it, it came out slow, like day-old lava, slowed but still scorching, still able to consume everything it touched. She could have kept it inside, made a joke, but she didn't.

I could see I shouldn't have asked. "Never mind. We can talk about something else."

But the women were still silent, eyes nailed on their friend, still waiting.

"No, you should know. You need to know what came before. You need to know how life changes the shape of the world. If nothing is said, in a few years, we'll all be gone and with us, all that made our world mean something. That's why we need to unlock rusty old secrets. Scrape out memories that live under the weight of years. They never go away. They just sink and become heavier every year. Maybe by sharing them with the young people we'll lighten our load and go on our way with a lighter heart. Maybe they'll help lighten your load as well."

She looked around at her friends and then settled her eyes on me. "You make sure you write down the stuff that's usually left out." She shifted her weight in her chair and took on a different pose. She cleared her throat and then began.

"Do you know about San Cristóbal? Thirty-eight it was, or maybe thirty-nine? Doesn't matter. It was long ago. That hurricane was all the evil of the world rolled into a huge wind that snatched the breath out of all our lives. No one was spared. It wounded, almost destroyed, the spirit of the people. That wound has never really healed. Some of us had lost too much to speak of. And so we didn't. But I remember.

Doña Pastora's Story

He was a big man, big and jet-black, and he had the whitest teeth of anyone in the barrio. And when he smiled, you felt it down here.... And kind, he was a kind giant. The children loved him. He carried little pieces of cane in his pockets and handed out sugar-sweetness to any child he met.

The first winds caught us on the way to your great-grandmother Mati's house. I waited and waited for him to come home but there was no more time. I took the children over, hoping to meet him on the road. When I got to the house, he was nowhere in sight. I tried to go out after him but the wind had just picked up so fast. I had the children to think about. I'd have to wait and trust him to find shelter on his own. I sat, gathered up my kids, and never stopped praying until I heard the wind die down and the noises stop. I heard screaming. I think it was your grandmother calling for Doña Mati. But in my head, I kept praying for my Moncho. There was no room in there for any other prayers. After a while, I heard nothing but the words in my head, *Dios mío, please shelter him, cover him in your goodness, hold him under your protective wing, guide him to a haven, keep him from all harm, deliver him into my loving arms, save him for his children's sake.* I don't know how long we were in there, but when we came out, the world had changed.

Everything I had known had been pushed away by San Cristóbal. Houses, trees, crops were all caved in, pushed out, flung about until nothing was left intact. Mud, mud everywhere, covering everything. That day, the side of the mountain slid down like a blanket and covered everything in mud. I heard a woman screaming, *Moncho! Moncho!* Later, when my throat wouldn't work anymore, I realized it had been me screaming all along. I sat down on a rock and leaned on my children. I sat and waited for them to bring me his body.

And they did. But it took many, many days to find him. They didn't want me to see him. My husband. I just looked at them and they knew. Nothing and nobody in this world could keep him from me. He was bloated, barely recognizable. His hand was so swollen, his wedding band pinched into his skin like a tie on a sausage. He still had on one of the new boots I had gotten him for his saint day. It was my Moncho, all right. Dead now for over a week.

They said some words to me and I nodded. I didn't know what they said and didn't care—until they had to break his legs to get him in the coffin. I started screaming again. Never did hear the words…not enough wood…makeshift coffins…many remains…no room…no space…

I don't remember anything else. Thank God! Someone fed me and took care of my children. One day, I got up and made his favorite breakfast and ate it all by myself. It tasted salty. I cried into that food the whole time I was eating it. After that I began to move about and do the things my body remembered to do. And sometime, I don't know when, the weight on my chest started to get lighter, or maybe I just learned to carry it better. One day, I smiled at the sun. I suppose that is what folks mean when they say that you begin to heal. I don't know about that. I just know that for many years after my Moncho passed away, I smiled less than I used to and when I did smile it seemed an unfamiliar movement.

* * *

The other women listened, not meeting Pastora's eyes.

* * *

Doña Teo was wearing a pink dress that day and had actually put on some rouge. The hanky in her pocket matched the dress and she was wearing shoes instead of the slippers she usually wore. That day she left her Jesus of Nazareth cardboard fan—the one that said FUNERARIAS GONZÁLEZ—at home. That day she carried her silk fan. She spread out her skirt and arranged herself on the cane rocker before beginning her tale.

Doña Pastora couldn't resist. She teased her mercilessly, "*La señorita* is going to tell us her story today. She has her Easter Sunday best on so this must be a good one." Doña Teo blushed to the roots of her silver-white hair.

"As a matter of fact, it is. *¡Sí, señoras!* This is a good one."

Doña Pastora, with a mischievous look in her eye, said, "*Muchacha*, with movies and television and all today, you know these children don't have any imagination. You'd have to give her some details." And she leaned forward in her chair to catch every word.

"You are all a bunch of *carifrescas*"—Doña Teo eyed them coldly— "but I'll tell you, *nena*." She turned to me. "We'll just ignore them."

With this, both Doña Pastora and Doña Gume pulled up their chairs. I could see Abuela standing at the doorway. They hung on every word. I couldn't help it. My laughter just came ringing out. These women had become teenage girls again, anxious to hear all the details of their friend's conquest.

They whooped, slapped their knees, and pulled up even closer. Doña Teo glared.

DOÑA TEO'S STORY

My story is about love. I was fourteen and in full bloom you might say. I wasn't always an old lady with flabby arms. You should have seen me then. I was slender and my arms were firm and strong and my bust stood out in front of me like round-tipped *piraguas*. Young men would look and look but I was very shy and my father very strict. So the boys looked and kept at a distance. But at one of the *fiestas patronales*, a man from another town came and looked. He looked and I looked and he talked and I listened. He asked me to dance a bolero and I don't know what got into me but I said yes. I know, I know, that was forward of him and shameful of me. But I didn't care. Once we started moving against each other to the music of the Trío Los Panchos, I thought that I was born to be led around the floor in those muscular arms. We walked away, under the low-hanging trees, yes, we did. And then he touched a little and then I liked it a lot and then…well, you can imagine the rest.

He was muscular and his hair was parted in the center and brushed back. Black and shiny with scented brilliantine. He had a neat little moustache to match that curled up at either side of his heavy lips. He had green eyes and his skin was the color of fresh milk. He wore a white *guayabera* and white linen pants. His belt cinched him in at the waist and you should have seen those butt…

He smelled of jasmine and had a deep, penetrating voice. I had never met anyone like him. I heard that there was an American movie actor named Roberto Taylor who looked like him. I couldn't keep my eyes, or my hands, off him.

One thing led to another and I knew my mother would never approve. He was ten years older than me and from another town and you know how Mamá felt about white men "sniffing" after *trigueñas*. It never worked out, she said. They just want to play with you and then marry their own, she said. Of course, I was in love so her words fell on deaf ears.

So, one night, we just ran away together. He had a brand-new car and we drove to Fajardo, where no one knew us. We stayed at a cabin on the beach. It was small and had no running water or electricity but it was only until he could make the arrangements with the priest. Then we'd go home and my Papá and his would have to accept us.

I was so happy! We had a wonderful week. We were to be married Friday afternoon. I would wear my fine green dress and white shoes, and gardenias in my hair. It was all planned. I could barely sleep on Thursday night. I finally fell asleep and woke up with the sun shining on my face. I stretched and smiled and hugged myself, all before I realized that I was alone on the bed. Something was very wrong.

I remember thinking that he must have just gotten up, because his side of the bed was still warm. I sat up and stared at the creases on the pillows. It was too quiet. Too still. I looked around and it was then I saw that his clothes were gone. It finally hit me that he, too, was gone. The last thing I remember was feeling wetness on my cheeks. I don't know when or how, but I woke up in my own bed at home. My mother walked in and out carrying food three times a day. She put the food down at the foot of the bed and walked out as silently as she had walked in. She never again spoke another word to me.

Days later, the priest came in as silently as clouds. He spoke to me about repentance, about cleansing sin, about penance. I turned my face to the wall and said, "speak to my mother." He shook his head and walked out. Then he spoke to my mother about young people making mistakes, about unconditional love, about forgiveness. She spoke to him about shame and about being betrayed by her own flesh and blood. After that, there weren't very many words in our house.

My neighbor's son, Cristiano, had been one of the boys who looked and looked and waited for me to look in return. I never had. He began bringing me a mango every afternoon—to sweeten my day, he said. He could read the bitterness in my mother's face and could feel the silence, see it sucking away what little life I had left. But I wasn't hungry and left his mangoes on the dining room table.

I knew there must be talk in the neighborhood. When I asked him about it he said that gossip fell around him like discarded leaves, unwanted and unneeded. I blinked and looked at him for the first time. That afternoon, I nibbled at a sliver of his mango.

One day he proposed and promised two things. He would always bring sweetness into the house and there would never be silence between us. We got married in a simple ceremony under his mango tree. My mother, who could easily see the tree from her porch, chose not to attend the wedding. She had shuttered the windows and doors early that morning and kept them closed even in the boiling afternoon sun.

I learned to love Cristiano and, with time, I grew to appreciate his quiet and unassuming ways. He never spoke of my youthful folly. Eventually, I worshipped my husband and he worshipped me. Life brought many lemons to our door, but he kept his word, bringing me a sweet every day. And we may have had more than a fight or two, as all couples do, but we never, ever had silence.

* * *

They told me of their lives and the lives of others—everyone in the town, in fact. They shared their dreams with me, and their disappointments. They celebrated their joys and whispered their failures. I looked at them with their limp aprons and their cracked feet in oversized men's slippers. I watched toothless, sunken mouths and listened to the words floating out through ill-fitting dentures. They told me stories I had never heard and stories they knew by heart. And as they did so, they suddenly turned into a group of young girls playing in the creek, young women sending their men to war, mothers-of-the-bride letting go of their no-longer little girls, old women sitting before their husbands' coffins.

The days grew into weeks and still I listened. They filled my days and my emptiness with their teeming lives. My grandmother told them I was writing down their stories and they smiled behind cupped hands and brought me more, trusting that I would be gentle with their tales.

"You're a good girl. You write this down and tell the truth about us."

They brought their stories in their pockets, their teacups, their photo albums, their treasure boxes. They brought them in lockets and broken picture frames and yellowed newspapers. They must have rummaged in the bottoms of their drawers, under the beds, between the old dresses in the backs of the wardrobes. They brought me huge leather-bound Bibles and yellowed christening gowns and pressed flowers. They brought me the pieces of their lives and bade me make them a quilt of words. When the world was moving too fast for them, they bade me stop time.

During those many weeks, I sat back and listened and wrote down what I was given. The idea of being a published writer started to take seed once again. It felt good, like a rediscovered family album. Everything seemed familiar. I woke up thinking of the tales, and the pen in my hand moved and kept on moving. I couldn't write quickly enough to capture all the words that swirled around my head. I took their stories and nurtured them, blended them with my own, and let them simmer.

26 NEW PERSPECTIVES

I sat in front of my grandmother in the dimness of the *balcón* at dusk. The only light came from the open front door. Abuela Concha had scraped out the pots and washed all the dishes before coming out to join me. The smell of *chorizos* was still in the air. I felt satisfied as she finally sat down to sip her rum-laced *coquito* from a teacup. Although I was raised up there in the cold, I could still whip up some *criollo* holiday treats. Abuela put the cup down and picked up the wide-tooth comb. I slid between her knees, welcoming the cool of the ceramic tiles beneath me. It felt good, surrendering my thick hair into her hands.

All day, I'd wanted to talk to her about the events of the previous night. I remembered the hushed voices of the women as they left my grandmother's back room. I'd heard the chanting and the voices. They sounded so familiar and yet made me uneasy. I had slipped into the room as Abuela was bidding the last of the women goodbye at the front door. Shadows slid along the walls of the candlelit room. The corners disappeared into darkness, creating the feel of an intimate bower. The long table was covered in a white cloth, and on it sat vases of flowers—freesias—and a bank of lit candles. The same legion of plaster Catholic saints that inhabited my mother's bedroom altar in New York City—La Caridad del Cobre, San Martín de Porres, La Milagrosa—stood guard here in my grandmother's back room in rural

Puerto Rico. And among these, other items—a huge carved statue of an African drummer, a coconut, a half-smoked cigar, a dish of copper coins, a bowl of seashells, yellow and white beaded necklaces, a huge bowl of clear water.

"Abuela," I started, "do you really believe in all that stuff in the back room?"

"*¡Claro que sí!*" You go to a big university and listen to teachers, I go to my back room and listen to the voices of the ancestors. We both learn."

"But that's ridi—" I felt a slight tug on the back of my head.

"*Cuidado.*" There was a note of warning in the word. My grandmother continued, "I hope your mother taught you more than how to prepare holiday foods. I didn't expect that from my own granddaughter."

"I'm sorry, Abuela. I didn't mean to ..."

"Just remember. I respect your ways and I expect you to respect mine. You have a lot of information in your head. And that is good. But along the way, you've forgotten some things. The ancestors speak to the heart. You have to learn to listen for them. This is a lesson I can teach you. When you stop paying attention to the ancestors, you cut yourself off. And then when you are in trouble, you are lost, have no way of finding your way back to yourself, like being lost in the forest without the stars to help guide you home."

I turned and looked at Abuela and realized that she was speaking from a totally different place. Her eyes were traveling somewhere beyond the porch in another time.

"*Pero,* Abuela, that's *bruje*—"

I never finished my sentence because the grandmother that I had come to know, the woman who was always ready to open her arms to me, suddenly changed before my eyes. In an instant, her body tensed. The soft lines in her face hardened. Her hands clenched into hard fists that were tightly contained in her lap. Her eyes flashed.

"Don't say it. Don't say that word." Her voice was raspy, harsh. She must have heard the edge in it because the voice that followed was more controlled, the edge less cutting. She took a deep breath before continuing. "That word has cost the women in this family more pain than you can ever imagine. Please, it would kill me to hear it come from your lips."

"I'm sor...I didn't know..."

"Then it's time you did." I watched as her fists relaxed. "And I guess it's up to me to tell you."

She spoke a long time about Fela and Mati and Cheo and Próspero and Romero. She spoke about herself, her fear of what she couldn't control, her need to be "normal," like every other young girl. In a quiet voice, she spoke about her pushing away her mother's teachings. She spoke of the terrible silences between her and Abuela Mati and the pain that the distance between them had caused. She spoke of her time of denial, her lost time in the hospital, and her time of healing. She spoke of the price she had to pay, of her regrets, and finally of her making peace with her life.

"The people who have used that word are people who hurt us because they fear our gift of hearing beyond words and speaking to the ones that came before, learning the lessons of the past and seeing the dangers of the future. Learn from my mistakes. We get only so many gifts in life. When we have been given one, it should never be squandered."

"But Mami never..."

"Your mother has always believed...even more than I. In my time of denial, it was she who never broke the line, she who kept faith with our past. It was she who kept us going when I got lost."

I thought back on my mother's quiet beliefs. She insisted that I go to church and make my communion but never went herself. I remembered her candles and her incense and her saints, but never to this extreme, séances and chanting and talking in tongues to spirits who brought messages from the dead. That was never a part of our home.

"There are many ways of knowing and many paths to the truth," said Abuela.

I searched my memories. Mami had told me many stories about Abuela Mati and Abuela Concha and the rest of the family. But she had never said anything about ghosts and spirits. Slowly, a tiny flower of a memory started unfolding in the back of my mind. I remembered Mami's dreams, the accurate forecasters of trouble. She seemed to anticipate every major event in my life.

She often related her dreams to me, called me with admonitions and premonitions. She pressed unwanted advice on me. I had always hated it, but in retrospect, I had to admit that she was uncannily accurate.

"*Nena*, we all carry an energy that makes each of us who we are. Your spirit, more than your name, tells the world who you are. What we call death is only the body wearing down. The spirit is still alive and waiting to reach out to the next generation. That's why we honor our ancestors. That spirit, what you call ghost and what I call ancestor, watches over all of us. Your mother's dreams? Those are just ancestors whispering in her ear while she sleeps."

Abuela continued as though she had heard my thoughts.

"In the daytime, when Elena's awake, her brain is too busy to listen. She relies on her book learning to guide her. But when she sleeps and her mind is at rest, that's when the ancestors come to her. Beneath all that book learning, there's a part of her that remembers to honor those other ways of knowing."

I didn't move, hardly breathed, not wanting to break the spell. Her words introduced me to a mother I was only beginning to recognize. And she put into words feelings I'd had in my most private moments and hadn't even named yet. Abuela's voice brought me back.

"I know, because I tried to turn away from myself when I was a young woman. I thought I knew better. Like you, I thought the old ways were just superstitious nonsense. And then when trouble came my way, I had nothing to hold me up and I was lost for a very long time. Now I listen all the time. I'm always open. Sometimes, I barely sleep.

"I'm an old woman and closer to the old ones than you young people. Maybe I hear them more clearly than you do. You have a lot of living, a lot of exploring, and a lot of learning to do. You want to *do* everything. And you want to do it *now*. The young are always in such a hurry, trying to change the world overnight, before they even really get acquainted with it. Maybe that's as it should be. I don't know. All I ask is that you honor what has come before…and that you never use that word that has brought so much heartache to our door."

Abuela pinned the last braid and kissed the crown of my head. She gave me a gentle push to let me know she wanted to get up. After picking the loose hairs off the comb, she pulled herself out of the rocker and began her slow shuffle, then her stiff limp, toward the front door. She scratched her head and pushed the comb into her own hair.

I watched her go, and thought that soon she may be one of the ancestors herself. I took her words and put them away. Later, in the darkness, protected by mosquito netting, I would take them out again and reconsider.

* * *

They walked in like swans, their words, like feathers, filling the air with their sense of entitlement. I had come in forty-five minutes early to my first class at the *universidad*. Would my Spanish be good enough? Would a black Nuyorican from the South Bronx fit in? Could I hold my own? I had registered for this course with so much enthusiasm. Suddenly, I wasn't so sure.

During the class, I noticed that mine was the only Afro in the room. There were several natural blondes and quite a few unnatural ones. There had been a raised eyebrow or two, but no one said a word to me.

I sat in this class on Puerto Rican history and culture for an entire semester. The words *"esclavos"* and *"esclavitud"* were rarely mentioned and then only in passing—like an unfortunate disease. Slavery was referred to as a regrettable period in our history. Much was made, however, of the glory of the cane and coffee that was the mainstay of colonial society. Who actually worked the cane and the coffee fields was not the issue. We learned about all the great Puerto Rican abolitionists who became great statesmen, but nothing of the slaves themselves. The times I brought up the question of race, I was assured repeatedly that all Puerto Ricans were treated equally and racism simply didn't exist in Puerto Rico. Looking around the campus, my eyes told me differently. But I waited for the second semester and the study of contemporary history and culture.

On the first day of the spring semester, the professor closed the windows on the noise of the *comunistas* and *independentistas*, bearded revolutionaries who threatened the Puerto Rican way of life. The student protesters carried large signs—VIETNAM PARA LOS VIETNAMITAS, WHY FEED THE YANQUI WAR MACHINE??, YANQUI GO HOME, and THEIR OWN SONS DON'T WANT TO GO, WHY SHOULD WE? They chanted, *"Arriba, abajo, los Yanquis pa'l carajo."* The professor shut out the noise and said, "Turn to page one fifty-six." There was a cartoon of a huge, benevolent Uncle Sam, taking a half-starved and dazed *jíbaro* under his wing and walking toward a sunrise. The caption read, "The Dawning of a New Day." It was a reprint from a turn-of-the-century newspaper. *Nothing has changed*, I thought. I closed my notebook, picked up my knapsack, and left the room. I threw the textbook in the trash basket on the way out, knowing I would never go back.

I pushed through to the front of the rally so I could get a better look at the stand. The chanting got louder and louder with each speaker. I didn't even hear the sirens until the police were on us.

They came with their clubs and their dogs and their handcuffs. The tear-gas canisters burst like white roses all around the crowd as policemen swung their clubs indiscriminately at whatever body presented itself. Soon gray gas filled the quad. People ran in all directions. Placards were trampled underfoot; a pregnant girl went down. I turned to help her up when I felt the first blow. After the second, I felt myself being dragged away. I made my body as heavy as I could. It made no difference. I was dragged a short distance and then into a dark room. I thought. *This is it. Secret beatings, electric shock, death. I've read about this.*

But the person who pulled me away was not a policeman. My rescuer was a woman, a huge black woman in her fifties or sixties. She was over six feet tall, and her pure gray Afro was stained red on the left side of her head. She was wiping her forehead as she bent over me.

I tried to move but she held me down.

"María Luisa Campos." The statement was actually her introduction. She was a photographer and had been taking photos of the clash between students and cops when she saw me go down. She had blocked the next blow and somehow gotten me away from the crowd, out to the street, and into her shop before the rest of the police detachment arrived. I now lay on the floor of her shop, across the street from the melee in the quad.

I felt the stinging as she cleaned my wound.

"*¡Coño, cabrones, hijos de puta!*" The string of curses flowed out of her effortlessly.

"Wha…?" I tried to get up, only to fall back. My head burst into a dozen explosions. "Jesus Christ, what happened out there?"

"*¿Una Americana?*"

"No, yeah, I mean…yes, I'm Puerto Rican, but I live in New York."

"Oh! *Una americuchi.* One of *those!*" She switched to English.

"What! What the hell does that mean?"

"I know the type."

"Listen, lady, thanks for the help but get off my case. You don't know a damn thing about me. If you'll help me up, I'll get out of here and be on my way." I tried to get up, but the pounding in my head made it impossible to move.

"Relax, *chica*. Just stay where you are, unless you want to get your head bashed in again." She glanced out of the front windows. "The cops are still out there. So it's me or them."

She got up and gave me a good look. She took in the boots, the knapsack, my own Afro and my University of New York T-shirt.

"What the hell are you doing here, in the middle of all this?" She gestured toward the scene outside.

"I came here to learn."

"To learn? To learn what?"

"To learn about me. About Puerto Rico. About the past."

"Oh! One of tho—" She watched me tense up again and put her hands up in surrender. "I'm sorry, sorry. Tell me."

"Forget it. What do you care?"

She pointed at her head. "I care enough to have my head bashed in."

"Okay, okay. I came to learn more about us. I've heard a lot of family stories but I wanted to know more. I especially wanted to know more about black people in Puerto Rico."

"I know. 'Black is beautiful' and 'Power to the people.'"

"Something like that. I needed to know more. So I came to the university."

She took another look out of the window, "*Pues*, there's your classroom going up in smoke."

I could smell the tear gas that stunk up the street even through the closed door of the shop. I could hear the sirens as, one after the other, police vans transported dozens of students away from the campus to some unknown place.

"Thanks for getting me out of there..." I tried to clear my head. "What's your name again?"

"María Luisa."

"Thanks, Doña María." I was alert enough so that my home training kicked in. She was an older woman meriting the formal title.

"Forget that Doña business. Just María Luisa, okay? And you are…?"

"Carisa Ortíz."

"*Mucho gusto.*" She held out her hand. Funny, how we revert to niceties without thinking.

"No, really. Thank you. I'd probably be in one of those police vans if you hadn't gotten me out of there."

"You're welcome." She handed me two pills and a glass of water. I hesitated. "Just painkillers. You're getting quite a bump there."

I finally sat up and looked around. The walls were covered with old photographs, most of them cracked and sepia colored. Some reproduced. A few recent portraits of children and old women sat on the counter. The display behind the counter housed dozens of old cameras. Heavy curtains covered a doorway, beyond which I could see part of a tropical backdrop.

"What were you studying before your life as a revolutionary?" María Luisa asked.

"History and culture."

"Hah! *Our* history and culture? In there?"

"Yeah."

"And you expected to find information about black people or the black communities in there."

"Yeah, I did."

"I guess you know by now you wasted your time and money."

"Yeah, sort of."

"So, how did you end up with your head smashed in?"

"Well, there seemed to be more history going on outside the classroom than in. So I came out to see. Besides, in there—blondes have more fun."

She gave me a sad smile and rubbed her hands over her own tightly curled hair.

"Yes, I know what you mean. Some things never change. Listen, *chica*. What you get in there"—she pointed to the campus—"that's the sanitized version of our country. You want to know the truth of life here, especially ours," she rubbed my cheek with the back of her hand—"here it is." She waved her hand all about her. "And it's free. No head bashing needed."

"You mean you'll be my teacher?"

"No, I mean you'll be my helper. I can't pay much. But you'll get an education you couldn't pay for with gold."

"But you don't know me."

"Sure I do. The cops introduced us."

* * *

Day after day I stood at María Luisa's window. I watched the clashes between cops and students, cursing the brutal policemen and cheering for the protesters. Every bottle they threw was my blow, every chant was my screamed protest. But I was too scared to go out there myself. Meanwhile, María Luisa went out every day, camera in hand, to record what she could of the protest.

One day at the end of my first week, while I went on and on about the injustice and the brutality of the scene outside, María Luisa walked up behind me.

"I know how you feel. It's like watching the war on TV without actually being there, a much easier fight."

There it was, an unspoken accusation, the questioning of my sincerity and commitment. Anger flashed through me, especially because she was so right. "What the hell do you mean by that?"

"Relax, *chica*. This is not your fight. You have your own fight at home…"

"This is my home. I was born…"

"I know. I know. Shut up and listen before you get ready to fight me. Yes, you were born here. And your roots are deep in our soil. But the reality is that you don't live our life. You never have. Your place is up north. You got on a plane and came here to recapture something you think you've lost. I respect that. You want to acknowledge the past, honor what and who came before you. I will help you do it because it's what I believe in more than anything else. Look around you. But you came here to study, not to live."

"I..."

"Listen. First lesson—the beginning of learning is listening. You may not like everything you hear, just like you didn't like everything you saw out there. This is no paradise lost, no panacea. This is the real Puerto Rico, not the post cards and the nostalgia of your parents. Here you will find racism just like you find it up north. You'll find intolerance, meanness, cruelty, hypocrisy—just like you will in New York. If what you want is to fight these things, you didn't need to come here. You can, and I hope you do, fight them wherever you live. But you didn't come here for that. So, I ask again, why are you here?

"Did you come to learn or to confirm? You probably came here looking for a dream. You're looking for your parents' memories of Puerto Rico, their 'truth,' sugarcoated with years of nostalgia. That Puerto Rico probably never existed, not even twenty or thirty years ago when they left. It certainly doesn't exist now. Our reality will kill a large part of your dream. Are you ready for that?"

My face must have given away my feelings, because her tone became softer, more sensitive to the damage she was doing.

"What you'll be left with in the end will sustain you much more than any illusion you may have brought with you. Because here in addition to all the problems of poverty, political intrigue, corruption, jealousy, and sociological and historical denial, you'll also find *familia*, *respeto, dignidad, amor, trabajo, cariño*. And yes, you will find racism, alive and well, just like you left it up north.

"All I'm saying is, stop and consider why you are here. When you know that, then to hell with me, to hell with anyone else. Find your ground and stand it firmly. That makes for a more fulfilling life; believe me, I know."

27 COLLABORATIONS

I knew absolutely nothing about photography—but I learned. There were several rooms beyond the studio, but I was introduced to one room at a time. I was shown the rooms I needed in order to do my work. At first, I only saw the bathroom, the supply room, and the studio. During my first week, I ordered supplies, kept the studio neat and clean, and set up backdrops for in-house portraits.

The work was not demanding, and although María Luisa never actually sat down and spoke to me about the photos that hung on the walls, I had plenty of time to examine them on my own. Most of them were portraits. All were washed with a layer of sepia, giving the subjects an almost mystical appearance, as though they were suspended in time. María Luisa often changed the actual photographs during the night so that when I came in the morning, I was never sure what image I would find in each of the frames, giving me the illusion that each image appeared temporarily and then receded into the past. Just when I got comfortable with each face, it seemed magically replaced by another, as though time was allowing me only temporary glimpses of what came before.

Although this was unnerving at first, it became an unspoken game. Each night, I would go home to Abuela's house and make up a story about one of the pictures. I tried to give the image a whole life—

family, friends, problems—before it was replaced by María Luisa's unseen hand. I added these stories to what I had come to call my "*Abuela Stories*," the ones I was collecting from my grandmother's friends, who still paid me the occasional visit. In this way, I started working on my first collection of stories of what would become my Puerto Rico period.

One day, near the end of my first month of work, María Luisa asked me to help her pack up some cameras, tripods, and other equipment and load them onto her truck. She locked the shop and told me to hop in next to her. She said little and gripped the steering wheel tightly as we pulled out of her driveway. From the equipment we packed, I could see that this would be a portrait job. But that was the first time I realized she did portraits in people's homes. I could see she wasn't about to volunteer any information, but I tried anyway.

"What's up?"

She was tense and terse. "I'm not one for much talk when I do location shoots. I have too much to think about and I don't like breaking my concentration, but this is your first time so you should know. *Mira, chica*, you're about to see another side of my life. This is not something I enjoy but it pays the bills and gives me the freedom to do as I wish with the rest of my time. Just follow my instructions, say nothing, and everything will be fine. I hope you brought your book. The trip will take a while."

"But where are we going."

"To another world."

She wouldn't say any more. Four hours later, we pulled up to a mansion in Ponce, the largest city in the southern part of the island. That was the first time I had ever walked into the home of a wealthy Puerto Rican. We were let in by a uniformed maid who led us through room after room, out onto a carefully manicured courtyard in the center of the house. Although it was scorching hot outside, here there was a hushed coolness that really did feel like another world. The courtyard was paved in mosaic tile. A huge fountain shot up from the center of an island of potted fern. The white wrought-iron furniture and large marble planters dotted the expanse of green that defined the perimeter of the courtyard. A huge rattan chair and a smaller bench had been placed among the flowering plants. The gardeners were just gathering their hoses when the woman of the house came out to greet us.

"*Buenas tardes*. On time as usual." She held her hand out to María Luisa and ignored me as I tried to balance the tripods and camera cases that I still carried.

A call for a servant brought out a pitcher of lemonade and some glasses. Another uniformed woman brought in a struggling child. They stopped immediately on seeing us. The little girl stared openly.

"Who are these people?" she asked.

"I told you I have arranged for our picture to be taken by a famous photographer. This is María Luisa Campos."

"Her? But she's a nig—"

"*¡Basta!*" This woman was not used to being questioned, but more than that, I think she was embarrassed at her child's obvious rudeness.

"I have very little time and won't put up with your nonsense. I won't be made late." She turned to us, face flushed. "Where do you want us, María Luisa?"

It took most of the afternoon to finish the shoot. The woman wanted to be photographed in different outfits and in several different locations within the grounds.

At the first opportunity, I asked, "A 'famous' photographer? What's that all about?"

María Luisa put out her hand to stop me. "Later. Away from here."

I held my tongue all afternoon. It was 6:30 that evening before we finally pulled out of the front gate. Since she said nothing, neither did I. She was quiet throughout most of our journey. When we were an hour away from home, she abruptly began.

"It started ten years ago. I was studying in New York and just beginning to make a name for myself. Then my father died. He left me a little money and the shop. I was almost broke, so I had to come home. Being a woman art photographer is difficult anywhere, but especially here. So I went back to the shop, taking pictures of weddings, communions, special occasions. Art photography was out of the question. I tried, but I'm not…socially connected or accepted… not part of the elite. I was barely making enough money to live on. So I stopped trying here. I started sending my work out to European and American shows under the name ML Campos. I got a lot of support from one of my former teachers.

"For a long time, I heard nothing but rejection. I had stopped trying, when I started getting reviews. Two of my photos were accepted for a major exposition in France. The reviews were glowing. My work was 'different,' 'exotically sensual,' they said; *'erotique noir.'* I won prizes. And my work started to sell very well. Soon there were wealthy collectors and requests for a solo show from an important Parisian gallery. One or two of my photos were purchased by important museums. I'm not rich, but I do have some name recognition."

"But then, why that back there?" I motioned in the direction of the house we had just left.

"You are so young! Celebrity doesn't always transfer into a constant income. Once I was recognized overseas, I became very popular at home as well. 'A new and undiscovered talent,' I think that's what they called me. And I took advantage of my 'fame.' Fame pays well, *chica*, but exclusivity pays even better. I work for the very rich and charge them outrageous fees. I sell my name to these people very rarely. Their fees are often enough to keep me going for long stretches at a time. Don't look so disgusted. Bills have to be paid every month. They can't wait until the next exhibition. Fine and noble principles almost landed me in the street once; it won't happen again.

"Yes, I sell my name. But it's not just the money. I do it because it buys me freedom and time. It guarantees that I will be able to do my real work without worrying about whether I can pay for an assistant or afford my supplies. I can take my cameras to the countryside. I can look for traditional people living in traditional ways, the true ways of our country. In the mountains, and in the small villages, away from the superhighways and the hamburger chains, I look for the face of Puerto Rico. I try to capture it in my lens and project it onto the world. And if I have to put up with an occasional afternoon like the one we just had, to me, it's worth the price.

"I'm not a crusader, *chica,* and far from saintly. I'm a woman that has a lot to say and is very much aware that she may not have much time in which to say it. So don't judge me too harshly."

* * *

One day not long after, María Luisa asked me to pack her equipment again. I braced for another visit to the world of the rich. I said nothing, but I was relieved to see that this time we prepared for wide-angle shots, and I could tell from the film she packed that we would be working outdoors.

Again we loaded the truck in silence and headed south. This time we went deep into the mountains. We climbed fences, crossed fields, and made our way through tangled brush to find a dilapidated structure in the middle of nowhere. I looked around. No one had been here for years. María Luisa, meanwhile, had pulled two machetes out of the back of the truck and was handing me the smaller one. I had never touched a machete in my life and barely knew what to do with it.

"This is my real work." She gestured at the ruin. "It was an extensive coffee plantation once. The man who owned it was a prosperous merchant who exported coffee all over the world. His forty to fifty slaves made him one of the richest men on the island. That probably doesn't sound like much to you, but remember, we are a small country and couldn't support, thank God, those giant plantations like the North Americans. What happened here was bad enough."

I stared at her in amazement, "You're kidding? This…"

"Don't look at me like that."

"But you never said…you never told me…"

"It's a surprise. I'd been waiting…making sure. No one knows about this yet. I wanted to get in here with my camera before the authorities come with their measurements and their classifications and the like. I wanted to listen for the voices of ghosts. I wanted to try to find them before all our progressive leaders sanitize it too much and put it on display for a buck or two. So don't disturb anything. I want it as is, all of it. Here"—she handed me a camera—"start earning your keep."

I turned and started exploring. I couldn't believe we were standing on the remains of an actual plantation. As careful as we wanted to be, we had to pull away vines and cut away impassable plants to get to the main house. A tangled mass of vegetation had grown around and through the buildings. Trees grew out of the center of an old mosaic floor, the roots pushing up old tiles to claim their space. In the remains of one room, a royal palm grew straight up into a trompe l'oeil vaulted ceiling. As I walked carefully through the ruins, I found remnants of their lives—an old pot, a hitching post, broken pottery, a cracked porcelain sink. In the back, where there had been a second story, now stood a staircase to nowhere. An old bed—springs rusted, mattress long decomposed—hung from a window in the air above the half floor left on this side of the structure. Nature itself had consumed the old mansion as, I assumed, it had consumed the bodies that once inhabited this place.

We took pictures all afternoon. By the time we got back to the truck I was exhausted. My arms hung loosely at my sides. I wanted nothing more than to lie down and close my eyes. At first I had been incredibly excited. This was such a find, such a step into the past. But after hour upon hour of standing in the midst of that world, finding the bits and pieces of the realities of their lives, I began to see and to feel and to cry. And then I didn't want to see anymore. It had been more than I could have imagined. By late afternoon I was drained and ready to go home.

"The first time I did something like this, I cried for a week," María Luisa said, coming up behind me. "But now, now I'm happy, so happy that it's all in here," she tapped her camera. "And if my plan works, it won't ever be forgotten."

When we got back, María Luisa went directly to her darkroom and I went straight home to bed. I woke up sixteen hours later, ate Abuela's food, and crawled back into bed for another ten hours before I could get up and deal with the world again.

A few weeks after the plantation visit, María Luisa took me into another of her back rooms. This room was all the way in the back of the building, behind a curtain. There she entrusted me with her most precious possession, her collection of historical prints, portraits, and landscapes taken by her father and grandfather.

"Very few people have ever seen this room and nobody has touched this collection. Some of these prints go back to before the turn of the century." She had pried open the corner of one box. I put my hand in and pulled out a half-dozen photos that sat near the top.

The first picture was a black-and-white shot of a young woman. Her white skin was deeply burned by the sun, not tanned and polished from lying on a beach but brown and lined from toiling in the outdoors. She was a young woman but her face and eyes were old. Her hair was plaited and the braids pinned across the top of her head, like a heavy crown. She sat leaning on the wooden wall of a train compartment, staring into space. She wore a print dress, a bit frayed, bodice held closed by a safety pin. In her lap she clutched at a dark hen wrapped in newspaper. Her hands, large and rough, were the only living part of the picture. I stared at the picture, dumbfounded. I hadn't even known there had ever been a rail system in Puerto Rico.

The second picture was taken in the train yards. A locomotive conductor sleeping in the cab was surrounded by a flock of white goats. The goats were feeding on the few blades of grass that had grown around the huge dark machines. The white bodies of the animals were startling against the big dark engines that sat just behind them.

The third photograph was a sepia studio portrait. A tall black man in a white linen suit stood erect, expectant, one arm resting on an ornamental post with the word RECUERDOS printed vertically down the front of the column. Behind him rose a country scene with faded palm trees and rolling hills. He stood, panama straw hat proudly displayed, unsmiling, intense eyes staring. On the floor just next to the column was a small, shiny suitcase. This picture could have been a parting gift to relatives left behind as he began his quest for a better life elsewhere. I wondered why it was still here, unclaimed and long forgotten.

I couldn't wait to dig into the dozens of stacked, sealed boxes that lined the walls of the room. They were labeled only by year. The ink was barely legible on some of them. Some were still tied with the original ropes. The tape sealing the cardboard boxes had curled back or cracked. Some were not boxes at all, but yellowed and stained suitcases. Before I could begin organizing and cataloguing these photos, I would have to wipe away the blanket of protective dust that lay over them.

I was fascinated, lost in the world of those images. Not one of the pictures I had seen was like those of the San Juan socialites, beauty queens, cotillions, or political leaders that hung framed and prominently displayed in the university administration building. We already had a disproportionate number of their stories. They all lived in marbled halls and were well enough protected.

I was totally immersed in these pictures because some of them could have easily been of the people in my own family stories, people with no public voices.

I looked from the photos to María Luisa and back to the photos again. Finally, I sat speechless.

She continued, apparently oblivious to my reaction.

"I know, I know. It'll be a lot of work. *Chica*, take your time. Some have been here a hundred years, a few more won't hurt. So go slow and be careful." She turned to leave the room and stopped just before reaching the doorway. I looked at her back.

"*Oye*, Carisa."

She had never called me by my name before.

"Those boxes are their lives' work, you know, my father's and grandfather's legacy to me. So they are my life, too. I haven't allowed even my closest companion to touch these."

* * *

For five years we crisscrossed the island. María Luisa was relentless in her search for unusual locations, socially invisible communities, or the quickly disappearing past. Her photographs sparked my words and I filled journal after journal with snippets of stories. I started carrying my journal everywhere and often recorded my thoughts while we were still in the truck.

One night María Luisa started speaking while we drove back to town at dusk. "So when are you going to tell me about the books?"

"What books?"

"Please, don't insult me. If you don't want to talk about it, you don't. But I'm not stupid."

"Well, they're not really books, just journals. I like to write stories about the people we meet and what their lives are all about, or at least what I think they're all about. When I don't know, I fill in the blanks."

"A fellow artist, a storyteller?"

"Well, not exactly an artist. I just scribble."

"Nobody keeps 'scribbles' as well guarded as you have kept yours. One day, you might want to share your scribbles. In case you haven't noticed, I have a good eye for more than just photos."

We drove the rest of the way in silence. I hadn't shown my writing to anyone in a long time. I still wasn't ready to do so, not yet.

* * *

We continued working on María Luisa's project. We went to see prisoners in La Princesa, a network of underground caves in Camuy, defunct plantations in Manatí, tiny Depression houses in Naguabo, prostitutes at the docks in San Juan, junkies in La Perla, fishermen in Vieques, *jíbaros* in the mountains. And everywhere, everywhere we went, she looked for *los viejos* and the very young. She captured wrinkled faces and painfully shallow young bodies in her lenses while I captured their stories in my notebooks.

Our pilgrimages became ritual: the packing of equipment, a silent journey and unspoken search for the elders, respectful requests for information. Not one of the people we approached ever refused us, as though they had just been waiting to be asked, waiting to contribute. Soon I had volume after volume of my story journals, each entry with a space at the beginning or end for the photo of the subject.

I remember the first time it happened. I was putting the final touches on my story of a fisherman we met in Fajardo. He was forty years old and had never been to the capital. Since he had been born and raised on the tiny island of Culebra, he considered Fajardo to be a confusing enough metropolis. He had spent his whole life ferrying between the mainland of Puerto Rico and the islands off the east coast. I wondered how such a life could exist in our modern world. I was still writing when María Luisa walked by and dropped his portrait on my book. By the time I looked up to thank her she was back in the darkroom.

Shortly after that, I began reciprocating by leaving my finished stories on her desk, also without commentary. It would have meant so much for her to praise my work. I wanted her approval. I know she read them but she never commented on them. I was too insecure to push it.

* * *

One day, while I was in the back of the store, I heard the front door open. When I went into the studio, a young man stood patiently waiting. He was beautiful with his shoulder-length black curls and eyes that seemed to see through me. He wanted a passport photo. That was an easy job that I had been doing for some time. I used the camera as an excuse to examine him openly. He wore jeans and a crisp white shirt, with rolled sleeves, open at the collar. There was a thin silver chain around his neck and he wore a silver ring, no stone. Most people sit stock-still for this type of picture. At most they spread their lips impersonally. But he couldn't stop smiling, a big flashy smile that lit up the room. I asked him to just sit and relax, but as soon as my back was turned, the smile was back. I gave up and snapped, flashy smile and all.

His name was Adrian and he was one of the new professors at the university. Five years before, he had been one of the graduate students arrested by the police. He was one of a number of graduates who went from protesting in the streets to lecturing in the classroom.

He said, "I understand you have a wonderful collection of historical photographs."

I said, "Oh, you want to talk to María Luisa. She's the owner and photographer. I think the collection you mean is the work of her father and grandfather."

"We want to do a retrospective of our native photography and would love to include some of her photos."

"You'll have to talk to her about that," I said.

"And what can I talk to you about?"

I ignored the flutter in my chest. "Your pictures will be done in an hour," I said, evading the question.

"Okay, when will she be back?"

"After lunch."

He smiled. "Lunch, that's a great idea. I'll pick something up and we can eat while I wait. What would you like?"

Then it was my turn to smile.

* * *

He spoke of his work and I spoke of mine. He taught cultural anthropology and sociology in the Department of Humanities, and the next time we met he introduced me to several young professors who were taking the department in a new direction. They were focusing on the sociology of the common man. They studied seamstresses, garment workers, stevedores, cane cutters, and tobacco workers. They recorded the stories of young girls who did needlework in factories. They took their tape recorders into the mountains and recorded music, the tales and reminiscences of people who had never been to the capital and didn't even own a telephone. They noted linguistic differences, attitudes, and home remedies. They spoke to the people no one else even thought about, much less studied. They took the word "slavery" out of the closet and breathed life into it, gave it faces, names, memories. They studied wills, certificates of sale, manifests, deeds, demographic records. Finally, I found answers to some of the questions that had brought me to the university in the first place.

They were excited about my work. It seemed to do with literature what they were doing in their own fields. It felt natural for us to join forces and create a multifaceted approach to our studies. Adrian went to his department head and secured me a graduate fellowship. When he told me, I was elated. These professors were my age, full of youthful vitality, enthusiasm. They held the keys to the future. I had been steeped in the past so long that this new approach seemed a breath of fresh air. I was ready to move on, to start building on what I had already learned. But to do so, I had to leave the photo shop.

I dreaded telling María Luisa. Ours was more than a simple working relationship. She had come to depend on me and had given me much more responsibility than that of a simple clerk. I had learned so much from her, and her work fed my own. But how could I pass this up?

The historical photo collection was classified and catalogued, and I had almost completed all the preservation work that could be done on-site. The fieldwork we had done had yielded her thousands of photos. There was very little portraiture work done anymore. The studio was more a gallery than an actual working studio. Almost all the work was done in the darkroom. María Luisa's exhibitions and gallery sales overseas afforded her a very comfortable living. I had to go sometime.

One morning I worked in the studio until María Luisa finally got up. She had worked in the darkroom late into the night. I saw the result of her work that day. We had been to Yauco and taken some wonderful shots of children picking coffee.

"These are great, as usual," I said.

She grunted, not fully awake yet. I waited until she had her breakfast. She stood at her worktable, holding some new lenses. I watched her and was surprised to notice that her gray hair had turned completely white. She still had an athletic figure, but she moved slower than she used to and she seemed very tired. Were my eyes playing tricks on me?

"You got a minute? I need to talk." My voice sounded weak and distant.

"Talk? About what, Storyteller? I just got up."

"Yeah, I know. But this is important."

"*Bueno*." She put down the cylinder she had been examining. "Go on, if it's so important." She was impatient.

"Well, you know Adrian?"

No response.

"You know he and his friends are doing this great work."

She just looked at me.

"Well, I decided to go back to the university. Adrian arranged for a one-year fellowship for me. Don't look at me like that. I really want to do this. It'll be wonderful for my own work. Collecting stories from a totally different perspective. A whole new way of…a whole new group of…a team…I would learn so…"

She put her hand up, as though shielding herself.

"Is it the work or is it the boy?"

"Wha…?"

"You know damn well what I'm asking, Storyteller. Don't treat me like I'm an idiot. So I ask you again, is it the work or the boy?"

I thought about it a moment.

"It's both, but more the work, really."

"Then you must go."

"But I…"

"*Mira*, Storyteller. Nothing lasts forever. When the music stops, you find a different fiddler."

"But I was thinking, maybe I could still work here on my days off. Maybe I could still help out with the fieldwork…"

"A dog can't have two masters. You'll have your own fieldwork to do, and those people aren't paying you not to be there."

Just then the door opened and Adrian walked in with his tape recorder.

"Buenos días."

His words hung in the air. I looked from María Luisa to him and back again.

"Like I said, you must go."

She picked up the equipment she had been working on and took it to the back of the store. Just before she closed the curtain to the back she turned and smiled.

"Good luck, Storyteller. I'll miss your stories."

"I'll come by often."

"Sure you will."

28 Endings and Beginnings

None of it had been easy. I'd finished my commitment to the university. Adrian had been offered a teaching position at Howard University. And I needed to find my way in a different direction.

"Absolutely not! What do you mean, you're going? Going where? To do what and with whom?"

"With nobody, Abuela. I'm going to West Africa. I need to go by myself and take my next steps alone."

Abuela stood, fists on her hips, refusing to accept what I was saying. "And what am I supposed to tell your mother? A young girl like you out by herself…"

"You don't have to tell her anything."

"What? Are you crazy? I am responsible. Have you talked to your mother about this?"

"Not yet."

"You're doing this, *¿sin permiso?*"

"Without permission, Abuela, I'm a grown woman. I'll let Mami know my decision. Things are different with us. Mami is used to me having my own life, making my own decisions. I've been responsible for myself for years. I love you, but I've made up my mind. I've bought my ticket and I leave at the end of the month. Please, I don't want to say anything hurtful. It's just time for me to go."

Abuela went into her back room and slammed the door. She wouldn't talk to me for three days. Every evening, I found my dinner awaiting me on the dining room table. But I didn't see my grandmother at all. Dirty dishes were gone, washed and dried by an invisible hand. The day before I left, I was surprised to hear her come into the kitchen while I was preparing my breakfast.

She pulled the ripe *plátanos* out of my hands, made a long slit in each one, and removed the peel. I stood aside watching her slice them in thin diagonal pieces and drop them into the hot oil. She said nothing. While they turned golden brown in the skillet, she cracked three eggs and fried them after removing the sweet-smelling bananas. As she watched the eggs fry, she began speaking.

"When will we see you again?" She sounded tired, defeated, and yes, a little fearful. "You'll forget about us old women. When you return, you'll go back to New York. Your life will be filled with young people and music and dancing and we'll never see you anymore."

"Abuela, you will see me. And when you do, you and your friends will still tell me your porch stories."

She shook her head, her slippers dragging as she shuffled away.

* * *

"So your answer is no." The pain in Adrian's face tugged at my heart. I had to remember to start breathing again.

"It's not just no, Adrian. It's 'no for right now.' There are things I have to do and things you have to do, too. You must go to Washington. Everything in your work has led you there. The things I must do have to be done somewhere else."

"But why? Research…"

"Adrian, you better than anyone should know. I have to talk to people, go to the source…"

"But…"

"If I can accept your need to go to Howard, why can't you accept mine to go to West Africa?"

"Are you going to turn this into a feminist argument?"

"An argument is the last thing I want. What I want from you is understanding…and patience. I'm trying to say I love you and want you to love me enough to understand. I'm trying to say that I can't ask you to wait for me but I really want you to. I'm trying to be fair. I'm trying to say it all and am not doing a very good job of it, am I?"

"I want us to get married now. I want a home of our own. I want us to work together."

I tried to maneuver my way around my rioting feelings. Of course I would love to marry him. Of course I wanted us to have a home. But I had work to do. I had to go back to the beginning. I had to find out more about what had been lost before it was all gone. I could see that the path that brought us together would now take us away from each other. Yes, I would love to continue working with him, but why did I have to give up my work for his? I looked at him for a moment before I opened my mouth.

"I'm going to ask you a question and I want you to think about what I'm really saying before you answer. Do you want to come to Nigeria with me so we can do *my* work together?"

I watched him working his jaw, digesting the layers of what I was asking him. I knew what the answer would be and so did he. There was no more need for discussion or arguing. When he finally looked up again, he was red-eyed and the lines in his face had all gone south.

"I suppose you don't know when you'll be back."

"No."

There was a long pause, and then, "Do you think you can take time out to mail me a letter or two a week?"

For the first time in this conversation, I felt I could smile. "I suppose I can manage that."

I took in the scent of his cologne as his arms closed around me.

* * *

I hadn't seen María Luisa in weeks. The last time I saw her, she had been dragging a heavy piece of equipment to the truck. I had called to her and waved but she didn't see me. I was about to run across the street to help with the cameras when I noticed a middle-aged woman in men's overalls lifting the last of the equipment before walking over to María Luisa. They embraced and kissed for a long moment before María Luisa released the woman, who walked back into the studio and closed the door.

María Luisa drove off before I could get across the street to her. I wanted so much to talk to her again. I had noticed that the shop was closed a lot of the time. There had been a retrospective of her father's work at the university and a father/daughter exhibit at the Cintron Gallery in El Condado. Finally, the photography dynasty was getting the recognition it deserved. I went to both exhibitions but she attended neither one. They said she had become quite a recluse.

A few days later, I caught up with her, told her of my work, and asked about her latest project.

"My latest project is me. There are things I should have done years ago that need care and attention now. I'm not a young woman anymore and maybe I should start living for today. All my life, I've recorded yesterdays and worried about tomorrow. And along the way I've neglected the here and now. I've decided to let the young take care of correcting history and planning for the future. And you are all doing that quite well. It's time for me to live my life one day at a time."

I listened quietly and then began, "You know, the study is finished."

"Yes, I know."

"The findings have been published and reports well received. Many of the professors have received offers from a number of universities."

"And your Adrian, is he one of them?"

"Yes, he is."

She looked at me for a while.

"That must be hard for you."

"Yes, I guess it is. But I've made some choices and I have my own plans. Soon I leave for West Africa. I need to go back further. I need to see for myself. My stories are going well. In fact, I wanted to give you something before I leave."

I had worked on the handmade book for weeks. It contained only half a dozen stories, each accompanied by the portrait that sparked the tale. They were all her photographs. She leafed through the book and looked up, shielding her eyes from the sun.

"You know, Storyteller. I don't think anyone has ever given me as nice a gift as this. I'll keep it by my bed and read it tonight. Thank you."

"No. I'm the one who needs to thank you."

"If I had ever had a daughter...well...I'm not one for a lot of advice. I've made many of the choices you are making now. I know the urgency. I know the call. But don't forget about your other needs, Storyteller. Don't forget that the artist still has to be a woman. Nourish them both. Do what you need to do, but don't forget that there are joys that can only come from finding the right person and sharing a life with him...or her. You have many years ahead, time to explore it all. I'm so envious...I wish you well."

For the first time in all the time I had known María Luisa, she slipped her arms around me and held me for the briefest of moments before she started to pull away.

But I wouldn't let go, not just yet.

She cleared her throat.

"Better be careful. You know how evil tongues wag."

She pushed away and I let her go.

"I'll be watching for your book," she said. Then she added, "Love you."

I waved and walked away.

* * *

"*¿Cómo?*"

"*¿Que te vas pa' donde?*"

"*¿Esta niña se ha vuelto loca?*"

"*¡Dios libre!*"

The chorus of questions and open outrage showered down on my head. The porch ladies couldn't understand my decision to leave for Nigeria. The word "Africa" brought them blurry images of wild animals, danger, and the end of the world. They thought about that show their grandchildren used to watch with the wild man swinging from tree to tree. They thought of people living in caves. They thought of the jungle, cannibalism, and human sacrifice. They thought of people who didn't have enough to eat and wild animals roaming freely. They had forgotten the place of memory and could see only the manufactured stereotype. They envisioned an unknown void swallowing up their little girl. Or maybe they just thought of me going away and never coming back.

I listened respectfully and tried to calm their fears the best I could. I tried to explain to them that their vision was skewed; that there were many aspects of the continent they knew little about. I sent them on their way, shaking their heads, with a promise that I would bring them pictures of modern Africa, so they could see the large cities, the museums and restaurants and schools and churches that dotted every city on the continent. I would have to replace the images put in their heads by TV shows of white men painted black and constantly saving the lives of stupid natives.

Abuela sat quietly in the corner rocker as I came in from the porch. I expected anger, but as she looked up from her embroidery, her voice came out heavy with concern.

"So far away, *nena*? Going so far?" They were the first words that had crossed between us in days.

I let myself down heavily on to the chair across from her and reached for her hand. "Abuela, you know I have to go. It's been coming a long time. I need to do this for me, for Abuela Mati and Abuela Fela and for you and Mami, too."

"I'm worried."

"Yes, I know. But I'll be careful, I really will."

"*Nena…*"

She turned to look at me and she had a gleam in her eye.

"*Nena*, from the first time we spoke of this, I've been so angry. I've been trying to understand but I just couldn't. Then your Abuela Mati started coming to me in my dreams and she told me that you will be fine. She reminded me of things that I never listened to when she was with us, things I had almost forgotten. And then something strange happened. A longing grew in here." She pointed at her chest. "And suddenly I was wishing that I was a little younger and my legs were a lot stronger and not so stiff and my…well, you know what I mean. I wish that I was still in the 'go out and discover' part of my life. If all those things were true, believe me, Cari, nothing would keep me from going off with you. I would be sitting right there next to you the whole way."

"Abuela, are you saying…?" I stared at her in amazement.

"*Nena*, I would give anything to see the place where Abuela Fela was born. I would go back there and look for the river and walk through old villages and stand under the moon. I would look into the faces of the people and see the lines of my own face in theirs. I would try to find in them what I would not take when given freely by my own mother. I would listen to the drumming and let the music pull my body. I would dance to the sun at sunset and the moon at midnight and I would soar in my imagination."

I stared at her in amazement and could almost see the twenty-year-old Concha there, beyond the stooped shoulders and swollen feet and arthritic, water-logged hands. I would love to have known that girl. We would have been best friends.

I hugged my grandmother with all my strength, shifting our weight from one foot to the other, doing a slow dance together. We danced around the room, memorizing the scent and shape and movement of our bodies.

"*Nena*," she said finally.

"Yes, Abuela."

"Bring me back a drum and take lots of pictures. Take pictures of the old women. I want to see their faces. Bring me their lives in your stories. I'll be ready when you come back. I'll go get new glasses so I can read them for myself."

Her words were the closest to words of encouragement I had heard. Her support was priceless to me. The only regret was that I could not take her with me.

"*Bendición*, Abuela." I wouldn't think of starting a journey like this without her blessing.

"*Que Diós te bendiga, m'hija.*"

Dear Cari,

It's been over a month since you called me about your trip to Africa, and I wanted this letter to get to you before your departure. I'm sorry I haven't written or called since then, but then I'm sure you remember that my reaction was not a good one. I regret that. I've been doing a lot of thinking since then and there are things that need to be said. You know I have always preferred writing to the telephone with its cold plastic and impersonal wires. I have always trusted words on paper. I guess you can understand that better than anyone.

My first reaction to your news was to forbid you to go. I was thinking of my baby, not the young woman you have obviously become. No mother wants to see her child move away. Your moving to Puerto Rico was bad enough. But at least you were with family. Regardless of my relationship to Mamá, I knew she would take care of you as I would. Besides, it was to be a temporary move and you were to be back within a few months.

Now, years later, you are going to the other side of the world, even further from me. My heart couldn't take it.

It seemed that the people I love are always leaving me; first Abuela Mati, then Mamá, then your father, and now you. I even dredged up all the feelings of your brother's death. A young child's death is never really laid to rest in a mother's heart. I'm still struggling with all those feelings of abandonment. I recognize where they are coming from. That doesn't mean I've dealt with them very well. Then I remembered Mamá's reaction to my leaving Puerto Rico all those years ago. I'm sure she felt the very same fears then that I am feeling now.

Today, I sit in this empty house in this cold city; a city that never accepted me, and one that I have never accepted as mine. It is a city in which I have lived temporarily for twenty-five years without it ever becoming home. Lately, I've had recurring dreams about being in Puerto Rico again. I find myself yearning for continual warmth, for mending fences with people I left behind. Mamá once said that the one thing she regretted most in her life was not valuing her time with Abuela Mati before she was taken away from us. I've learned a great lesson from that. Cari, I don't want to wake up an old woman who let her life stories, as you would call them, slip right through her fingers.

So I've made some important decisions you need to know about. First, I plan on an early retirement. By the time you come back from your trip, I should be living in Puerto Rico once again. I've already put the house on the market. You must let me know what things you want me to store for you.

Last, but certainly not least, I want you to soar. I want you to go out and find your path and create your own story. I envy you your courage. I will be anxious to read your work, see Africa through the eyes of youth. Abuela's words have become legend. Yours will have the ring of today's truth. I am so proud of you.

My fear for you is still with me. Take care of yourself for my sake. I don't know what I would do if I lost another child, but I trust you. Please let me know when you'll be landing in New York. I know you'll have a three-hour layover between flights. I'll bring you something good to eat and we can trade stories. I'll bring the stone with me. It's fitting that it go back with you. After all, it all began with the stone. You should take it home.

Love,
Mami

I remember looking down at a tiny group of people as I walked away from the gate. I turned one last time to wave goodbye, and there they stood. Adrian, tall and serious. He didn't wave at all. I knew even at this distance that the muscles in his jaw were tight with his effort to hold that stony stare. No emotional displays from him. He was surrounded by four old ladies. Their white heads bobbed around as the women stretched their necks, searching for me in the crowd. Each woman was dressed in her best—an embroidered linen dress in a pastel shade. In one hand, each carried an umbrella that would protect her from the harsh sun on her way home. In the other, each clutched a short-handled purse. They held their bags close to their bodies because they had heard of the terrible crimes that plague the cities. I knew there was nothing much in those bags. But they were of the opinion that well-dressed ladies carried matching accessories.

On Adrian's left side, Doña Pastora and Doña Teo leaned on each other and pointed. Yes, they could see me. They waved their tiny hankies and giggled. On his right stood Doña Gume. I was amazed to see her out of her environment. She had come out to see me off after decades of refusing to leave her safe world in San Antonio. She seemed confused by the mass of people, but finally found me and smiled an uncomfortable smile. She clung to Abuela, the rock of their world, who stood impassively. I knew it was Abuela Concha's ambivalence that kept her from waving. Her face was full of love.

"Last call for American flight five forty-five for New York's Kennedy Airport."

I moved through the gate quickly, pressure building up behind my eyes. I focused on what came ahead rather than the people I was leaving behind.

Now I am flying high over the Atlantic on my way to Lagos, Nigeria. I don't know what I'll find. But I hope I will find a way back to older stories. I leave behind so many people I love. I leave them for a little while to find treasures to share when I come back. I close my fingers over the smooth black stone with the inner glow. I lean back, close my eyes, and find her there. I recognize her even after all these years.

She walks a path that is clearly marked. She knows her way. She remembers the markers. The *griot's* stool is abandoned on the hill. She picks it up, dusts it off, and takes a seat. She grinds her hips into it. It fits well. It is her journey's companion. She opens her mouth and starts to sing. She knows I am watching. When she turns her face to me, I see that the Lady has my face.

POSTSCRIPT

My name is Carisa Ortíz and I am a teller of stories. It is what I do. It is who I am. I have collected many stories. They have been given to me freely. And now, I give them to you. All I ask is that you listen with your heart and, if you have a mind to, that you pass them on.

Reader's Guide to
Daughters of the Stone

1. In which ways are the characters informed by their dreams?

2. What is the legacy passed on by Fela? Is it a gift or a curse?

3. What are the different ways of knowing in the novel?

4. In what ways do they change as we get closer to the present?

5. Who is the Lady and what role does she play in their lives?

6. In what ways are the women outsiders and what price does each pay for being different?

7. What does the stone represent to each of the main characters?

8. How does African mysticism/spirituality manifest itself in the life of each woman? How does it change with the move to each different culture and time period?

9. In what way does guilt/remorse affect each of the main characters?

10. How does language change/evolve from book to book within the novel?

11. How is language acquired, lost, and reclaimed throughout the women's lives?

12. How do the different characters express their creativity?

13. Sleep plays a major role in this book. What is the function of sleep in each of the main characters' lives?

14. How would you characterize the Tomás/Fela relationship? Is Mati born of love or rape?

15. What is the significance of storytelling in this family?

16. How does "the gift" manifest itself in each woman's life? How does it change over the course of the novel?

17. The structure of the novel is cyclical. Why does it begin and end in the same place?

18. What does the stone symbolize to you?

19. Escape is a major theme in the novel. How does each main character deal with this issue? What is she escaping from and what is she hoping to find?

20. Mati rejects traditional schooling for her daughter, yet there are many mentors in the narrative. Who are the mentors, and how is knowledge passed from one generation to the next?

21. Who/what is the antagonist in this narrative? How did the protagonist fight back?

22. There are many ways of resisting. How do characters in this book resist?

23. Are you from a culture different than the one explored in the book? Do any of the relationships/situations in the book remind you of people you know? How does a different culture inform the same type of relationships/situations?

24. Is there a strong woman in your life that has had to struggle to assert herself? What was her struggle? How did she fight back? What did she win? What did she lose?

25. What is the most important legacy left to you by your ancestors? What has it meant in your life?

26. What legacy would you like to leave behind for the next generation? Why?

BIOGRAPHY

Dahlma Llanos-Figueroa was born in Puerto Rico and raised in New York City. She is a product of the Puerto Rican communities on the island and in the South Bronx. She attended the New York City public school system and received her academic degrees from the State University of New York at Buffalo and Queens College-City University of New York. As a child she was sent to live with her grandparents in Puerto Rico where she was introduced to the culture of rural Puerto Rico, including the storytelling that came naturally to the women in her family, especially the older women. Much of her work is based on her experiences during this time. Dahlma taught creative writing and language and literature in the New York City public school system before becoming a young-adult librarian. She has also taught creative writing to teenagers, adults, and senior citizens throughout New York while honing her own skills as a fiction writer and memoirist.

The 2009 hardcover edition of *Daughters of the Stone* was listed as a 2010 Finalist for the PEN/Robert W. Bingham Prize. Her short stories appear in the following anthologies: *Bronx Memoir Project, Latina Authors and Their Muses, Chicken Soup for the Latino Soul,* and *Growing Up Girl.* Dahlma's work also appears in various literary magazines such as the *Afro-Hispanic Review* and *Kweli Journal.* Since her retirement, Dahlma continues to dedicate herself to her writing, speaking engagements, and workshops. She resides in the Bronx with her husband, photographer Jonathan Lessuck.

Instagram and Facebook @DahlmaLlanosFigueroa
Twitter @writer1949
www.DahlmaLlanosFigueroa.com

CPSIA information can be obtained
at www.ICGtesting.com
Printed in the USA
LVHW110736180820
663481LV00001B/20

9 781732 642409